THE
DUPLICATA

THE DUPLICATA

Catch Me If You Can

A MYSTERY A LOVE STORY A THRILLER

DAVID THORNHILL THOMPSON

THE DUPLICATA
Catch Me If You Can

DAVID THORNHILL THOMPSON
Copyright © 2012 by David Thornhill Thompson
All rights reserved
Electronic edition: January 2012

AUTHOR'S NOTE
This is a work of complete fiction. It does not depict real events, persons, products, or other protected entities. Descriptions of such matters are the product of the author's imagination or are used fictitiously and any resemblance to actual persons, living or dead, business establishments, events or locales is entirely coincidental.

Published by
Adventures Press
P.O. Box 510453
Melbourne Beach, Florida 329512

Published in the United States of America

CONTENTS

To Jane Lee
A great ride, my love
All the better for your company

"I am always doing that which I cannot do, in order that I may learn how to do it."
Pablo Picasso

ENERGY = MASS TIMES VELOCITY

My most frightening memories of the crash are the dreadful silences that separate each crescendo—upside down at 200 miles per hour, tumbling violently over and over, as the laws of physics attempt to systematically destroy what has become a random object. The senses all become focused like a microscope—no, like a laser.

The video tape of the incident shows that—like a giant, silver, tail-dancing marlin—it took the car a full 13 seconds to consume its entire store of twelve million pounds of kinetic energy by completing a *pas de bouree*. The program concluded with six rolls, one vertical leap into the air, four revolutions on its own longitudinal axis, three end-over-end cartwheels followed by four more rolls and five 360-degree flat spins.

Of course, everyone thought that I'd died along with the car—either from the multiple impacts, or from the explosion of fuel that occurred at the end of the car's spectacular, gymnastic dance of death.

I had not.

That's where the horrifying silences come in. I have

this recurring rhythmic dream sequence that goes like this.

Wham! Unh! Silence.

Wham! Unh! Silence.

Wham! Unh! Silence.

It took me nearly a year after the crash to understand it. No doubt, the doctors were right to tell me that my mind was avoiding the horror all that time, but that advice didn't ease the curiosity. *What the hell is that sequence?*

I know now that inside that race car, I was squeezing my entire being into the smallest possible, tiny, hiding-from-everything, please-don't-hurt-me anymore, oh, God, make-it-stop, when-will-this-end, little ball.

I know that *Wham!* was the shedding of another ton of kinetic energy, as the car returned violently but only momentarily to the pavement. And *Unh!!* was my grunting on impact, the separation of cartilage in the rib cage, the fracture of the collarbone under the safety harness, the dislocation of the hip as the leg jammed in the pedal bracket, the disintegration and rearrangement of 19 small bones in the foot and ankle, as nature's irresistible forces conquered another infinitely moveable object. You get the idea.

But the silences? The horrifying, dreadful power of those unbearable, looming, nano-seconds of fear dragging on between the *Unh!* and the next *Wham!* — they're the worst.

And, of course, the smell of high-octane fuel and its pungent promise of the ultimate pain — fire — is no better.

Adrenalin stimulated senses, all of them, work like they never did before. Eyesight is more precise. Hearing is more acute. Smell is stronger. Touch is more sensitive.

However, the body and mind can stand only so much of this 50,000 watt, clear channel, stereophonic, Dolby surround sound intake of the senses. Then, it shuts down.

At the end of the crash, as I endured the last and most petrifying silence of all — disturbed only by the quiet ticking of cooling metal, the terrifying smell of burning fuel and rubber, and the growing heat of the fire — I had preserved enough adrenalin to begin a one-handed struggle with the safety harness.

Just when I began to think that I would lose this final battle, I heard and saw the approaching Course Marshal with fire bottle in hand.

It was a measure of all the frightened relief within me that, as he raised the face shield on my helmet and I looked into eyes more frightened than my own, I asked very quietly in French, "Alors, comment se fait-il des points de style?"

"So how was it for style points?"

Then, I fainted.

HOSPITAL

In my mind, the single most incriminating piece of evidence in the case against the existence of a benevolent God is the human conscience.

The conscience is the most easily programmable, user un-friendly, fiendish device of torture on earth and must have been invented by the Devil. No benevolent, loving God would subject mankind to the pain of conscience.

Thus, during the course of my 13-second contest with the forces of nature and the gods of fate, my damnable conscience would, from time to time, interrupt the regular programming to bring me another bulletin.

What the hell am I gonna tell Rod?

Jesus, I hope Arthur didn't see this.

This is going to make for another of those wonderful Thanksgiving Dinner conversations with Uncle Robert and Mother about my career and life ambition.

Isn't it wonderful what the conscience can produce in the middle of life-threatening disasters? As yet another ligament stretches and another bone fractures, conscience demands attention to my car owner, my editor and my relatives.

I should explain. I'm Edwin Hartford Pearson; Ned, to almost everyone but my own family, or at least the stuffy ones. My profession is journalism. My hobby is motor racing. I wish it were the other way around but it isn't. Oh, I get paid modestly to drive race cars and I compete with the stars but I'm one of those "almost was" racers who couldn't find the money when he was young enough to get a real professional ride and develop it into a full-blown, high-paying career. Racers are like all athletes—lots of good ones but few great ones. The difference between nationally ranked and world class is a lot more than a transatlantic plane ticket.

So, I drive for what are called privateers; those affluent team owners who love the sport and squander fortunes, waiting for that rare day when all the factory teams break and the determined dark horse wins.

On any given day, I'm good enough to turn any single lap with the front-runners—that's if my equipment were equal; or if I had spent as much time testing the car as they had; or if I had as many laps at that specific track. *If, if, if...*

Still, I'm happy getting paid modest fees plus expenses and spending time at racetracks with racers. And because racing doesn't pay all my bills, I write. Conveniently, I'm Senior Correspondent for International Motor Racing Monthly, which is what its title says it is. I'm mostly very happy, despite my family's conviction that I'm being kept by some Italian Countess or secretly selling drugs because no one could earn a proper living my way.

I'm happy, that is, until I wake up in a hospital in suburban Le Mans, France and realize that I have rolled up a $450,000 Porsche 962C belonging to my owner, Rodney Walker Evans of Pebble Beach, California into an ugly, mostly useless little ball.

I missed my story deadline for the 24 *Heurs du Le Mans* issue of International Motor Racing Monthly, thoroughly pissing off my editor/publisher, Arthur Bathgate of London, England.

And I probably scared the hell out of my poor mother, Barbara, who will get another call from my Uncle Robert Barker Pearson III suggesting that we all sit down for a little talk as soon as I return to New York.

And, oh yes, there's the issue of what to do about the pain. It's everywhere. In addition to the specific pains in the areas of trauma — the shoulder, the ribs, the hip and the ankle — I feel like something got inside me with a hammer and tried to beat its way out. I hurt all over.

Happily, the trauma specialists brought to this world-class event have treated dozens of crash victims and understand the situation only too well.

As soon as my blood pressure and heart rate stabilized, they began intravenous feeding, occasionally laced with painkillers to allow the body to withstand the enormous all-over pain — as well as to sleep.

The crash occurred around eleven o'clock in the morning on Sunday, 19 hours into the race. I must have awakened on Monday, but I'm not sure when. It was Tuesday when I struggled up from a fairly dreamless sleep only to have the strong sense of being watched.

Slowly, I turned my head toward the window and looked into the somber gray eyes of Colin McDonald, my crew chief. Colin and I go back a long way to my first days in racing Formula Fords, the training wheels of Grand Prix racers. We're about the same age and Colin had scraped up enough savings from his job in a British Leyland Motors dealership to buy a brand new Crossle Formula Ford. Colin's goal was to rent the race car to a beginning racer, develop their racing program together and eventually move up to Formula 3 and Formula 2 and maybe even, some day, to field a Grand Prix Formula 1 team. He hadn't made it yet, but that's another story.

Colin barely smiled and said quite coolly, "Damn lucky, mate."

He never asked, "How are you? How do you feel? What's the doctor say?"

He already knew all of that because he wouldn't come in the room without knowing everything that could be known. There was no wasted motion — no dither, no blather.

"Damn lucky, mate."

I knew he was right, of course. But I also knew he had more to say. So, I replied, "Why?"

"Why? Well, for starters, lad, there ain't two damn square feet of open space left in that bloody cockpit, that's why. Then there's the fact that by some bloody miracle, every time the damn car returned to earth it lit on a corner and not on your head so most of the energy was absorbed in tearin' the damn corners offa' the thing and not offa' you.

"You're gonna love the video on this one, alright. You'll be on everybody's crash and burn films for the next ten years.

"There's also the fact that the 40 gallons of Shell's finest 114 octane petrol still in the tank when it burst was spewed around in the prettiest ring-of-fire circus trick you ever saw because the damn car decided to flat spin five times before it quit dancin'. Therefore, lad, all the gas to barbecue your Yank butt got left in the green, green grass."

By this time, I began to realize my worst fears. No matter how hard I tried, I could not fend off the giggles. And as they rose inside me, I knew I was about to pay a dear price for this man's friendship. He was going to make me laugh and it was going to hurt like hell.

My God, did it ever. With my free hand, I put one of the pillows over my face, as I choked, gagged and suffered thousands of tiny damaged nerve ends re-rupturing in a cascade of pain.

"Stop, you bastard. You're killing me," I said through gritted teeth. At that, his face lost some of the merry twinkle that had risen steadily as he talked. It returned to the somber, solid stare to which I awoke.

"I'm glad you mentioned that," he said quietly. "Another reason you're damn lucky is because at the tire stop before the crash, I told Bobby to put the run-flat tires on the front. I thought the debris would start fallin' off all the damn cars after 15, 16 hours and we weren't gettin' caught and we weren't catchin' anybody either, so I thought I'd play it safe."

Run-flat tires are basically a tire within a tire. If you puncture the outer tire and lose all the air, there's still enough strength in the inside casing so that the tire doesn't go completely flat and tear off the rim. At 200 mph, a tire blowing out or suddenly deflating can tear the suspension right off the car. A run-flat lets you safely slow down and return to the pits.

I thought for a minute and said, "Colin, if the tire didn't deflate, what the hell put me on my head? The car swerved violently, first right, then left, then right again and then snapped over into the rolls. Do you know what caused that?"

"I think I do, Ducky. I think I do. In the first place, when you accelerated off that corner, all the weight transferred to the rear and the nose came up a little, taking weight off the front tires. Then you reached the end of the straight and reversed the process by coming off the gas and onto the brakes. That's when the front went down, the car pulled to the right and you turned the wheels back to the left. The tire came off the rim at that point and the rim dug into the pavement, tossing you on your head.

"The wheel rim? You mean the tire came off the rim?"

"Right-o, my boy. Off the rim. Did you ever hear of a run-flat comin' off the rim?"

"Of course not. We get a bad tire?"

"That's what I suspected, laddie. At first, I was afraid that by the time I could get there from the pits, the damn Course Marshals and the clean-up crew would have destroyed the wreckage so I could never figure out what happened. I knew it had to be a tire but I couldn't believe a run-flat would do that. I found the mark where the wheel rim dug into the pavement and the car flipped.

"So I went and got Jimmy from Goodyear and we went lookin' for the tire. They had it in the impound area, along with the rest of your trash. There's a hole in the tire. I saw it before Jimmy and decided to tell him that I'd found a puncture hole so he'd let it go at that."

"What do you mean, 'Let it go at that'? At what? What did you find, Colin?"

"You know what day it is?"

"Yeah. It's Monday, isn't it?"

"No, Ned, it's Tuesday."

"Jesus, I'm tired."

"You should be, lad. On Monday, after we got the transporter loaded and the crew away, I called a friend here in Le Mans. He's a flic…a local. I took the tire over to his farm in Bruton and asked him to look at it. I'm gonna show you somethin'." Colin produced a section of a racing tire from his bag and brought it over to the bed.

"See these two holes?"

I nodded.

"Do they look alike to you?"

Again, I nodded.

"Exactly the same?"

"Yes, Colin." I was beginning to be annoyed.

"My friend, the copper, is also a hunter and gun collector. He shot this tire with a 9mm NATO assault rifle, lad. Once. This hole on the left is his."

My mouth fell open, while the increase in heart rate and blood pressure caused a very faint warning signal of pain from a body that wanted no interruptions.

"Are you saying… Colin, do you think…?"

"Laddie, I think somebody's tryin' to kill you."

That was late June. The story actually began in the mountains west of Lake Tahoe in late March.

FAMILY

You choose your friends.

You inherit your family.

Being ever interested in the origin of things, I've always thought that perhaps this was the original *good news, bad news* joke. For reasons so complex that even I can't completely explain them, I'm simply not comfortable around most members of my family. My Dad, John Hartford Pearson, has been gone for some time and I've always gotten along fine with my mother, but the rest of the family pretty much sets my teeth on edge.

The Pearsons and the Hartfords, the Williams and the Barkers, are descendants of those early New England families that, through energy, intelligence, guile, deceit, monopolies, restraint of trade and whatever else it took, ended up dominating the commercial and financial activities of early America. They set up the great merchant banking houses and fleeced the burgeoning ranks of entrepreneurs with loans and capital investments that guaranteed their own success. They funded the arts, endowed great educational institutions and created closed societies to insure the preservation and purity of the breed stock.

And they never stopped believing that theirs was the "right way" to do things, while their descendants clung to their isolationist ways.

My dad, the third child of Robert Barker Pearson II, and brother of Robert Barker Pearson III — Uncle Robert — was a gentle person produced by a string of sharks. I think that my distaste for my relatives is at least partly rooted in a feeling that started in the seventh grade; a feeling that nobody had much respect for my Pop, or Jack as his brothers and sisters called him.

Certainly R.B.II and Grandmother Pearson, Margaret Baines Hartford, loved my father and the family did everything it could to make him an investment banker, the likes of which even the old bastard, R.B. the First, my great-grandfather would be proud. But Pop preferred the piano.

Jack Pearson took his first piano lesson at the age of 5 and it effectively ended his chances of becoming a first class moneylender. He flat fell in love with music. So, the family indulged him and, in exchange for his willingness to complete his economic studies at Yale and his business studies at Wharton, he was granted his musical eccentricity.

And, every chance he got, he played the piano — in college combos, in church productions, at the end of the evening at cocktail parties, at Union League Club dinner dances — every chance. People smiled and applauded because Pop was good. And he was also likeable. Meantime, the sharks were downstairs at the Men's bar, carving up the factoring trade and fixing the price of the latest IPO.

When R.B.II and R.B.III would call him in to review

his portfolio, sort of like his report card — how much he had lent to whom at what interest for what security — they always did it in private. It was not so much that they cared about making a public fool of him. No, I don't think they actually gave a damn about his feelings. What was at stake was their own standing among the Partners. As a member of the family and son of the Senior Partner, only Pop could avoid the public hazing, the smirks, and the downcast eyes suffered by a poor performer made to stand in the Partners Arena.

So, they kept private track of his progress — or lack of it. They occasionally finessed some good accounts into his portfolio for appearance sake and kept him out of trouble.

And eventually, they killed him with their kindness; kindness that chained him to a place he didn't want to be, doing a thing he hated to do, and without the strength to break away.

I drive racecars and write magazine articles, along with the occasional book. And I travel around the world — catch me if you can.

And boy, does it annoy the Pearsons — which is why I was mildly surprised when I got back to my upper West Side apartment in New York one Tuesday in late March after the Brazilian Grand Prix, only to find a message from my mother on my answering machine.

"Edwin, please call your Aunt Blake. She'd like to talk to you about something personal, if you have a minute. Please don't forget. As a favor to me. By the way, how are you? Where are you? You really should let someone know your plans. Where you can be reached? I mean, people worry about you. And people do get sick, you know. And die, sometimes. Well, please call Blake. I think it's important."

I love it. "By the way" means the same as "I almost forgot," or "I just remembered." The telephone is sometimes as effective as truth serum or the lie detector in raising the truth to the surface. Disembodied and impersonal, it brings out our real priorities in priority order. Mother could have said, "I'm calling about your Aunt Blake but you would think me rude or uncaring if I didn't ask about you, so I will but then I'm entitled to bitch a little at you just to get even with you and maybe coerce you into paying more attention to me because I'm going to die and make you feel guilty." The fact is that Mother knows perfectly well how to reach me in any emergency — or any time at all, for that matter. It's one of the many reasons why I admire and respect my boss, Arthur Bathgate. He is caring enough about his minions to understand the psychological beatings taken by people who travel for a living. Forgetting for a moment, loneliness, bad food, separation from family and the more overt effects of regular travel, there are the constant naggings of guilt about those you leave behind, along with questions about what's fair to you and what's fair to them. And, of course, "they" have no doubts whatsoever that you have abandoned them.

Arthur understands all this and he also understands the value of happy, worry-free correspondents — like me. So *International Motor Racing Monthly* provides a 24-hour, 365-day staffed message center for its people. It's not optional, by the way. Arthur believes in two-way streets. He provides it so that you can stay in touch and so can he. So wherever you go, you leave with the Message Center a contact point — hotel, racetrack, business office, whatever. The goal is to be able to reach you somewhere within six hours. And, of course, you can reach the message center anytime.

There's also a special deal for V.I.P.s. You can give a three-digit number to anyone you choose that will authorize the message center to tell that person where you are and give them a phone number or address so they can reach you directly. Some messages are not for everyone's eyes or ears.

Mother is number 123. In the seven years I have worked for RW, she has used it once. It is not the way of a Pearson to go electronically chasing one's errant offspring around the world. They will come home, if they have any sense.

As I shuffled through a week's accumulation of mail, mostly junk, I really couldn't focus on the envelopes. Aunt Blake wants to talk "about something personal." What the hell could that be? I tried to remember the last time I had talked to Aunt Blake and I guessed that it might have been Christmas, a year ago.

I dumped the junk mail into the wastebasket under my desk and noticed that Josie, my housekeeper, needed another reminder that dirt and dust get under things and steadfastly refuse to collect in neat encampments in the center of the rooms where they can be efficiently removed by relaxed, smiling, sanitation personnel. You have to go look for dirt…in dark places, under things. And while you're there, please empty the goddamn wastebasket. Thanks, your $100 is in the envelope.

I dropped my bag on the bed and stripped, dumping everything into the big wicker basket that serves as a laundry hamper. I was pleased to see that it was empty, which meant that Rico's Dry Cleaners would soon have some clean underwear and socks for me.

Many of the knotty issues in life begin to unravel

under the pressure and warmth of a strong, hot shower. I don't have any profound understanding of man's affinity for warm water. Some say it's because we started out as fish and we secretly want to return. Yeah, right. Maybe it just feels good, relaxes you. Whatever, I do some good thinking with hot water pounding on the back of my neck and running in sheets down my body. I don't even feel very guilty about wasting water — very.

I like Aunt Blake. I even forgive her for marrying Robert Barker Pearson III. He's not bad looking. None of the Pearson men are, present company included. She probably couldn't have known that he'd turn out to be a rapacious son of a bitch, single mindedly devoted to the multiplication of his own and his family's absurd fortune at the expense of anyone who resisted. I imagine when he was 22, he seemed only vigorous, ambitious, handsome and that quaint icon — a catch. No one knew that the years would add to that such qualities as being cold, ruthless, cunning and domineering. Oh, well.

Aunt Blake is one of those reasonable women who have grown old without becoming antique. No soft cotton prints with embroidered borders for her — no, sir. Coco Chanel grew up dreaming of an Aunt Blake as the perfect example of what time and money could mean. Oh, sure, she has wrinkles and liver spots and body shape changes but somehow you just don't notice them in the glow of health she exudes and the power in those clear blue eyes.

This is a positive person. And when you're with her, you slide into a belief that you are really important and that she really wants to know everything she's getting you to tell her. It's only upon later reflection that you realize what a gushing babbler she made of you.

So, it was difficult to imagine what "personal" something Aunt Blake would want to discuss with me. Over the years, though she never said it straight out, or even hinted, I had the strong feeling that she understood what I do and why. She didn't necessarily approve, but she understood — and accepted.

And, I think that's the strength and the power of this woman; her ability to accept and understand someone else's different ways — without the need to approve or disapprove; to modify; to advise; just accept.

And, by the way, Aunt Blake is one of the few members of my family who call me Ned.

Still, I wanted a little more information before I spoke to her, so with a screwing up of my courage and resolve, I called Mother.

She answered on the third ring.

"Hello?"

"Mother, it's Ned."

"Edwin! Where have you been?"

"I was in Brazil, Mother, covering the Grand Prix."

"Of course. A motor race, isn't it?"

"Yes. It's the first event of the year for Formula I."

"What's Formula I?"

"It's a kind of racing, Mother…a class."

"Like in the Olympics?"

"Well, the same principle."

"Were you racing?"

"No. I was just covering the week for the magazine."

"Good. Have you given it up?"

"Not yet, Mother."

"Oh, Edwin, I wish you would. I don't know where

you got your fascination with such a...such a..."

"Coarse pastime? Were you searching for something along those lines?"

"Edwin, you know that your father and I always supported you, whatever you chose to do. It's just that I don't know anything about what you're doing and my friends tell me that it's very, very dangerous and you're always gone somewhere and you don't seem to have an office or a regular schedule or friends. You don't even have a..."

"Wife? Mother, please let's not get started with this. I just called to find out what it is that Aunt Blake wants."

"Oh, that. Well...there you are! It seems that no one in this family can rest peacefully after years of trying to raise their children along paths of good sense and responsibility. I mean, as a parent, you just never know anymore what's going to become of a child, even after they seem to be well on their way to a proper and successful life. Do you see what I mean?"

"No. Mother, what are you talking about? Does this have something to do with me?"

"Oh no, dear. It's Willie. Your Aunt Blake is worried about Willie."

Oh, Sweet Jesus, Cousin Willie. William Barker Pearson, the first son of R.B.III and Grandson of R.B.II. He is ten years older than me and has always been my childhood cross to bear. I never got to know Willie very well because I hated him with regularly increasing intensity, beginning with my first hearing of the words, "Willie would never do a thing like that."

Willie, the President of the Class. Willie, the National Honor Society winner. Willie, the Baker Scholar at Harvard. Willie, the youngest Vice President at Pearson and Partners, Inc. Willie, the darling of Silicon Valley. Willie, the collector of rare automobiles. Willie. Willie. Willie, eat shit and die!

From everything I could quietly learn from mutual friends and acquaintances over the years, to those who didn't know that Willie was my cousin, Willie wasn't really a bad guy. Years of leading the parade and accepting the pats on the back may have convinced him that he was as important and good as he thought he was. It may have blinded him to vast reaches of the human condition. But, no one I ever talked to thought Willie was a bad guy. He was pompous, maybe. Boring, maybe. Shallow, maybe. But rich as hell, and a nice guy.

It's funny how mega-money splits personalities. Most rich people I've known are either very nice or quite rotten. There isn't much plain vanilla.

But I hadn't actually seen Willie in maybe ten years. It was clear to me long before my parents accepted it, if they ever did, that I was not going to be like Willie. I was probably half glad and half sad about that. But in either case, I certainly didn't seek opportunities to bask in the glow of Wonderful Willie — or continue to be exposed to comparisons.

It became easier to avoid Willie when, with the firm's blessing, he cashed out of Pearson and Partners and went west to make his second fortune floating common stock issues and debentures in support of Silicon Valley's entrepreneur whiz kids. I could stop worrying about bumping into Willie at the rare family gatherings that I attended. No longer would I have to endure barely disguised expressions of benign contempt for my life and lifestyle. Questions like, "Well, Cousin Ned, how's the glittering, glamorous life of the daring *pilote* going these days?"

Rightly or wrongly, I took this to mean, "Are you still pissing away your time hanging out with a bunch of jet set riff-raf and generally acting like an adolescent instead of getting a real job and contributing to the Pearson legend and the Gross Domestic Product?"

Maybe it was just Willie's self-conscious way of breaking the ice, but the ice only thickened — and more so, of course, if he did it in front of members of my immediate family, who could quickly take Willie's overture as the dropping of the green flag in the race to see who could get on my case the fastest.

"Mother, what about Willie is Aunt Blake worried about? What's happened?"

"Well, I'm not sure. You really must talk to her, but I think it has something to do with his collection…you know, all those cars."

With his interest in valuable cars and his carefully assembled collection of Ferraris, Aston Martins, Bugattis, Maseratis and other investment-quality exotic cars, Willie and I should have been good friends. My problem was right there in that word "investment." I didn't believe for a minute that these cars — machines that give some people goose bumps just to look at; cars that make small boys drool, the sound of which can make some men shiver or smile or make some women want to take off their clothes — meant one damn emotional nano-bit to Willie.

They were a set of numbers and rates of appreciation. He didn't drive them. Hell, he didn't even touch them, as far as I knew or believed. And so what I cared for and understood as a piece of priceless craftsmanship, even art, Willie bought and sold like Series E Bonds, bid and ask. I didn't like that.

"What about the cars, Mother?"

"Edwin, I said I don't really know. Will you call Blake and talk to her? It won't hurt to help someone in your family, will it?"

I realized I'd gone too far. "Of course not, Mother. I'll call her right now. Are you okay? How's the arthritis?"

"Oh, about the same. I've got some new pills from Dr. Samuelson and they seem to help. Are you in New York for a while? Can we get together?"

I should be here for a few days," I lied. "I'll call you later this week to see what you're doing this weekend."

"Oh, I'm going out to your sister's this weekend, but maybe next week?"

"Okay. I'll call. I'm going to call Aunt Blake now."

"Thank you, darling. I'm sure you can help and she sounded so worried. Talk to you soon."

"Bye, Mother." *Click.*

Somehow, my conscience would not allow me to tell my Mother that I didn't have Aunt Blake's phone number. So, I looked it up. The R.B. Pearsons of upper Fifth Avenue was what I was looking for. If I'd had two tin cans and a long-enough string, I could have stretched it right across Central Park and into their window. New York is funny that way. People are so near and yet so far. I think it was E. B. White who said, "New York offers the gift of loneliness."

While my neighborhood and four-room apartment are exactly 2,722 feet horizontally and 125 feet vertically distant from the Pearson's of upper Fifth Avenue, I may as well have been in Tibet. I can look out my window and see their building across the Park, but I don't know their phone number — or address. Life is funny, or is it the people?

"Aunt Blake? It's Ned...Ned Pearson."

"Oh, great. Thanks for calling, Ned. How are you?" she asked in that throaty, solid, confident voice that I'd forgotten.

"I'm fine, Aunt Blake. Mother left a message, asking me to call you. Something about Willie?"

"Yes, I wanted to ask your advice on something. Unfortunately, I've got a bunch of people here right now. Let me ask you something. Could you have lunch with me? Maybe tomorrow?"

"Well..."

"If tomorrow isn't good, pick another day."

"No. Tomorrow will be fine. Where and when?"

"How about Le Cirque? It's close and I can always get a quiet table from Sirio. Say, one o'clock?"

"Fine," I said, thinking, of course, *I can always get a quiet table from Sirio.*

Le Cirque is one of the most expensive, exclusive, three-star restaurants on the upper East Side. *God, the Pearsons know how to live.*

"Great. I look forward to seeing you, Ned. It's been a long time."

"Me, too. See you tomorrow. Bye."

After hanging up, I realized that I was actually looking forward to seeing Aunt Blake again. Although I had assiduously avoided contact with most of my relatives during the last ten years, there seems to be in mankind some instinctual, primordial connection that can never be completely broken. There are many childhood friends and schoolmates about whom I never, ever think, but my relatives seem to pop up in thought and dreams like bobbers or nautilus missiles, appearing from nowhere at unexpected times.

So, the prospect of a great lunch with a relative I actually liked presented a pleasant muse only improved by the likelihood that R.B. III would ultimately fund the pleasure.

With that raffish satisfaction on my mind, I finished opening my mail and went back to working on the feature article previewing the upcoming World Sports Car Championship season due on my editor's desk in London in less than a week.

LE CIRQUE

Le Cirque was just off the lobby of a residential hotel on East 65th Street, west of Park Avenue. It is almost impossible for a tourist to get dropped off in front of the restaurant because the cab drivers all come up Park Avenue, make a U turn at 65th and face downtown on Park because they want to join the race for the next waiting southbound sucker. The cabby then gives you the international sign of apology—a shrug—and dumps you on Park, so you can sprint 50 yards up 65th Street in the rain and really wreck your best tie before meeting Ms.or Mr. Big for a fancy lunch. You could argue, threaten, try to get them to back up or go around the block, but you'd probably lose and definitely ruin your day. The trick is to tell a white lie and ask for 65th and Madison, then stop the cab as it gets into 65th Street and smile all the way into the restaurant.

Le Cirque is typical of those three or four very fine restaurants in world-class cities that have an air of permanence. Such restaurants share three common traits. First, the owner is in the house—no absentee ownership, no amateurs, no hobby seekers. Second, price is no object. What it costs is what it costs. From carpet to carpaccio, only the best. Third, the restaurant is more important than the patrons. Oh, of course, if you're a star or a statesman, you'll be treated better than if you're not. What the hell, stars are good for business and business is what these people do. But, whoever you are, there'll be someone equally or more important than you sitting in that chair tomorrow night, so enjoy the attention tonight. And, don't forget where you are. There are worse tables in the house and you wouldn't want to be seen at one of those, would you?

As for me, I walked. It was still March, but clear and brisk, fairly calm. It was one of those days in New York that seem to sparkle and hide the dark side of the city. So, I locked my apartment, walked across the Park, down Fifth Avenue and across 65th Street. I still have enough good manners left and respect for my elders to be on time — especially when they're paying. So, I was a little early.

Sirio, the owner, often greets the guests personally and, whether he does it naturally or learned it in acting school, he wears a slightly sardonic, knowing smile that makes you think that he might think he actually knows you — even when you know he does not. It works for everyone. If he ought to know you, you are flattered that he remembers. If you think he might remember you because you were there on your last trip two years ago, you are amazed. If you know he couldn't know you, you wonder what famous person you resemble and you are secretly thrilled at the thought.

"I'm meeting Mrs. Pearson," I told him.

Just an ever so slight flicker of the eyes and the

twitch of the jaw muscle told me that we would indeed get that quiet table. He smiled just a bit more broadly and said, "Of course. We are just preparing Mrs. Pearson's table. May I offer you an aperitif at the bar, while we finish?"

I agreed and moved toward the small bar that faces the main room from its station along the wall to the left of the foyer. Happily, I was able to get a stool at the far end where I could comfortably watch the comings and goings of Le Cirque's creme de la creme clientele. When the bartender came, I ordered a tonic with bitters and lime that the French call an Anglais and the English call a Tropic. Don't ask.

I don't drink anything but wine during the racing season and not too much of that. Even though I hadn't started my season yet, I knew that Aunt Blake would order wine and I also knew the quality of Sirio's cellar. I decided to relax and enjoy myself. I sat back to examine the room, while I waited.

I love watching people from a distance in settings like restaurants and cocktail parties, where everyone gets to play their part on a tiny stage. At moments like that in those surroundings, we are only what we say we are. If we choose our audience carefully, we can be whomever and whatever we choose—debt free; happily married; on the Fast Track; pursued by the opposite sex; influential; powerful; clever. It all depends on the story we tell and how we deal with the stories of others.

Waiting there and watching, I saw one well dressed but fairly plain middle aged businessman lose, regain, lose again, regain again and finally abandon altogether control of the lunch table conversation in favor of a visit to the men's room. When he left, the remaining three

at the table engaged in a clearly disapproving conversation about the dearly departed. Surely, whatever he
was after that day, they weren't buying his act. Unfortunately, I didn't see the last act because before the star
returned, Aunt Blake had arrived.

She opened the door briskly, as the Maitre d' realized who it was, and rushed to recover from a lax moment of inattention. "Ah, Mrs. Pearson," he purred,
"So very nice to see you. Let me take your coat."

Even at 73 and even at Le Cirque, Aunt Blake still
turns heads. At five feet seven and a hundred and thir-
ty pounds, she still has the bearing of a model that she
never was. The camel colored cashmere Versace suit
over the burgundy Prada pumps and the single strand
of cultured pearls say heavy-duty lady.

Aunt Blake simply smiled and nodded. By now,
Sirio appeared as if by magic with the 100-watt version
of the knowing smile and extended his hand as if to a
long lost conspirator.

"Sirio," said Aunt Blake, smiling back, "How are
you?"

"Bene, Bene, Mrs. Pearson. And you? And how is
Mr. Pearson?"

"He's fine, Sirio. Right now, he should be in Frankfurt, but he'll be in Milan tomorrow I think."

"Ah, Milano. How I envy him, although the weather may not be so good, eh?"

"Probably not, but he'll be on his way back on Friday, so it doesn't matter."

"Your guest is at the bar, Mrs. Pearson." This
wasn't actually true because as she came in, I waved
for the bill, the bartender waved *no bill* back to me and
I made my way toward Sirio and Aunt Blake, arriving
just as Sirio made his comment.

"Actually, I'm right here, Aunt Blake."

She turned and, once again, I was physically affected by the strength in her clear, china blue eyes. They say that the eyes are the window to the soul. If so, when you look into Aunt Blake's windows, you instantly know that this person is here and now.

She is the kind of person that after an absence of years, you feel completely natural embracing lightly and murmuring, "It's great to see you again," even in front of a room full of strangers.

She stepped slightly back, smiled up and asked, "You hungry? Sirio, do you have our table?"

As we followed Sirio down the aisle along the bottom of the inverted L directly toward the banquet, we passed what is known as The Brokaw table. Tucked away in a corner formed by the short wall of the foyer and the front wall of the restaurant, this comfortable haven from the bustle of the restaurant's open spaces performs the illusionary feat of seeming somehow private, while being in plain view of the entire dining room. This is probably because of its namesake, Tom Brokaw, who demands and gets this table almost at will. He is often seen huddling there with one female network news anchor or another, presumably providing her with on-background insights to be read into tonight's 7:00 news camera, and him with a fresh supply of ego gratification.

Faithful to Aunt Blake's request, Sirio marched us right past several hundred million dollars worth of coolly examining eyes, all sitting in the high-priced seats—those where you can see and be seen—and around the corner toward the kitchen. There, we came upon a beautifully set table for two that, by some act of unseen nudging, had been given ever so little extra room on both sides. It was the quiet table.

And waiting by the table were two starched and formally attired waiters, with smiles that said, "We arose this morning, dressed and came to work just to prepare this table and no other. Does Mrs. Pearson approve of our labor?" Each held out a chair. As Sirio did a little backward step and a hint of a bow, waiter number one beckoned Aunt Blake to choose his lucky chair, which she did. F. Scott Fitzgerald wrote, "*The rich are very different than you and I,*" and he was right. The restaurant ruffles and flourishes are embarrassing to some people who then get into a clumsy passage of "after you...no, after you...no, I insist" and draw unwanted attention to them, while ruining the whole game. Aunt Blake, to my everlasting gratitude, accepted the fawning with a big smile and played the game of queenly attention with business-like efficiency. We were smoothly seated with crackling, starched napkins being unfolded and placed on our laps, while Sirio asked for a drink order.

"Would you like some wine Ned?" asked Aunt Blake with a smile, "or are you in training?"

Feeling grateful for the sensitivity that would remember to ask about such a detail, I said, "No, not till next month. I'd love some wine, but will you choose? You know the list. You must have some favorite."

"Fine," she said, turning to Sirio, "Bring us that Sancerre Martha and I had last week, Sirio, please."

"Of course, Madame, the Sancerre. And shall we bring the menu?"

"No, let's wait for the wine. Don't you think, Ned?" she asked me, while turning to Sirio with a smile. "We have some catching up to do."

"Of course, Mrs. Pearson," he said, and with that,

he was gone to perform whatever was his next act at another table in the constant juggle required to give every guest his obligatory 60 seconds in the spotlight of the owner's smiling attention.

"Well," said Aunt Blake, taking a deep breath, "how long has it been? Christmas, a year ago?"

"I think so," I said. "At mother's," I added, wishing I hadn't.

"Yes. Have you seen your mother lately?"

"Not since this Christmas, no." Then, feeling guilty and to end this line of conversation, I lied, "I'll be up there next week, though."

"Good, Ned. She misses you. And she worries, I suppose. Now, tell me about your racing and your writing. You spend quite a lot of time traveling, don't you? When were you last in Europe?"

I proceeded to give Aunt Blake a thumbnail sketch of my travels during the last six months, including the month in Japan and Brazil covering the last two Formula I races for the world championship. She seemed really interested in the Japan part and occasionally asked an insightful question about how the entire circus of crews, equipment, race cars, drivers and media manage to move efficiently from country to country over distances like those involved in the world championship.

Between my description of the three chartered jumbo jets that carry the equipment, and some funny stories about customs clearance problems, the captain took our orders and the parade of delicious, meticulously planned and prepared dishes began to flow on and off the table.

For all of my family issues and annoyances, I try never to forget some of the privileges I've enjoyed being raised as a Pearson. One of them is an exposure to really good food. Happily, my work often puts me in the way of the best in the world, so I get to prove my affection regularly.

When Aunt Blake ordered the Sancerre; a dry, crisp white from the head of the Loire valley, I decided to choose my food to match. Happily, my anticipation was not in vain, as I discovered a perfect first course on the menu — boudin blanc; the milk-white, very tender, poached sausage of pureed young veal and herbs. It came to the table gently steaming, aromatic and smelling divine on its coulis of leeks.

Between mouthfuls, Aunt Blake and I continued to talk about my travels and I nearly forgot about her request for some "advice." With her bright and curious mind and her obvious interest in the human side of things, the conversation flowed on as comfortably as if I were talking to Arthur Bathgate, my editor, or one of the team managers.

I was having a very good time in this humming, warm, good smelling, well served, gracious setting. And I think Aunt Blake was, too. She never looked at her watch or the other guests — only her food, the waiters and me. And, she showed no sign of distress or worry, only enjoyment.

When our main course arrived, the captain poured more wine, asked if there was anything needed and left us.

My Sole Duglere was perfect and so was this conversation with a wise and gracious woman who seemed *genuinely* interested in my prattle. By and by, with dessert declined, two cafe filtres ordered and the table cleared, I thought it time I quit taking advantage of this generous opportunity to talk only about myself.

"You said you needed some advice, Aunt Blake," I said, totally unprepared for the sudden appearance of tears in those blue, blue eyes.

"Excuse me for a moment, Ned. I'll be right back." She stood and moved quickly down the aisle toward the alcove that obviously contained the lounges. I sat stunned and frightened. *What in the world could bring such pressure on this strong, seemingly secure woman to cause that sudden tearful reaction?* I wondered. *And what could it be that I can do or know anything about that would help.*

Whatever it was, she had been holding it tightly in check and now I had clumsily unleashed it. But, damn, she had seemed so calm and comfortable, there was no way I could have known. *Well, Boyo, you better get your shit together now because this looks serious and there'll be no slip sliding if you want to look yourself in the mirror down the road.*

Before I noticed, she was back with a waiter beside the table, smiling and sliding into her chair. I rose as much as I could and fell back into the chair. She nodded quickly and looked into my face. She seemed back in control, with just the faintest redness around the rim of the eyes to suggest the passage of tears.

"Are you alright?" I asked.

"Yes, I'm sorry. I was completely surprised at that. I guess I didn't realize how much I've been worrying. I hate teary old ladies and you must be scared to death by now, but I thought I might lose it completely if I stayed at the table. I'll be alright now, I promise."

There it was again, that first concern for others in the midst of her own pain. I was continuing to love this woman, and becoming desperate to know what was the problem.

But long distance racing has improved my control over a sometimes-destructive impatience. Sometimes, you just have to wait and let the competition and the race come back to you. Lap after lap, you wait. And they slow down, or they break. Or, they spend all that time in the pits. And they come back to you, lap after lap. Then, you have the lead. And occasionally, you win. I wasn't exactly holding my breath, but I was being very still. Finally, she said, "It's about Willie...and Jennifer." And I waited.

"I know you don't like Willie very much," she said. As I raised my eyebrows and began my protest, she said, "Oh no, I understand. You've never said anything and no one's told me anything. It's just an instinct that mothers have. They know who will and won't like their children because they know their children's strengths and weaknesses so well."

I decided to continue waiting.

"I sometimes find myself apologizing for Willie and then I'm ashamed of myself. No mother could ask for more in a son. As a boy, he listened to us, he took direction, he tried to please us most of the time and he achieved. God knows, Willie is an achiever."

And then I knew once more why I liked Aunt Blake, realizing that she knew what I know. But still, I waited.

"St. Pauls. Harvard. The firm. And now, this thing he's doing in California. His divorce from Catherine was a shock and I never really understood the reasons he gave, but no one can ever really know what goes on inside a marriage, can they? So, I accepted it and tried not to make him uncomfortable about it. If he knew how I felt, he never mentioned it. I was delighted when he met Jennifer. It put a stop to that period I understand all divorced men go through. What do they call it...sport fucking?" At that, she blushed and so did I. "Excuse me, but I think it's so funny...like some kind of athletic contest. Like a softball game in the park. Anyway, I guess it's to prove they're still attractive to women or something. But these days, it's a dangerous sport.

"I know Jennifer is younger and some think she's too ambitious and is more interested in Willie's money or family connections. But still, they seem well suited. They have common interests and she's very good to Willie's children, so I say leave well enough alone."

Now, I was really puzzled and beginning to mentally form a question. "I know," she said, with a rueful smile. "So, what's the problem?"

So, she's a mind reader, as well.

"The problem is...I think Willie is in some kind of serious trouble, but I don't know what it is and so far he won't tell me."

"What makes you think he's in trouble?"

"He said so."

"He did? What did he say?"

"He's been acting strangely the past few months. You know how dedicated to business he is, always in his office early, lots of meetings, a full schedule, no time for play. You know the type. Like his father, your Uncle Robert. But a couple of months ago, I tried to reach him at the office and they said he wasn't in and wouldn't be in that day. I asked if he would be calling in for messages and they said that they didn't know."

"Now, Ned, that's not like Willie. He's got phones everywhere and fax machines and whatever new electronic toy is available. He is constantly in touch with everything and everybody."

"So, what did you do?"

"I called Jennifer but she wasn't in her office either, so I left a message for her to call. The next day, Willie called back. We talked for a while, but he didn't mention where he was the day before and, of course, I couldn't ask. I mean, it's really none of my business, is it? Then he asked me why I called Jennifer and I told him that I was looking for him. He was very quiet for a moment and then he said, 'She wouldn't have known, anyway.' At the time, I was feeling guilty, as if I were prying, so I didn't respond and he changed the subject. But later, I thought, *Why would he tell me that? What was his message?* After a while, I forgot about it. Then, a couple of weeks later, I tried to reach him again and the same thing happened. Only this time, his secretary assured me that she could reach him if it was an emergency. I told her it wasn't; just to have him call me when he had a chance. This time, he didn't call back the next day. It took two days.

"Ned, in 20 years, it has never taken Willie two days to return a call. When he called, I asked him if everything was alright. He said it was, but he wasn't convincing. He sounded worried and depressed. When I asked about Jennifer, I got the same kind of…I don't know…half-hearted answer.

"Finally, last week, the whole thing happened again. I tried to reach him. Couldn't find out where he was. Tried to reach Jennifer and couldn't. Willie called back and sounded awful. I told him point blank that I sensed there was something wrong; that he sounded unhappy and that he didn't seem to be keeping a normal schedule. I asked if something was wrong in the business, or with Jennifer or what."

"What did he say?"

"Ned, I'm not sure, but I think he cried. He didn't

actually sob, but he struggled and spoke very slowly. He said he would be in New York next week and would tell me about some 'things' that were happening when he got here."

"That's it? Just things?"

"Well, he did say he was going to see some lawyer here and that he had a meeting with Sothebey's, the auction house. He didn't say why, but I know he's collected some valuable things over the years. God, I hope he's not in some kind of financial trouble...having to raise money or something."

"Well, Aunt Blake, I hope so, too. But I'm sure Willie can work it out, whatever it is," I said, thinking unworthy thoughts about comeuppances and the like.

"But, what I don't understand is, how can I help? What did you want me to do?"

"Well, Ned, I can't talk to Willie's father about this. He's like a bull in a china shop. He'll be on the phone in a minute, or worse yet, on the next plane to California. He's never quite gotten used to the idea of Willie succeeding on his own, without the fine hand of R.B. III in the background. I never would have asked your mother to call you, except for one other thing that Willie said."

"What's that?"

"Toward the end of our conversation last week, right out of the blue, he asked if I ever saw you anymore. Did I know what you were doing; 'were you still into cars,' I believe were his words. I told him I thought so, but that it had been a year since we talked. Then, he said, 'I don't think Ned likes me much, but I may need his help.' He then asked if I would find out if you were going to be in New York next week. I promised to call your mother and here we are. Will you be here next week?"

I had actually planned to fly to London on the weekend to finish off my story. But the last hour and a half reminded me that things change and people change and severing all contact with your relatives might not be the perfect answer. And it reminded me that Aunt Blake had never done anything but accept me for what I was. Anyway, I could do my editing and rewriting by e-mail. In a pinch, I could even access some computer files in London for background material. All writers with half a wit thank their respective lords for the computer. What I do can be done anywhere — under water, on the moon, in town or out. The computer and the modem give a writer incredible geographic flexibility. Yes, I have to be at the event to describe and report it well, but in between I can plug into the Internet for any additional research.

"Sure," I said. "I'll be here all week. When do you think Willie will be here?"

"He didn't actually say, but my guess is the middle of the week."

"Well, no problem. I'll be in and out, but I'll give you my number and you can just leave a message on the machine if I'm out, okay?"

"Thank you, Ned. I'm really worried and I'd like to get to the bottom of this. I hope you're not too uncomfortable about this."

"No, Aunt Blake. Maybe it's time for Willie and me to take another look at each other. It'll be fine. I'm happy to help however I can."

The bill came in its little gift box, as if it was something that management prepared just for your after-dining pleasure; something so lovely and valuable that it should be wrapped and boxed appropriately. Aunt

reviewed the bill, gave it the obligatory once-
, as if to say 'I don't sign anything I haven't read,'
ned it over and signed it. She had a charge account
it Le Cirque. Ain't it great? Makes you proud to be an
American.

We rose to say our goodbyes and thank yous, and
moved toward the door where our coats were waiting.
"I hope everything was alright?" Sirio asked.

"Lovely as always," Aunt Blake assured him.

As Aunt Blake passed, he looked at me, decided I
was hired help, nodded, gave me the number three
smile and moved away. You pay, you play. That's the
rule and I hadn't paid. Fair is fair.

We moved on to the street and I hugged Aunt Blake
again, this time feeling real affection. We walked over
to Park and I hailed a taxi for her, since she had sent
her car and driver home when she arrived. I opened
the door as the cab slid to a stop and, as she gathered
her coat around her and stepped in, I said, "Now don't
forget to call. I'd like to help. Please call even if he
doesn't come in, just so I'll know what's happening."

"I will," she said, "and thank you, Ned."

"No problem," I said. "And, thanks for lunch."

The cab pulled away and I decided that the day was
too nice to be inside, so I would walk over to Fifth and
down to the main New York library at 42nd Street and
Fifth to do a little search for material I needed for a
book I was working on called *The Bridesmaids*. It's
about the wacky, wild entrepreneurs who stormed into
the automobile business in the twenties trying to get
rich and eventually got forced out or acquired by Hen-
ry Ford and Alfred E Sloane of General Motors.

As I hurried west along 65th, I kept thinking about
what problem Willie could possibly have that had any-

thing to do with me.

Of course, the only connection I could think of was the cars. But surely he knows, I thought, that I just race them and write about them. I'm not an expert on collector's cars. *Maybe he thinks I know someone who can unload something?* And, finally I gave up the musing, and decided to wait and see.

I sped up my pace and enjoyed the crisp sunshine. I watched the passing parade of faces; young, old, rich and poor, business people and tourists all going somewhere up or down the canyons of Manhattan.

As I traveled south on Fifth past Tiffany's, I remember that my last thought about Willie was, *Willie'll be all right. He can take care of himself.*

That was Wednesday afternoon. Two days later, I was reminded of that thought at about six o'clock on Friday evening when the ringing phone interrupted my finishing touches on the WSC Championship Preview. It was Mother.

"Edwin!" she almost yelled into my ear. "Edwin?"

"Yes, Mother, What is it?"

"Do you have cable?" she asked loudly.

"What?"

"Do you have cable?" she asked louder.

"Yes. Yes. Why?"

"Turn it on now. Get CNN. Your cousin Willie's been killed."

HEADLINE NEWS

"This just in from our San Francisco bureau. Mary Jackson has the story.

"Mark, according to reports from the California Highway Patrol, multi-millionaire computer industry financier, William Barker Pearson, died a violent death this afternoon somewhere in the Sierra Nevada mountains just west of Tahoe, when his million dollar sports car plunged off the side of a mountain, tumbled some 250 feet down the mountainside and burst into flames. It is not clear from early reports whether or not he died from the impact, or the ensuing fire. Authorities believe he was alone at the time.

"Apparently, he had left his lavish ski chalet near Lake Tahoe and was returning to his home in Palo Alto. We were unable at airtime to reach his office or his home, so we don't have further details.

"Mr. Pearson was well known for his successful financing of a number of corporate computer hardware and software firms in California, including Compucal, BitWare, SoftCorp and others.

"He is survived by his former wife, Catherine of

Sonoma and their two children, Arthur and Linda, as well as his second and present wife, Jennifer Paterson Pearson. Back to you, Mark."

Jesus. Jesus. Jesus. The talking head droned on about other things, as I sat there staring at the screen, thinking, *This only happens in the movies or novels. It doesn't happen to real people. People that you know. That you talk to. That you're related to. Jesus. Am I dreaming, or is this actually happening?*

And if it is, what the hell should I do now?

The answer was, answer the phone, because it was ringing and I didn't know for how long. I picked up the receiver semi-automatically, still staring at the screen.

"Edwin? Are you there, Edwin?"

"Yes, Mother, I'm here. Uh, are you alright?"

"Absolutely not. I'm terrible. Did you see it? Did you get CNN?"

"Yes, I saw it. I can't believe it."

"Oh, it's awful...just awful!"

I suddenly realized that I hadn't spoken to her since lunch with Aunt Blake and I had no way of knowing whether or not she knew about Willies 'troubles' and Aunt Blake's concerns. I decided that there was no purpose in laying that on her, if it hadn't already been done. So I asked, "Have you talked to Aunt Blake?"

"No," she said, "not since she called last week to ask about you." Then, a little hurt, she added, "I was hoping that one of you might call and tell me what it's about. I mean, did you ever call her?"

"Yes, Mother. We had lunch."

"I see," She replied in a chill tone. "Maybe we could have lunch sometime?"

"Mother, why don't you call Aunt Blake now," I

said, stupidly. Realizing that could be a terrible idea, I then said, "Better yet, call Uncle Robert."

"Edwin, why don't you call Uncle Robert? What are you afraid of?"

Since I couldn't answer that question and I was tired of screwing around, I said, "Fine. I'll do it right now and if I learn anything, I'll call you right back."

"Thank you, Edwin. Oh, this is so upsetting. Do call me. Please?"

"I will, Mother. I promise."

As I dialed the office of Pearson and Partners, I worried a lot about two things: *What if no one has told R.B. III about Willie?* I sure as hell didn't want to be the one to do it for about two hundred reasons, not the least of which was the likelihood that he would hate me for the rest of his life — and understandably so. The second reason was that I didn't have a clue as to how I was going to begin the conversation. What does one say, "Hi, Uncle Bob. I know we haven't spoken in well over a year, but I was just calling to find out how you're taking the news of the death of your eldest son." *Jesus.*

As the phone rang, I looked at my watch and realized that it was already six o'clock so I might have missed him. Of course, my next thought was that I probably wasn't going to be that lucky. Then, to my severe disappointment, someone answered, "Pearson and Partners, may I help you?"

In an instantaneous takeover by the subconscious, my brain produced a completely unrehearsed, improvised plan B. My ears heard my mouth say, "Mr. Pearson's secretary, please."

"I'm sorry. She's gone for the day. Can someone else help you?" asked the professional voice.

"Well, I'm not sure," I stammered. *Damn.*
"Who's calling, please?"
Do I want to do this? Where am I going with this?
"Sir, by any chance is this in reference to Mr. Pearson's son?"
Holy Jesus. This may work out.
"Well, yes it is." *Please, please help.* "Uh, has Mr. Pearson been, uh, informed about his son?"
"Of course he has." The voice was indignant. "May I ask who this is?"
"Oh, thank you. That's all I wanted to know. This is a member of the family and I just heard the news on TV and wanted to find out if Mr. Pearson had been notified. That's all. Thank you very much. Goodbye now." *Click.* The relief flooding over me from the knowledge that I wouldn't have to talk to Uncle Robert under these awful circumstances more than compensated for the rising tide of disgust at my cowardice.

But I would have to talk to Aunt Blake and now that it was clear I would not be delivering the terrible news, I also knew I should do it now. So I did.

The housekeeper answered on the third ring. I imagined that the phone was ringing a lot.

"Pearson residence," she said.

"This is Ned Pearson, her nephew," I said. "Is she there?"

"Yes, sir. Just a moment please." I heard her walking across the marble foyer toward the parlor.

"Ned, is that you? I take it you've heard?" Her voice was flat, with little emotion.

"Yes, Aunt Blake, and I'm very sorry. Are you alright? Is Uncle Robert there?"

"Yes, dear, he's here. He's lying down right now, but Doctor Abramson came over and we're fine. Linda is on her way in to spend the night."

"Good. Good. Is there anything I can do?"

"I don't think so, Ned. We're going to California in the morning. I've talked to Catherine and the kids, and to Jennifer. Oh, Ned, nobody can believe it. He wasn't a careless driver. In fact, he hardly ever drove at all and hardly ever in those sports cars. Jennifer, of course, wasn't with him. She said he'd gone to Tahoe to work on some complicated deal that he needed to think about. I don't know. I just don't know."

Her voice just trailed off in that bone weary way that comes after you've re-thought the situation again and again, and ugly reality just won't go away.

The most difficult part of talking to the victims of tragedy is your own helplessness. Every encouraging word must be stopped at the gateway out of the mind and examined for authenticity. Most fail the test and most remain unspoken because they're false. It will *not* be all right. Tomorrow will *not* be a better day. The dead are dead—final, forever.

So, you just do the only thing you can do—fill time and space, while the wounds heal and the victims absorb and eventually outgrow the pain. It is an agonizing process but the only one there is.

And so it was that I realized that Aunt Blake and I were just sitting silently, connected by telephone wires and waiting for something useful to say. Nothing came. Finally, Aunt Blake said, "Maybe sometime you could ask someone you know how such a thing could happen? If we understood that, it might ease the pain for Robert and me."

I said, "Sure. I can do that." I thought, *Maybe she'll forget about this because by the time I could learn anything—even if I could learn anything—the pain should be buried and better left alone.*

"Thanks for calling, Ned. I'd better go look after Robert now. Maybe we can talk when we get back?"

"Bye, Aunt Blake," I said, and hung up feeling totally inadequate and angry at my inability to do anything useful for her. I wasn't helped much by the realization that I had no reason to assume that I had any power to help, or that no one expected me to help. I still wanted that woman to be freed from her misery and I just couldn't stop thinking about it.

I don't know how this process works, but by the time I had called Mother and told her the little I knew about Aunt Blake and Uncle Robert and then taken a long hot shower to soak away the stiffness of an afternoon of tension, I'd already made the decision.

As soon as possible, I'll go to California. I'll look at the car. And I'll try to find out what was bothering Willie. After all, I'm a journalist, aren't I? I'm supposed to search for truth. So that's what I'll do — at least for a little while.

FLIGHT 29

I'd suddenly gotten very busy with the magazine and it was three weeks later that I found myself sitting in a very comfortable first class seat on a 747, hearing, "Nonstop service to San Francisco's International Airport." It was then that I realized how little I really knew. It had been three weeks since the funeral and I still had no plan at all. So, like the good journalist that I am, I started making a list of what I knew and who I knew. The list was pretty short. First, I knew Aunt Blake, who started this whole thing in the first place. Then, of course, I knew Willie who was the center of the puzzle, but would be of little help in my search for truth. Next, I knew Jennifer who I had met just once at some family gathering or other, and whom I really didn't know at all. Beyond that, I couldn't think of a single person whom I could call and say, "Hey, I'm in town and I'm trying to find out why Willie was acting strangely and what he was feeling so much pressure from. Can you help me?"

Just then, the flight attendant came by to inquire about my preference for dinner. I rejected all the one-liners that came to mind—like, "good food"—and asked for the fish, and some Napa Chardonnay. I have this theory about airline food that goes like this: Either they don't know what good food tastes like, or they simply can't find a way to overcome the mechanical problems involved in the process of getting food from the kitchen to the table with a pause in an airplane galley. So it's best to choose the dish they screwed around with the least before sending it off to you. The fish wins this little game every time. And it's also the dish that will add the least number of inches to my beltline, so at least I don't have to suffer the indignity twice — once, when I eat it and again, when I look at myself in the mirror the next morning.

Whatever works for you, I guess.

So, sipping my wine, I returned to my musing about a plan of action once I arrived in sunny California. The first list being so short as to be almost useless, I started a second list of those people whom I thought might have even the slightest idea of what was going on in Willie's life that could cause him to change his behavior so suddenly. It went something like this:

Jennifer
The people at his office
Catherine, his first wife
Anybody these people could think of that I couldn't

I also decided that I'd better talk to the State Police just to see what they might have found or heard in their investigation of the accident.

I had one other person on my list that I was looking forward to interviewing, someone who was the economic basis for my trip. Just in case I haven't made it clear, I really do work for a living. There is no way that I could afford to just pick up and fly off to the West Coast on the spur of the moment, if I had not so carefully chosen my profession many years ago. Again, I have to thank my publisher, Arthur Bathgate, for coming to my rescue. When I called him in London to tell him of Willie's accident and to let him know that I felt I had to do something to ease Aunt Blake's pain and concern over his strange behavior right before his death, Arthur immediately offered his sympathy and asked if there was anything he could do to help. Before I could demur, he said, "Ned, I have an idea. It's time we did a piece on these auctions. You know, where they're getting these outrageous prices for so-called collector cars."

"Well," I said, "Arthur, I don't really know much about that business..."

"Nonsense," he interrupted, "You've seen them all at one time or another somewhere on a racetrack, I'd imagine. And those you haven't, you can surely find someone to tell you about." His enthusiasm was compelling and it would be fun to write about something other than the prima donna, multi-millionaire rich kids I normally follow for much of the racing season.

Arthur interrupted my thoughts again to say, "What I was thinking, Ned, was that in order to follow up on your cousin's accident, you would have to go to California, wouldn't you? And while you were there, you could pop down to Monterey and see this fellow, Rod Evans. You know...the one who runs those fabulous auctions at Pebble Beach and Palm Springs and all? That way, you could kill..." Realizing where that was going, he had the presence of mind to stop for a breath.

Still, I thought it wasn't such a bad idea. For all I knew, Willie may have known Evans. He may even have bought something from him. So, I agreed. And it wasn't too hard to do since this would mean that the magazine would pick up a substantial part of my expenses for the trip. In plain talk, that means most of them. Now you know why I was sitting in First Class.

Arthur, generous soul that he is, pays for business class for his faithful Senior Correspondents. I, in turn, use my Frequent Flier miles to upgrade to First, if I can't find some friendly airline employee to do it for me.

So I added to my list one Rodney Walker Evans of Monterey, proprietor of the world's most successful automobile auctioneering firm and accordingly, multi millionaire. By all accounts that I had heard, Rod Evans was a man to be reckoned with. He had the reputation of a man no one would call dishonest, at least not to his face, or in front of strangers — that is, witnesses. But on the other hand, you wouldn't send your mother down to Ol' Rod's place to do a deal all by herself, either.

Just before I left New York, I made a few calls just to prepare myself for my interview with Evans. I had an editor once who growled at me after a disastrous interview, in which I carelessly confused the subject's wife with someone else's, and turned the interview very frosty. "Sonny, cold calls are for encyclopaedia salesmen. If you want to come back with the story on your tape, you better go out with a lot of facts in your head."

I do my homework.

My homework told me that Rod Evans was a fairly typical, self-made man, more successful than most, but following the pattern, nonetheless. Evans had grown up in Southern California in the Fifties, spending most of his spare time building street rods and diggers, anything to get you from A to B in the least amount of time with the maximum amount of sturm and drang. While the other young studs at Buena High School in Ventura were playing stick and ball games, surfing, cruising or squeezing zits—local legend has it that if you asked the wrong person if they went to a "good school" in Ventura, you could get a punch in the face—young Rod was looking for another clapped out '40 Ford coupe that he could work his magic on, turning a $500 investment into a $1,000 profit. He developed a reputation among the best looking girls at Buena as a guy with a fairly single-minded attitude about girls. As it turns out, there were a fair number of them who shared his fascination with the delights of a balmy Pacific evening spent in the steamy confines of the front seat of Rod's latest project. Though no one who knew him in those days would have described Rod as a gentleman, the occasional girl who thought that she might acquire the reputational spice of a date with Rod without actually playing the game was in no danger of being treated with anything less than courtesy. However, she might have to strain her creative faculties to explain to her parents or friends why Rod was seen back at the A&W root beer stand, alone, by 8:00 pm on the night of their date. Of course, all Rod would ever say was, "boring." Thus, a system of rewards was born for those who cooperated with Rod, and subtle punishment for those who did not. This very system was developed and refined over the years, and eventually served Rod well in dealing with matters of much greater portent than simply getting laid reliably.

To the extent that the young men in Rod's middle-class neighborhood knew anything about or even noticed the fast-growing phenomenon called sports cars, they dismissed it scornfully as the product of the hoity-toity, rich kids—something stupid and foreign and not to be trusted. Road racing was virtually non-existent. Everyone who had any sense raced either on dirt or paved circle and oval tracks, or perhaps in the desert.

Except Rod had heard and eventually read about racing in Europe where they raced both on public roads and on special tracks called "road courses" built just for racing.

What almost everybody who knew Rod in those days overlooked was the man's ambition. Everyone knew he was fascinated with cars and would spend endless hours polishing, filing, buffing, sanding, whatever it took to make this car look better than the last one. They all said he was a perfectionist and they thought he really loved cars. He did not. He loved money.

Each sale he made was bigger than the one before it. Each time he closed a deal, he took a third of the money and put it in a bank account that nobody—not even his mother—knew he had. He took the other two thirds and bought another project car. He was pyramiding and nobody but Rod knew it.

The other thing that nobody knew was that Rod decided that he was going to be rich. He had made that decision one bright Spring day in 1956 when he had driven over to Pasadena to a body shop where he had heard there was a young genius doing really hot designs in layers of lacquer that were winning awards at car shows all over the Valley. While he was there, a truck and trailer arrived and the crew from the body shop came out to unload the trailer. In no time, they had ramps up the back of the trailer and were rolling out the most beautiful automobile Rod had ever seen. It was a fiercely red car with fat black tires on brilliant chromed wire wheels and a nose like the mouth of a Pacific shark.

Rod stood transfixed, as the unloading was completed. While be watched, a young man just slightly older than Rod arrived in an immaculate Lincoln convertible. He stepped out, wearing yellow linen slacks and tasseled loafers, and strode over to the crew that was unloading the car. He spoke briefly to one of the men who had arrived in the truck, who reached in his jacket pocket and produced a set of keys on a leather fob. The young man opened the door of the topless red car, smoothly slid into the fat, banana yellow, leather seat and inserted the key into the ignition. The engine made preliminary whining mechanical sounds, as it turned over with increasing speed until, with a sudden cough, the first of its twelve spark plugs fired. This was immediately followed by the remaining eleven, producing a rumbling, gurgling, blubbering sound of mechanical symphony that made the hair on the back of Rod's neck stand on end. Then, the young man made two quick stabs at the accelerator and the engine gave two piercing, ripping shrieks of sudden anger. Rod took one step back in awe.

The young man smiled comfortably, turned off the ignition and stepped out of the car. Looking at no one in particular, he said, "Sounds great, doesn't it?" and then walked into the office.

As soon as he could catch one of the crew alone so he wouldn't look dumb, Rod asked him, "What kind of a car is that?"

"That, pal, is a Ferrari."

"Where's it from?"

"Italy."

"Italy," he repeated, "What's it worth?"

"Oh...six, seven."

"Hundred?"

"Yeah, sure. Seven grand!"

"No kidding...seven grand?"

"Yeah, it's mostly handmade."

"What's it for...I mean, do they race them or what?"

"Yeah. That car finished second last month in Italy in a thousand kilometer race."

"How far is a thousand kilometers?"

"620 miles."

"Jesus Christ! 600 miles. And it looks like that?"

"Yeah, they cleaned it up, but we're going to redo the whole thing."

"Yeah? What's that going to cost?"

"I don't know, probably two grand."

"Two grand? My God! Who owns that thing?"

"That kid who was in it, that's who."

"That kid? Who is he? I mean, where does he get that kind of dough?"

"His name is Lance. He's Barbara Hutton's kid. You know, the heiress."

"Yeah? And how'd he get the car? Did he go to Italy?"

"No. There's a guy in San Francisco who brings 'em over."

"I'll be damned. Seven grand, you say?" And that's exactly when Rodney Walker Evans decided that he was going to be rich. Well, actually it was about half an hour later. He was westbound on the Ventura Freeway, thinking about the sexiest, most outrageous car he had ever seen. He remembered the sound of that lovely twelve-cylinder engine in the hands of the rich kid.

All he said was, "Shee-it." What he meant was, 'Piece a' cake."

JENNIFER

Sometimes, I plan a trip thoroughly. Sometimes, I
don't. It usually depends on how sure I am of what I'm
doing. If I'm working on a story that's well developed
and I'm just adding the last few elements, then I'll
probably plan the trip in detail because I know almost
exactly what I want to accomplish. Other times, times
when I'm just on a fishing expedition, I make almost no
plans at all. That, of course, explains why I was making
lists on the airplane. This was definitely a fishing trip.
It also explains why I had made no reservations anywhere. I had a lot of ground to cover and I didn't know
how long it would take or where it would lead. It's
called, "staying loose."

As I waited for my luggage to make its way from
the plane, I dialed the number I'd gotten from Aunt
Blake for Jennifer's office. One of the nice things about
early morning flights from the East is that you often arrive on the West Coast before lunch. This means that if
you're lucky, you can sometimes catch your contact in
time to offer lunch, which often means that you can do
two interviews on the same day that you've traveled

three thousand miles for—one over lunch and one in the afternoon. Playing these little efficiency games is one of the ways to break the boredom and drudgery of frequent long distance travel, and I play them as often as I can. I hate sitting around a hotel room waiting for a day and a night to pass so that I can do an interview that I could just as well do while I'm sitting there.

As the phone rang in the Merrill-Lynch office in Palo Alto where Jennifer traded stocks for the portfolios of a dozen or so Silicon Valley junior millionaires, I reflected on the conversation she and I had before I left New York. Of course, she didn't know me very well, nor I her, so that could explain the note of almost professional reserve I detected in her voice when I told her that I was coming to California and would like to see her. There are times when you believe you can almost read minds, even over a long distance line, and this was one of those times. I was sure I heard the word, "Why" spoken in her mind but not from her mouth.

Even so, I said, "I'm working on a story and I promised Aunt Blake that while I was there, I would try to learn as much as I could about what was worrying Willie before he died."

"Well," she replied quickly, "That's fine, but I've tried to make Mrs. Pearson—*why not Mother or Blake?* I wondered—understand that Willie was under a great deal of strain about an underwriting that was going badly. Also, he suspected one of his employees of serious misuse of company funds. I know she had calls from Willie that upset her just before his...his accident, but I'd hoped that with the benefit of some time, her grief would heal and her worries would recede. I hope you're sensitive to her need to put this behind her, Ned?"

I wanted to give this newly widowed woman every bit of sensitivity she deserved and I certainly had no right to stick my nose into her life just to satisfy my own curiosity or that of her recent mother-in-law, but...

One of the differences between the good journalist and the hack is an extra sense or two combined with stupid bullheadedness. While the sensitive side of me was reasonably pleading, *What do you say we back off a little here?* But the reporter was asking, *Does she know something I don't know that she'd like to leave that way?*

So I said, "You're absolutely right. The sooner Aunt Blake gets this off her mind, the happier she's going to be. We should do everything we can to get past this tragedy. Maybe I can help if I knew just enough about Willie's problems to assure Aunt Blake that I'm convinced it was nothing for her to worry about now? Tell you what...I'm not sure exactly when I'm coming out there, but when I do I'll give you a call and maybe we can have lunch or something just to reintroduce ourselves."

"That would be very nice," she said, in a tone I took to be sincere. "Willie liked your work. He used to show me articles you'd written and sometimes where you'd won a race. Are you still racing?"

Willie's interest, of course, was a complete surprise to me and the flattery had its effect, so I told her I was and repeated my promise to call her when I arrived.

Now, standing in the airport not 20 miles away from her, I was anxious to see how this next step would go. The receptionist answered with the firm name, wished me a good morning, looked at her watch, changed it to afternoon and inquired after my needs. I asked for Jennifer and was told, "She's not in the office. Do you wish to leave a message?"

"Would you know how I could reach her?"

"May I ask who's calling?" That question never fails to cause my mental computer to default to responses like, "The IRS," or "Her husband's attorney" — you know, code words for "*Just answer the question.*" If the helper works for a man, I occasionally say, "It's his next door neighbor and I want to know what he's going to do about my wife." That's a sure-fire, never-fail way in; no further screening questions asked, thank you very much.

In this case, wishing to burn no bridges, I caved and said, "This is a cousin of her late husband and she's expecting my call. I'm at the airport and I'd like to reach her this afternoon, if I can."

The helper digested this and decided where the greater risk lie — helping or not helping. She made the prudent choice and responded, "Well, I'm not sure but you could try her at home," and quickly added, "But I can't give you that number unless..."

"I have it, thank you," I said and hung up.

As I dialed Willie's home number, also courtesy of Aunt Blake, I wondered why Jennifer would be at home at noon on a Thursday, and then realized that there could be a dozen logical reasons. Then I wondered why I was constantly having suspicious thoughts about Jennifer. I finally decided in a rush of self-support that it was probably logical to wonder about the surviving spouse of a wealthy man who has died a violent death. I'm not a cop, but they sure would have questions.

"Hello?"

The heavy breathiness of Jennifer's voice made me shift my mental gears. She had what could only be called a bedroom voice, no matter what time of day or night you heard it. There is a commandment about your neighbor's wife that I'm sure applies to your cousin's wife, as well, and Jennifer had the kind of voice that instantly made you start thinking about Right and Wrong, Miss Manners and other means of self-control. No one will ever convince me that women who have that soft, silky, slow-paced murmur haven't a clue in the world about its affect on men. I'm convinced that only the pencil sharpener, 4th octave TV nose talkers are oblivious to the aural pain flowing out of their air horns. On the other hand, I don't know if the purring is intentional, if it can be learned and manipulated, but it sure gets my attention.

"Jennifer, it's Ned. Am I catching you at a bad time?"

"No, not at all. Where are you?"

"I'm at the airport."

"Where, in San Francisco?"

"Right."

"Uh, I see. Where are you going?"

Here we go, I thought. "Actually, I just landed and I called your office to see if I could catch you before you went off to lunch. They told me that I might find you at home and here we are. Do you have time for something to eat?"

"Well, let me think for a minute," she said. I held my breath and crossed my fingers. She had every opportunity to say that she was busy, had an appointment, had to go back to the office, a million possible excuses to avoid my ambush. Just when I began to suspect that the delay was now long enough for her to have chosen the one she thought least offensive, she blindsided me by saying, "That would be lovely," in that soft, throaty voice that made an instant believer out of me.

"Do you have a car?" she asked.

"I will in about five minutes," I answered.

"Good," she said, crisply. "Ask for directions to Half Moon Bay. That's south on I 280 and west on 92. It shouldn't take more than 30 or 40 minutes. Do you like Mexican food?"

"Love it," I said, obediently.

"Fine. There's a cute little cantina there and they make great margaritas. It's called Fonda del Mar and it's on the right hand side of Highway 1, about a half mile south of the intersection of 92 and 1. Think you can find it?"

"I'm sure I'll have no problem," I said, wondering if my intelligence or my masculinity or something was being tested — *or is this woman playing the coquette?*

"Fine, Ned," she said, "then I'll see you around one o'clock."

"Look forward to it," I said, and I did.

HALF MOON BAY

What I didn't bother to tell Jennifer is that a long time ago, Half Moon Bay was a special place for me because it was the closest place that I could get my feet into the Pacific Ocean after landing at what the airlines refer to as SFO. When I was a boy, I thought it phenomenal that you could walk in the Atlantic and the Pacific on the same day. I actually did it once, although I never told anybody about it because they'd have thought me weird. Nonetheless, Half Moon Bay was the spot I picked and I remember coming over the top of the hills that separate San Francisco Bay and the Pacific. I stopped the car to gaze out over that bright blue water to remember the way the Atlantic had looked at sunrise on the same day.

I also knew that the Half Moon Bay of my youth was no longer there. The open sweep of uncluttered beach had been replaced with the claptrap of development; the standard assortment of tract houses, fast food stands and beach merchants.

And, so it goes. Still, I was intrigued with Jennifer's choice of meeting place, almost like a trysting place where you wouldn't expect to see any one you knew. Finally, I decided that maybe I was fantasizing too much. I decided that I should start preparing myself to learn what I could about Willie's last few weeks from this woman who really meant little to me but would have to be treated with care.

With that on my mind, I accepted the car rental agent's apology for losing my reservation, along with his gift of a two-class upgrade for my aggravation, at no extra charge, of course.

Jennifer lied. The margaritas were not just great, they were fantastic. I hate Roses lime juice, that sickening concentrate of lime flavored cough medicine the tex-mex amateurs of the Mexican food world try to pass off as proper flavoring in a margarita. If they hadn't scoured their taste buds into stumps with CarboCola and MacGreasyfood, they might know that the Mexicans don't use limes in margaritas, they use lemon juice. And the sweetness comes from the Triple Sec.

Anyway, the bartender at Fonda del Mar knew. I was halfway through my first and thinking about the next one when she arrived. And that's what she did — arrived.

When she appeared in the dining room's doorway, the noise level created by a half dozen simultaneous, active lunchtime conversations temporarily ceased. It snapped off suddenly, like when a priest enters a study hall. It began a comeback, as one-by-one people realized that their mouths were still open but no sound was emerging. If she was hoping not to be noticed, she must have been sorely disappointed. Not only did the entire room do a mouth-breathing doubletake, two waiters who thought they could beat the other to her chair were smartly kicked in the ankle by the owner, who decided to exercise his management privilege and hoard all the sunshine for himself. He smoothly stepped in front of them to deliver his deepest bow, reach for her hand and croon, "Ah, Mrs. Pearson, how very nice to see you again."

Well, I'll be damned, I thought, *She's known here. Well then, it's not a tryst. Oh Pooh.*

"Ned," she said, extending her hand, "It's very nice to see you again. You've come a long way for lunch."

I shook her hand, gently, becoming uncomfortably aware of its warmth. Just as I was beginning to lose my focus, she removed her hand from mine and accepted the chair being held adoringly by El Capitan and his friends. As she was seated, the owner asked with a dazzling white and gold smile, "Something from the bar, Senora?"

"Yes, Ricardo, one of those, please..." She pointed at my nearly finished drink. "And another for Mr. Pearson, I think. Right, Ned?"

As I nodded my agreement, I caught the brief look of puzzlement in the eyes of old Ricardo who was slipping his clutch trying to figure out why this Mr. Pearson didn't look much like the other Mr. Pearson. However, being in the business he was in, he'd probably seen it all, so he gave up for the time being and moved off to fetch our drinks and take care of the rest of the business.

There is a phenomenon in life which, as a contrarian, I call now-you don't, now-you-see-it. Sometimes, when I lose something and look for it unsuccessfully, I later find it in plain sight exactly where I'd looked before. It also works occasionally on people. You see someone for the second time and it's like you hadn't seen them at all the first time. As I sat at the small table with its red cotton tablecloth and glowing oil lamp in the muted indoor light of the cantina, I kept thinking that this woman couldn't be the same one I had met a few years ago. I could not understand how my memory of this woman could have been so vague and nondescript. The woman across the table from me was anything but nondescript. Jennifer Paterson Pearson, widow of the late William Barker Pearson, was living, breathing proof that money can buy almost everything.

Certainly God or Mother Nature or Good Luck produced the fine, high cheekbones, the clear green eyes, the satin complexion and the 69 inch frame. But it was after-tax profits that produced the tan, healthy glow, the radiant, honey blonde hair, the soft wool Givenchy suit, the mauve silk blouse and the heavy silver bracelet opposite the ladies diamond Rolex.

And, of course, she had an attitude. No, not the "tude" of ghetto fame, but the attitude of a mature, very wealthy and secure woman about to share a meal with a reasonably attractive, possibly unattached, possibly interesting member of the opposite sex. I wouldn't call it anticipation, but perhaps active curiosity — as in, *I wonder where this might be going.*

Appropriately, the first thing she said was, "Now tell me what it was you wanted to see me about."

I decided I had no choice but to let Jennifer be responsible for her own level of sensitivity when talking about Willie. In other words, while I didn't want to be heavy handed, if something bothered her I hoped she would just say so and I would back off. Otherwise, I was just going to follow my nose in trying to make sense out of Aunt Blake's concerns.

"Well, Jennifer," I started, "I was wondering if you had noticed Willie acting differently in any way in the weeks before his accident. You know…preoccupied, tense, distracted, anything like that?"

"What did Aunt Blake tell you about that, Ned?" she replied. At the moment, I wasn't sure whether or not this was a diversion on her part or just an attempt to organize her thoughts.

"Well, she said that she tried to reach Willie a couple of times during those last two or three weeks and couldn't connect in the usual way. Each time, he called her back a day or so later, which, I guess, was unusual. At least, Aunt Blake thought it was." For no particular reason, I decided to leave out the part about Aunt Blake trying to reach Jennifer and failing, and the part about Willie saying that Jennifer wouldn't have known where he was. I guess I thought that would seem as if Aunt Blake and I were somehow keeping track of Willie's and Jennifer's lives; prying into things that were no business of ours. I just felt uncomfortable about that information.

I began to wonder about this woman's psychic powers when she said, "Willie started disappearing for odd periods of time."

"Disappearing?" I repeated.

"Yes. He would just drop out of sight and contact for one, sometimes two days at a time. When I asked him what was going on, he would say that it had to do with some investigation he was conducting…something connected with the business." Then, she very quietly dropped her eyes, looked into her lap as if ashamed of something. "I thought maybe he had grown tired of me and was having an affair or something, but I couldn't believe he would be so clumsy or cruel. Anyway, he denied it when I asked."

When she looked up, there was the tiniest tear in

the inside corner of each eye. As she looked squarely into my eyes, she smiled just the smallest bit.

I quietly died. My death was attended by Ricardo who showed up at that perfect moment. For this, *he* should have died. Instead, he was successful in delivering the menus. Jennifer sat back to dig in her bag for a tissue, while I tried not to make eye contact with Ricardo for fear that I might leap out of my chair and bite his silly, smiling face. To his credit, his short range antenna was sufficient to pick up the unspoken, electric signals emanating from our silence; the signal reading, "Vamoose...now!"

And vamoose he did, without even trying to deliver the specials of the day, if there were any. When he was gone, I looked over at Jennifer who had now composed herself. For the moment, I decided to change the subject. I really didn't know how to console this lovely woman, whose husband had died without warning after suddenly becoming a mystery man in an unfathomable way that suggested that maybe he didn't love her anymore.

"Sorry," she said, "I'm pretty much in control now, but every once in a while the pain wells up and I have to hang on very hard to stop it."

To hell with Amy Vanderbilt and all the rules, I thought at that moment. *Hang on to me, Jennifer, dear, oh do hang on to me.* What I said was, "I understand."

What I *wanted* to say was, 'Listen, this must have all been very hard on you and don't you think you need some time away from all these familiar and depressing surroundings. Like, I mean, wouldn't a couple of weeks in Maui be just what the doctor ordered to get yourself pulled together and ready to face the lonely life of a rich, gorgeous widow? I don't have anything on my plate that should take priority over lending my counsel and comfort to a member of the family. How soon can you leave?'

Did I say, psychic?

She said, "I probably should get away for a little while, but there've been so many things to look after. With the will and the company and all, I just haven't been able to do it. And I don't have a clue where I would go."

Now tell me about your benevolent god. Is this the sort of oriental torture designed by someone with my best interests at heart? This is the recent widow of my cousin sitting here looking absolutely exquisite, vulnerable and reading my mind.

We were interrupted again by Ricardo, inquiring about our selections from the menu. This time, I was actually glad to see him because I was about to say something to Jennifer that could start us down a truly uncharted path; a path that I could only imagine would produce regret in the end, but one that would certainly be interesting along the way. The other reason for gratitude over Ricardo's return was that the second margarita on an otherwise empty stomach was beginning to make its way to my head. Loss of control was not something I often experienced, and I certainly had no intention of allowing it to occur here and now.

Jennifer ordered *ceviche*, the refreshing Peruvian dish of raw whitefish diced and marinated in fresh lime juice, chopped peppers and cilantro. I chose the *ropa viella*, veal cooked slowly for a long time until the meat collapses into that shredded state similar to last week's pot roast. However, lest you think it tastes like old meat, let me assure you that the aromatic spices not only give the meat its fabulous aroma and taste, but combined with the slow cooking, they also tenderize an otherwise common piece of beef to the point that it melts in your mouth. Ah, peasant ingenuity. Some of the best food I've ever eaten was the product of necessity mothering delicious invention. This dish is no exception.

With Ricardo on his way back to the kitchen with our order, Jennifer turned and said, "Ned, I'm sorry I can't be more helpful than that, but I just don't know what Willie was after. And I don't know how to find out more, even if I wanted to."

Not wanting to press the issue too hard, I phrased my next question as delicately as I could. "Er, is there anyone at the office who could shed some light on Ned's behavior?"

"Well, Bob MacIntosh, who was Willie's right hand man, should be able to. But for all I know, he might be part of the problem. You know, Willie and I didn't share a lot about the business. For one thing, there was always the possibility of a conflict of interest because I was often trading in the stocks of companies that Willie was helping."

Not being much of a Wall Street Journal reader and majoring in English Lit, I didn't get a perfect picture of what she meant, so I asked, "What do you mean?"

"Do you know how Willie and I met?" she asked.

Not wanting to admit to my total ignorance, or have Jennifer think that she had been of no interest to me when she married Willie, I replied, "Not precisely." This, of course, was a polite lie. I didn't have a clue.

Jennifer did as most people do. She took me off the hook by telling me what I didn't know. "Willie and I met because I had a client who's personal investment portfolio I had been managing before his own company began to grow so fast that Willie spotted it and offered to take it public, you know, issue shares of stock in the company to public investors. My client came to me and asked me to liquidate his entire portfolio, so that he could buy more of his own stock prior to the public offering. Well, in addition to the tremendous tax problem that was going to create, I wasn't even sure that what he was proposing was legal. I asked him a few tough questions that he couldn't answer. Finally, he said that he wanted to put me together with this genius investment banker who was going to make him richer than any stock broker ever had. So, with that wonderful introduction, I agreed to a meeting with Willie in his office. I went there, determined to expose this unethical, unprincipled, unscrupulous villain I had created in my imagination and prepared for battle. And battle, we did. We must have argued for three or four hours. At first, I thought he was just a crook. Then, I thought he was a brilliant crook. Then, he showed me some regulations that I had never seen or heard of, and I began to think he was just plain brilliant.

"In the end, I was exhausted but convinced that his recommendations to my client were correct and that I'd have to go admit that I was wrong. At that, I got mad all over again, thinking that Willie had just cost me a very good client."

As she told her story, she took on a shine and then a sparkle of good humor that made her lose the look of pain that had come over her earlier. Once again, I began to feel that powerful attraction that began with her earlier arrival.

"Then, he floored me," she continued. "He said, 'Look, why don't we get together with Al,' Al was our mutual client, 'and tell him that we've worked out a plan for him and that it's very complicated. We'll finish the details later and bring it back to him. That way, in a little time, he'll forget what either of us had recommended earlier and he won't care anyway, as long as we both agree. That way, nobody has to back off in front of Al.'

"I couldn't believe my ears. Here's a man I figured for a typical chauvinist pig, a con artist and maybe a crook, who had just clearly proven that I had given our mutual client less than the best advice. He now had me in a bad professional corner and he was proposing to cooperate with me in a plan to get me off the hook in the eyes of the client. By now, it was late and he asked me if I'd like to get something to eat on the way home. Frankly, before I was married, I got that sort of invitation quite often. I knew it didn't just mean let's have a bite and continue our business. Usually, it meant a different kind of business. And usually, I declined. In this case, however, I was really confused by what had happened and I didn't want to insult him, so I said, 'Sure, as long as we go Dutch.'

"I know," she said, smiling at me ruefully, "that's old fashioned as hell. But it works on everyone except the cretins, and for them I just say no.

"So we did. We drove in separate cars to a little Italian place in Redwood City and ate pasta and drank a half carafe of dago red. Willie never made one funny move. We talked a little more about the business and the market and new issues, you know, shop talk and then drifted, as strangers do, into questions about each other and our backgrounds. I don't know how well you knew Willie. I guess you weren't very close. Otherwise, you and I would know each other better, but he was a very sad man. He told me that he and Catherine had separated six months earlier and that he missed his children very much. He didn't seem clear on whether or not he thought they could or would work out their problems, and I really didn't want to get too far into that subject anyway. And that was it. We finished the meal, had a cup of coffee, split the bill and went out into the parking lot. We stood by the cars and agreed to arrange a meeting with Al, the client, in about a week, shook hands and left. I remember wondering the next day if he would follow through on his offer to avoid telling Al that I had screwed up. I decided that I'd just have to wait and see what happened when we got together with Al. Well, the meeting day came and my secretary buzzed me to tell me that Willie was on the line. When I answered, he said, "Hi. Just calling to remind you that we've got a meeting with Al at eleven, and to see if you remember that we were going to tell Al that we have jointly worked out his problem and will get back to him later with the details."

"You bet," I said, and we hung up.

"Wow, I thought, *a straight arrow*. Sure enough, we had the meeting and it went exactly as planned. Al was tickled that he didn't have to spend any more time worrying about the details and that two people that he liked were apparently getting along and taking care of him, which was true. Nonetheless, I wasn't prepared for Al to say at the end of the meeting, as we were saying our goodbyes, 'Hey, you two should find a way to get to know each other better. Jennifer and I only have a professional relationship, but if I weren't happily married I might have tried to change that.' He shot Willie a big wink and game me a fatherly smile. Normally, I'd have been annoyed at the personal comments in a business environment, but Al seemed a

harmless product of his generation and Willie had acted in a sensitive way, so I joined in the smiling. We shook hands and left."

At this point, Ricardo slid up to the table to inquire about our satisfaction with the food, as well as our interest in coffee and dessert. We ordered espresso and a flan with two spoons. I don't know what Jennifer was thinking, but I think sharing dessert with a beautiful woman is one of the sexiest things there is to do with your clothes on. Of course, there are other ways but never mind.

She continued, "I'm not sure whether or not I was hoping that Willie would follow up on Al's suggestion, but I do know that when my secretary told me about a week later that Willie was on line one, I had such a rush of confused emotions that I told her to tell him I'd call right back in five minutes. I sat in my office with the door closed, wondering what the hell was happening to me. Finally, I dialed his office and was put through to him right away. He came on the line and, in that quiet voice of his, he said 'Listen, I've been thinking about what Al said last week and someone has given me two tickets to the opera, Aida, I think, and I don't know much about it. Would you like to go? It's Friday night.' I said, 'Yes. Would you like to pick me up?' And I gave him my address. I don't remember that much about the opera, but I do remember that we went down to the wharf for a late supper. Then, he drove me home.

"He left my house on Monday morning. His divorce was final six months later and we were married a month after that. That was two years ago."

Well, I thought, *a lonely man in the company of a delicious, intelligent woman. What else is new?* She hadn't told me a thing about herself and her reasons for marrying Willie, but I could speculate on a few — starting with, *Willie was probably smarter than the other men who floated through her life. And, he was gloriously rich. And, in need of friendship. Which leads to intimacy. Which leads to love. Which leads who knows where.* This reminded me that I might be standing in exactly the same place Willie was when the lightning of lust struck him right in the testosterone locker, which in turn reminded me that I'd better get back to my task which was to find out what was up with Willie just before he died.

"Jennifer," I asked, "Willie had quite a collection of fine cars, didn't he?"

She looked at me quickly with wide eyes, a bit startled I thought, but she recovered quickly and said, "Yes, he did. I'm just starting to make arrangements to dispose of them. He didn't trust Catherine to manage that well, so in his will he left her much of his other property, including about 40 million dollars worth of investments and his stock in the company. He left me quite a lot of cash, plus all the complicated investments, thinking that I could better sort them out. I knew he was doing that and I decided not to argue with him, even though I'd rather not have to go through all the hassle that's involved. The only good thing is that Catherine's lawyers have told her that she's better off having things with a known value than some of the intangible stuff that I got. It's depressing to talk about it."

"How do you plan to dispose of the car collection?" I asked.

"I've contacted one of the leading auctioneers in the country who deals with antique and vintage automobiles," she said, "And he's going to give me a proposal,"

Well, well, well, I thought, *Small world.* "Who is that?" I asked.

"It's a man named, Rodney Evans," she said, "Ever hear of him?"

"You're not going to believe this, but one of the reasons I came to California is to interview Evans for a story I'm doing about the vintage car business."

"Incredible!" she said, with a big smile, "Ned, could you help me with these arrangements? I mean, I don't know anything about these cars and you must be an expert."

"Not really," I said. "I know enough to be dangerous, although I do have some contacts that might be helpful checking out any proposal Evans might make."

"That's great," she said. "I've been putting this off because I didn't want to make any mistakes, and I wasn't sure how to begin. I'd feel much better, if I knew I had you to help me." She gently reached over and touched the back of my hand.

There is a moment just at the apex, the middle, of a 170 mile per hour curve, when the race car becomes extremely light and the steering becomes almost perfectly neutral. The lateral G-forces are at their peak and, very soon, the driver will know whether or not the car will continue on its present course, or if it will try to fly off the track or begin a fatal spinning move. At that moment, one stops breathing in order to concentrate on the car's behavior during the next full second. If, in the first three tenths of a second, the car begins to move its rear end outward—which is called oversteer—it's telling the driver that a spin is about to begin. At that point, the brain calls for a steering correction and a throttle correction. Each change must be made with the care and gentle touch of a surgeon working near the aorta. One sudden move, and you and the car are finished—for the day, or maybe longer.

When Jennifer touched me, I felt that same instant requirement for calm. I also stopped breathing in order not to do anything sudden, as if I might frighten her. As for myself, I was scared to death. Why, I don't know, except to guess that somehow a relationship in balance might go out of balance and spin out of control, if I made a mistake now. As I was beginning to decide whether or not I dared to look into her eyes while that feathery touch lay on my hand, she suddenly withdrew it and waved for Ricardo and the check.

Hayzoos Kreestos, I thought, *my man, you've got to get a grip on yourself. This woman is fogging your goggles. You need to back off and slow down.* That seemed to do the trick and we both watched as Ricardo made his way toward us with the bill. As I reached for it, Jennifer smoothly intercepted and said with a grin, "No, I insist. I'm retaining you as my official advisor on matters automotive, and this was a deductible business luncheon under IRS regulation something or other."

I sat back, smiled and thought, *Ah, liberation. Long may your banner wave. I'll accept a free lunch from a drop dead blonde every chance I get. My number's in the book.*

After she'd finished paying the bill, she turned and said, "Listen, the cars are kept in a garage on our, I mean, my property, not far from the house. Would you like to see them?"

I can't say exactly why but a little warning light blinked quietly near the back of my mind and made me pause to think about my answer that logically and under normal circumstance would have been, "Hell yes, let's go!" I am, after all, a car freak and almost any car, no matter how modest, holds some interest for me.

In other words, I should have jumped at the offer. But somehow, I had this nagging feeling that I was wandering along near the edge of something and if I didn't begin to plan each step carefully, I could easily step off that edge and into something completely beyond my control. I get the same feeling sometimes in a race car when I'm right on the edge of the outer limits of the car's performance envelope. There are little indescribable feelings; some based on subtle readings of the information coming back from the car's behavior and some based on all that experience filed away down there in the subconscious. More than once, I've been chasing another driver and realized that lap after lap, he's getting closer to the edge, or what's called "ten tenths," and then been able to predict on what lap and at which corner he would finally spin the car out. My crew goes crazy when I do this on the radios that we use to stay in touch. I say something like, "I think Duvallier's tires are going. He's been missing the apex on seven for four laps. He'll go off in the next two laps." Sure enough, not every time, but often enough to make you respect what you're seeing, he goes off in the next two laps.

So you learn to pay attention when that little warning signal says, "There's something you should know about. Pay attention."

As we made our way out to the parking area and stood between our two cars, I decided that I really didn't want to go back to Jennifer's house with her. Perhaps, I was fantasizing too much or perhaps my ego was working overtime, but I just had this uncomfortable feeling that I should get some space between us and sort out my plans. I made an instant decision to tell a little white lie. She hadn't asked and I hadn't said what my schedule was, or where I was going next. Thankfully, I realized that we just hadn't gotten around to that so I was free to invent whatever excuse I needed. I said, "Boy, I'd love to but I'm due in San Francisco around four. I've got a meeting with an old college friend who works for the Chronicle. He has some friends at State Patrol Headquarters in Sacramento who he thinks might be helpful."

Her eyes widened ever so slightly and her nostrils imperceptibly flared, as she breathed inward. I thought, *Damn. Now she thinks you're going to do an "I'll call you sometime," number and disappear on her.*

"Listen," I said, "Here's my schedule." I completely made it up as fast as my mind would work, so this lovely creature who was asking for my help would not think I was brushing her off. "I have this meeting in San Francisco. Then I promised Aunt Blake that I would stop and see Catherine in Sonoma just to hear whatever she might have to contribute to the puzzle. I also thought that if you didn't mind, I would take a look around the ski lodge at Tahoe. That's where he was before he...he had the accident, wasn't it?"

During all of this, her face was unreadable — calm and placid, but watchful. However, when I mentioned the lodge, her eyes widened just a little and she put her lower lip under her upper teeth, softly. I thought she might be preparing to tell me that she'd rather I not go to the lodge, but all she quietly said was, "I have an extra set of keys I can give you."

"Great," I said, and I was so relieved when she no longer seemed upset that I decided I could modify the schedule a little bit to accommodate what she really wanted — to get started on dumping Willie's collection.

I suggested, "Why don't we see if we can see this guy Evans in Monterey tomorrow? Maybe I could pick you up and we'll drive down in the morning and have lunch, depending on what his schedule is."

At this, she brightened like the sun coming out from behind a cloud. She said, "I have his number at the house. I'll call him as soon as I get home. Where will you stay tonight? The guest room is always made up. I never knew when Willie would show up with one of his software geniuses to spend the night, talking about the next generation of microprocessors or something."

I quickly told another lie. "I'm staying with my friend and his new wife who he wants me to meet. I guess we're having dinner." I hated this routine, but I needed some space to sort out where this was going.

"Alright," she said, seemingly resigned to the fact that I was definitely leaving.

Now I felt like a real shit for dragging Willie's death out of the box again. "I'm very sorry to bring all this up again," I said. This time, I reached over and took her hand in mine just to let her know that I really was sorry. I shouldn't have done that because there was that warm, soft touch again, making the heart rate rise and the mind wander. At five nine, she was tall enough so that we could look into each other's eyes without much bending of the neck. This also meant that I could feel her breath rising gently with the slight aroma of alcohol and caramel from the flan, all mixed with the scent of the elegant cologne I'd first noticed when she sat down at the table. This time, the warning light did not blink. It flooded my brain.

I took one step backward, smiled broadly and reached for the door of her car. It was a spectacular, pearlescent, eggshell white, Mercedes 500 SL roadster, which costs about a hundred and five thousand, tax and title included out the dealer's door. "Don't forget the lodge keys," I said, trying to get us to move away as quickly as possible from that abyss I knew was waiting for just one misstep.

She reached into her purse and quickly produced a set of four keys on a ring. She explained each of them, "Front door, garage, side door and storage locker." I nodded that I understood her explanation, anxiously wanting to get this over with and down the road so I could sort out my confused feelings. She handed the keys to me, letting the tips of her fingers drift across mine just ever so lightly as the keys dropped into my palm. She looked up with a warm smile and said, "Promise you'll call me tonight? I'm really looking forward to tomorrow. I mean, I've wanted to get started on this and I really need your help. I just can't do it alone. Do you know what I mean?"

I was terribly afraid that I did — know what she meant, that is. I said I would call her and moved over to my car.

As I got in and started the Mustang, she backed out, swung the Mercedes around and accelerated onto the highway northbound toward Rte 92. I got one last flash of that golden head and she was gone, leaving me to take my first deep breath and begin to organize my thoughts and plans. All of these, of course, I had invented on the spot in order to get away from a Beautiful Rich Widow who seemed to like me very much, so much that she wanted to take me home with her. I, of course, declined the invitation.

I, of course, could be an idiot.

SAN FRANCISCO

As I pulled out of the parking lot and pointed the Mustang north toward San Francisco, my mind was a maelstrom of confusing thoughts. First among them was my reaction to Jennifer. I don't know that I had any specific expectation in mind as I planned this trip, but I certainly did not expect to find someone so attractive. There, I've said it. I was attracted — very!

I mean, if I had known that she would look and sound and feel like this, then I might have been prepared to deal with it a little more, how shall I say it, distantly. I mean, I was there on an errand of mercy, so to speak, just trying to give Aunt Blake a little piece of mind. I really had other things in life that I must do and I just didn't have time to get involved with a Beautiful Rich Widow — no, my late cousin's Beautiful Rich Widow — which makes it even more complicated.

I also realized that I was being very egocentric. I was assuming that Jennifer was sharing the attraction when it was quite possible that she was just a stressed out, grieving person who needed a little support in a time of extreme duress. *Yeah, right.* Damn, I was confused as to the signals I was receiving.

I made myself a promise to keep a tight rein on my feelings tomorrow and to try to find out more about where Jennifer was coming from and where she might be going.

I also realized that I'd been so taken by Jennifer's presence that I'd done really very little thinking about the real purpose of the trip, that is, what happened to Willie. I decided that as soon as I had found a place to stay, I'd call this fellow MacIntosh at Willie's office and set up an appointment.

I knew that I should also call Catherine and let her know that I was in town and wanted to see her. A little notice would be polite and also prudent in case she had travel plans of her own.

Finally, I began to think about our trip tomorrow and this fellow, Evans. I was looking forward to meeting him and I needed to begin thinking about a story line for the article. After all, Arthur deserved something decent for his thoughtfulness.

By this time, I had reached the sprawling, southwestern suburbs of San Francisco and begun to make my way to the little Japanese hotel I prefer whenever I'm there. It's a little out of the way — that is, it's not right in the heart of the business district, but that's part of its attraction for me. I can't ever recall hearing the words "fast track" or "career path" spoken in the tiny little teak paneled bar off the lobby. Also, they usually have a room on short notice which is a boon to free spirits like me who feel about reservations and advanced planning the way lumberjacks feel about white shirts with starched collars.

In a fairly short time, after pulling the Mustang into the underground parking garage, I was in a very comfortable room on the fourteenth floor with a lovely view of San Francisco Bay to the east. This being truly a Japanese hotel — owned by, designed by, and operated by — the room was decorated in that cool, simple, serene style so favored by the oriental psyche.

And it contained the ultimate luxury — the Japanese bath. Living as the Japanese have for so many centuries, on too little land to properly feed and house the population, they learned long ago something that has managed to escape many in Western civilization — people stink. They breed germs. And they pass them around.

Accordingly, the Japanese have developed the bath into a high art. And my room was equipped with tools of that art; a square porcelain tub of generous proportions fed by two shower heads, a three legged stool on the platform adjacent to the tub and several firm brushes for scrubbing away the wrapper of dying epidermis we all walk around in.

And, of course, there was a selection of perfumed soaps and emollients with the spices and fragrances of the Orient. The drill is to start the water running in the tub as hot as you can get it, pour in a little of this or that and enjoy the fragrant mist as you turn on one of the shower heads. Then, sitting on the stool, you scrub the bejesus out of your whole body with strong soap and a firm brush. Front, back, top and, heh-heh, bottom. Palms of the hands. Soles of the feet. The whole nine yards. Just when you've got the whole thing tingling and glowing, you pop it into the hot tub and let all those frustrations and disappointments, all the struggles of life, all the things that just didn't quite work out get melted away and replaced by a whole new, fresh stock of peace and optimism. *Aaahh...nice.*

All of this took me about an hour, so I still had time to make my phone calls. My first was to the number I had gotten from Aunt Blake for Willie's office. As the phone rang, I prepared myself to talk to a total stranger about whom I knew very little, other than that he was a business partner of Willie's who, in Jennifer's words, "Might be part of the problem." For all I knew, MacIntosh hated Willie's guts and would have no interest in talking to a cousin from the East Coast who might be here to muck around in affairs he knew nothing about and even further complicate an already unpleasant situation.

After identifying myself to the receptionist, I was put on hold for a while. Then I heard the change in signal strength that identifies the opening of new circuits. In other words, my call was being transferred. Then a second, more mature voice came on the line to say without preamble, "Mr. MacIntosh will be right with you, Mr. Pearson." I remember being impressed with the professional tenor of that voice and the confidence that I was, in fact, actually on the line without asking. I waited. Then, a strong voice in the middle range and no accent that I could detect said, "Mr. Pearson, what can I do for you?" It was the same voice that lawyers use to speak to total strangers who may be the firm's next wealthy client, or nothing more than a brief interruption in a busy day — noncommittal but correct.

"Mr. MacIntosh, I've come to California to inquire about my cousin's — *damn, I couldn't think of a word that didn't sound like an investigation* — uh, activities before his death."

He paused, evaluated. "His activities? I'm not quite sure what you mean, Mr. Pearson."

"Well, Mr. MacIntosh, Willie's mother, Blake Pearson…do you know Mrs. Pearson?"

"I have met her, of course, but we haven't spoken since Willie's passing."

"Well, Mr. MacIntosh, Aunt Blake had some conversations with Willie during the weeks before his death that were, shall we say, concerning to her in regards to Willie's happiness, his state of mind. She's asked me to get a little more background on those conversations just to clarify for her what Willie might have meant by some of the things he said."

"What sort of things were those, Mr. Pearson?" It was the same flat, arms length voice.

I decided that I needed to sharpen my pencil a little with this guy. "Actually what I was hoping, Mr. MacIntosh, was that I could stop by your office and discuss this with you in some detail while I'm here."

"How long will you be here, Mr. Pearson?"

Ah, the salesman's old 'how much do you have to spend' question. "As long as it takes, Mr. MacIntosh."

"Well, of course. I'll be happy to help Mrs. Pearson in any way I can, but I'm a little puzzled as to exactly what it is you're looking for."

"I'll try to explain that when I see you, Mr. MacIntosh. When could we get together?"

"Well, I'm really not sure. My schedule is quite full…what, with all the adjustments we've had to make in Willie's absence. Isn't this something we could do on the phone?"

Why is this guy being so cold? Is he just not sure of who I was and afraid to talk to a stranger? Is there some problem between he and Willie's family that no one's told me about? Or is he hiding something? I decided I had little to risk by turning up the heat a little to see what would bubble. I took an educated shot in the dark and said, "Mr. Mac-

Intosh, am I correct in assuming that you are the second largest stockholder in the firm after Willie's estate?"

"Why yes, that's true," he said, "but I don't see what that's got to do with what you were asking about a minute ago."

"Well," I said, loosening up my best tone of insinuation, "it probably doesn't, but I was just thinking that if the firm was in any difficulty, if Willie was, for some reason, under duress, you know, some money pressure or something that would explain unusual behavior... well, I was just thinking that you, as a major stockholder, would have been quite concerned. You see what I mean?"

It worked. Now the tone was a little thinner. "What kind of problem were you thinking of, Mr. Pearson?"

"Oh I didn't have anything specific in mind, just something that might affect the reputation of your firm. Look, why don't we stop wasting each other's time and set a date. I'm obviously not going to discuss this over the phone and it may only take 15 minutes out of your busy schedule and the whole thing will be finished. I'm really just doing Willie's mother a favor. Why don't you humor me a little and I'll he out of your hair in a jiffy." The part I left unspoken was, 'tightass.'

"I could spare a few minutes on Friday morning, say eleven?"

"That'll be nifty, Mr. MacIntosh. I'll see you then."

As I hung up, I had mental images of the next half hour in old MacIntosh's life, as he did a high speed check on who the hell Edwin Hartford Pearson was and what he was sniffing around about. But he'd have to be damn careful because if I was telling the truth, if I really was helping Willie's mother and old MacIntosh asked the wrong question in the wrong place he had to know that R.B.II, Willie's father, would soon be on the case, as well. This would not be good. I'd have to wait and see whether or not MacIntosh had something to hide, or was just naturally an anal personality. Either way, my job was to get to the truth and I'd had lots of practice at that.

I hoped that my next call would not be quite so abrasive. As I dialed Catherine Pearson in Sonoma, I thought about the last time that I had seen her. It was at least five years ago, obviously before the separation from Willie. I certainly didn't feel close to Catherine. Over the years, I had spent a few hours in the same rooms with her at family gatherings. I'd always found her pleasant enough, but of course she was always in the shadow of "Willie the Great," as he was known in my youthful resentment. An attractive woman, but with no distinguishing features, Catherine was the perfect wife for a young tiger on Wall Street. Bennington and the School of Fine Arts at Columbia gave Catherine sufficient social credentials to admit her to the finer circles in Manhattan and led to a well-ordered, affluent life of child-rearing, charitable works and the occasional business entertainment. No one would ever have thought to ask, "How are Willie and Catherine getting along?" It was clear that Willie was an enormous success in investment banking and that just automatically assured everyone that Catherine must be thrilled to death with her life. After all, she never complained, did she?

Thus, their world of friends and acquaintances was rocked when the news of the separation quickly spread. Of course, almost everyone attributed the problem to some sort of mid-life crisis of Willie's. Why this affliction is almost exclusively a disability of men is a phenomenon to me. I've never heard anyone say, "Oh, they're not getting along because *she's* experiencing a midlife crisis."

In any event, it was generally understood that Willie had left Catherine, but no one believed that he was fleeing to someone else's arms. That this partially softened the blow for Catherine was the common wisdom. Old Willie, therefore, was not lost forever, it was thought. He'd come home wagging his tail behind him, by and by.

No one planned on Jennifer. And no one planned on Willie dying.

My muse was interrupted by a cheerful voice saying, "Hello?" with that rising question mark at the end that seems to signify, "I don't know who you are yet but I'm happy you called. Let's proceed."

"Catherine, this is Ned Pearson, Willie's cousin."

There was a pause.

"Ned, how are you?" she asked, with the same enthusiasm as she had answered the phone.

"I'm fine, Catherine. I'm in San Francisco and I was hoping I could get to see you before I return to New York. Actually, it's about Willie's death." *Damn, I wish I'd rehearsed a smoother way into this conversation.* I didn't have a clue as to what Catherine's feelings were about in all of this. I was operating on the standard male assumption that Catherine was probably some kind of grieving first widow or something.

As I struggled to find a way to continue, she interrupted in a more somber tone and asked, "What is it about Willie's death that you wanted to talk about, Ned?"

"Catherine, please forgive me. I shouldn't have just

jumped into this without asking how you are feeling. How are you feeling?"

"I'm fine now, Ned. Of course, it was a terrible shock and it's going to take a while for the kids to heal. First, they had to go through the separation and now his death. It's almost too much to ask of teenagers, with all the other adjustments involved in simply growing up...to have to deal with the loss of your father, as well. Do you know what I mean?"

"I do," I said, "You might not remember this, but my dad died when I was 19. My world ended, at least for a while. It was awful. I dropped out of school for a year and just moped. I had some pretty dreadful moments when I wasn't sure if I could go on living."

"Oh Ned, I didn't know that. Well then, you can see why I'm so worried about William. He's 18 and just finishing his first year at Stanford. He wanted to quit and come home, but I've asked him to finish the year and then decide about the future. I don't know whether or not he's going to make it." Then, kind of as an afterthought, she asked, "Ned, would you think, I mean, would you be willing to talk to William about your experience? You know, tell him you understand how he feels and that it will get better with time, and that he shouldn't just stop now because staying busy is the best way to deal with the pain? You know, I try to tell him these things, but it would mean more, I think, coming from you because you're a man and you've been where he is and all..."

This all came gushing out and I thought that maybe she wouldn't stop for fear that when she did, I'd say no for some reason. Instead, I interrupted her to say, "Catherine, I'd be happy to talk to William and I'm sure it could do some good."

"Oh, Ned, that would be such a relief to me to know that William could talk to someone about his feelings and not be left alone to work out his problems. I can't tell you how worried I've been...what, with all this teenage suicide you read about. Thank God Linda is still here with me and I can spend time with her day-to-day.

"Oh that's just terrific," she said, brightening up again, as if a great weight had just been lifted from her shoulders. Now tell me what it is that you're concerned about Willie's death. Just so you understand, Ned, or maybe I should say so you don't misunderstand, the separation occurred a long time ago and it was mutual. As I grew older, I realized that Willie and I had very little in common, except a social circle and two children. For a long time, it seemed essential to keep the marriage together just for the sake of the children, but eventually Willie was away so often and for such long periods that he became much like a visiting parent in a divorce. We ultimately decided that we should try living separately, so we did. Then, he met Jennifer and that was that."

All of this was delivered in such a matter of fact way that I began to be relieved of the guilty feelings I'd experienced at the beginning of the call.

"Well, Catherine," I said, "no one ever knows what really goes on in situations like this. People only speculate. I'm glad to hear that you're surviving this. What I'm interested in is finding out more about Willie's behavior just prior to the accident. Aunt Blake thinks that he was acting strangely. Did she mention it to you at the funeral?"

"Yes, she did, and I told her that I could only think of two things."

"What were those?"

"Well, the first is that Willie became less punctual than normal. You know, one of the things that eventually drove me crazy was that for years Willie was the original efficiency expert. Everything had to run on a pre-planned schedule. Bless his heart, he recently began to become a little unpredictable, you know, showing up late. And once, and this was not funny, he completely forgot about one of Linda's school programs and didn't show up at all. Can you imagine?"

I couldn't because I didn't know Willie that well, but I'd take Catherine's word for it. "What was the other thing?"

"Well, Ned, he used to take the kids skiing a lot. He'd pick up Little Bill at Stanford, drive up here, pick up Ann and take them up to the lodge at Tahoe. After one of those trips, Ann told me later...and after that Little Bill confirmed it; Willie behaved in a strange way. Apparently, he was not interested in skiing at all, telling the kids to go ahead without him. And when they returned, he had all of his car books spread out on the floor and was making notes about something."

"Did the kids say what about?"

"No, that's the strange thing. He wouldn't say when they asked. I didn't pay much attention when they told me. It's only when you and Blake asked about Willie's behavior that it occurred to me."

"Hmmm. Well, the changed habits are consistent with what Aunt Blake felt. I guess we'll see what else I learn, if anything."

"Where are you staying if I think of anything else?"

I gave her the name of my hotel and we hung up wishing each other good luck. I was happy to learn that she was not the victim I had thought.

That taken care of, I looked up Jennifer's number again and dialed. *By now, she should have had time to reach Evans and try for an appointment.* She answered on the third ring. Once again, I had a small physical reaction to that velvety voice. "Hello?"

"Hi, Jennifer. It's me...Ned."

"Oh, terrific. I was hoping you would call before I had to go out. We have an appointment with Rod Evans at 11:00, tomorrow morning. He's invited us to lunch, if we're free. Can we stay, do you think?"

"I have the time, if you'd like to," I said.

"That's great. I think it would be fun and you said you wanted to interview him anyway, didn't you? I thought we could kill two birds and all that."

I was mildly alarmed and asked, "Jennifer, did you tell Evans that I was a writer?" I don't think much of ambush journalism as a practice and I had planned to let Evans know over lunch that I wanted an interview for my publisher, but I also wanted a little look-see before he got too much of an opportunity to polish up the act for the media.

"Oh no," she quickly replied, "I just told him that you were a relative of Willie's and interested in cars, and that you were helping me decide what to do with the collection. Is there anything wrong with that?" She sounded a little wounded and I thought maybe I had been too rough.

"No, not at all. I just wanted to know what he would be expecting. I'll tell him myself tomorrow."

"Fine," she said, "now you'll need some directions to my house, won't you? I mean, we'll drive down together, won't we?"

"You got it. How do I get there from the city?" I asked, trying to slow down my rising pulse rate, as I thought of the prospect of a leisurely drive in the country with a very pleasant feminine companion. She gave me the directions, we agreed on the time we needed to leave her house for Monterey and the time it should take me to reach her house in the morning. We then said our goodbyes, assuring each other that we were both looking forward to tomorrow's trip.

After I hung up, I found my mind wandering back over the conversation and eventually got to the part where she said that she was glad I'd reached her before she had to go out. *Out where?* I wondered. It was almost seven o'clock by now. *Where would she be going at this hour? Out for dinner? To a meeting? With whom?* And suddenly, I realized what was happening here.

My God, I thought, *I'm jealous. I've gotten possessive. I've known this woman for one day and I'm wondering who she's spending her time with. Get hold of yourself, boy. This is going to be a whole lot of trouble, if you can't stick to your knitting. Finish your business here and get on with your life...your happy, carefree, single life.*

And recognizing sound advice when I hear it, I dressed and went over to Ernie's, ordered the Whiskey Steak medium rare, a bottle of Zaca Mesa Vintner's Reserve Sirah and got quietly shitfaced.

Then I went back to the hotel and slept the sleep of the truly content.

WOODSIDE

The next day, a Thursday in late April, turned out to be one of the most wonderful days of my entire life. No matter what happened later, no matter where this would all lead, that day was simply exquisite.

I hear people say that they have no regrets, that they would "not change a thing." Frankly, I generally think that's dumb. I mean, if you have no regrets, it must mean that you have either no ambition or no imagination. Either you don't wish that something or other had gone better than it did, or you simply can't imagine that it could have. I mean, wouldn't one have at least wanted to be richer or smarter or better looking or something? Having said that, I must admit for that one day, I have no regrets.

I was up early that morning, partly in anticipation of the day ahead and partly because of a little jet lag. My body was still a bit on East Coast time. This was fine with me because I needed to get organized and down to Jennifer's house in Woodside by 8:00 or so, in order to leave time to take a look at Willie's car collection before we left for Monterey. This was a work day and the freeway would probably be slow going down past the airport.

I opened the drapes on the sliding window that led onto the tiny terrace facing East and the sunlight flooded the room. I slid open the glass door and stepped out into the cool Bay air. I took a deep breath, admiring the view across the peninsula, out to the Oakland Bay Bridge and south across the Bay, itself.

I love to travel and one of the things I love most is the early morning in a new city when the people are just beginning to stir. The air has been washed overnight by the winds from last night's falling temperatures, maybe leaving some dew on the surface of streets and buildings. Everything looks and smells fresh, as if it were on display in a greengrocer. Of course, some cities smell fresher than others and San Francisco is the freshest because of the water on both sides.

Having filled my lungs with that fresh, slightly salty air, I left the door open to air out the room and went in to take my shower and get organized. Afterward, I dressed quickly in fresh, pressed jeans, a cotton polo shirt, a raw silk blazer and a pair of Bally loafers. In other words, I was California chic. After all, I was going traveling with a smashing blonde to meet a bucks-up auto tycoon in one of the world's poshest ports. One should dress properly.

I also threw my Nikon in a small bag with some other odds and ends that I thought I might need during the day. I considered and then rejected the idea of taking my trusty laptop computer, thinking that I wouldn't be doing any actual writing today and it would be excess baggage. I took one last look around the room and closed the door, checking to make sure that I had the keys. I walked to the elevator and went down to the lobby.

I decided to let the hotel know that I would be staying a few more days and that would at least include the weekend. This news was received with appreciation, since most business hotels absolutely die on the weekends. That re-established my credentials as a preferred customer, which got me an invitation to the continental breakfast offered to friends of the house. I accepted and was pleasantly surprised to find that the fruit and pastry were both fresh and of excellent quality. With coffee and grapefruit in my tummy and a cheese Danish in my hand, I went down to the garage thinking that if I didn't put the brakes on the calorie intake soon, not only would I not be able to get into my driving suit, I wouldn't be able to get into the race car.

On the way to Jennifer's house, I thought about the day ahead and what Evans might be like, along with the angle I might want to pursue with the story. *Do I want this to be mainly a personal profile, or should it be more about the business of collector cars — what are now being called "investment grade automobiles?" Jesus*, I thought, what have we come to? There isn't a shred of doubt that Herr Daimler, Mr. Ford and even Ing. Ferrari in the beginning thought that they were designing and producing something that would eventually wear out and be disposed of. They hadn't a clue that their creations might someday become "investment grade" — like a municipal bond, or a warrant, or a pork belly. But they have.

I remembered reading that Ferrari had produced less than forty thousand cars since he began in the late forties and that the combined prices of all those cars when they were first sold was about a billion and a half dollars, or less than forty thousand dollars per car. Then, I'd read in the last ten years that collectors had bid the prices of those same cars up to an average of four hundred to five hundred thousand dollars each. Some of them were selling for five and six *million* and some Jap was supposed to have paid twelve million for one.

Think of it, I thought, *twenty billion dollars worth of cars. And that's just Ferraris. Doesn't include Mercedes, Bugattis, Maseratis and God knows what all that the high-rollers are trading around like prize horses or fine art.*

And our boy, Evans, sitting right in the middle of all that juicy commerce. Must be a buck or two sticking to him, I thought. *This could be very interesting.*

Before I knew it, I was at the exit I needed for Jennifer's place in Woodside. Following her directions, I soon arrived at the entrance to a drive marked *Pearson,* with a field stone pillar on either side. Turning in, I drove up a long, slightly curving driveway, which eventually branched with the left fork continuing past the house and the right one turning into a small circle at the near end of the house and bounded at the rear by a multi-car garage. The circle was covered in off-white pea gravel like that of the driveway. On one side, there was a low timbered rail that indicated the parking area. As I parked the Mustang, I could see into the yard behind the house, where there was a swimming pool, large bathhouse and lovely formal gardens. All-in-all, it was nothing too dramatic, but *large and comfortable* was my first impression. The house itself was cloned in the California mission style, with lots of redwood and fieldstone. A wide, low veranda ran across the front, with that deep Spanish-style overhang for avoiding the hot western sun. There were climbing roses growing from pots at the base of each of the pillars and some hanging pots of a beautiful yellow flower I didn't recognize between the pillars. The veranda came around the side of the house in my direction. In the shade under the overhang, I could see a wide screen door leading into the house in a direct line from the short, red-tiled walkway that lead up from the gravel onto the veranda.

As I finished taking all this in, the screen door opened and Jennifer stepped out into the sunlight with a big smile. She walked straight up to me, stuck out her hand, offered her cheek for the familiar air kiss and said, "You're a very prompt man. I thought maybe you wouldn't be here for another 20 minutes or so."

All of this happened quickly; too quickly for me to deal with the rush of competing thoughts like, *Jesus, she's just as gorgeous as I thought...There's that warm hand again...Nothing suggestive in the air kiss...Oh, am I early?*

"Well," I said, "I wasn't sure how long it would take to get here and I wanted some time to look at the cars. I wasn't sure how long it would take to get to Monterey...." And I realized that I was babbling and Jennifer was grinning. I just shut up and grinned back. I decided that this was the time for some of my famous patience, time to let Jennifer lead, so I kept my mouth shut long enough for her to say, "Good, I'm glad you're here. We'll have plenty of time. How 'bout some coffee? Have you had breakfast?"

"Love some coffee, and yes, I had breakfast at the ...."

Oops, I almost said 'hotel' when I told Jennifer I was staying with friends. "...the Johnsons."

One of the reasons I so seldom lie is because it's so much trouble keeping track of the lie, so that you don't contradict yourself in a careless moment. Jennifer glanced at me briefly and started toward the door. I couldn't tell whether or not she caught the stumble, but then I decided that it didn't make that much difference. Probably the worst she could imagine is that I had a date or something I didn't want to talk about.

Over her shoulder, she said, "Come on in. I just made fresh coffee. It should be ready by now. Then we'll go down to the barn and look at the cars."

She had on a white silk jersey pullover with three-quarter sleeves, a scoopneck over faded jeans and a pair of the most expensive looking, dove gray, hand-tooled, calfskin cowboy boots I'd ever seen. With the long legs in the tight, well-worn jeans and the wonderful affect that high heels have on a woman's rump, I was having a marvelous time on this all too short trek to the kitchen.

She had the walk of an expensive runway model — no vamping, no wiggle, no rock and roll. It was just a fluid, feline, headup stride with a hint of the athlete — and all woman.

All too soon, we reached the kitchen; a large, sunny, wood, stone and tile room designed by someone who loves food and cooking. With a big chop block in the middle and pot racks everywhere, we might have been in the kitchen of a fairly good sized restaurant.

As Jennifer set out the cups and poured the coffee, I asked, "Do you cook?"

"Not so much anymore," she said, without looking up. "It's not so much fun cooking for one and, even before Willie, uh, died, he was away an awful lot so l kind of lost interest."

"Are you a good cook?" I asked, which may sound rude or stupid, but I've found that for some strange reason, people rarely delude themselves about this or try to fake it. Most will tell you straight out if they're good or no good without much embarrassment. Jennifer was no different.

Without hesitation, she said, "I'm pretty good. You should let me cook something for you sometime."

"I will," I said, while my brain flew out the window and around the house a couple of times, praying she wouldn't say, "When?" I didn't think I could stand much more of this and might just lose my grip. *I might beg for breakfast and a place to lie down. Now. With her? Stop it!*

Instead, she asked, "Cream or sugar?"

"Black," I replied, as I calmed down a little and took the offered cup.

"Shall we walk down to the barn?" she asked, moving toward the opposite end of the kitchen from where we had entered. I nodded my agreement during a sip of my coffee and set off after her again. This time, I decided that my viewing pleasure should be confined to the back of that golden head and the interior of the house we were passing through.

The rest of the house was just what the kitchen and the exterior would have suggested — lots of adobe, Spanish tiles and exposed beams. There were thick, wool, native rugs and throws everywhere in the strong colors of the southwestern desert. The furniture was large, boldly designed and fit well in the great open spaces of the house. It was a warm, secure house; a place to read and recharge the batteries. And Jennifer looked like a bright bouquet of spring flowers moving through it.

We finally reached another door at the far end of the house that opened on to another broad veranda.

Only this one overlooked two barns, some paddocks and an equipment shed that fronted a very tidy and compact riding ring. In one of the paddocks, two sleek and handsome chestnut quarter horses stood. "That's Martha and her son, Toughy," said Jennifer.

I'm not really into horses, so I don't understand the science of choosing their names. All I know is that if people named their dogs the way people name their horses, the dogs would bite them in the face — and rightfully so.

"Do you ride?" asked Jennifer.

"No, I'm afraid not," I said.

"Like horses?" she asked.

"I like them fine," I replied, "I just don't care a lot about riding them," thinking, *I hope I'm not failing some important test here.*

"Willie wasn't very interested, either," she said, "I wonder why women are more interested in them than men?"

Not me, Baby. I'm not touching that with a ten foot pole, I thought.

"Gee, I never thought about that," I said, adding, "Are the cars in one of the barns?"

"Right," she said, "the one over there." We began to walk in that direction.

I could see from where we were that one of the barns was actually closed more tightly than the other, apparently to seal it from the weather and the dust of the farm. That would make sense, if you were trying to preserve several million dollars worth of machinery from the ravages of time and the environment. As we drew closer, I could see that new windows had been installed and there was evidence of some kind of ventilation system on the roof.

As if reading my mind just like yesterday at lunch, Jennifer said, "Willie spent a fortune weatherproofing this old barn and installing a climate control system to protect the cars. It always seemed a little silly to me to bring them here in the first place if they were so fragile, but Willie didn't want to leave them in storage in one of the commercial facilities set up to care for them. He wanted them where he could look at them once in a while, and even occasionally drive some of them."

Now there's a news flash. I'd thought that these things were strictly a commodity to Willie, like debentures or bushels of wheat. I never thought that he actually gave a damn about using them for what they were made to do—driving them. It was turning out that there was a lot about Willie's life that I didn't know.

As we neared the door of the barn, I saw that there was a key pad on the wall beside it. Jennifer punched in a series of five numbers and there was a quiet, metallic *snick*, as the lock bolt slid back out of its socket.

Pretty slick, I thought. *Serious business.*

"Willie had this system installed so that the mechanics and caretakers could come and go without having a set of keys. Also, it's electronically controlled so that we can change the combination from the house. Once in a while, you have to let a stranger in and you don't want them leaving with the combination so you give them a temporary, one-time code. If you have a disgruntled employee who has to be fired, you just change the code. You can even change it by phone." At that, she giggled, "Isn't that silly? All this nonsense about a bunch of old cars?"

Actually, I didn't think so at all. I thought it was damn smart. But there was no way I was going to disagree with this lovely creature on this sunny, Spring morning. "Boy, this must have cost a fortune," I said, avoiding the issue of silly or not.

"Well, it did," said Jennifer, "but Willie was smart. He got most of the cost back by convincing the insurance company that he should get a lower rate because the cars were so well protected. I forgot to tell you that there is also a fire alarm system included, with a direct line to the local fire department."

"Very smart," I agreed.

By this time, we were inside the barn. Jennifer touched some more switches on the wall and the barn was flooded with bright overhead light. And there, parked neatly on a bed of sparkling white gravel in three angled rows, were approximately twenty million dollars worth of rare and exotic machinery. I was stunned.

Of course, I had been to museums and other public collections of automobiles and seen interesting cars with interesting histories, but I had never seen a private collection in a setting like this. The idea that these beautiful machines were the possessions of one man — now woman, I reminded myself — that they had been carefully chosen, purchased and brought here to be displayed as a representation of that man's interests and affluence, like a collection of rare books or lithographs, somehow made the cars themselves more powerful as a collection than they might have been individually. I just stood there and gaped.

My reverie was interrupted by Jennifer asking, "Do any of these mean anything to you, Ned? I mean, do you recognize any of them especially?"

Ah, dear heart, I thought. Do I? Indeed I do.

"I sure do. Jennifer, these are some of the most well-known cars in the world. Willie knew what he was doing. My God, he's got a GTO!" I exclaimed. "Look, there's a Daytona Spyder. Jesus, Jennifer, this is incredible!"

I realized that I had been talking about the cars, as if Willie were still alive. I calmed down for a minute and began to walk up the aisles between the cars in order to get a better look. I was aware that to the average person who couldn't care less about cars, GTO probably meant some Pontiac made in the sixties and Daytona was a small Dodge coupe. They wouldn't know that these names—in Detroit's typical "fuck you, sue me" fashion—were stolen from two of the world's most famous Ferrari race cars and applied to tinny American fakes by some marketing genius and the advice and counsel of some legal department.

Well, well, well, I thought. *So Willie actually did like the cars.* And he obviously knew what he was doing because from the looks of it he had started to put together a collection of the really important models.

"Who takes care of these cars?" I asked.

"This Evans' firm," she replied. "They come and take them away somewhere. They do the work on them and then bring them back."

"Jennifer," I asked, "do you know when Willie started this collection?"

"No," she said, "I really don't. It was before I met him, I know. But we went to some auctions together. That's how I knew about this fellow, Evans. I mean, really Ned, you should see some of the people who show up at these things. And Ned, some of them are carrying suitcases full of cash. I saw one man open his attaché case to get some paper or something out, and underneath it there were stacks of hundred dollar bills. I'll bet he had several hundred thousand in his lap. I told

Willie about it and he just laughed. He said that he'd heard that a lot of drug money was getting laundered that way, but maybe he was just kidding. There were also lots of stars around and lots of Arabs and Japanese. Bizarre, really."

"Well," I said, "whatever was going on, Willie bought himself quite a collection. This is going to be worth a lot of money. He must have paid a fortune. Do you have any idea of the value here?"

"I haven't had it appraised. That's one of the reasons I want to talk to Evans. It's carried on the books for its purchase price that is a little over $20 million dollars, but it may have gone up since the cars were bought."

"I would guess so," I said, "if some of these were in his collection before you and Willie were married."

Jennifer looked at her watch and said, "I think we should get going if we're going to get to Monterey on time. Have you seen enough?"

"I sure have. This is incredible. I had no idea that Willie was into this thing so deeply." I turned and moved toward the door. Jennifer paused to turn off the lights and followed me out into the sunshine, which by now was beginning to warm the morning air.

We walked back up to the house, each occupied with our own thoughts. For no particular reason, I began to wonder if somehow Willie's behavior before his death had something to do with this fabulous collection of rare automobiles. I decided that I had no basis for that thought, when we were on the veranda once again.

Jennifer said over her shoulder, "Let me get my sweater and my bag, and I'll be right there. If you're interested, there's a loo right off the kitchen hallway. I'll see you at the car."

I walked on through the house toward the kitchen, admiring again the warmth of the rooms. While having a brief fantasy about firesides in winter, I soon reached the bathroom. I decided to take her offer given the upcoming drive and my morning's coffee consumption. Afterward, as I passed through the kitchen on the way to the car, I noticed something out of the corner of my eye. I paused. At first, I couldn't figure out what it was that had caught my attention. Then, the lighted button on the wall phone over by the pantry door went out. As I continued on out through the screen door and down the path to the car, I couldn't stop my mind from beginning its jealous interrogation again. *Who was that'? Why didn't she say she had to make a call? Did someone call her? Who? Oh stop it, you dope.*

And then, thankfully, Jennifer came through the screen door and down the path. Once again, my heart rate rose a little at the prospect of spending the day with this stunning woman.

She smiled into my eyes and I had the feeling again that she was reading my mind. Although, when a dog looks up at you and wags its tail, it isn't really mind reading to conclude that the dog likes you. It's pretty obvious — which is what I feared I was being at this point.

But never mind. As usual, she got me off the hook by asking, "Do you want to drive, or should we take my car?"

There I was with a chance to spend the day in one of the world's most desirable automobiles, Jennifer's 500 SL, and my male ego jumped. *Me, driven around by a woman? No way.* I had to be stupid and say, "Oh, why go to the trouble of getting yours out. The Mustang will be fine." *In a pig's eye, you dope!*

But maybe the god who takes care of drunks and fools was hanging around that morning because Wonder Woman gave me a second shot at the right answer. She said, "Have you driven an SL? I just love it."

Finally getting my brain to override those other things that cause me to give dumb answers sometimes, I replied, "No I haven't, but some of my Formula I friends have them and rave about them."

Bingo. Jennifer said, "Listen, the drive down to Monterey is beautiful and the day is going to warm up. Why don't you drive the Mercedes since you like driving anyway and this would give you a chance to try it. On the way back, we can put the top down."

Thank you, god of drunks-and-fools. "Oh," I said "that's a good idea. That would be fun." I quietly breathed a sigh of relief at having escaped the consequences of my own stupidity.

She reached in her purse, removed a small key case, aimed it at the garage door and pressed a button on the case. The door began to rise and then she pressed a second button. I'd heard about this, but had never actually seen it. The Mercedes started its engine, immediately settling into a smooth idle.

I laughed and said, "Show-off."

Jennifer just giggled. Then she said, "Willie discovered this. How can I say it, this *kid* who is a genius with microprocessors and he had patented this technology for electronically operating motors and things by remote control. Of course, there have been garage door openers and remote TV controls for years, but they were never safe for cars because of the possibility of one of them going out of control somehow. You'd have a dangerous situation. What this kid had figured out was how to build in some sort of override device that would cancel the signal if the machine being controlled acted in some way beyond the limits that were programmed in. I don't understand it all, but anyway this made it possible to get government approval to install these in cars. Willie took him public and here we are."

She handed me the keys and went around to the passenger side, opened the door and gracefully slid into the yellow leather seat. I got in the driver's side, fastened the seat belt and very carefully shifted the automatic into reverse and backed the car out of the garage.

As we drove out of the driveway, she asked, "Do you know your way back onto I 280? I think we'd better take the quick way down, just to make sure we're on time. Maybe we can take the long way home and see the sunset on the Pacific?"

That's what I mean about this being one of the all time great days. I mean, I felt like I might have been watching a movie or something where the smashing blonde says, "Darling, let's take the long way home." *Is this for real?*

MONTEREY

In fact, I did wonder what was on Jennifer's mind. I kept getting the feeling that something was being offered, something being suggested. And yet, she hadn't done a single thing, said a single thing that could be construed as anything other than friendly, proper and appropriate under the circumstances. I mean, how was she supposed to act? Like I was some sort of enemy? Maybe an encyclopedia salesman or something? The problem, of course, was that I was so attracted to her, found her so...so female, that I suspected I was finding some special meaning in everything that she said or did. And I had a hard time keeping my eyes off of her. The driving was a welcome distraction.

I finally left this line of thought and concentrated on getting us down to Monterey. We had about 90 miles to go and about 90 minutes to do it in, so there was little time for puttering. Happily, the big Merc V8 was not a puttering sort of motor and we were soon humming along, doing about 80. I was enjoying that feeling of power and complete security that the Germans have been building into their cars for decades. Sure, the Japanese have caught up, but it's the Germans who drew the map.

I looked over at Jennifer and smiled. She had been quiet for a few miles and I wondered again what she might be thinking.

"You look like you're enjoying yourself," she said.

"Am I ever," I responded. "This thing is outstanding. I appreciate the test drive."

"Anytime," she quipped, with that sparkle in the eye and a slight holding of my glance that set me to wondering once again, *What's that supposed to mean?*

We made the turn for Los Gatos and, on the other side, climbed up to two thousand feet and crossed over the crest of hills into Santa Cruz County. We would come down out of the hills soon and bypass Santa Cruz, emerging onto the flat run down to Castroville. It was home of the artichoke sandwich, ranking right up there with those other American culinary triumphs like ice cold red wine and corn dogs.

I began to see familiar landmarks from the last time I'd been here; a trip several years earlier to Laguna Seca, a racetrack located on the grounds of the Fort Ord Military Reservation. I spent the next several minutes in a reverie of that particular weekend that ended with me wrecking the racecar but falling in love. *Ah, but that's another story*, I thought, *and Buster, you need to see that it doesn't happen again. You have major fish to fry and very soon.* I was thinking about the fact that in a week I would be going to Europe to begin the racing season, something that I was looking forward to after the relatively quiet winter.

Jennifer broke into my thoughts, asking, "When will you be racing again?"

Damn, I thought, *this is starting to feel like a lot more than coincidence.* "I have to go to Italy the first week in May," I told her, "the season begins at Monza with the first race in the World Sports Car Championship."

"Oh, that's exciting," she said, "are you driving?"

"No. I don't have a contract yet. My sponsor from last year went to jail for securities fraud in Switzerland, so the race team folded. I think he's found a buyer, though, so maybe there will be some good news when I get there."

"Securities fraud?" she said, with raised eyebrows. "What did he do?"

"I don't really know," I replied, "I think it was something technical and the Swiss are very tough, as I guess you know. Apparently, they wanted to make an example out of him. He'll be out in three months, they tell me."

"Is he in the securities business?" she asked, "I mean, is it someone I might know?"

"No, he's not. He's in the fashion business. He manufactures a line of women's clothes. His name is Reuter. Klaus Reuter. Do you know him?"

"No, I don't think so," said Jennifer. She looked out the window, apparently thinking about who Reuter was, or the fashion business or whatever.

By this time, we had reached the exit for the center of Monterey and I asked Jennifer if she had gotten directions to Evan's office. She had and quickly related them to me. The route was not too complicated, taking us through a heavily populated area of suburban homes and shops down toward the original waterfront area of this venerable, old fishing port. *Venerable, indeed.* Steinbeck's Cannery Row disappeared sometime in the sixties, swallowed up by the forerunners of the great wave of gentrification and over-population that has washed over every fishing village from Bar Harbor to Key West on the Atlantic and from Puget Sound to La Jolla on the Pacific.

Still, the city fathers had eventually put on some brakes, so the old city center of Monterey was not without some attractive architecture. There was enough room left to make it livable. We parked the Mercedes under the admiring gaze of a pair of college kids, locked it with Jennifer's clicker and walked the block to the address she had been given by Evans.

The carved, gold-filigreed, wooden sign standing in the small grassy yard of the meticulously restored Victorian house read, *The Rodney Walker Evans Company, Auctioneers.*

A black, wrought-iron railing guarded the three brick steps leading up to the short brick walkway and the first of two more wooden steps onto the covered porch. The entrance consisted of wide, beautifully varnished double doors of honey colored oak with shining brass brightwork, the kind usually seen only on very well maintained yachts. A small brass plate read, *Enter.*

I held the door for Jennifer. Immediately, we were standing in a large foyer looking at and being looked at by an attractive, dark haired receptionist who smiled and asked, "Mrs. Pearson?"

Jennifer said, "Yes, and this is Mr. Pearson." She quickly looked up at me and blushed. I had thought she was gorgeous the moment she walked through the door at La Fonda del Mar yesterday afternoon. Now, I almost couldn't handle it. In her embarrassment, ten years went out of her face and I had an overwhelming urge to take her in my arms and tell her that it was alright, not to be embarrassed.

I was saved from myself by the receptionist saying,

"Yes, Mr. Evans is expecting you. Won't you have a seat?" With that, she turned and went up a flight of stairs and disappeared from view.

As soon as she was out of sight, Jennifer started laughing and then I got the giggles, too. I was afraid that the receptionist would return to find these two baboons with tears running down their cheeks and unable to speak. However, we got ourselves under control just in time, as the receptionist returned to the top of the stairs and said, "Won't you come up? Mr Evans is in his office."

I immediately got the message. There are two kinds of executives. Those who require a display of rank and those who don't. The former always sit at the head of the table, so everyone will know who is in charge. They also carefully distinguish between those visitors who deserve to be met at the front door and those who are to be brought to the throne room like mendicants. Apparently, Evans was one of those and judged Jennifer and me not worthy of VIP treatment. *Okay*, I thought, *this may get interesting.*

We dutifully climbed the carpeted stairs and followed the receptionist down a hall that seemed to perfectly bisect the house from one side to the other. As we reached what I assumed to be one end of the house, we came to a door on the left that would lead back toward the front of the house. As we came through the door, I instantly understood why we had been brought here.

The entire front wall of Evans' office was floor-to-ceiling glass for a distance along the front of the house of perhaps 20 feet. The effect of this was to appear to be standing on a terrace overlooking the entire Monterey Bay with the foreground filled with houses falling away down the hill. In the middleground, there was the harbor with its fishing fleet and wharves, and in the background the blue Pacific, sun-dappled and stretching away to the horizon.

Absolutely breathtaking. Evans stood at the corner of his desk that was strategically placed, so that he could enjoy both the views of the harbor and of his duly impressed guests. Jennifer, as I recall, was strangely silent but I couldn't restrain a quiet "Wow," as I took in the view. I slowly turned toward Evans, who said in an almost professional and somber voice, "Mrs. Pearson, it's nice to see you again, although I am very sorry about the circumstances that bring us together." He looked at me. "And you are Mr. Pearson's cousin, is that right?"

"That's right," I replied. "Ned Pearson"

"The journalist, isn't that right?"

Well, I thought, *I should have known. Either Jennifer did tell him, or he's enough in touch to have seen my byline.* "Yes, that's right," I said, deciding that I needed to go very slowly with this man. I had that feeling that I imagine divers get when the sharks show up. No sudden moves become the order of the day.

"And the driver, as well?" he asked.

Either this guy does his homework, or I'm better known than I realized, was my next thought.

"Yes," I said, "also true."

"Yes, indeed," he said, "must be an interesting life." There wasn't a hint of censure or admiration—just a flat statement.

"It suffices," I responded, thinking, *if cool is what we're gonna' be, brother, I'm cool.*

He met my eyes, and the corner of his mouth dimpled ever so slightly. There was a little twitch of muscle way back along the jaw line. He then turned to Jennifer and said, "Won't you sit down, Mrs. Pearson, Doris will he along with coffee in a moment.

RODNEY WALKER EVANS

As advertised, Doris arrived with a silver serving tray, well set with bone china cups and saucers, silver sugar and creamer, sterling spoons and coffee. As she set about the ritual serving process, I was thankful for the chance to take a good look around Evans' office and a few exploratory peeks at the man, himself. Because of the spectacular window forming one side of the office and the door at one end, most of the furniture was at the other end or along the side away from the window, much as it would be on a terrace. Evans desk was at the far end. It was, a fairly simple construction in modern glass and what looked to be cypress. To the left was a complicated computer station that also contained a printer and a fax machine.

High tech, I thought, *but I wonder if he really knows how to operate this stuff, or is it just for show?*

We were sitting in a cluster of two club chairs in saddle leather and a love seat in chocolate colored suede cowhide surrounding a coffee table cutely constructed of a sparkling chromed wire wheel on which a round glass top was laid. In turn, this assembly was standing on a pedestal formed from a shortened axle. *Very automotive. Hmm.*

The entire wall in back of the love seat was covered floor-to-ceiling with framed photographs of well-known figures, seemingly enjoying the company of our hero, Mr. Evans. *The classic vanity wall.*

Evans was on the wall no less than 50 times in the company of movie stars, tycoons, rock stars, politicians — fewer of those because, I supposed, they couldn't be seen too often tooling around in one of Evans mega-buck specials — and assorted other famous people. Suffice it to say, Rodney Walker Evans had put his friendly hook around some swell people, and he wasn't about to hide the fact.

I must say, in fairness to Rodney's photomates, he was not bad material to be seen with. On the basis of his looks, he would have easily qualified to be the star in the pictures. Rod Evans was one of those California beach boys who started life looking good and improved with age — another good reason to dislike the guy.

Now in his middle fifties, the full head of healthy blonde hair had retained most of its straw color, except at the temples where it was turning to silver. The lines in the face had begun to define themselves more sharply, so that they now implied strength rather than friendliness. The skin shone with the glow of exercise and just the right amount of California sunshine. And Mr. Evans had obviously kept himself in shape.

The six foot two inch frame must have been carrying no more than 200 pounds and the stomach was flat. *Quite a package*, I thought, and glanced at Jennifer to see if she had a reaction.

I was surprised at the look in her eyes, as Evans approached the club chair on his end of the setting. She seemed to be looking right at him but her face was completely blank, as if he wasn't there and she was focused well beyond him. I couldn't make up my mind whether she was simply thinking about something outside the room, or just trying not to look Evans in the eye.

My thoughts were interrupted, as Doris finished serving and asked, "Hold your calls?" After getting a nod from Evans, she left.

He began the business of the day by saying, "Now, Mrs. Pearson, please tell me how I can help you. I know that you are seeking counsel on the disposition of your late husband's collection and we can certainly be of assistance there, but I need to know a little more about your goals in doing so. For example, I need to know whether or not there is any urgency in the matter, perhaps some requirement to meet tax obligations or financing issues? Or, on the other hand, do you wish to time the disposition to maximize your appreciation? There's also the possibility of charitable contributions that would take advantage of the highest possible appraisal value as a deduction from other income."

Jesus H. Christ! I thought, *the man is an absolute snake charmer. This is not the trade school, body shop, self-taught, diamond in the rough, up from the street kid I've been told about. This guy is straight out of a Wall Street board room. He talks like a Harvard lawyer,* I thought. *How in hell did he transform himself into this…this chief executive officer?* I wondered.

He continued in this vein a little while longer and then asked, "Have you given any consideration to such questions, Mrs. Pearson?"

I wondered what Jennifer's answers might be since

we had certainly not discussed them. She said, "Not really, Mr. Evans, but I can tell you as far as I know that there are no serious tax issues, or any reason to hurry."

Good for you, I thought. I could just see this shark sniffing around for a distress sale in which he could convince the seller that she was getting the best possible deal, while he makes a quick and easy sale.

"Good," he replied, "Because this is not the peak of the market. Prices are a little depressed right now. This would not be a good time for quick and easy sale."

I'll be damned, I thought. *Maybe this guy is straight?*

"Mrs. Pearson, would there be any advantages to donating some of the collection, say to a respected museum?" he asked.

I couldn't see how Evans could make any money on that deal, so I was really confused as to where this was going.

Jennifer said, "You'd really have to talk to my accountants to determine the answer to that. I just don't know, but I'd certainly consider it if they recommended it."

"Fine," replied Evans, "I should get a contact there before you leave. We often work with accountants in doing valuations for estate tax purposes."

I was beginning to get the idea that we were not dealing here with your regulation used car salesman.

Then he asked, "Mrs. Pearson, are we discussing here the entire collection or just parts?"

"Oh, I don't really know," she said, looking at me as if to say, 'What do you think?'

I didn't have a clue, so like a stiff, I said, "That's something to think about, isn't it?" I immediately felt like a fool.

"Well," said Evans, "that can wait. It's not critical

just yet, but we may want to try for a private sale of the entire collection. Sometimes, that will net the seller a better overall return than selling the cars one at a time, especially if there are some particularly desirable cars in the collection, as in your case."

I noticed the use of 'we' in Evans remark and thought, *How swiftly he cooks the meat. I wonder when it'll become 'our' collection?*

Jennifer said, "Ned and I don't really know much detail about the cars, themselves. Are there some special cars in it?"

I saw just a moment's hesitation, as Evans thought about his response. *Choosing between the whole truth and something less?* I wondered.

He rose from his chair and moving around the desk to the computer console, he said, "Let's see what we have here," and began working on the keyboard. After several entries, the printer began to make its electronic mutterings and slid out two sheets of paper that Evans picked up and brought over to Jennifer and me.

To my astonishment, he had a complete listing of every car in Willie's collection with entries after each describing the car itself, its history, when and where it was purchased, the seller, the price paid and several other pertinent details. My mouth was hanging open.

"Mr. Evans," I began, "this is incredible. You know more about this collection than Mrs. Pearson does. How do you come by this information?"

He smiled and took the opportunity to say, "Please, most people call me Rod. May I call you Ned?"

I nodded, waiting to see if he was going to answer the question. He was.

"Ned," he said, "it's our business to know these things. In the first place, we helped Mr. Pearson make many of the acquisitions in his collection. Some of them were made at auctions we produced, some at other auctions where we are represented. One way or another, most of the investment grade automobiles in the world pass under our scrutiny. We've just been diligent enough to record what we see."

Holy cow, I thought, *this guy is really something*. I asked, "Do you have similar information on other collections?"

He smiled the smile of the man who has just been dealt the fourth ace in a game of five-card stud. However cool this cat was, he was not cool enough to avoid the gloat in his voice when he replied, "Ned, we have in our confidential files, detailed information on over 6,000 investment grade antique and vintage cars. At the most recent sale price the combined value of these cars exceeds three billion dollars."

I may not be a genius, but even I can see the spider and the fly. Sitting here smiling at me was a man who had in that little personal computer the names, addresses and phone numbers of the owners of most of the world's most desirable rare automobiles. And, he also knew exactly what had been paid for them and what they might be worth on today's market. *And I'd bet he'd be willing to part with a little of that information under the right circumstances, like, say a small commission, maybe ten percent, for getting party A together with party B in a little transaction to unload one of those beauties just when party A needs to raise a few hundred thousand quickly or party B gets sick of the braggart at the club and decides he needs his own collection to brag about. Let me see, I thought, ten percent of three billion is three hundred million. Yes, sir, Ol' Rod is definitely sitting in the catbird seat and he knows it.*

And that was just the private transactions. It didn't count the buyers premium from public auctions where the new collectors usually began their hobby, or where the owners not suffering from urgency could see what their prizes were worth on the open market. Nor did it include the other services like appraisal fees and other things Evans had alluded to.

This is going to make some story, I concluded happily, *although Rod might not like spotlight shining too much on this enterprise.* It seemed to me that some of these high-rolling customers might get the idea that they were simply supporting this guy's expensive habits.

At this point, Evans interrupted my train of thought by asking, "Did you plan to stay for lunch? I've made a reservation at Lila's, which is right on the water. It's such a lovely day, so I thought that you might enjoy it if you have the time."

Jennifer looked at me, as if seeking my approval and I nodded. "I don't see why not. Think they'd have some Abalone?" Abalone is a favorite of mine and only available in California. It's a big mollusk that clings to the offshore rocks in the Pacific, wearing a shell much like a medium sized box turtle. Divers with flat tire irons sneak up on them, quickly slip the flat iron under them and before they can get a sufficient grip on the rock, pop them loose and put them in a net bag. Pounded flat like a veal cutlet, dipped in egg and floured, and then quickly sautéed, they taste like the finest, buttery tender veal you've ever eaten.

"They're a specialty of the house," Rod replied, with a smile at Jennifer.

Boy, is this day going great, I thought.

"Well," said Rod, "what do you say we continue this conversation at lunch?" We all stood and moved out of Rod's office, down the hall to the stairs and out the back of the house, following Rod's lead to a gleaming Rolls Royce Silver Cloud parked in the rear of the building. To his credit, he made no silly apologies or other inane comments, as he held the door for Jennifer and I got in the back seat. To my credit, I didn't either, even though it was only the second time I had ever sat in one of these beauties; the first being in London when a wealthy race car owner had his driver fetch me 'round to the owner's club where we agreed to the terms of my contract to drive his race car.

The drive to the restaurant was brief and I barely heard the conversation between Rod and Jennifer in the front seat, as I enjoyed the smell and feel of the Connolly hides upholstering the back of this luxurious behemoth and tried to come to some conclusions about this remarkable man.

We arrived and were taken to a lovely table overlooking the ocean. Once again, I was reminded of the advantages that my life enjoyed. The meal was everything I'd hoped for, including the Abalone. We drank a local sauvignon blanc and talked about those things that newly met people in a business environment do — the weather, the latest international incident, the food — nothing very personal as people get used to each other. We managed to avoid the subject of Willie, but I felt that he was hovering somewhere nearby since he was the link between us all.

Jennifer and Rod seemed comfortable with one another, but I thought it mildly odd that they never referred to any events or occasions from earlier times. I assumed that Jennifer must have been with Willie at least once in a while when he was adding to the collection with Rod's help. Therefore, they should have had something to talk about. I finally concluded that they were simply avoiding the Willie connection and sympathized with them.

When the coffee came, I thought it about time that I tell Rod that I intended to do a story about his business. When I mentioned it, he didn't show much reaction but asked, "Do you mean the collector car industry, the auction business or my company?"

"I haven't decided yet and I have to discuss it with my Editor, anyway. But I found our conversation this morning very enlightening. Your work is much more sophisticated than I imagined," I said.

Flattered, he smiled slightly. "Well, let me know what you decide. There are a few secrets that we can't share with you or our competitors, but we'll cooperate any way we can. Now what I'd like to do is take you out to our main facility and show you the various services we provide for our customer's."

I looked at Jennifer. She nodded slightly, so I said, "Let's go."

Evans signed the back of the check. We rose and filed out of the restaurant, smiling at the maitre d' and assuring him that everything was keen. Once in Rod's car, it took only ten minutes to arrive at a large, enclosed compound surrounded by a chain link fence and containing two handsome red brick buildings; one with only a row of narrow windows high up on each side and the other with a row of garage doors facing the sister building and what appeared to be offices across the front. Two overhead doors, one the normal size and one that looked as if it would admit a tractor trailer, were at the far end of the side of the building without many windows. The distance between the two buildings was sufficient to permit a tractor trailer to be driven directly in or out of that large door in one motion. This could permit loading and unloading away from prying eyes, if it were desirable.

In the work bays of the opposite building, mechanics were performing various maintenance and repair operations, although I noticed that over half the bays were empty.

Rodney took us through the various departments: Maintenance, Repair, Restoration, Appraisal, Research and Event Management, explaining as we went that his company was designed to provide the serious collector with a spectrum of services from identifying and appraising a possible acquisition to restoring it after purchase to disposing of it when the customer wished to trade or sell it. He also pointed out that the Company had a Transportation and Storage Division for those who wished to exhibit their cars at the various events around the country, including vintage races where Mr. Bucks Up could really give himself a thrill by hurling his little half-million dollar trinket around a racetrack with 15 or 20 equally wild and crazy guys, risking not only the toys but life and limb, as well. The Rodney Walker Evans Company was prepared to help you spend your money in many diverse ways.

I found the entire tour absolutely fascinating and knew that Arthur Bathgate would definitely get his money's worth on this assignment. It seemed as if Jennifer was enjoying herself, as well, as she was very quiet during the tour. She asked few questions, but looked everywhere with apparent interest.

We wound up back in a reception area of the building with offices and I asked to see the storage facility. Evans explained that they were unloading an extremely rare car and that he was contractually bound not to reveal its presence because it might set off rumors that the car was being sold. His explanation for the secrecy was that since these cars were often used as collateral for business loans, bankers were nervous about their portability and the potential for theft or other unpleasant transfer of such collateral. After all, it's not easy to carry off, in the night, a 20-story mortgaged building and sell it to some foreigner who will take it out of the country. The bankers like to know where their collateral is and what's being done to it.

Journalists hate to take no for an answer and that was what I was getting in a very polite way. Normally, I would press but we were having such a nice day, I saw no reason to spoil it. Besides, I figured that I'd be back to finish this story and I could see the storage facility then. *No need to get pushy.*

By this time, it was getting late and I figured that Evans had other business to do today other than just acting as a tour guide, so I asked, "Jennifer, have you seen enough?" I then turned to Evans and asked, "What do you suggest as a next step?"

"I think what's in order here, if you'll permit me, is for me to give Mrs. Pearson a proposal for the disposition of the collection since it seems that she has no long-term interest in retaining or expanding it. Am I correct, Mrs. Pearson?"

"Yes, quite," said Jennifer. He then looked at me. "Don't you agree?"

I nodded, thinking, *Heavens, I'm now on the Board of Directors of this enterprise.*

"Would a week from today be soon enough?" asked Evans.

Jennifer said that would be fine and we all went out to Evans' car for the trip back downtown. As we made our way, I was left again with my thoughts and pondered the number of unoccupied desks and the empty bays I saw on the tour. *Well, maybe the business is seasonal or something?* I concluded. I also noted that there were no identifying signs at the compound, probably to keep the thieves from developing any interest.

Soon, we were beside Jennifer's Mercedes and saying goodbye. Evans reached back to shake my hand, met my eye and said, "A pleasure meeting you, Mr. Pearson. I hope we can be of service. By the way, you drive professionally, do you not?" As I nodded, he continued, "I have clients who sometimes wish to see their cars in competition. Perhaps I could introduce you sometime when it's appropriate?"

Great, I thought. In this business, contacts are everything. I also recognized the implicit — you scratch my back and I'll scratch yours. "That would be appreciated," I said, "I'm always willing to talk to people with a first class operation." *Don't want this guy to think I'm some kind of racer bum with a helmet bag under my arm and the itch to go fast.*

He smiled and nodded, getting the ego message and then turned to Jennifer. "It would be a pleasure to be of service, Mrs. Pearson," he said in that undertaker voice.

For a moment, I thought that Jennifer was going to giggle. I could see the red rising on the back of her neck but whatever she was thinking, she stopped, offered her hand and said, "I look forward to hearing from you."

THE LONG WAY HOME

We got out of the Rolls and into the Mercedes. I wheeled it around and pointed it out of town. We retraced our steps back through Castroville and on up to Santa Cruz. This time, however, I swung a little westerly, looking for the Pacific Coast Highway. I was going to take Jennifer up on her suggestion to take the long way home. Soon, we found it and were sailing along with the blue Pacific below us on our left and the hills rising to our right as the road followed the undulating contours of the coastline. This is the road you see in all the car ads and it never fails to delight me. To find myself flowing along in a spectacular car beside this lovely woman amidst this poster setting was almost too much to believe. We hadn't said much to each other all day, being too involved in the conversation with Evans, but I had the feeling that we were communicating any-way — and waiting for some sign. I didn't know what, but I thought, *Soon.*

We had stopped and put down the top because, as she had predicted, the day had warmed nicely. She was curled up in the seat facing the sea and it was just windy enough to discourage conversation. So we travelled that way, mile after mile. When I would see a seal or sea lion, I would point. Occasionally, she would touch my sleeve and point out to sea at a boat or a bird. And I would look at her and just smile at this marvelous, peaceful time. And she would smile back. We just didn't need to talk.

The 50 odd miles back to Half Moon Bay drifted by without measure of time. We floated along on a mood, content with each other's company, thinking our own thoughts, occasionally coming together in a shared view or scenic surprise, but never interfering with words. I'm sure I knew what was happening, but I kept it out of my consciousness because I didn't want to deal with it, I suppose.

Once, when the road dipped down to the level of the water, we stopped and walked a way along the beach, listening to the surf in the warm spring sun. As we walked, saying little, our arms would touch or a hand would brush against another from time-to-time, and my awareness of her would grow and my thoughts become more confused than ever. But it didn't seem to matter. We were there. And it was fine.

I wanted it to never end but, of course, it had to. We arrived at the turn eastward toward the hills and away from the shore. Soon, we were climbing toward the ridge on the other side of Jennifer's house. I stopped the car one last time at an overlook where we could turn and look back at the setting sun, changing from gold to red and spreading its soft pink blanket across the sky. We looked at each other and smiled, but said nothing. But we knew.

I started the car and pulled back on to the highway. A few minutes later, we were pulling into Jennifer's driveway. After waiting for Jennifer to use her clicker on the garage door, I pulled the Mercedes into the garage. We got out and moved outside, while she closed the door.

We hadn't said much to each other following the sunset smiles and I was beginning to feel a little awkward. I mean, I just wasn't sure what to do next. Jennifer broke the gridlock by asking, "What are you doing for dinner? You said you'd let me cook something for you. How about now? If you don't have plans?" she finished, offering me a way out if I wanted it. I didn't.

"No," I said, "that'd be great and we can talk over the meeting today and maybe decide how you want to handle the collection. But you're sure it's not too much trouble?"

"Not a bit," she assured me. "How would you feel about some giant prawns on the grill?"

"Excellent," I replied, and thought, *May this day never end.*

We went into the house and she offered me a drink. We settled on a bottle of Chinon Blanc from Sonoma that had been chilling in the refrigerator. We took the bottle and our glasses out on the patio in the back of the house overlooking the pool. She threw a switch and soft, underwater lights gave the pool and the surrounding area a warm glow. The gardens were just beginning to blossom and the early evening air was filled with that smell of new growth and fresh earth that only comes in Springtime.

We talked of nothing much for a while, as we enjoyed the wine and the waning dusk. Finally, she said, "Well, if we're ever going to eat, I'd better get myself into the kitchen."

"Can I help?" I asked.

"Sure can. If you don't mind, you could start the fire. The charcoal is in the locker to the left of the grill. There should be starter and matches in there, too."

I went off to do my duty, while she donned an apron and began to put the meal together. When I'd finished with the fire, I picked up my glass and went into the kitchen to watch. She was very efficient and quite competent, as she went about trimming greens for a salad and preparing the shrimp for the grill. I watched with a certain fascination, as that lovely face was set in total concentration. She occasionally nibbled on her lower lip, as decisions were made about quantities and ingredients; another Jennifer that I hadn't seen before.

The meal was delightful. Jennifer had basted the prawns with olive oil, while they sizzled on the grill. A salad of bib lettuce, arugula, and endive with its vinaigrette dressing was a perfect foil for the succulent shrimp. We sopped up the drippings with crisp French bread and the plates were soon empty.

As we ate, I asked her where she had learned to cook and she told me that an aunt had taught her, following her mother's death when she was ten. Her face became sad for the second time since I had met her and I felt bad for having raised the subject. But then, I thought, *How could I know?*

I guess to compensate as much as anything else, I told her about losing my own father at a young age. We talked for a while about the effects of such tragedy. As I think about that conversation now, I still can't believe that she could have told me only the half of the story that she did, without any indication of the other half.

As we finished our wine and the candle flames began to shiver in the light breeze of the cooling evening, I realized how little I really knew about Jennifer. I was about to ask more questions about her background and then changed my mind because I feared that I might ruin the marvelous mood of the day. As I was searching for a safe way to ask about her life before Willie, she asked, "How about some coffee?" This broke my reverie and my chain of thought.

"Great," I said, "and while you're doing that, I'll clear the table." As I gathered up the dishes and took them into the kitchen, I couldn't help thinking how domestic this scene was and how wonderfully comfortable I felt within it. I wondered again, for perhaps the millionth time, if I would ever marry again. They say that second marriages are the triumph of hope over experience and I supposed that we probably never really give up hoping. *Well*, I thought, *Jennifer is certainly someone who could keep hope alive.*

She brought a tray to the table with coffee service, two snifters and a pony of cognac. "I thought you might like something to ward off the evening chill," she said, with that quiet smile. She poured the coffee and the cognac and raised her glass. "To newfound friends," she said.

I raised mine and said, "Hear, hear" in my best, stupid House of Lords accent.

I must admit that I wasn't sure whether her choice of toast was a message or not. It did occur to me that she might be trying to tell me that we were friends, period — and to expect nothing more. On the other, more hopeful hand, she might be saying, "I'm glad we found each other."

I was too confused about my own intentions to deal with hers, so I just kept moving.

In fact, I changed the subject. I asked her what she thought of Rod Evans and the day's business. She looked at me closely when I asked and I had the feeling that she might be annoyed at the question. After furrowing her brow, she said that she thought his operation was very impressive, but she wasn't sure how far he could be trusted. Since those were my exact thoughts on the matter, I didn't prolong that line of conversation. We agreed that we should reserve judgment until we saw his proposal.

Then she asked me if I had learned anything that would help answer Aunt Blake's questions. I realized then that I hadn't asked Evans any questions at all about his relationship with Willie, and whether or not he could shed any light on Willie's behavior. I excused myself on the grounds of sensitivity to Jennifer's feelings and the inappropriate timing of such questions during our business meeting. I told Jennifer that I would give Evans a call later.

By now, the wine and the cognac were beginning to work their magic and I realized that it was time to say goodbye. I had to see MacIntosh in the morning and get up to the CHIPS in Sacramento before closing time.

I finished my coffee, drained the last drop from the snifter and said, "Well, dear lady, it's been a wonderful day and this was a terrific meal, but I should be getting along while I can still navigate."

She leaned into the candlelight, so I could see the smile in the green eyes and said, "I meant what I said yesterday. The guest room is made up. You're welcome to stay."

It was the moment of truth; the point where you choose between good enough and perfect. *If I stay*, I told myself, *I'm pretty sure I know what will happen and boy, wouldn't that be great. But what will I say to myself on the plane back to New York? Congratulations, you found yourself a lonely widow who trusts you because you're her dead husband's cousin and which dead husband was apparently not paying too much attention to her before he died and you smiled at her a lot and made her know that you cared and got to jump in her bed?*

Is that gonna make you happy? Or, if on the other hand, you think this might be someone you'd like to be around for a long time, would it maybe be a better idea to give it a little time and space so you can both clear your heads of any confusion as to where you're going and why. What say, Big Guy, quick and dirty or nice and easy?

She stood up and came around the table toward me with her chin up and the question in her eyes, face shining with candlelight and cognac. Quick and dirty had an early lead.

I instinctively held out my hands and she walked right past them and into my arms. She looked up and said, "I know what you're thinking and I want you to know that whatever you decide is fine with me. I know about men and I trust you."

I believed it—all of it. And nice and easy won the photo finish. I looked down at her and said, "Well, my broker always advised me to look for long term gains. What do you advise?"

She said, "Shut up and kiss me." So I did.

If, as they say, the body has no memory for pain, then it should have no memory for pleasure, should it? Thus, I can't explain the memory of that kiss, but it exists and I can't forget it, no matter how I try.

That soft warm mouth, redolent of cognac and sweet breath, pressed upward on my lips until the heat spread gently through my entire body. There was not a

hint of lust, just sweetness and honey and giving openly. And as the length of her firm, long body folded softly against mine, I thought I might faint. And I just
didn't care.

About a century later, I felt her gently withdraw
and I opened my eyes to see that smile again, the one
that asks, "Wasn't that nice? We should do that again
sometime."

I cannot definitively say much about what happened next, other than I spent a little time somewhere
among the planets and eventually returned to earth
northbound on I 280 approaching a sign that read,
Downtown Next Exit –which meant that I was almost
back to the hotel.

I do remember telling Jennifer that I had a meeting
with MacIntosh in the morning and one in Sacramento
later in the day. I also promised to call her when I got
to the ski lodge and let her know if I found anything.

But the kiss...the kiss, I remember. I wished that the
day would never end. And in my mind, it hasn't—in
spite of everything I have done to forget it.

PALO ALTO

I slept the sleep of the innocent that night. Perhaps it was getting over my jet lag, or maybe it was the dream that kept floating in and out of consciousness all night; the one with the smiling green eyes and the face with the California tan that said so softly, "I trust you."

I hadn't left a wake-up call because I wasn't due at MacIntosh' office until late morning and I let myself drift for a while, thinking about the delicious yesterday and that face and how good I felt, warm and right all over. But eventually, I decided I'd better get on with it, so I got myself fully awake, got out of bed and began my morning routine which included another dose of that tangy Bay air and some morning sunshine to brighten up the room.

After my shower, I put in a call to the magazine offices in London just to catch up on my messages and to talk to Arthur. I was disappointed to learn that he was on the Continent somewhere attending some sort of conference. I wanted to fill him in on the meeting yesterday with Evans and tell him that I thought we had a great story at hand. I also wanted to ask him to get the

Research Department started on a project to determine if there were any operations in Europe like Evans', or if Evans had a worldwide lock on this business. Although it was a pity that Arthur wasn't there, I had enough swag with the research folks that they would go ahead with the work and get Arthur's blessing later. After briefing them on the target, I transferred over to the harried woman who does all the administrative things, like booking hotel rooms, securing press credentials and all the nitty gritty stuff of managing a crew of traveling reporters. She gave me a couple of updates and schedule changes, and then I was on to the Message Center to see who was looking for me. Nothing earth-shaking there, mostly people getting back to me on the latest developments in the "Silly Season," that time of year when the drivers play a multi-million dollar game of musical chairs with their driving contracts and sponsorship deals.

Having gotten completely up to date, I opened my trusty laptop to begin revising my files. I not only use it to produce the several thousand words a month that are my keep, but as my traveling secretary, as well. In it, I keep itineraries, calendars, appointments, expenses, all the things a normal person would keep in a desk at an office—something I don't have, thanks to God and Arthur Bathgate.

I finished modifying several of these files and making some notes of things I wanted to follow up on. I closed the laptop, put it in the bag with the Nikon and finished dressing. Then I went downstairs to partake once again of my host's freebies. In the elevator, I had a nagging, vague thought about something I had seen in the files, but I couldn't seem to focus on anything specific so I forgot about it, as I stepped off the elevator and headed for breakfast. Then I went down to the garage, retrieved the Mustang and made a leisurely trip in mid-morning traffic down to Palo Alto.

On the way, I thought about my earlier conversation with MacIntosh and decided to give him the benefit of the doubt. *After all, I thought, if I had been number two to Willie for a while and then he died suddenly, without warning, and I was confronted by friends and family wanting to know about a lot of things that were previously the exclusive province of me and my deceased partner, I might be a little testy myself. No one likes having more than one boss, if that.*

I also decided that honey would get more from this meeting than vinegar.

I was right on time arriving at MacIntosh's office and they only kept me waiting for ten minutes, which I decided would be all right unless it became eleven. As if on cue, MacIntosh came rushing into the reception area and apologized for keeping me waiting, saying, "I'm very sorry. I had to take this return call from Paris. I've needed to reach this man for days and he was just about to leave for the weekend."

I checked my mental time zone map and realized that he was right. I said, "Not to worry, I just got here," which wasn't true but what the hell.

He took me back to his office, ordered coffee for both of us, offered me a chair and said, "Now Mr. Pearson, how may I help you?"

I had already decided to give him the benefit of the doubt and his manner today was very different than on the telephone two days ago, so I took the plunge. "Mr. MacIntosh," I began, "we have a curious situation here. I have no reason whatsoever to think that Willie's death was anything other than a tragic accident. However, both his mother, Blake Pearson whom I assume you know."

He interrupted to say, "We've met."

"And his wife," I continued, "believe that his behavior just prior to his death was abnormal. They both speak of unexplained absences, but neither has any concrete evidence that something was wrong. As his closest business associate, I was hoping that you might have observed something that would put this to rest, particularly for Willie's mother."

As I spoke, I watched MacIntosh' face carefully to see if I was producing any reaction. At one point, he turned and looked out the window at the southern tip of the Bay. I had the feeling he was making up his mind about something. When I finished, he turned back to me and said, "Mr. Pearson, based on our earlier conversation, it would not surprise me if you found me somewhat defensive, perhaps a bit churlish. I believe 'tightass' is the popular phrase." And he smiled.

Well, well, I thought, *what have we here?*

"Since that conversation, I have had the opportunity to confirm that you are indeed acting at Mrs. Pearson's behest."

"Which Mrs. Pearson?" I interrupted.

"Blake," he replied.

"Really? You spoke to her?" I was a little surprised.

"No," he said, "I spoke to Robert. We have a business relationship. Does that also surprise you? You see, whereas Willie was escaping from his father's influence, I, on the other hand, have found it profitable to maintain a discreet alliance with Eastern sources of funds through Mr. Pearson."

Well, I'll be damned, I thought, *and I'll bet old R.B.III loved having a conduit into the office next to Willie's.*

"So Mr. Pearson, I'm prepared to cooperate with you completely in your search for information...on one condition."

Off went the alarm system that lives in every journalist's head. All of us hate the offering of not-for-publication information. It always leads to moral, ethical conflict down the road when you have accumulated even more information but can't use it without violating the earlier agreement.

"What's the condition?" I asked.

"That whatever you learn remains confidential and that the name of this firm will not appear in print in connection with your search under any circumstances." Seeing the look on my face, he quickly added, "Let me explain. We deal every day with trade secrets and financial information worth billions of dollars. Most of our clients are inventors of one kind or another. All of them are paranoid. Every one of them thinks that someone is out to steal their ideas and in some cases that fear is justified. We have spent years nurturing a reputation for trustworthiness and confidentiality. If Willie's death was seen to imply that there was a problem in this firm, it could have seriously damaging effects on our business. I will not let that happen."

Well, I thought, I can see his point, even if I think some of the paranoia may be contagious. And after all, I'm not doing an article about this anyway.

I said, "No problem. I take your point. What can you tell me?"

"Probably not very much, but I can tell you that I believe Willie was distracted in the month prior to his death."

"How, specifically?" I asked.

"Well, it's mostly a collection of little things. For example, once in a while, his attention would drift off in a conversation. You could say that's normal, but it wasn't for Willie. One of the ways he accomplished so much was that he had enormous powers of concentration. Meetings with Willie were usually very brief and to the point. He would ask a few questions, make a decision and move on to the next subject. Near the end, he became vague from time-to-time."

"Anything else?" I asked.

"Yes. Normally, Willie was first in the office in the morning and last out at night unless he had left for a meeting. That pattern changed. Finally, Mr. Pearson, there were the unexplained absences." He was beginning to sound like a Headmaster I once had in boarding school—very disapproving.

"Tell me about those," I said.

"We all prepare a weekly schedule that we share, so that each of us can know where the others will be on any particular day in case we need the other person for some matter or other. Actually, Willie initiated that practice, as the firm grew. Recently, he violated it a number of times, simply not filing his plan. When I asked him about it, he apologized but he did it several more times."

"So this would confirm Aunt Blake's experience, I take it?" I said.

"Yes, indeed, and I can tell you it got embarrassing when one of Willie's own clients would try to reach him and we didn't know where he was."

"Well, I can imagine, Mr. MacIntosh. You must have been very uncomfortable." *Poor, uncomfortable thing*, I thought. *Asshole, did you ever try to find out what was happening to your partner, the guy who made you rich?*

"Very much so, Mr. Pearson," said MacIntosh, completely missing the irony in my voice.

"But you have no idea what could have been bothering Willie?" I asked.

"None whatsoever. I never saw it as my place to inquire into personal matters, you understand."

Of course not, I thought. *See no evil, hear no evil, eh, MacIntosh? And cover your ass. Not your problem. No way. Not your brother's keeper and all that.* "Of course, I understand, Mr. MacIntosh. Is that it, then? Is that all you observed?"

"I'm afraid so. I wish I could be of more help, but I don't see how."

I thanked him for his time and, as he walked me to the reception area, I admired some beautiful original art displayed on the walls along the way. As we reached the lobby, I commented on the quality of the art and MacIntosh proudly accepted the compliment and then said, "Oh, that reminds me. I chose most of these pieces and I'm regarded as the art investment partner in the firm. The other partners look to me for guidance in this area. Willie did ask me a puzzling question sometime in the two weeks before his death. I'd almost forgotten it."

"What was that?" I asked.

"Well, let's see if I can get it right. It was something about forgery. Oh, I remember now, he wanted to know what the effect would be on the value of an artist's work, if widespread forgeries occurred. I found it very puzzling because that was the only time I can remember that he ever showed the slightest interest in art. Would that mean anything to you?"

"Not a thing Mr. MacIntosh, not a thing. But thanks again for your time and please let me know if anything else comes to mind."

And I left this tightassed little man, as fast as my feet would go.

SACRAMENTO

As I drove out of the parking lot, it was close to one o'clock. I realized that if I hustled, I might actually be able to get to Sacramento in time to find someone at the California Highway Patrol (CHIPS, for the hip) office who could fill me in on Willie's accident before they all ran off for the weekend. To do it, I'd have to cover the nearly 140 miles to Sacramento in less than three hours to have any hope of someone responding to my query before closing. *Ah well, never up, never out,* I thought.

Certainly, the 5.0 liter SVO Mustang would be up to the task of a 75 mile an hour average speed. As for the U.S. Interstate Highway System, the specifications exceed those of the Nazi Germany engineers who built the Autobahns for speeds up to 200 miles per hour. Certainly, they should present no problem for a mere 75 mile per hour average. The only flies in my ointment, however, were traffic, politicians and the police.

The lies of government regarding the fuel and life saving benefits of the 55 mph speed limit are Brobdignagian.

For decades, in much of Europe, there were no

posted speed limits. Regulations require a "reasonable speed" for weather, road and traffic conditions. It may come as a surprise then to some, that in these unregulated conditions, the public, driving on express highways designed for very high speeds, voluntarily record an *average speed for all vehicles* of, you guessed it, 70 miles per hour. In other words, they drive at a speed that is comfortable, not one that is mandated by some politician from New Jersey whose total contemporary driving experience is a cab ride to the train station in Trenton and another cab ride to the Senate Office building in Washington. The politicians should have to commute 50 miles each way on the San Diego Freeway.

In minutes, I was moving down across the toll bridge from San Mateo over the Bay to the mainland. I decided, *What the hell, even if I'm too late today, I can always go on to Tahoe, so go for it.*

And so I did. Some people hate to drive, some don't care and some love it. No different than most other lifetime activities, it takes all kinds. I'm a lover, of course. I'll drive anything that moves—any time, any place. You name it, I'll drive it. I've driven everything from lawnmowers to a Greyhound bus—bulldozers, tractor trailers, thrashing machines, go karts, taxicabs, police cars, pickup trucks, anything with wheels. If it moves, I'll drive it and enjoy the experience—which explains why I found so much to do on the way to Sacramento. I can find plenty to amuse and amaze myself, cruising along between 70 and 80, listening to Willie Nelson, Floyd Cramer or Dave Brubek and trying to deal in a civil way with the left lane bandits. You know them, they're the same people who jump the line at the movie to join their friends or show up in the 10-items-or-less line at the supermarket with a week's worth of groceries for a family of four—and then pay by check without an authorization card.

Years of being frustrated by these folks have worn away my will to resist, so I mostly follow a policy of avoidance. This is probably why I came to be singled out for the special attention of the California Highway Patrol; invited by flashing red lights to a friendly road-side conference; encouraged to discuss such things as frequent course deviations and appropriate velocities and asked to produce certain credentials like a driver's license and registration.

This conference occurred just after I had passed the northern outskirts of Stockton. I had just recalculated my time-to-target estimates and concluded that I still had 57 minutes to cover 42 miles. *Piece of cake. Unless we dally, officer.*

And dally, we did. These days, virtually all state police cruisers carry on-board, computerized commu-nications systems that allow an arresting officer to key in the particulars of your driver's license and automo-bile registration. Then, over the airwaves, they can dump this data directly into a Cray or some other inor-dinately expensive civil servants choice, taxpayer pur-chased mainframe. In short order, the officer will re-ceive a report in his cruiser detailing the shabby history of your driving record, when you made your last mortgage payment, and the date of your last pap smear for all I know—that is, unless you're out of your home state and driving a rental car.

Computers and telephones being what they are and the public out there tearing around like mad persons and then getting themselves apprehended, the line at the tattle tale window is sometimes long. Mother Computer is programmed to persist and it will happily redial till the cows come home, if you and your officer friend have the time. He does — have the time, that is.

So the officer and I sat there and waited. The hostage experts will tell you that after the initial anger and tension wears off, what follows emotionally is a state of sympathy that develops between captor and captive. The captive begins to excuse the captor for simply doing his job and the captor is grateful that he is not being actively hated for it. This probably explains why the officer eventually asked, "What do you do back in New York?"

"I'm a journalist, a writer," I replied.

"Oh yeah?" he said, with curiosity, not disbelief. "What do you write?"

"I work for *International Motor Racing Monthly*. I cover the Formula 1 Championship, mostly."

"Hey, wait a minute," he said, "Are you the guy that races the sports cars uh, uh, what do they call it, Group, Group...

"C."

"What?"

"C. They call it Group C. It's an international racing classification."

"And you're the guy. Well, I'll be damned. I've read your stuff, but I'm not into that foreign stuff much," he said, with a slight note of apology. Writers are always meeting people who are initially excited to meet someone whose words actually appear in print. They then become embarrassed to realize that they are about to fail the test of familiarity with the material, itself. I guess it's much like I feel when seated next to a priest at some function. I'm interested in what he has to say, but I hope I don't have to expose my ignorance of the bible and his religion which I don't dig.

But as I said, I love machines and driving them and, as a journalist, I've got a lot of curiosity about all forms of motorsport. So I asked him, "What kind of racing do you like?"

"I'm into desert racing. Some of my buddies got together and we built a Class A dune buggy we run in HYDRA and Score events."

I knew that he was telling me that his racing was "big time" by referring to the two major off-road racing sanctioning bodies. "What's the longest race you've run?" I asked, hoping that it was long enough to be respectable and not embarrass this guy who was holding my driver's license in his left hand.

"I did the Baja 1,000 two years ago," he said, with that small grin that says 'I know you're gonna be impressed and shucks, it wasn't that big a deal but I'm sure proud of myself.'

"Solo?" I asked.

"Yep. A bitch," he responded.

"Yeah, really," I said. I looked at his face to find the grin still in place. "Yeah, well, we finished third in class and seventh overall which wasn't too bad for us." In racer's code, this means: 'We kicked ass on some of the factory teams whose budgets are six or seven time bigger than ours. Not too shabby for a kid.' I was appropriately impressed and said so without fawning. We talked a little more about the race vehicle, while the radio and on-board computer crackled and hummed away in its quest for truth.

His nametag read *William Harmon* and he asked, "Mr. Pearson, what brings you to California? Are you working on a story or on vacation?"

I told him that it was a little of both, and then it dawned on me that I'd been sitting here for ten minutes with someone who might be able to help me. Feeling like a dunce, I said, "Listen, the main reason I'm here is the death of my cousin, William Pearson. Does that name mean anything to you?"

He looked at me for a few seconds, obviously doing his own computer search and said, "No, I don't think so. Why?"

"Well," I said, "he died in a crash up near Tahoe. The car went off the side of a mountain."

"Oh, Jesus," he exclaimed, "Is that the guy? I mean, is that guy your cousin? Oh, I'm sorry, I didn't connect the name. I mean, you know, in this business you see a lot of accidents and you can't remember everybody's name, you know?"

He was obviously very embarrassed as people often are when talking to the relatives of the recently deceased.

"Of course not," I said. "Do you know anything about the accident?"

"Yeah, I do," he replied quickly, "Although I wasn't there. That area is covered by Troop J, but I heard a lot about it. Gee, I'm sorry. Were you and your cousin close?"

"Not really, but his mother, my aunt, asked me to look into the accident because she was worried about her son just before he died. So when you stopped me, I was trying to get to your headquarters in Sacramento before closing so I could look at the accident report and maybe talk to someone familiar with the accident."

Officer Harmon looked at his watch and said, "Well, you'd have to get there before four o'clock. Gee, I wish you'd said something earlier. Uh, listen..." he said, reaching for the computer, "This damn system is obviously backed up or the main computer is down or something, so I'm going to cancel my search request. I have to issue a warning because I've already reported a violation, but you can ignore it. They don't share warnings with the national record system, so it's no problem. Were you going to meet with someone in particular when you got there?"

"No, I was just going to follow my nose until I found the right department."

"Well, maybe I can help a little bit. When you get there, go to the second floor and look for the Accident Investigation Division. Ask for Detective Allen Andrews. They call him, Andy. He's a good guy. Tell him that Bill Harmon sent you. I'm sure he'll give you everything you're looking for. By the way, what are you looking for? I mean, was your cousin in some kind of trouble? He was pretty wealthy, wasn't he?"

News travels fast, especially where money is involved. "I'm not sure what I'm looking for, but I'd just like to know a little more about the accident. It was apparently quite a mess."

He looked at me to be sure it was okay to talk about it and apparently decided that the issue was not too sensitive to talk about. He said, "Yeah, quite a mess. The car, it was a Ferrari, wasn't it? It went over a 250 foot slope, real steep. My buddies from J Troop tell me it was nothing but a burned out ball of junk when they got it back up the slope. Hey, listen, I don't know how much of this stuff I should be telling you. You better see the AID and talk to Andy. What I know is just hearsay, anyway." He nodded. "Well, I gotta get after the perps," he said, "I got six more hours on my shift, so I'll see you on your way. Pleasure meeting another racer. I'll be watchin' the papers to see how you're doin'. Take care now, you hear?"

We shook hands. I said my goodbye and got out of the cruiser and walked up to the Mustang, thinking, *Well, the day wasn't a total loss. I got some information, a good contact and a reference and I beat a speeding ticket. Not too shabby. Never up, never out, indeed.*

And, oh yes, there was still the matter of the Lovely Lady to sort out over a good meal and a half bottle of the Napa Valley's finest. *Onward, then.* I fired up the Mustang, put on the left turn signal and pulled back on to I-5 to cover the last 40 miles into Sacramento.

Officer Harmon turned off his flashers and pulled out behind me. Then he put the hammer down on the 340 horsepower Police Special V8 and moved smartly around me, giving me a quick military salute as he passed.

Nice guy, I thought, *Nice, helpful guy.*

Little did I know.

CHIPS

The mind is a curious device. Like the computer, it stores and retrieves information, along with managing other pretty important functions like breathing, taking your hand out of fire, and making love. However, unlike the computer, it does not always work on command. Sometimes, it will not give back a piece of information you know is in there; a very frustrating trait. Other times, without warning, it spits up a piece of information you never asked for. This was one of those times.

I was tearing along like the hammers of hell, secure in the knowledge that my racer buddy, Officer Harmon, was up there ahead of me somewhere, so I could safely thumb my nose at the old 65 mph signs along the highway in my effort to get to Detective Andrews before closing time.

Suddenly, I knew what had bothered me this morning in the elevator; the thought that something was odd about my laptop. I got the whole picture in a rush of déjà vu. The software I use presents all of my files in alphabetic order by whatever name I have given them.

It also does something I never have to ask it to do. It automatically records the date that I last entered that particular file. This is useful sometimes when you are trying to be sure that the information in the file is up to date. I suddenly realized that what was bothering me in the elevator was that some of the dates on the directory were wrong.

This all popped into my consciousness so suddenly that I flinched and looked in the rearview mirror to see how I could get the car off the road quickly and get out the laptop to check it out. If the angry honking of horns was any indication, I'd pissed off a few of my fellow motorists by blasting by them at a "rate of knots," as Colin would say, and then suddenly diving for the shoulder in a cloud of dust.

I got the car stopped, reached over the seat to my traveling bag and withdrew the laptop. I popped up the lid and screen, and quickly punched in the characters required to get me to the directory. And there it was. Of the seven files that run my life's schedules and details, four of them carried, after the title, today's date, indicating that I'd used the file today, which I had after my phone call to London.

The other three carried yesterday's date. Believe me when I say, computers don't make mistakes, people do. Garbage in, garbage out is the defensive cry of computer proponents when people complain about faulty records and such. If the computer puts in yesterday's date, then either the clock and calendar in the computer are wrong or the date is correct. I looked up at the top of the screen and the date and time shown matched those on my wristwatch. There could be only one conclusion. Those files marked with yesterday's date were opened yesterday.

The problem was that yesterday, I spent the entire day with Jennifer — without my laptop.

I had glanced at it in the room and decided not to take it to Monterey. And I never touched it when I arrived back at the hotel late last night.

Someone was peeking into my life and it gave me the chills. I cursed the system that had changed the dates on the other files, since now I'd never know if those had been opened, as well. But I was damned sure they had been.

I could have locked up the laptop or entered some secret passwords to protect the files, but for crying out loud, I thought, *who the hell would care?* I'm not carrying around a lot of confidential corporate data or something, and anyone would know that. No, whoever went in there was looking for information about my life and schedule. *But why?*

After confirming that none of the other files had been entered yesterday, I put the laptop away and pulled back onto the road. I couldn't shake the eerie feeling that someone was watching me. And I couldn't figure out why.

As I puzzled over this new aspect of my life, I hardly noticed that I had reached the junction that Officer Harmon had told me to look for on the way to State Police Headquarters. At the last possible moment, I realized where I was and cut across two lanes of traffic to get in the proper lane to exit, thus annoying yet another couple of my fellow motorists. I was having a world class day in the department of terrorizing the traffic and looking like a Nit-Wit on wheels.

Happily, I only had another mile to go and I managed to get my mind back on my driving enough to complete that without further incident.

Harmon's directions were precise and excellent, including those that took me to the second floor offices marked, *Accident Investigation Division*. As I approached the frosted glass door leading off the long hallway, I suffered those feelings of dread that occur at the end of a long trip; the fear that the person you need will not be there. With fingers crossed, I opened the door and entered a large bullpen area, organized with rows of government grey desks, many topped with CRT's and stacks of paper in all varieties of official formdom. I was standing in a small reception area separated from the bullpen by a waist high railing and containing two straight-backed chairs with a low table between them. On the table were the well-leafed remains of a couple of last year's news magazines and parts of a daily paper, all, I guessed, compliments of visitors who had finished with them during their wait.

A young man on the other side of the railing at the desk nearest the door looked over at me and asked, "Can someone help you?"

I was too uptight to try any of my stupid one-liners on this guy and said simply, "Could you tell me if Detective Andrews is in?"

"Which one?" he replied.

Damn, I thought, *probably the wrong one*. I said, "Allen."

"I don't think so," he speculated, the sort of standard operating response of any civil servant when you tell them what you're hoping for. They must be drilled for weeks in the art of saying "I don't think so," and "Probably not." It makes me crazy.

"I'll see," he said, and got up from his desk. He made his way down the aisle between the desks toward the area where partitioned cubicles began and ran out of view toward the far end of the offices. He disappeared from view and I fidgeted with the tension of waiting. Eventually, he reappeared and made the agonizingly slow walk back to me, with no expression on his face that I could read. By now, the suspense had me wanting to choke him and say, "Hurry up, dammit! Is he, or isn't he?'

When he got within earshot, he said, "Well, he's in but he's on the phone and he says he's leaving as soon as he finishes the call. Could you come back on Monday?"

Modern man is a curious creature who insists on exploring everything that he can get his hands on using a couple of taxpayer dollars to pay for it. One of the areas being probed by the scientists is what makes certain kinds of people tick—people like jet pilots, policemen and racers, among others. In every study of the psychological makeup of the professional race driver, one particular personality trait always stands out from the others. The typical, successful racer has an almost pathological, nearly anti-social drive to achieve a goal. He or she always ranks abnormally high on characteristics like determination, focus on objectives, endurance of intentions, ingenuity in the face of obstacles, things like that.

Thus, it is ill-advised to tell them, "Come back Monday." To them, Monday is the next century.

I looked at the man and summoned up every bit of friendliness and polite respect I could find laying around in an otherwise steaming mind and said, "Listen, I've just driven from Palo Alto and I have to go back to New York on Sunday. It's about my cousin who died in a wreck over near Tahoe and Trooper Bill Harmon said I should ask for Detective Andrews; that he could help me if he was here. Could you just ask him, if he could spend five minutes with me? Please?"

I know the guy wasn't carrying a high-speed computer between those pink ears, but he sure put out some smoke slipping his mental clutch trying to think of a way to say no without being a prick. Finally, he looked at me, sighed and gave up in the face of superior desire. He rightfully concluded that, "No" would not be the last word on the subject. Off he ambled to try once again and soon he was returning, preceded by a guy who clearly was on his way to get rid of this annoying interference with his regular TGIF prayer meeting and beer blast with the other senior guys from the office.

As he arrived at the railing, I never gave him a chance to state his case. I looked right into those clear blue Scottish eyes and said, "Detective Andrews, I'm really sorry to come in here so late. I know you must want to get home to your family and so do I, but I promised my dead cousin's mother, who is just destroyed by his death, that I would get some word from a responsible public authority that my cousin's death was merciful and quick. She needs that reassurance, Mr. Andrews."

He took a long, hard look at me, moving his eyes slowly up and down, while I held my breath. Then he looked at me and asked, "Did Bill Harmon really send you here?"

"Absolutely," I replied.

"How tall is he?" he asked.

"Why sir, I'd guess he's about six two or three," I said, knowing I'd won.

"Okay," he said. "Come on back. I can give you ten minutes, no more."

As I passed through the gate in the railing and followed Andrews back to his office, I could not refrain from looking at the clerk's dour face, and giving him a smile and a small shrug as a message of condolence. *Not to worry*, I thought, *on Monday, there'll be a fresh supply of victims for this guy to obstruct.*

As we entered Andrews' cubicle, he indicated that I should take a seat and asked, "Now which case was this?"

I told him and he turned to his console and typed in the name *Pearson* and the month of *February*. He studied the screen for a moment and then asked, "And what exactly did you want to know? And by the way, you can forget about that bullshit in the lobby. What's really on your mind?"

"Well," I began, "it *was* a little thick, but I was afraid I was going to get turned down and the truth is that my cousin's mother did ask me to find out more about what happened." Then I told him what I had learned about Willie's behavior just before he was killed.

He listened with apparent concentration and from time-to-time, glanced back at the computer screen. When I had finished telling him everything I had learned on my trip but leaving out the part about my laptop, he sat quietly for a moment and then asked, "Mr. Pearson, are you suggesting foul play?"

I thought, *My god, this really is a movie. I thought only Sherlock Holmes said 'foul play?'* I said, "I'm not suggesting anything, really. I'm just trying to find out if the police saw anything at the crash scene or anywhere else that would suggest a cause for Willie's death or some connection with his abnormal behavior prior to his death. At least some people think it was abnormal,"

I quickly added.

"Well, Mr. Pearson, we're not in the business of looking for signs of foul play at an accident scene, so the fact that none were reported doesn't prove anything. We routinely examine the car in a case like this for signs of alcohol or drugs, and this report doesn't indicate that any were found in your cousin's car. Do you know if your cousin was a user of either, Mr. Pearson?"

"I know he drank wine, but as to grain alcohol or drugs, I doubt it. He was pretty conservative."

He glanced again at the report and said, "All the blood tests were negative, so it doesn't appear that he was DWI. Other than that, Mr. Pearson, I don't think there's much else I can tell you. The area of the accident is pretty remote, so there were no witnesses except for the person who saw the fire and reported it. She didn't go down to the car because she's elderly and was afraid of the steep slope. She apparently heard no cries or anything from the victim and the condition of the car would suggest that your cousin died from one or more of the impacts, as the car tumbled. I can tell you from the report that he had severe head injuries."

I sat there feeling worse and worse about poor Willie. And at the same time, I was beginning to decide that enough was enough and he should be left in peace. I could just tell Aunt Blake that the police said he died a sudden death from a blow on the head and that's that. This whole thing was beginning to pall. I asked where the accident occurred and Andrews told me, "Three miles north of Vade on Fallen Leaf Lake Road."

Finally, I said, "Well, thank you for your time, Mr. Andrews. I guess this is a dead end. I don't suppose there was enough left of the car to tell you anything, either?"

"It doesn't look that way and there's not much we could tell anyway unless we had something definite to look for. Incidentally, he may have been asleep at the time."

"Why do you say that?"

"Well, because the car was traveling very fast."

"How do you know that?"

"It punched a hole in the armco. You know, the guard rail."

"Punched a hole?"

"Yes. At less than 50 mph, the car would have rebounded. The car weighs about 2.800 pounds, so he'd have to have been going at least 70. And, there's one other thing. There were no skid marks."

"Really?"

"None. That usually means driver asleep or..."

"Suicide?"

"Yep."

"Jesus."

"Has the family mentioned that as a possibility?"

"No. Not at all. Well, I'll have to think about that. Again, thank you for your time. You've been very kind."

"Not at all, Mr. Pearson. I hope his mother will be comforted. It's really too bad but sometimes the average citizen gets a hold of too much car and gets in trouble. Who knows?"

"Oh, that reminds me," I said as an afterthought, "do you know where the car is?" I thought that the police would still have it in impound.

He turned back to the console, typed in some more instructions, waited and said, "It's been released to the insurance company."

"Oh," I said, "Does it say which one?"

He gave me the name and address of the company, which I wrote down. Then I got slowly to my feet, thinking, *Well, that's it. Nowhere to go from here.*

Andrews interrupted my gloomy thoughts and asked, "Can I walk you to your car? I'm going now myself."

We walked out together and I thanked him again. Then I gave him one of my cards and asked that if he thought of anything else, would he please get in touch with me. I didn't believe for a minute that I'd ever hear from him and I didn't think I really wanted to. *This should be put to rest*, I thought. I mean, I sure wasn't going to touch the suicide theory with Aunt Blake, or Jennifer or anyone. *It's bad enough as it is*, I thought.

Wrong again.

HOTEL

For several minutes, I just sat there in the Mustang. This was not my idea of the way to end the perfect week. The things that I had learned from Detective Andrews were mostly depressing. Though I did believe that I had now fulfilled my promise to Aunt Blake and could honestly report some of the findings in a way that might be a little comfort—even if not a complete answer to her questions about Willie's behavior. After all, white lies—or in this case, a few judicious omissions—would serve a worthwhile purpose.

On a more selfish note, in Rod Evans I had come upon a story that would justify Arthur Bathgate's generosity. And finally, I had met a very special lady who darn well might change my life in many wondrous ways.

Now I had a decision to make. I had originally planned to go directly from Sacramento to Tahoe to take a look at the scene of the accident and Willie's ski lodge; all in hopes of finding further clues to the puzzle. But I was starting to hate the puzzle and this poking around in the gory details of poor Willie's demise.

One of the dark sides of my profession is the death and injury of fellow racers. The sport has made incredible strides in driver safety and crash survivability. It used to be called a blood sport like bullfighting, but it isn't anymore. Still, death and injury occur. But I like the way the members of the sport deal with it. Death and injury are always treated with enormous respect. Cool, professional analysis is performed after every incident and the facts are used to make adjustments for the future so that bit-by-bit, the safety of the sport improves and the experience is not lost or the sacrifice wasted. On the human side, the survivors rally around the families of the victims, support is provided where needed and the show of life goes on with each member accepting the risks in exchange for the rewards in a rational balancing of good and evil—just like space exploration and astronauts. The idea of daredevils just doesn't fit anymore.

My problem here was that there didn't seem to be a future into which I could factor whatever I could learn about Willie's accident. It seemed like an ugly, random act with no logic and nothing to be learned. I couldn't bring him back and I had no lessons learned to pass on to the future.

I decided that maybe Tahoe could wait—possibly forever.

At least for now, I was just not up to the trip and more immersion in this dreadful reality.

I started the car, checked my map and headed back to San Francisco and the comfort of my Japanese bath.

It's only 90 miles from Sacramento to San Francisco, but this was Friday night and the traffic was dreadful. In the end, what should have been a 90-minute trip took close to three hours, so I didn't get in the room until nearly eight o'clock. I'd thought of nothing but a hot bath for the last hour, so I never even glanced at the telephone and its blinking message light until I had spent another hour soaking away the weariness that a day immersed in sadness can produce. When I came out of the bath I finally noticed the blinking red light on the phone and dialed the message operator.

"What room?" she asked and I told her. "Mr. Pearson?" she asked and I said yes. "You have a fax message Mr. Pearson. Would you like someone to bring it up?"

Damn, I thought, *a fax wouldn't be from Jennifer. She'd call. It would be simpler.*

"Mr. Pearson?" said the voice.

"Oh yes, send it up, please."

Well now, I thought. *Who would be sending a fax on Friday? If Arthur wanted me, he'd most likely phone and leave a return number since he travels like I do. He wouldn't want to be interrupted in the middle of the night; time zone differences and all that. Who could it be? If there were a family crisis, I'm sure they'd use the phone. Hmmm.*

Then there was a knock on the door. I grabbed a dollar off the dresser and went to open it.

"Your message, sir," said the smiling bellhop, and tried not to look at my hand as I offered the tip. "Thanks."

I closed the door and immediately popped open the envelope containing the fax. I searched the bottom of the paper for a signatory. *Hey! It's from Colin. What the hell*, I thought. *How did Colin find me?*

Then I began to read his message:

Good news, Mate. Reuter has found a buyer for the team. Company named IEM. Some kind of electronic engine management systems, I gather. Guaranteeing five races mini-

mum, ex Le Mans (too expensive, it seems). Here's the rub. Company is Italian. They insist on doing Monza. A deal breaker, I fear. Practice starts Wednesday. I can get the car there. Can you possibly get to Milan on Tuesday to sign contracts? Deal depends on everything being tied up Tuesday P.M.

Do try, Mate. Mouths to feed and all that. Could be winning effort. Equipment is good and word is this is only pilot effort for them. If satisfactory, new cars next year.

Call me or fax me at Hereford Green. We have our fingers crossed. Regards, Colin

Well, well, well, I thought. *Maybe things are looking up.* Poor Colin was practically begging because this deal would guarantee a season's work for him and for the crew. More importantly, it would keep their work in front of the media and the other owners, something essential for continued upward progress in racing's hierarchy.

It would also be alright for me, although I had some other offers on the back burner so I hadn't been panicking about not having a ride at Monza. I assumed these people would not try to nickel nose me on my fee, so the least I would get is what I got last year — not spectacular but respectable for a non-factory ride.

All-in-all, I thought, *a better deal than going to work at the last minute for a strange team.* Colin and his guys were a known and reliable element. We'd all had a year's worth of experience with the car and with each other, so this would be an advantage over the other privateers and the new factory teams. *Hey, this could be fun,* I thought.

I picked up the phone to call Colin and say yes when I realized that it was 5:00 A.M. at the Hereford Green shop. No one would be there, so I sat down and wrote a fax. In it, I asked him to leave an address for the meeting in Milan on my machine in New York, which would solve the time zone problem and let me get some sleep which I was going to need very soon.

Once done, I began to make a plan because I had to accomplish a lot in a very short time. The days of floating along and waiting to see what was around the next bend in the river were gone for a while. I had to make some decisions.

The first one was what to do about Jennifer. I assumed that Jennifer already knew everything she wanted to know about Willie's accident. She seemed to me to be ready to put that all behind her and move on. I didn't think that she would be upset that I was, in effect, abandoning the search—at least temporarily. If that was the case, then the next question was what about Jennifer and me?

I was completely stumped. During the 24 hours since our dinner at her house and what I had been mentally referring to as *The Kiss*, she had been in and out of my mind constantly, chased away only by the events of the day that demanded my immediate attention. I'd been running the films over and over: *The way she looked coming into the restaurant. The feathery touch of her hand on the back of mine. Her eyes filled with tears. The sunset glowing softly on her cheeks. Her giggle. Her silky voice on the phone. And the candlelight flickering in her green eyes as she said, "I trust you."*

I wondered what her reaction would be when I told her that I had to go to Europe for the better part of the next month. And with that thought, the flood gates of déjà vu opened up and I was back in a hotel room somewhere, on the phone, telling Laura that I had to spend the next month in Europe and why couldn't she join me for much of the time. Without warning, the terrible memories of that conversation — and all the others that eventually led to the separation and then to the divorce — cascaded into my mind. I suddenly felt the way you do when you turn on the radio in the car and someone has left the volume switch up too high and you're frantic to find it and turn down the sound. My mind was crying, *Stop!*

Laura is my ex-wife. I'll be brief. We were married the week after she got her BA in English Lit. I was a teaching assistant working on my Doctorate that I never got. I got a job writing for a magazine, while I kept trying to make it into Formula I or Cart. She got a job as a secretary in a law firm. She could type and that's what those with undergraduate degrees in English Lit. were offered in those days.

Laura is not the secretarial type. Within months, she realized that she was about 50 percent smarter than most of the young lawyers in the firm. She also realized that she was blessed with the kind of logical mind that flourishes in the legal profession and, of which, there is a short supply. We decided that she should go back to school and get a law degree. She did. She did it so well that upon graduation, she was offered a spectacular position in a very prestigious firm on Park Avenue. From that day forward, our marriage was doomed. We were successfully traveling in two different directions; she in an ever upward climb to responsibility, stability and loss of flexibility and me toward the life of a well-paid gypsy.

It never could have worked, but it took us three more years to figure that out. One day, we realized that we had slept in the same bed just 40 nights out of the last 150. Under our circumstances, there was no possibility of children, neighbors, common friends, or all the other trappings of a normal life.

We were faithful to each other in the absences; at least I know I was and I'm pretty sure she was, too; but eventually, she grew tired of explaining at client cocktail parties and corporate functions why she was unescorted. In the beginning, she really tried to catch up with me on the circuit, but the better she performed at work the more they demanded her presence. As marriages often do, ours died from neglect.

Each of us was satisfying the insidious urge to be somebody and that left little room for us to be each other. We buried the marriage peacefully. Neither wished to inflict more pain than we'd already suffered, and we held a wake over a spectacular five course meal at Lutece. In my grief, I got well and truly bombed and Laura was kind enough to see me safely into a cab and on my way home.

That was five years ago and we have remained great friends. Laura may well be my best friend. She certainly has seniority. A couple of times, she has thought that she'd met Mr. Right and then, for a while, I wouldn't hear much from her, but it hasn't worked out yet. Success is a demanding master and she enjoys hers.

So what the hell was I going to do about Jennifer, the first woman I'd met in a long time that I had anything like an inkling of permanence about? Of course, I'm not a celibate person by nature and my work puts me in the way of many fleshly temptations. I try to partake with a certain degree of discrimination, although certainly not where race, creed or color are concerned. I definitely practice equal opportunity. But rarely does someone appear who looks like a keeper — except when they're being happily kept by someone else.

So what was I going to do? Fly off to Europe, saying so long, catch you later, Baby? Or was I going to say to Colin and the money guys, hang in there while I sort out my intentions toward this Wonder Woman I just met. I'll get back to you on your kind offer a little later?

Damn. This dog won't hunt, I thought.

When faced with this kind of dilemma, I resort to my secret weapon — the truth. Plain, unvarnished truth is often the only answer. I decided that I could not just abandon a career that I'd invested years in and I couldn't, on the other hand, make any promises to Jennifer, so all I could do was be completely straight with her and hope that she would understand. If so, she'd try to give me time to work it out. If not, well, then I'd beg or something.

As I picked up the phone to call her at home, I decided that this was not a message to deliver over the phone. I'd done that once before and it didn't work. The phone rang for a while and just when I thought that I'd get an answering machine or no answer at all, there was that silky voice saying, "Hello?" with a little sleepiness in there somewhere.

"Hi," I said. "It's Ned. Gee, I hope I didn't wake you. I didn't realize how late it was." *It was ten o'clock and I'm an idiot*, I thought.

"No, no. I was reading and I nodded off, I guess. Are you alright?"

"Oh, I'm fine," I said, "I had a very busy day. I went up to Sacramento after talking to Bob MacIntosh and talked to the State Police."

I thought there was an odd tone in her voice when she said, "What did you find out?"

"Not much," I replied. "I think you already know

the details of the accident and MacIntosh just confirmed that Willie acted distracted those last few weeks, but hasn't a clue why."

"Do the police still think it was an accident?" she asked.

I was surprised at her question and said, "Well, yes, don't you?"

She quickly responded, "Oh, of course, I do. It's just that, I don't know…I thought maybe they'd find something odd or something."

"Well, Jennifer, I don't think there's much more that I can discover and I've pretty much decided that I'm going to tell Aunt Blake that she should just not worry anymore and get on with her life as best she can."

"Oh, Ned," she gushed, "that's right. I'm so *glad* to hear you say that. I mean, what's done is *done* and we all have to move on. Don't you agree?"

The force of her emotion puzzled me, but I thought, *Maybe she's just relieved that I'm not going to drag her all through the problem again?*

"Yes, I do. It's time to get on with life. Speaking of which, can you have breakfast with me tomorrow morning? I have something to tell you that I'd rather not do over the phone. Are you busy?"

"Tomorrow's Saturday. No. I mean, yes, I can have breakfast with you. Where? What's it about?" Suddenly, she seemed frightened.

"Well, it's nothing bad," I said, "just inconvenient. I have to go back to New York suddenly and I want to see you before I go. I have some things I want to say. And I'll be back." Well, it wasn't a total lie. I didn't say soon and I *was* coming back. I just didn't say when yet.

"Oh, Ned, that's a shame. I'd hoped I'd see you at least once more before you left." And she sounded really sad.

"Well, let's have breakfast and talk about the future."

That seemed to encourage her and she said again, "Where?"

I said "I've got to catch a 9:30 plane, so could we meet near the airport?" She suggested a place about two miles from the airport. We agreed on eight o'clock and said goodnight.

After calling the airline for a reservation, I packed my bags for the trip and made a few notes in the laptop of things I needed to attend to in New York.

I left an early wakeup call and asked that my bill be ready at the same time, so that I could leave quickly in the morning. Then, I tried to go to sleep, even though my mind wanted to stay up and rehearse my breakfast speech to Jennifer. Eventually, it capitulated and I returned to dreams of green eyes and downy hair behind small, delicate ears.

MILAN

Getting almost anywhere in the world these days is relatively easy and Milan is no exception. Except that in this particular case, the first step, leaving Jennifer, turned out to be the most difficult.

We met at a coffee shop close to the airport. I'm not often early for appointments, but in this case I had a dual motivation; a plane to catch and an explanation to make. I was halfway through my first cup of coffee when she walked in. I must admit that it does wonders for your ego when all eyes in the room finally have their curiosity satisfied with the conclusion that the most lovely creature in the universe is going to sit at your table and smile into your eyes, not theirs. *Life's a bitch, guys.*

She was wearing something Springy, cotton with a big flower print, the skirt just at the knees so that you got a great look at those fabulous wheels. It was that kind of dress that sings, *"I Enjoy Being a Girl."* It didn't hurt the effect one damn bit that she had her hair swept up in back and pinned with a large tortoise shell comb that left wisps of that soft blonde hair floating around like a billowy cloud. *This is not going to be easy.*

She walked up to the table. I rose and extended my hand. Once again, she stepped right up to me, kissed me lightly on the lips and stepped back to get my reaction. I actually blushed. *Shit.* In front of the whole room at 8:00 A.M. on a Saturday morning, I went full flush red. She laughed and sat down. To escape, I signaled the waitress for more coffee and menus.

Then, she said, "Hi. I've been thinking about that for 30 miles. It was nicer than I imagined it would be. How are you?"

"I'm terrific," I said, "you look great. Do you always look like a flower garden on Saturday mornings?"

"Only when I'm meeting a special person," she said. I nearly blushed again.

The coffee and menus interrupted us, so we ordered and the waitress went away. Jennifer looked around the room and then at me and said, "I hope nothing serious is wrong back in New York. I mean, you sounded concerned on the phone. It's none of my business, of course, but I worried last night after we hung up."

"No, no," I assured her, "It's not like that. It's mainly business. Uh, I've got to sign a new contract."

Now, why the hell are you dissembling? I thought. Why don't you just tell her the whole truth? Because, dammit, she's going to be upset and she's going to think that I'm not interested in her feelings. Don't rush me. I'm going to tell her.

"So, can you tell me what's happening?" She smiled.

"Yes, well, the reason I had to see you is because I have to go do something that will keep me away for a while and it's come at the worst possible time. I mean, we have just really met and I was hoping that we could spend a little more time getting to know each other. At least I did and I kind of thought that you did, too. But now this thing has come up and it's going to interfere with that, if you see what I mean."

"Ned, are you married?" she asked right out of the blue.

"No. No, I'm not married. Why would you ask that?"

"Because you act married. You act guilty as hell, as if you had to explain your life to me, as if you had done something wrong. Why don't you just tell me what it is that has you so worried and then we can sort it out together."

I wanted to go around the table and kiss her right then and there. *Who is this angel,* I thought.

"Okay," I began, "Here's what's happening. I got a fax last night from Colin McDonald, he's our team manager, the racing team, you know? Remember I told you that Reuter was trying to sell the team? Well, he's done it and the new buyers are Italian and one of the conditions is that we race at Monza next Sunday. In order to do that, I've got to get to Milan and sign my contract by Tuesday. So that's why I have to leave now." I waited quietly and fearfully for her reaction. It knocked me out.

She looked up and said, "Ned, that's marvelous! I could tell in the car the other day that you were worried about your racing future and now something's happening. Is it just this race or the season?"

"No," I quickly responded, forgetting momentarily that the crisis had passed. "It's five races at least and maybe more, and if we do well they'll re-up for next year with new equipment."

At this outburst, she beamed. "You should see your face. You are so excited, you can hardly stand it. It's wonderful to see someone so enthusiastic about their life."

"Well, yes, I am pleased," I admitted, "but I'm also disappointed to have to leave so suddenly. I mean, we've just met and I feel really good about you, and I want to see more of you, that is, if you're interested, and I'm afraid you'll think I'm some kind of flake if I run off to Europe. But you see, it's my career, it's what I do and it makes me happy, so I don't have easy choices. Can you understand any of this?"

She smiled that soft, warm smile and reached across the table and took my hand in hers. This time, I didn't flinch. I just sat there feeling the warmth of her touch and her smile, and waited. She said, "Ned, I told you that I trust you. What that means is that I know you will not do anything to deliberately hurt me and that's all that I ask of you. Each of us is a grownup and we have to live our lives doing what's best for ourselves. If we're lucky, we'll find someone whose life will comfortably fit with our own and we can share life with that person. Maybe you and I will fit? Maybe not? In the meantime, you must do what makes you happy and not worry about making me happy. That's my responsibility and not yours. If we make ourselves happy, then maybe we'll make each other happy, too? That could be glorious, but only time will tell."

For once, I had the good sense to keep my mouth shut. I had just been handed the keys to the kingdom, a license to steal and the golden goose in one sweet package. I grinned.

For the longest time, I grinned.

The waitress came with the food and we ate quietly, talking mostly about the details of my trip. I considered asking Jennifer to come with me or join me, but I decided that it probably wasn't a good idea. This was going to be a very tough week — meeting new owners, getting comfortable in the car again, getting familiar with the track and all the stresses associated with major league racing. It would not allow much time for being an attentive lover and friend. And besides, I needed to concentrate on putting my absolutely best foot forward for the new owners. Million-candlepower distractions like Jennifer Paterson Pearson I did not need — not this week.

We finished breakfast and I looked at my watch, realizing that I'd better get moving or I'd miss my plane. I got the check and left money on the table, rose and gave my hand to Jennifer. We walked out to the parking lot, with me sneaking peeks to see how many jealous eyes were watching Jennifer. The answer was — all of them.

At her car, we stopped and she asked, "Ned, will you call me and tell me how it's going?" I promised I would and then came that moment of awkwardness before every leave-taking when neither one of you knows exactly what to say, but this time I knew. I simply reached for her, took her in my arms, folding that long, soft body against my own and kissed her. We just stayed that way, letting the feelings flow through each other until the breath was all gone. She tilted her head back, grinned up at me and said, "Hurry back, darling. I want more."

Whoowee, Baby. Like I said, I nearly missed my plane — by 24 hours.

I helped her into her car, watched it move into the

stream of traffic and then cleared the fog enough from my brain to become aware that I'd have to get moving if I were to catch that plane. In the end, I did and it wasn't until we were climbing through twenty thousand feet that I was able to tilt the seat back and start to re-run the incredible movie of the week. I could still taste her lips.

I got back to my apartment around 7:30 that night, not too much the worse for wear. After I dumped my bags in the bedroom and the mail on my desk, I hit the message button on my answering machine to see if Colin had gotten back to me. He had.

"Good on you, mate," he said in his best imitation cockney, "Oy new oy could cownt on yeh, down't yeh new." He continued in a normal tone, "It would be best if you caught the Sunday night flight if you can, my friend, because you don't want to be negotiating a contract after an overnight flight. I wouldn't, anyway. Also, we're going to begin testing on Wednesday and I'd like to have you over your jet lag enough to do a whole day. Are you in shape? We'll see."

Good old Colin. He's already in the driver's seat and starting to push, I thought. But that's his job — to get the team moving toward the goal line and that's how you do it, making sure everybody is ready to go. In this business, preparation is everything.

He continued with his reminder list and finished with the time and address of the contract meeting as I had asked.

There were a couple of other calls, nothing important so I called the airline and booked a flight to Milan on Sunday night, as Colin had suggested. That would put me into Milan on Monday morning and gave me a chance to catch up on the sleep lost on the flight. I decided to stay at the same hotel where I already had a reservation later in the week, when I was planning just to cover the race for Arthur. It was convenient to the track and that's where I'd be for most of the week, anyway. I called the hotel and even though it was the middle of the night, the night clerk spoke sufficient English to assure me that they could extend my reservation back to Monday night from its original Thursday start date.

That done, the only other detail was laundry and that could wait till Sunday. Having satisfied myself that everything for the trip was in order, I walked over to Broadway and had a beer and a giant, medium rare, barbecued cheeseburger. It was the last of those I'd see for a while. Then I went home and pulled one of my racing books off the shelf, one that had a diagram of the race track at Monza, and took it to bed to study.

There is a process called visualizing included in every modern training program for almost any sport these days. The object is to create in the player's mind a mental image of the successful execution of the task. Take a pole vaulter, for example. If he can see in his mind's eye, what the bar looks like at 20 feet and can imagine himself clearing it and all the motions that lead up to it, then he has a very good chance of actually doing it in reality. Basketball players refer to "looking" the ball into the basket. It's the same thing here. In a race car approaching a 90 degree right turn, at say 180, and the curve has a maximum speed of 130, the driver must choose a spot to begin braking, a spot to turn into the corner and a spot to begin accelerating out of the corner. To do this again and again, achieving the maximum speed each time requires him to have a picture of that corner in his mind so that the choice of when to take each action becomes almost automatic. He no longer has to think about each decision. It just flows out of his mind and occurs at the proper time. And lately, there are actual videos of all the major tracks so that you can practice on your couch.

The whole process becomes as mindless as making the bed. Repetition is the key—and visualizing—so that you can actually practice the steps without being there. That's what I did until I fell asleep.

The next 48 hours would be called uneventful, that is, if you're a regular international traveler. I arose on Sunday with that wonderful feeling of anticipation that comes with almost every trip, but especially so when a race week is beginning. Before I knew it, I had gone out for breakfast, gotten my laundry done, packed my bags, paid some bills, written a couple of letters and gone to the airport. The flight to Milan was smooth. I ate very little because now was the time to start getting lean and mean. The serious business was about to begin. Monday morning at Malpensa Airport is no one's favorite place to be, but I was able to clear customs fairly quickly and proceed to the counter to pick up my rental car. No game playing here. I had a reservation and it was honored, no problem. A quick check of the map and in a flash, I was away to my hotel up north and happily, on the same side of town. Well, a sludge would be more like it. Nothing on earth surpasses rush hour in a big Italian city.

Once at the hotel, I was quickly registered and shown to a very comfortable room, sighing the sigh of the traveler who has successfully negotiated the trips and traps of the journey and is now happily ensconced in a safe harbor.

My first thought was to call Jennifer. Then I realized

it was 1:00 a.m. in California. *Not a good idea.* So I called Colin in Hereford Green, where it was 9:00 a.m.. *Somebody better be at the shop.*

Colin answered, "IEM Racing."

"IEM, indeed," I laughed, "what became of McDonald Engineering?"

"Ah my, lad, the venerable firm of Colin McDonald Engineering, Ltd. presently enjoys the many luxuries of commercial sponsorship, and accordingly, a modest adjustment in identification to please the Lords and Ladies of largesse, don't you see. And where the hell are you, might I ask?"

I found myself as usual, falling into the pattern of banter that Colin always created with his warmth and good humor. I replied, "Why, I'm sitting on my ass in a foreign land not 20 kilometers from a famous race course, wondering where in hell are my crew, my race car, and my sponsors. I've little to do alone in my room."

Colin roared, "Well, ring up room service and see if they might have a comely crumpet on the menu. Seriously, you're in Milan, are you?"

"Indeed," I replied, "When will you be here?"

"The transporter left an hour ago. Gilly and I will fly down this afternoon. Will you be available for dinner, lad?"

"Wouldn't miss it for the world. You can fill me in on my new employers and tell me how to squeeze a couple of extra quid out of them."

"That I'll do, but I wouldn't set my hopes too high, my boy. They're no fools and they're very cautious. But I hear they're straight, so there's that to consider. I think they're serious about this. I hope we can give them enough of a show to keep them interested. I'll call your room when I get in. If you're going out leave me a message, won't you?"

We rang off and I decided that now was the best time to catch up on the lost sleep, so I pulled the blinds and climbed into bed. As I drifted off to sleep thinking about all that had happened during the past week, I thought, *Life is full of surprises, isn't it?*

I didn't know then that I'd only seen the first act.

IEM

Colin and his wife, Gilly, arrived as scheduled and we had an early dinner in the hotel. I listened carefully to his descriptions of the people I would be meeting in the morning and thought about his quiet advice not to get my hopes up too high about the fee, although I had already decided that last year's level would be alright, at least for starters. We agreed to touch base again on Tuesday afternoon to start planning for Wednesday's practice. Barring any mishaps, the transporter would complete its 800 mile journey across the Channel at Calais, down through France to Lyon and over the Alps into Italy by late afternoon on Tuesday. The crew would be up late Tuesday night, unloading the car and several tons worth of tools and parts in order to be ready to run as soon as the track opened on Wednesday morning.

I arose on Tuesday, a little anxious about the day. I'm not an especially social person. Strangers make me nervous and I was, without benefit of introduction, about to meet my new employers — employers, that is, if we could agree on terms. I dressed in suit and tie because I assumed that the IEM people would be doing the same. My conservative upbringing encourages conventional behavior. I generally dislike being dressed wrong. I can't help it. Blame it on my parents. Besides, I knew that these people would be evaluating me not only as a racer but also as a spokesperson for their company. Sponsors often use their drivers in advertising and public relations for their product. I can see their point in wanting to hire someone who can actually put together three consecutive complete sentences in at least one recognized language. I could manage it in two, although Italian was not one of them. I can handle menu Italian and race car Italian. In other words, I can eat and get my car fixed. But the Italians are impressed by any American who has bothered to learn a second language, even if it's French.

In other words, I thought I'd pass muster in the department of, "Would we want to invite this guy to a cocktail party with our best customers?"

So off I went to my meeting with the sponsors, hoping that it wouldn't be too painful and we could quickly get on with what I really came for — driving the race car. Excluding the hour in traffic to get to IEM's downtown office and find a parking place, the next few hours were a complete and delightful surprise.

I entered the fairly modern building and followed my instructions to find the receptionist on the twentieth floor. There, I introduced myself to a great looking receptionist who's fluttering eyes and demure smile suggested that she had been warned to be on the lookout for the American racer. The Italians feel about drivers the way the Spanish feel about bullfighters. She offered me coffee and a seat on the softest leather couch I'd ever touched. After she brought the coffee and went away to announce my arrival, I looked around the reception area and concluded from the design and quality of the furniture and decorations that perhaps IEM had both money and good taste. *A promising beginning,* I thought. When Miss Adriatic returned, I was able to get a more complete view of a wonderfully generous bosom lovingly restrained by a soft, brown, v-necked cashmere sweater that cascaded down over a tweed skirt and medium length, nylon clad strong legs. *A lady for a cold winters night,* I thought, and apparently my eyes had lingered a little too long because when I finished my reflections, I found her smiling directly into my face and waiting. Her expression seemed to ask, "Well, what's the verdict?" Of course, I didn't have time to get into detail on that, so I just grinned. Then she said in quite passable English, "Please come with me, Signor," and I was only too happy to oblige. I followed her at a respectable distance down a carpeted hallway to a door marked, *Conferenza* that she opened and held to let me by. As I passed her and moved into the room, the confines of the doorway space forced us to an electric proximity. As I passed, I got a disturbing swirl of warmth and perfume and a quiet smile, as she said, "Momento, prego."

Ah, I thought, *God love this land of passionate women.*

It was, in fact, just a moment when the door opened again and two people appeared—a man and a woman. He was the older of the two, about 40, I guessed, and apparently senior. She was in her thirties and very good looking in that aristocratic, northern Italian way; tall, built like a model with long lines, smooth olive skin, dark hair and surprising blue eyes. *The heritage of some ancient Teutonic invasion,* I supposed.

I was standing at the time and I realized that we

were almost eye-to-eye, as she spoke first, extending her hand and saying in excellent, only slightly accented English, "Mr. Pearson, I am Victoria Antonini and this is Vincent Gammino. Thank you for coming on such short notice. We're very happy to see you."

Well, well, I thought, *civilization.* In my profession, you get a wide range of reactions from people you meet. Some of them expect a mouth breathing Cro-Magnon and accordingly put on their Cro-Magnon manners. Once in a while, you get treated as if you were an equal. This was looking up.

"I'm pleased to be here," I said, truthfully.

"Won't you sit down, Mr. Pearson," said Gammino, indicating a chair at the conference table and moving around to the other side. "I see that you have coffee. Would you like more?"

I shook my head.

"Well then, shall we begin our discussions?" he asked, and began. "Mr. Pearson, I am the Executive Vice President for Marketing of IEM. Signorina Antonini is our Vice President for Public Relations. IEM is not the actual Italian name of our company but since English is the international language of technology, International Electronic Management is our public name."

I was not suffering too much from jet lag or the language barrier to catch the "Signorina." — in other words, Miss Antonini. *Goody, goody.*

"Together," Gammino continued, "we have convinced our President, Signori Malandrino, that the most effective way to publicize our new, electronic engine management system is to demonstrate its effectiveness on the race track. We have quietly done two years worth of testing and we are convinced that our system will perform competitively in your form of racing. If we are successful, we expect to become a major supplier to automobile manufacturers worldwide. Perhaps you can see how important this is to us?"

Wow, I thought, *this is very big.* I said, "Yes, I certainly can," thinking, *Stay cool now, friend. There's a big moment coming here any minute.*

"We are not without resources or alternatives when it comes to developing a racing program, Mr. Pearson. We have offered technical support to teams in many different series over the years here in Italy. But this would be our first international effort. So when we first conceived of this program, we contacted a number of people who we have found to be reliably informed about the various racing teams in the sport. When it was reported that Klaus Reuter's team might be available, we expressed an interest and here we are."

I was impressed with the efficiency of this guy's presentation. *Not much wasted. Probably some engineering in his background. But not unfriendly*, I thought, *just straightforward. This must be what Colin was referring to.*

I still thought that this was a time to be listening and not talking, so I maintained my polite, interested silence. Gammino continued, "So, Mr. Pearson we have only one piece of unfinished business in our preparations, the matter of contracting with a driver." He smiled.

It wasn't exactly a crocodile smile, but it was full of meaning nonetheless. The message was, is it going to be you or someone else? *Well*, I thought, *I can play a little poker when need be, so let's do it, Vincent, old buddy.*

I said, "Well, I'm obviously available and well qualified," with what I hoped was the right tone of carefree confidence. *Don't think I'm going to grovel, Mr. Gammino.*

"Indeed, Mr. Pearson," he said "we agree with that

and we hope that we can reach an agreement quickly. Perhaps in the spirit of negotiation, I should not be telling you some of these things..." He glanced at Antinori. "...but we have decided to be very, how do you Americans say it, up front?

"So here is our position. We have good reports on your driving record and your abilities. We are particularly interested in your ability to provide our engineers with feedback from the performance of our system on the track.

"Mr. McDonald was very complimentary on that score. We also hope to be able to use our driver as a spokesperson for our company and our products, although we realize that this is beyond the scope of the basic driver's contract. You have a reputation as well educated, reliable, and intelligent, Mr. Pearson."

By now, I was beginning to be a little embarrassed as this stuff flowed out and Antonini sat there smiling ever more openly. *Jesus*, I thought, *this is certainly a new experience.* I managed a grateful smile as Gammino continued.

"Mr. Pearson, it boils down to this. You are our first choice for this position. You are familiar with the car and the crew. You have an excellent competition record and you appear to have the personal skills to fulfill the non-racing requirements. Unfortunately, we have only today to conclude this matter, if we are to have the benefit of our new product announcement at this race, the only one in Italy for this season. We realize that this puts unusual pressure on you, but it cannot be helped. If you decide to reject our offer, we have made arrangements to meet with our alternate choices later today."

Holy Moly, I thought. *These guys are incredible.*

They're supposed to be Italian, running around like a Chinese fire drill. Instead, they've got this thing organized like a space launch. Who are these people? And what am I gonna do now?

"So, Mr. Pearson, in an effort to simplify this matter, here's what we've done. Signorina Antonini has here a draft agreement for your consideration. As part of our purchase agreement with Mr. Reuter. we obtained copies of all contracts with his team from last year. The contract we are offering you here is an exact duplicate of last year's contract, except in two respects."

Oh, oh, I thought, *now the bad news.* I remained silent.

"Signori Malandrino, our President, is a very enlightened manager. It is his belief that happy employees are inexpensive and unhappy ones are worth nothing. This leads us all to find ways to strike positive agreements with which both parties are happy. Because of the short notice and our desire to have a positive relationship with our driver, we have modified your contract with Mr. Reuter as follows. First, we are increasing the annual fee by ten percent. Secondly, we are offering a performance bonus of ten percent of the prize winnings of the team. All other aspects of the agreement remain the same, including travel expenses, accommodations, etcetera."

I don't know if my mouth was hanging open or not, but my mind sure was. I was still trying to catch up with this unbelievable message when Gammino stood and motioned to Antonini to give me the large envelope she had been holding. She offered it to me and I took it from her hand, gazing at it as if it were alive. Finally, I regained my composure enough to say, "Well,

Mr. Gammino, that seems...that seems very fair. I'm, uh, I'll look at this right now. I mean, actually...that's more than I, uh, expected."

Now both of them were beaming. She said, "If you would like a few moments to read it, Mr. Pearson, we can leave you alone here. What do you think? When you're finished, just let the woman at reception know and she'll find us. Okay?"

"Yes, that'll be fine," I said, "it shouldn't take long."

They left me to open the envelope and read. I did read the thing, but I really wanted to whoop and holler and go squeeze Miss Adriatic or something; maybe call Jennifer and tell her she was a good luck charm. Instead, I calmed myself down long enough to see that everything was as they'd promised and I was in roses for this season. *Unbelievable*, I thought. *What a week.*

I went down the hall to Miss Adriatic's desk and, while trying to sneak a peek down her sweater, asked her to find Signorina Antonini. I don't know if she knew what I was doing, but she straightened up and leaned back, delivering a serious threat to the side seams of the sweater. *Mama Mia.* She smiled and I smiled, each for our own reasons.

By the time they returned to the conference room, I was busily signing the three copies of the agreement that they'd left with me. When they came in, I stood and extended my hand to Gammino and said, "Signor Gammino, this is very generous," indicating the contract, "and I'm signing it as is, and with great enthusiasm. You have an interesting way of doing business."

He smiled and shook my hand, saying, "Excellent, Mr. Pearson, and now that we are on the same team, please call me Vincent. And may I call you Ned?"

"Of course," I said, as I turned to the woman and

asked, "And what may I call you?"

As we shook hands, she replied, "Please call me Vicky, Ned." And I hoped that Vincent didn't notice that Vicky held my grip and my eye just a fraction of a second longer than necessary. *My, my,* I thought, *ain't life grand.*

"Now Ned," said Vincent, "would you have time for lunch with Vicky and me to discuss the announcement we will make this afternoon concerning you and the team?"

"Absolutely," I said, "I'm not due back at the hotel until late afternoon."

"Excellent," he said, and he and Vicky went off to make arrangements and gather their papers.

The lunch was pleasant. We had some wonderful, fresh ravioli sautéed in a little butter and parsley and a salad of arugula. We talked of their plans to announce the new product and their involvement in racing at a series of press conferences later in the week where my presence would be required. They also had planned a giant cocktail party for Saturday night before the race, where they would host a couple of hundred people from the automobile and related industries plus the press. Colin and I would be asked to say a few words about the upcoming season and our involvement with IEM—all pretty much standard stuff. It was no big deal for me and I looked forward to seeing the news of my new contract in print. *Fame is fun.*

We soon finished lunch and I thanked them again for the contract and told them that I looked forward to working with them, which I honestly did. Straight, enthusiastic people who believe in what they're doing are uncommon and refreshing. Their enthusiasm was contagious. We agreed that I would next see them at the track and I gave them my room number at the hotel, so they could deliver an information packet that would more fully brief me on IEM and its history. Then I left them, retrieved the car and went back to the hotel where I found a message from Colin.

MONZA

The crew had made better than expected time with the transporter and were already at the track unloading. I couldn't wait to see the car and the crew and to tell Colin about my morning, so I raced upstairs, tore off my suit and changed into jeans and a sweatshirt and roared off to Monza. I had no trouble finding the crew, although the transporter still had last year's sponsor logos on it, a problem that I knew Colin would be frantically trying to correct.

To me, the Autodromo Nazionale di Monza is, in its own way, as impressive as the Indianapolis Motor Speedway and equally venerable. Monza, as it is simply known, was opened in September, 1922. It is huge by most racing facility standards with an original layout consisting of two circuits; one a banked oval nearly three miles around and the other a road course of over three miles in length, both of which could be combined to create a ten kilometer course.

The early twenties were the golden age of motor racing when the major European factories all began to compete for the Grands Prix, the big prizes, as stipulated and organized by the Automobile Club de France. As the center of racing in Italy, Monza created a mystique as powerful and enduring as the cars and drivers who raced there; cars like Alpha Romeo, Ferrari and Maserati in the hands of men like Ascari, Nuvolari and Taruffi.

So I was thrilled to be there and looking forward to the season with Colin and IEM.

It was like old home week with all the familiar faces and everybody feeling great about the new sponsor and the beginning of a new season. Man is essentially an optimistic creature and no matter what his experience might tell him about his prospects, every Spring is a renewal of faith that this year will be better than the last. We were all happily breathing the fresh air and feeling strong.

The week went reasonably well. We managed to keep the car on the track throughout our testing on Wednesday and Thursday, and moved steadily through the series of tests that Colin had planned. I was stiff and sore. This was my first time in the car since late last year, but I had kept myself in reasonable shape over the Winter and the race was only 500 kilometers, about 300 miles, so I wasn't worried about my stamina. *Looking good,* I thought.

Thursday night, I finally got a chance to call Jennifer. Since it was nine o'clock at night in Italy, I called her house in Woodside hoping to catch her before she went to the office. *No such luck, darn it.* I was really tired from the two days of testing and I had to get some sleep before Friday's practice sessions, so I just left a simple message that I had called and would call again on Friday and that everything was fine.

Friday brought the first rain of the week and I was

delighted. That may sound crazy, but rain—especially in qualifying—is the great leveler. I don't mean pouring rain which is dangerous but the light misty kind. The driver's skills come much more into play in the rain and I've seen banzai drivers who couldn't be touched in the dry, turn into pussycats in the wet. Since we definitely did not have the fastest car in the dry, I hoped that the wet track would help us close the gap. And it did. We ended Friday's practice sessions third on the grid, which Colin and I figured was at least two places better than we could have done in the dry.

Everyone was delighted, particularly all the people from IEM. Of course, these were early days and the knowledgeable ones knew the results were artificial, but it still felt very good and their decision to sponsor the team was looking like a good one. No matter what happened, even if we moved back on the grid tomorrow's qualifying, we appeared to be competitive and it was early in the season.

Saturday was dry but overcast. We adjusted the car back to the settings for dry conditions and hoped for the best. Two cars that should have been quicker than us in the dry had mechanical failures in the morning warm-up and weren't back together in time to get a full session in the afternoon. And just when they were getting up to speed, the session was cut short by a terrific crash that closed the course for the remaining time in the session. *Bad luck for them, good luck for us.* "That's racing," is the racer's response to almost every quirk of fate. You just never know.

As a result, we moved back just one spot to fourth, outside second row. It was an outstanding beginning for a new season and the sponsors were standing around clapping each other on the back.

We had time after the session for a quick trip to the hotel for a shower and to change for the IEM cocktail party. I had that pleasantly weary feeling one gets after a strenuous but successful day, and actually looked forward to the party. This was something unusual because I really don't like people in groups larger than six. Then they become a mob—and act like it. But I knew it would be fun to see the sponsor's happy faces enjoying their purchase. There would be other, less auspicious moments, I knew, and I should enjoy this one. I suddenly wished Jennifer were here to share this. *Oh well, maybe later.*

The party was held in a hospitality suite at the track and it was just as festive as I imagined it would be. When I arrived, Vicky quickly took my arm possessively and steered me past a lot of expectant faces toward a short, round man in his late fifties who was surrounded by a group who were obviously listening to his story. As we approached, he turned and saw Vicky and me. He smiled, as Vicky spoke in rapid Italian, the only word of which I clearly understood was "Pilota." Then she said, "I would like to introduce you to Signor Arturo Malandrino, our President."

He offered his hand and said, "My sincere congratulations, Mr. Pearson and welcome to the IEM family. Your performance today was, as we say in Italy, formidable." The accent was on the second half of the word.

I made a half bow, smiled and replied, "Thank you for the compliment and I should say that I'm very pleased to be here. I'm looking forward to the season."

"As are we, Mr. Pearson." He turned to Vicky. "My dear, when will the program begin?"

Vicky knew a direct order when she heard one, no matter how politely put, and responded, "I believe that everyone is here, so we should begin at once." She took my arm and led me toward a small platform at the front of the room where Vincent, Colin and some others were standing near a microphone.

What followed was a series of predictable welcoming speeches interspersed with introductions and polite applause. Colin and I were introduced and made the appropriate remarks, thanking IEM and its people for their support and promising an interesting season. Several industrial luminaries were then pointed out in the crowd and welcomed by Vincent. Finally, Signor Malandrino took the microphone and expressed his confidence in the racing team and his engineers, and thanked everyone for coming.

After the speeches, I got myself a Pelligrino from the bar and tried to circulate politely like a good corporate citizen. I accepted congratulations from a number of people and tried not to get locked into any deep discussions about what it's like on the race track because most people don't really want to know, even after they ask. They get bored about half way through any serious explanation.

After a while, I noticed that one particular man kept appearing in my vision, always a few feet away but seemingly interested in whatever conversation I was engaged in at the moment. I was thinking about finding Vicky and asking her who he might be when he showed up at my elbow and smiled in a friendly way, as I turned and noticed him there.

He offered his hand and said, "I am Piero Romano. I've been looking forward to meeting you." Puzzled, I mumbled my name and waited to find out more, not believing that this guy just wanted to meet an American driver. He was quite well dressed, in his fifties I guessed, and spoke excellent English. "I am with the firm of Ferrari," he said, with the gravity and reverence only the Italians can muster when speaking of the prancing horse from Maranello. "I knew your cousin. You are the cousin of William Barker Pearson, are you not?" he asked, with raised eyebrows, slightly less self-confident now.

"Yes, I am, but do you know that he was killed in an accident?"

"Yes, of course, and please forgive me for not saying so, that is, I wanted to meet you and offer my condolences. I knew your cousin quite well."

"Oh really?" I had met few people outside the family who had known Willie, so this was a novel experience. "How was that?" I asked.

"As I presume you know, Mr. Pearson was a collector of Ferraris. Are you familiar with his collection?"

"As it happens, I am, although that's a very recent situation. Willie and I were not close. I live in New York and Willie was on the West Coast. And we are not the same age, so I haven't seen that much of Willie in these past few years." I stopped, thinking, *You don't need to tell this guy your life story.*

"I see. And how did you become familiar with the collection?"

I began to get the feeling that this was leading somewhere, though I didn't have a clue where. But I felt as if I had been stalked and now I was being questioned. It was uncomfortable, but I had no reason yet to be brusque or rude. In my business, contacts are everything and here was a guy from Ferrari wanting to talk to me. *I'd better listen*, I thought.

"I've just come from California where I was assisting Willie's widow to make arrangements for the dis....

the future of the collection." *I'd better be careful what I say to this character,* I thought. *I haven't a clue who he is and for all I know I could inadvertently say something that could affect the value.*

"Do you know what Mrs. Pearson's plans are?" he asked, his eyes narrowing ever so slightly.

That's it, I thought, *this guy may already know where I came from. Evans would know this guy and he could be sniffing around for information.* I suddenly felt as if I was in the middle of some spy novel or something. I was also suffering an attack of paranoia.

"Mr. Romano, might I ask what your interest in all of this is?" I tried for a low key, friendly tone but he got the message.

"Mr. Pearson, please forgive me. I've been careless and now you think me to be prying. I have no particular interest. We, at Ferrari, are always interested in the disposition of our cars and your cousin was a meticulous collector in whom we had great confidence. He was the kind of collector who will insure the future preservation and integrity of the Ferrari heritage, you see. Now, unfortunately, he is gone and we are simply interested in the future of the collection. I should have said so in the first place, but as you must know we Europeans do not subscribe to the American approach, I think you call it..."

"Up front," I interjected, thinking, *Well, some of you do,* remembering my new friends at IEM.

"Yes, that's it. Again, please accept my apologies. I meant no offense."

"No problem," I said. "Mr. Romano, when did you last see Willie?"

"Well, let me see, I believe it would have been in February, sometime. Yes, that's right, not too long before his unfortunate accident."

I'll be damned, I thought. "Where was that?"

"Oh, in my office in Modena."

"Really?" and then I thought, *Back off, guy. You're about to get into family business again.*

As I was trying to frame my next question, we were interrupted by Vicky and Signori Malandrino who arrived with Malandrino smiling at Romano and saying, "So, you two have met have you?" He turned to Romano. "Piero, I have only just acquired the services of this gentleman and already you are conspiring to seduce him away from me, is that it?" he asked, beaming at his own joke.

Romano smiled down at Maladrino and replied, "Honestly, Arturo, I hadn't thought of it, but based on today's extraordinary performance, you have given me an excellent idea for which I thank you."

Malandrino roared, turned to me and asked, "Mr. Pearson, will you join us for dinner, or must this be an early night for you?"

I thought, *This is either the nicest or the most manipulative man I've ever met. He knows that I have to race tomorrow, he wants me away from Romano for some reason, so he offers dinner and an easy excuse to leave if I want it.*

I don't like cocktail parties, anyway. It was getting late and I was weary from the week. I took Malandrino's lead. I looked at my watch and said, "Well, Signor Malandrino, you are kind but it has gotten late and I do have a busy day tomorrow." I grinned. "Perhaps, I could have a rain check?"

He looked puzzled and Vicky said something in Italian. He smiled at me and said, "Of course, of course."

Romano saw what was happening and pulled out a

card case, saying, "Mr. Pearson, I enjoyed our conversation. If you or Mrs. Pearson need any help with the collection, do let me know." He then said goodnight and moved away. I glanced quickly at the card and put it in my pocket.

I then said goodnight to Malandrino and to Vicky who walked me to the door and asked, "Mrs. Pearson?"

I smiled and said, "The widow of my late cousin."

"Bravo," she said.

THE RACE

Sunday, race day, was a day of bad news, good news. The weather turned balmy and Spring-like, which was bad news for our competitive hopes. The good news was that the car hung together for the full 500 kilometers, which was not the case for many of our faster competitors. I got a good start and held my fourth place position for the first half hour or so, but eventually Colin realized that the car would probably not last the race at this pace because I was pushing it very hard to run with the leaders and fight off the attackers from behind, those two cars that hadn't got to qualify well on Saturday.

So we backed off a little and settled in for the long haul, at least knowing that the car wasn't a complete slug, while giving the sponsors and friends something to cheer about.

By and by, attrition began to set in and we moved from our position in seventh back up to fifth. Then, with less than 50 kilometers to go, as I exited the turn leading on to the start-finish straight, I could see the car ahead of me and realized that I was catching him. The crew had been giving me interval times as we went along, but now it looked as if he was slowing. I decided to step up the pace just a little to see if the gap would close further and sure enough it did. I radioed Colin to see if he wanted me to risk the car this late in the race to get another position and he decided to go for it. "Softly, softly, catchee monkey," he said into my ear. And off we went. Soon, we were on him and I realized that people in the stands had begun to rise to their feet each time we reappeared around a corner. I was pretty interested to see how this would turn out, too.

The car was now beginning to show signs of the increased effort. The needles on the exhaust temperature gauges began to march from left to right across the dials and the water temperature rose to threatening levels. The guy was putting up a valiant fight to protect his position, letting the car drift over in front of mine at the entrance to every corner, so as to block my attempts to pass.

We were now down to less than four laps to go and my blood pressure was beginning to rise from a combination of worrying about the car's ability to stand this late-race punishment and the frustration of this guy's blocking my every move. Further fuel was added to the fire when a quick glance in the rearview mirror showed me that all this cut and thrust had slowed both of us down and now here came a third car to start trying to pass me. *Oh shit*, I thought, *we're going to blow this whole thing in the last three laps, if I don't do something soon.*

At this point, we had just exited the chicane on the back of the course and were approaching the 120 degree right hander that leads back on to the main straight. I made one of those never up, never out decisions, as we screamed down to the corner at 180 miles per hour. As we approached the braking point, the point where you lift off the throttle and get hard on the brakes to slow the car for its entry into the corner, I moved over to the right as if to try a pass under braking on his right side. As he had lap after lap, he slid over to block my attempt. I then moved back behind him and he resumed his normal line. Just as we got to the corner, I feinted again to the inside and as I hoped he would, he took the feint and moved sharply down into the corner to block me. As he did this, I pulled the car to the left and began passing him on the outside of the turn, while saying my prayers.

I prayed for good judgment that I'd not gone in too fast. I prayed for traction, that off line as I was, there would still be enough grip to keep the car on the track. And I prayed for fatigue — his. I hoped that he'd be so tired at the end of the race and the pressure of our scrap that his reaction would be too slow to block me coming out the other side.

He almost caught me — almost. At less than the last minute, he realized that he'd been tricked and he tried to recover and move back to the left, but fatigue beat him and I was, "by, home and dry," as Colin says. And I got a bonus. In his attempt to recover, he slowed abruptly in front of my pursuer and they came together hard. The threat to me was gone and I could now concentrate on getting the temperatures back down and coaxing another two laps out of this wrung out machine.

When I was able to look around again, I saw that the Tifosi were really on their feet now and I realized that after all, to them this was an Italian car, even though it was built in England and had an American behind the wheel. National pride is funny.

To crown the day, as I started the last lap, I came upon a car running slowly, well off the racing line. After I passed by, I slowly realized that it was the same car that had sat beside me to my right on the grid before the race—the third place car! Just as my tired brain assimilated that information, the radio crackled and Colin said, "You've just copped third, lad. Try to bring it home without clouting the walls, would ya?"

Of course, that last lap is agonizingly long and my imagination was hearing dreadful noises from the bowels of the car, with almost certain knowledge that it would fail at any second. My main concern was my rearview mirror and the assurance that no one was sneaking up to steal my prize. Finally, I rounded the final corner and accelerated down to the start finish line. I took the checkered flag to a thunderous spate of cheering that would have convinced an uninformed observer that I'd won the damn thing.

After crossing the finish line, I carefully slowed down and hoped that there was enough fuel remaining to return the car to the pits. With this crowd of crazies, I definitely didn't want to walk home. There was and the course marshals were protecting the pit entrance, so I was able to get the car all the way back to our pit where the mechanics were all slapping each other on the back and generally grinning like fools. When I arrived and almost before the car had fully come to rest, the door was ripped open and they began pummeling me with joy. This was nice, but all I wanted to do was get out of the thing and I wasn't sure when this could begin. Finally, Colin shooed them away and helped me unfasten the radio line and oxygen fitting attached to my helmet and the safety harness, so I could drag myself out.

My getting out renewed the celebration and then the officials showed up to escort me to the winner's podium. We made our way through the garage and up the back stairs to an elevated balcony on which there was a three level platform. The first and second place winners, both from factory teams, were already there. Since I had never been on this podium before, it was all new and exciting and I found myself wishing that I weren't so tired so I could enjoy it more.

We all stood quietly, while the winner's national anthem was played. As the newcomer, I wasn't ready for the champagne attack launched by the race winner against number two and me to the delight of the crowd. Soon, we were totally soaked, with our eyes full of stinging champagne. *Boys will be boys*, I guess. We then exchanged shoptalk about the events of the race. After a brief interview or two, I finally returned to the pit to find Colin and thank him and the crew for all their hard work during the week. All of the IEM people were there—except for Malandrino, for whom I reasoned the trip from the sponsor's boxes atop the stands down to the pits was a bit too strenuous.

Colin walked back with me to the team motor home; the giant traveling motel room we use for dressing, conferences and some peace and quiet at the race track. He wanted to talk with me, while I took a quick shower and changed out of my driving suit. "Well, laddie," he said, "that's a helluva beginning. I'd not of put a farthing on anything better than fifth going in. You hustled that sled pretty good, lad."

I wasn't going to get any higher compliments than that from Colin and I was pleased.

"Tell me," he continued, "while it's fresh in your

mind, what do we need to do for Silverstone?"

"Install an extra 30 horsepower," I quipped. One of our weaknesses versus the factory teams was sheer horsepower since they had million dollar engine development programs which we could never afford.

"I'll do that, lad. Maybe in your right foot," he kidded back, suggesting that maybe I wasn't pressing the accelerator hard enough.

"The only thing I can think of right now, Colin, is that if we could get a little more down force on the front end, I might be able to come off the high-speed corners a little harder. It's really pushing up high." What I meant was that the front wheels were not sticking as well as the rear in high-speed corners.

"We'll figure something out," he said and that was that.

"By the way," he continued, "I hope you brought plenty of clothes because you did so well today that our good friends from IEM came to me after the race and asked if we didn't need a backup car. They saw what happened to some of our unlucky friends this weekend and all by their little selves, bless their hearts, they figured out two things. One, this team has a chance to do well this year and two, if you put a foot wrong and prang our race car, we're up shit's creek for that race weekend. So they've agreed to invest in a backup car."

"Colin, that's terrific!" I shouted. One of the privateer's problems is that he can't take chances in testing and qualifying because if he crashes the car, he's often finished for the weekend and gets no points. With a backup car, you can do all your experimenting with it and then transfer your learning to the number one car that remains fresh for the race.

"Indeed it is, lad, but it means you're not going to see the good old USA for a while."

"What do you mean?"

"I just happen to know that there's a sister car to ours sitting at the Lola factory, as we speak. Simmons is here and I'm ordering it from him in an hour. It'll be in Hereford Green by the time the lads return with the transporter on Tuesday. I want it on the track at Silverstone by Thursday. A helluva thrash, but we can do it.

"We'll have three days to sort it out and two days to transfer the settings to the first car and be back at Silverstone on Wednesday for official practice. What do you think of that?"

My head was spinning, but I was very excited. The race at Silverstone in the English Midlands was two weekends away. This was turning out to be possibly the best shot I'd ever had at first rate equipment and a competitive budget, which meant that it was my best shot at eventually getting a coveted factory ride. "Colin, I think it's crazy, but if anyone can pull it off you can."

The problem was, of course, what was I going to tell Jennifer? I kept extra clothes in London for just such a contingency, but there was no way I could sensibly fly to California and back and keep to Colin's mad schedule. *Well, maybe she can come over here?* I thought, hopefully, and returned to excited thoughts about the possibilities ahead.

It took another two hours to finish with the well wishers and get back to the hotel. I looked forward to a long hot bath, a room service meal and early to bed. I was exhausted. But first, all week in the few quiet moments when I wasn't focused completely on racing, I had been missing Jennifer terribly. Now, I had a chance to hear that silky voice again and to tell her of all the good fortune of the week. As I dialed, I thought about asking her to come to Silverstone. She answered on the third ring.

"Hello?" It was lovelier than I'd remembered.

"Hi there. It's me."

"Oh Ned, where have you been?" she asked, making me smile.

"Earning my keep."

"Are you alright? I mean, how was the race? I've been thinking about you all morning."

"The race, dearest, was nothing short of awesome. We finished third when we should have finished sixth and the new sponsors are so happy that they bought us a second, brand new car."

"That's wonderful. Who'll drive that?"

"I will."

"You will? How can you drive two cars?"

"No silly, the second one is a backup car, a spare."

"I see," she said, but didn't.

"Trust me. It's a very good thing."

"I do. I told you, didn't I?" Her voice lowered slightly and the desire to touch her poured through my body.

"Jesus," I said, "I just had the most powerful longing to be with you."

"Me, too. When?"

Oh shit. This moment's come too soon. I'm not ready. "Jennifer, this week has been filled with absolutely wonderful surprises for me, but there is one piece of bad news. I can't get back to California for at least two weeks, maybe three. Could you possibly come over here?"

"Well I can try. I'm just not sure. I have some obligations at work and some meetings on the estate and a court hearing. Let me see what I can do. Where is 'here?'"

"It would be in England. The next race is at Silverstone, which is in the Midlands. It's beautiful. Have you ever seen it?"

"Sounds lovely. I promise I'll try. Now tell me about your week."

So I did. Ad nauseam, probably, but I was so excited to be talking to this glorious creature and so happy about the last two weeks of my life that I just couldn't shut up. From time-to-time, she would interrupt to ask a question or make a comment and she seemed really interested in my whole story. Finally, I ran down and she said very quietly, "I can see your face. You are so excited and it's wonderful. I wish it was right here, so I could kiss it again."

The sound and tone of her voice left me breathless and my heart just fluttered. "I miss you very much," I said.

"I miss you, too. I miss having my arms around you and feeling you against me."

I'm going to faint, I thought. "Hush," I said, "you're going to start something we can't finish for too long a time. Get over here."

She giggled. "I know how you feel. I feel that way. I'll try."

I couldn't stand much more of this or I knew I might ruin a perfectly good career, so I asked her what she had been doing. She told me that things were pretty routine and that she had gotten Evans' proposal and wanted me to see it. I gave her the Hereford Green address because that was the next place that mail could reach me.

We went on a little longer, running out of things to say after a while, but not wanting to leave each other. Finally, she said, "You'd better get some sleep. You're going to be a busy boy and I don't want to find you in a rundown condition when I see you." She giggled.

"Hussy," I said, "you shall regret your careless words."

"I hope so," she said.

We said goodbye, promising to talk again when I got settled in England. After I'd hung up, I felt bad that I hadn't told her everything that was on my mind. I hadn't told her that I was falling in love with her, even though I knew that I was. But somehow, I just didn't want to say it on a long distance telephone line. I wanted to be looking into her eyes when I said it. I wanted her in my arms. And I wanted to show her how much I loved her after I said it. So I waited.

I slept well that night and, since my plane to London wasn't till early afternoon, I had a leisurely morning. Before I'd left the track yesterday I'd gotten a copy of the lap chart for the race and the official summary of the event. With those notes in hand, I did a first draft of my race report for the magazine, while it was fresh in my mind. I'd be in Arthur's office on Tuesday and I was looking forward to seeing him after several weeks.

As I packed for the trip, I went through the pockets of my suit and found Piero Romano's card from Saturday night. I remembered then what it was that I'd been about to ask him when Maladrino interrupted. Having a little time and realizing that reaching him from Milan would be easier than from London, I stopped and dialed the number. After some passing around, I was finally put through.

"Mr. Pearson," he came on the line breathlessly,

"sorry to keep you waiting."

"No problem," I said.

"My hearty congratulations on your excellent performance on Sunday."

"Thank you. We were very lucky,"

"Perhaps, Mr. Pearson, but in Italy we have a saying, 'It's amazing how lucky you get when you work your ass off.' "He paused for my laughter.

"Were you there, Signor Romano?"

"Yes, I was and I saw what you did in the end. A very bold move. But beautifully done."

"Thank you."

"Well, what can I do for you, Mr. Pearson?"

"I was wondering. At the party, you said that you had seen my cousin Willie just before his death. I believe you said in February."

"Yes, that's right. He was here in Modena."

"Signor Romano, can you tell me what it was about because his family apparently doesn't know that he was here or why."

"Oh, I assumed that you knew, that he would have discussed it with others. I'm glad to learn that he did not because these rumors crop up from time-to-time and we make every effort to discourage them. After all, not once has anyone proven that it has been successfully done. We have examined every incident thoroughly and I can assure you, Mr. Pearson, that it has never happened."

What the hell is this all about? I thought.

"What has never been done, Piero?"

"Oh, of course. You don't know. Your cousin thought that he had acquired a counterfeit Ferrari."

Jesus H. Christ! A counterfeit Ferrari? No wonder Willie was acting strangely. "What kind of counterfeit Ferrari,

Piero?"

"A 1962 GT250 California spyder. But Mr. Pearson, let me assure you, it was not so. As I said, rumors such as this surface from time to time but they are never true."

"Yes, of course, but how do you know?"

"Certain measures have always been taken to insure against this possibility. Of course, these are confidential. For obvious reasons, I cannot discuss them with you or anyone else."

Right, I thought, *I think it was Nixon who perfected this tactic. Executive privilege or something.* "So you're sure Willie was wrong?"

"Positive."

"Did he tell you where he got the car?"

"No, he didn't. In fact, he swore me to silence about this and I was only too happy to agree. I've only told you because you are a member of the family and the professional community, and I hope I can rely on your discretion."

I made an instant decision not to rock the boat and said, "Of course, Piero, you can count on me. But I may have some more questions later. I hope I can come back to you."

"I would be happy to help in any way I can," he said, and sounded relieved that I wasn't going to press him further now. He asked about my plans and I told him I was on the way to England to begin testing the new car and he confirmed that the IEM people were very excited about the team. He asked me to stay in touch because, as he put it, "Ferrari is always looking for promising drivers." While I was delighted at the hint that Ferrari could be interested in me, I didn't miss the old quid pro quo in his comment. In other words, keep your nose clean and something good could happen. *We'll see,* I thought, and rang off.

I'll be damned, I thought, *Willie thought he had a $10 million dollar fake on his hands and he came here to sort it out and got turned away. No wonder he was up tight. If it could be done once, it could be done again, couldn't it? What the hell was I going to do about this? And wait till I tell Jennifer? And Evans? Whoops. Where did Willie get the car?*

With my mind spinning, I finished packing, checked out and went to the airport to catch my plane. Somewhere over France, I had a chilling thought. I wondered if the person who had tampered with my laptop was trying to find out exactly how much I knew that I wasn't supposed to know.

And then I realized that it was getting worse.

Later, I discovered how much worse.

ENGLAND

She never made it. At the end of that first week, it looked as if she'd arrive just before the following weekend; the weekend of the race at Silverstone. Then she called Hereford Green and said that the court hearing had been re-scheduled for the following Monday, and that her lawyers had insisted that she be there. If I hadn't been so consumed by the overwhelming schedule of testing and re-testing we were going through to get the cars ready for qualifying, I'd have been heartbroken. As it was, I tried to take the bad news philosophically.

She asked if I was coming back to New York after Silverstone and could I come to California then. Since we had a two-week break between the race in England and the French championship, I was sure that I could.

She said, "Goody. I might just have a little surprise for you then," and wouldn't tell me what it was, despite my pressing.

Each time we spoke, I considered telling her what I'd learned from

Romano about Willie's trip to Italy, along with his suspicions about having a counterfeit car. But each time, I couldn't find the right place to interrupt and drag out all the old, unhappy bones of the recent, unpleasant past. And besides, I didn't know where to go from here with the information, anyway. Each time I hung up, I felt a little guilty for not telling her and then excused myself by deciding that it would be best if I were with her when I told her.

Something else I didn't tell her about was the conversation I'd had with Sotheby's, the international auctioneers of fine art and antiques. I'd gotten the idea to see them when I found myself with some free time on Tuesday afternoon in London. Actually, it was something that Arthur said at lunch that day that triggered my memory.

I'd gotten to London late Monday afternoon and checked into a small, relatively inexpensive residential hotel just up the way from the south end of Berkeley Square, where the offices of the magazine were situated. After unpacking, I'd gone over to the offices to see who might be back from the various assignments of the weekend and to catch up on all the latest office gossip. Arthur was out, but had left word that he'd like me to join him for lunch the next day.

Several of my journalist friends were busily cranking out their reports on the weekend's racing activities around the world, but my arrival caused a great uproar of welcoming and congratulations on the new sponsorship and the Monza results. Finally, someone put forth a motion that we all move the meeting "down the road" to The Bleeding Hearth, a three hundred year old pub that is the magazine staff's "local."

Once there, I was obliged to buy everyone a round of drinks in celebration of my good fortune and I was happy to do it.

I spent the next two hours in the warmth and comfort of friendship, and common ground talking shop and rumors, love lives and war stories — the things that pubs were made for.

I went happily back to my hotel room and settled down to finish my Monza race report, reflecting comfortably on how well life was treating me.

The next day, I spent some time with Arthur catching up on the past several weeks in both our lives. Arthur is very special in my life, well beyond his role as my employer and my publisher. To me, he's kind of a cross between surrogate father, kindly uncle, friendly coach and sage advisor. When we'd got pretty well caught up, we turned to business issues and worked out my assignments for the next three months during the racing season. We also talked some more about Rodney Walker Evans and Arthur promised to tell me over lunch of some things he'd learned in his inquiries.

We went up the mews in back of Bruton Street to The Guinea for lunch. We both ordered the steaks and treated ourselves to a glass of wine. When the waiter had gone, Arthur looked back at me and asked — quite innocently I'm sure "What's new in your love life?"

I had the feeling that Arthur had seen something in me that prompted the question. I wondered, *Am I wearing my heart on my sleeve again?* Nonetheless, I began what I'd planned would be a simple description of Jennifer and our time in California, but Arthur is my friend and he was the first person I'd had a chance to tell since I met her so the story ended up taking all the time until our steaks came.

Just before we each popped the first piece of steak into our mouths, Arthur said in his quiet way, "Sounds serious, my boy." As we chewed and looked at each other, I realized how right he was. Jennifer was in my mind constantly. And maybe, it was time in my life to let myself get serious about someone again. *We'll see*, I thought.

Arthur asked me a couple more questions about the California trip and what I'd learned about Willie's behavior. That's when I told him about my conversation with Piero Romano in Italy. He quietly smiled, as he chewed and listened to my description of Romano's insistence that no one had ever successfully counterfeited a Ferrari.

"Sounds to me like a little whistling past the graveyard," he said. "I can surely see why they wouldn't want it to be true. It might put the entire market in a turmoil. One of the reasons they can command the prices for the new models is that everybody assumes that down the road they could, as most fine cars do, appreciate instead of depreciate. In other words, Willie's discovery, if true could have a nasty economic effect on a lot of people. It behooves them to sweep it under the rug, so to speak. What are you going to do now?"

"I'm not sure what to do, Arthur. For Jennifer's sake, I don't want to keep mucking around in the painful past. She's got a lot on her plate, dealing with Willie's estate without worrying about the damn collection that she wants to get rid of anyway. But I do have an obligation to Willie's mother, Aunt Blake. I don't have a clue how to go about checking out the cars, do you?"

"No, but I have a friend at Sotheby's who tells me that they have an entire department devoted to authentication.'

"Of course! That's why Willie told his mother that he was seeing Sotheby's in New York. I'll bet you that he was trying to get some advice on how to go about quietly checking out his suspicions. Arthur, do you think that your friend could get me an interview with the right department?"

"Sit tight, my boy. We'll see." Arthur went off to find the telephone.

As I waited for him, I began again to review what I had learned in California, which I thought was damn little. But often, when I'm writing an account of a race for the magazine, the process of mentally re-running the tape produces memories that I'd forgotten the first time through.

As I did my mental step-by-step, I arrived again in MacIntosh's office, went through the interview and my departure and...*Bingo...there it is!* MacIntosh had told me about a strange conversation he'd had with Willie in which Willie had asked MacIntosh about forgeries in the art world. *There it is again.* Willie trying to figure out what to do about something he had discovered — and getting turned away.

I didn't know the exact time sequence but that could be what had driven Willie to seek help from the Sotheby's people in New York.

By this time, Arthur had returned, sat down and asked, "How's three o'clock this afternoon? That fit your schedule?"

"Perfect, Arthur. What's the deal?"

"You're to ask for an Alan Simpson. He's one of their authentication people. He specializes in objects, not paintings and such, so he should be helpful. By the way, in case you're concerned, my friend tells me that these kinds of questions come up all the time and you needn't fear telling them what you know. They have to be very discreet with their client's sometimes dirty little secrets, if you know what I mean."

"Great," I said. "Arthur, what do you think I should do about Rodney Evans? Should I involve him or not?"

"I don't think so, Ned. Not yet, anyway. It appears that your cousin may have got the cars from Evans in the first place. It could be very awkward for you to come along with a second hand story that Willie thought one of them was a counterfeit, don't you see?"

"Yes, I guess you're right, Arthur. I'll wait a while. But sooner or later, this is going to land on his doorstep, I'm afraid."

"No doubt," said Arthur. "By the way, I assume you know that the prices of these things have dropped dramatically in the past 18 months. That could be putting some pressure on your Mr. Evans' pocket book, now couldn't it?"

I thought that Arthur might be right, which might explain some of the empty desks in Evans' offices. Soon, the waiter came with the check. We paid and walked back to the office. I called Hereford Green to check in and find out whether or not the new car had arrived. It had. The crew was not back yet, but Colin had heard that the transporter was on a ferry from Calais earlier that morning so they'd be along soon.

Happily, Sotheby's was in Bruton Street just above New Bond. All of this was across Berkely Square and within easy walking distance, so I enjoyed the warm Spring afternoon and strolled across the square. I looked in the window of the "Roller" dealership and the outrageous red Rolls Royce cabriolet was artfully displayed to attract the wayward entrepreneur with thoughts of love on his springtime agenda.

I arrived at Sotheby's punctually at 3:00, and asked for Mr. Simpson. I was quickly shown to a conference

room, where I was introduced to a surprisingly youthful man dressed in conservative tweeds and wearing a
full beard that I assumed was compensation for his apparent youth.

It turned out that looks were deceiving. Alan Simpson, I learned by piecing together some stories he told,
had been at his trade for some 20 years, which made
him older than me. The meeting lasted an hour. He listened attentively, took some notes and waited patiently
for me to finish. When I had, he cleared his throat and
began, "Mr. Pearson, your story is a fascinating one,
although you must realize there is little we can do
without a specific article to examine. I take it that you
are not even sure that there is a counterfeit car or if
there is, which one in the collection it might be. Is that
essentially correct?" I nodded.

"Well then," he continued, "about the best I can do
for you is suggest some ways you might find out if one
or more of the vehicles is less than genuine. If I were
you, I would begin by examining the various serial
numbers that can be found on the car. I'd make a list of
these and ask the manufacturer to check his records
and tell me if they are genuine and what they indicate
about the car's date of manufacture and origin. This
method will often turn up discrepancies that can then
be further pursued.

"The second thing I would look for is material in
the car such as plastic, certain kinds of metals and other substances that are not consistent with other, genuine models of the car. Often, someone trying to duplicate an original cannot easily obtain the original materials and takes a shortcut.

"Finally, Mr. Pearson, you should be aware that certain manufacturers of rare, high quality merchandise

try to protect their customers' investments by building in anti-counterfeiting devices. Unfortunately, these are not issues that they are willing to discuss in public because they would rather that no one even think about the problem except the criminals. Also, if they tell anyone what the devices are, then the criminals will know how to circumvent them, you see. It is as you Americans say, catch 22. Do you suppose you could get Ferrari to tell you what to look for?"

At my frown, he said, "No, I suppose not. Well, I'm not sure whether I've helped you. My hands are tied, I'm afraid. But I can tell you this. I would start with the serial numbers and after that, I would look for materials that don't match."

I thanked him for his time and promised to let him know if I discovered anything further, so that he could add it to his experience. Then I walked back to the hotel to pack for my drive to Hereford Green.

There was something nagging me in the back of my mind. It just hung there, unspecific and unreachable, but I knew that sooner or later it would move forward into the light of consciousness and I would deal with it then. It happened on the M 40 just past High Wycombe. The question stepped out of the shadows and I didn't like it at all. It was an ugly thing that had been worming its way around in my subconscious mind since Romano had told me the purpose of Willie's secret visit to Modena. I'd known it was there, but I didn't want to look it in the face and now here it was.

Why, when Willie discovered whatever it was that made him believe that one of his cars was a counterfeit and began to worry about it to the point of distraction, did he not tell Jennifer? Or did he? And if he did, why had she not told me?

Shit.

NEW YORK

The next ten days were among the most taxing I've ever experienced in racing. Everyone worked night and day to get both cars ready for practice and qualifying at Silverstone.

The fact that we got through it without a punch up or any serious friction was a tribute to Colin's steady hand and sensitivity to when enough was enough and it was time to call for a break.

Testing can be such drudgery. You take the car out for two or three laps, and then bring it in and measure things. Fluid levels and temperatures, tire temperatures, dozens of variables that indicate whether or not you're getting closer or farther away from the optimum setup, the maximum speed for the conditions of the day. Then you decide to try something else, perhaps more radical, and the car must be modified overnight for tomorrow's testing.

And tenth by tenth, the lap times come down until you stop making progress and then you think of something else to try. And so it goes.

In the end, all of the hard work to set up two cars

paid off. In the morning practice session on Saturday, I had a very fast, clean lap going, when a back marker failed to see me overtaking him into a high speed right hander. As I moved under him going into the corner, he turned down into me and we had a horrendous crash.

Without the backup car, we'd have started Sunday's race in twelfth position because on Saturday afternoon everyone else improved their times. We could not have been ready for that session. As it was, we simply rolled the backup car out of the transporter and were able to move up one place to fifth on the starting grid.

Once again, on Sunday, the higher horsepowered factory entries took advantage of Silverstone's sweeping, high speed corners and long straights to pull steadily away from us, as the race wore on. This time, Colin chose a conservative strategy, knowing that if we tried to maintain the pace we might well not finish at all. In the end, his plan paid off. The day was unusually warm for an English Spring and attrition of the faster cars gave us the gift of two positions in the last 40 laps. We finished fourth, overall, which kept us at third in the series standings.

Because of the hard work of the previous three weeks, Colin wisely decided to give everybody much of the following week off. The crew would come in on Thursday to begin rebuilding the wrecked car and prepping the backup car for France. I wouldn't have to be in France to begin practice until a week from then.

I went directly from the track to Heathrow, where I stayed overnight before catching a plane back to New York. After I was safely settled in the room, I placed a call to California. For a while, as the phone rang, I began to think that I'd missed her but finally she answered, all out of breath and sounding excited.

"Ned, is that you? Oh God, I was afraid you'd hang up before I got to the phone. I'm up to my ears in potting soil and I look like a ditch digger. I've been planting pansies and petunias and I'm a complete mess. How are you?"

I smiled, thinking about how gorgeous she must be with her hair up and her face flushed with the glow of the sun and the sprint to the phone. I ached to be there and take her into my arms. "I'm fine," I said, "We took fourth, which leaves us at third in the standings."

"That's wonderful. Are you pleased? You should be, you know. Oh Ned, are you going to be able to come out here? Please don't tell me you can't. I miss you and I want to see you. Now. Please?"

"My sweet. I have important news."

"Oh, what's that?" she interrupted, fearfully.

"My boss is demonstrating his appreciation for my devoted labors of the past three weeks by giving me the next ten days off. What do you think of them apples, Blondie?"

"Oh Ned!" she shrieked, "Are you coming? Are you?"

"Please, my dear, watch your language. These calls can be monitored."

"Oh you. Stop teasing me. Are you? Are you?"

"My plane leaves for New York at eleven o'clock tomorrow morning. I'll be on the nine o'clock flight to San Francisco on Tuesday and I have to be at Paul Ricard on the following Wednesday."

"That's spectacular!" she shouted. "Okay then, Mr. Smarty Pants, I have a little surprise for you, too. One of my best friends has a fabulous beach house just north of Santa Cruz. She's going to be in Europe for the next two months and guess who has the keys."

"Little Miss Muffet."

"Give that man the Kewpie Doll. Isn't that fantastic?"

"It's wonderful. I really need to rest after the last three weeks. It sounds perfect. Can you get away from the office?"

She chuckled. "Oh, I'll work something out, darling. You can count on it," she said in that low silky voice that brooked no doubt.

I promised to call again to make final arrangements and get directions, and we reluctantly hung up. I spent an hour working on my report of the Silverstone event before I began to get sleepy and make mistakes. Finally, I turned out the lights and climbed into bed. Just before I fell asleep, I realized that I was still smiling, as I thought about a week with Jennifer.

The next morning, I arose. And after my morning routine, I packed and put the final touches on the Silverstone report. Then I went downstairs, checked out, caught the limousine to the terminal and boarded the plane for New York. I arrived at the apartment about 4:00 that afternoon after a no-hassle trip.

I went through the usual routine with the mail — that is, I threw most of it away and then listened to the answering machine for the accumulated messages of the last three weeks. Mother had called again, as had Aunt Blake, and I realized again that a long time had passed since I had spoken to either of them. *I must call before I went to California and back to Europe.*

There were messages from sellers of things I didn't want; one from the office in London that I ignored since I had been there since the message was left; and one from an old girlfriend that I noted but didn't plan to return for obvious reasons. And then there was one near the end of the tape a message that made me sit up and scribbling frantically.

The voice said, "Mr. Pearson, this is Detective Andrews from the California State Police. You were in my office several weeks ago asking about the death of your cousin, William Pearson. You gave me your card and asked that I get in touch, if we learned anything new about the case. Something has just come up that you may be interested in. Please give me a call at this number. I'm usually in the office between 3:00 and 4:00 every day, out most mornings. Thank you. Have a nice day."

The call had come in the preceding Thursday. I looked at my watch and was disappointed to see that it was not quite 5:00 in New York. *Too soon to call Andrews in California. Damn,* I thought, *I wonder what this is about and I'm just going to have to wait to find out.* So I combined the thing I hate most — waiting, with the thing I hate second most, paying bills. That easily killed an hour.

At the stroke of 3:00 in California, I was on the phone dialing Andrew's number. He answered on the second ring, "Andrews."

"Yes sir, this is Ned Pearson, You called last week?"

"Pearson? Oh yeah, it's about your cousin, right?"

"Right."

"Hold on," he said, paper shuffling in the background. "Here it is. Yeah, now I know how you and Bill Harmon met. He told me he stopped you on your way to my office. Is that right?"

What the hell is this? I wondered, *Am I gonna get a ticket by mail or something?* "That's right."

"Well, you apparently made quite an impression on young Bill because he remembered you pretty well. You drive race cars or something?"

"Yes I do."

"Well, I guess that's it. That must be why Bill remembered you because he called me last week wanting to know if you had ever gotten to see me. I told him you came here and, uh... used his name to get past the clerk to see me."

"Right," I said, thinking, *When are we going to get to the point of this?*

"What kind of race car do you drive?"

Christ on a crutch. "Sports Prototype, International Group C."

"That like the Jaguars and the Porsches at Daytona?"

"Exactly."

"Oh, I see. Well you sure impressed Bill."

"Did I?"

"Yep. I suppose that's why when he heard these guys talking about your cousin's accident, he perked up his ears."

"What guys were those, Mr..., should I call you Detective or what?" Now, my ears were perked up.

"Call me Andy. It seems Bill was in a tavern over by Placerville near his brother's place having a beer with his brother, when some guys at the next table were talking about a car going off a cliff. Bill heard it and asked them what they were talking about. It seems that one of the guys is a logger and those guys get really deep in the woods. They make their own roads as they go, so he was apparently working on the other side of the ravine where your cousin's car went in."

I winced at that phrase "went in" because it sounded like an airplane crashing. But I guess that's what it really was.

Somehow, Andrews sensed my feelings because he said, "I hope this isn't too gruesome for you, Mr. Pearson, but you said you wanted information."

"No, not at all. Please go on."

"Well, it seems that the logger saw and heard most of the crash. The problem was that he was halfway up the other side of the ravine, maybe a half-mile away and there was no way to get across. Not that it would have made any difference. Like I told you, it looks as if your cousin died from the initial impact. But the logger thinks something was very unusual about the crash."

"What's that, Andy?"

"He claims he's seen other vehicles go over the side of a mountain, trucks and heavy equipment, stuff like that. What he thinks was different about this is that he thinks the motor was running wide open when the car went over."

I was puzzled. "Well.... didn't you say that you thought that Willie could have been asleep? I mean...could his foot have been on the gas?"

"Yeah, maybe. But here's what the logger said he saw. From where he was, he could look up across the ravine and see the road running around a corner up above, down alongside the mountain and down to the curve where your cousin should have turned right but instead went straight off. He says he heard the car coming down the mountain before he saw it and then he saw it come around the first corner, sort of coming right at him. Then he says the motor got louder and the car seemed to pick up speed and went through the guard rail and over the cliff."

Jesus Christ, I thought, *a stuck throttle*. The worst

nightmare of the racer is a stuck throttle. You are hurtling toward the end of a straight with your foot buried in the throttle waiting till the last possible moment to lift, trying to carry your speed as far into the corner as your courage and good sense will allow. And then you finally lift.

And nothing changes. You will certainly crash because there is no time to do anything other than brake but it's far too late. Your only hope is that you can turn the car sideways enough so that you will not be a cripple for the rest of your life as a result of a head-on impact; an impact that will dramatically shorten the car and your legs.

It was the worst nightmare and apparently it happened to Willie. *My God, what must have gone through his mind as that car hurtled through space. Oh Willie,* I thought, *you poor bastard.*

"Mr. Pearson, are you okay?"

I guess I'd gotten quiet.

"Yes, yes, I'm okay. I was just thinking how awful it must have been for my cousin. It looks like he wasn't asleep after all."

"Real tough, Mr. Pearson. I'm sorry. But there is one more thing that you should know. I mean, I know how difficult this must be but I thought the family should know everything that we've learned."

"Sure. What's that Andy?"

"The logger said that what made him wonder most about what he saw was that it never stopped."

"What never stopped, Andy?"

"The motor. It kept on running even after the car crashed. The logger said they usually shut off after the first impact but this one kept on running, even after it finally stopped rolling. Would that mean anything to you, Mr. Pearson? I mean, from your racing experience would that sound right?"

"I don't know, Andy. I'd have to think about it." All I really wanted was to get off that phone. This was just awful news.

"Okay, Mr. Pearson. I just wanted to get back to you on this. I thought you'd want to know."

"Absolutely, Andy. I really appreciate it and please thank Bill Harmon for passing it on, will you?"

"You bet," he said, and we hung up.

I knew immediately that this was trouble with a capital T. In the first place, I knew that I could no longer walk away from Willie's death like I wanted to. That meant that Willie was going to continue to hover around Jennifer and me when I just wanted him to go away. More practically, it was going to postpone — for at least a day — the moment when I could have that lovely confection in my arms again. That day was the one I was going to spend at the lodge at Tahoe looking for something that would explain what happened to Willie.

I thought for a moment and then went into the bedroom and dug down in the bottom of my carryall bag, down under the camera and the laptop and there they were. When I left California three weeks ago I'd forgotten to return the keys to the lodge to Jennifer.

I called the airline and changed my reservation to Reno where I'd get a car and drive up to the lodge. Then I called Jennifer with the news of my changed plans.

She was not happy. "Oh Ned," she said quietly, "I thought you were going to drop that and move on. I was so happy just to forget about it and now it's back. What's happened to change your mind?"

I felt rotten, but I still did not want to get into this on the phone. "Jennifer, please trust me on this. I promise I'll tell you everything when I see you. It's just that I know it's painful and I don't want to do it over the phone. Can you bear with me for another 24 hours?"

"Alright, darling. You do what you think you must and I'll see you on Tuesday. I just wish you'd hurry. And Ned? Let's get this behind us soon. Please."

"Scouts Honor," I said, and she laughed which made me warm inside again. "I'll be there in a jiffy."

"Well, we'll just have to get you out of it then." She giggled and I knew it was going to be alright.

TAHOE

I must say, even though I'm a part of it, the media gets it wrong too often. CNN had called Willie's ski lodge at Tahoe "lavish." It was not. Comfortable, yes. Spacious, yes — but it was not lavish. In fact, it was a bit Spartan — just the place to get away from the complications of modern commercial life and reflect on the basics. I could understand why Willie would want to retreat there when problems got too big to handle easily.

It was a place to think things through.

I'd arrived in Reno in late afternoon after changing planes in Denver. I'd rented a car in Reno and driven down through Carson City, around the southern tip of the lake and up into the mountains. I'd had to do a little reverse remembering because I was approaching the place from the opposite direction than what was given to me by Jennifer and Andrews. But once I got to Vade and turned north toward Fallen Leaf, there was no mistaking where I was. The road climbed steadily upward toward the 9,000 foot ridge in a series of undulating switchbacks. If I hadn't been preoccupied with my destination, if I'd just been out for a drive, I would have had a blast flinging the Camaro I'd rented around these unforgiving, banked curves. But I was looking for something specific and I soon found it.

There, where I'd expected it to be, on my right as I approached a left hand corner leading up the mountain, was a shiny new length of Armco barrier spliced into the weathered original. This was the place where Willie'd left the road. I went past it up the road for a hundred yards or so, and turned the car around looking for a place to park. I found a place, pulled off the road on the right, got out and started walking back toward the curve and the new barrier.

I looked back over my shoulder up the incline and began to calculate the speed of the car at full throttle by the time it had reached the barrier. Knowing what I knew about the car's weight and horsepower I figured that it must have been going at least 90, maybe more. Willie must have been so busy trying to shut it off that he never had a chance to stop it or turn it before it plunged through the barrier and over the side, and became an airplane without wings—no, a guided missile hurtling down into the forest below in screaming terror.

Jesus Christ. I was starting to get sick to my stomach thinking about it. I stopped almost at the bottom of the incline, stared at the shiny new metal and thought, *How did this happen, Willie? What went wrong here? This is not fair. You didn't deserve this, my friend.* And then I realized that my eyes had filled with tears and I just let myself weep with the sadness of this terrible tragedy.

I went back to the car, turned it around and went back up the mountain looking for the turn into the driveway of the lodge. I found it after a series of very tight, slow turns and drove up to the gravel parking area in front of the rustic log structure. I left most of my luggage in the car, except for an overnight bag and my carryall. I climbed the stairs to the deck that ran across the front of the lodge. The sound of my heels on the solid redwood planking rang clearly in the cool, thin mountain air. I felt very alone.

The lock worked smoothly and I let myself in. I turned on the lights with the switch by the door. The light showed me an ample, L-shaped sitting area dominated by a huge stone fireplace, soot blackened from regular use. The room smelled of wood and wax and the residue of warm fires. In one corner, there was a study arrangement consisting of a desk, a corner of built-in bookcases from floor-to-ceiling, a reading chair and lamp. There were stairs leading up to a second floor balcony that extended over a third of the sitting room. Along the balcony were doors that I presumed led to bedrooms.

Back downstairs, the remaining quarter of the first floor was devoted to a large kitchen and eating area, furnished with solid antique country furniture.

I put my bags down and decided to tend to first things first. I went directly to the kitchen to see if there was any food in the house that could serve as dinner. Between the pantry and the freezer, I decided that I would not starve to death before morning and that I probably wouldn't make a major improvement in my lot with a ten mile round trip back down the mountain to the small store and gas station I'd seen on the way up.

That curiosity satisfied, I settled down to see if I could find anything that would further my search for an explanation of Willie's last days on earth; something that would put an end to this search for a simple summary chapter on Willie's otherwise orderly life. I decided the most promising place to look would be the bookshelves. Books always say something about their owners. What were their professional interests? What did they do for fun? Were they high-minded or just ordinary folks?

Apparently, Willie and Catherine had owned this lodge for a long time because the shelves contained an unusually wide range of books and publications. There were a collection of children's books that I assumed reflected the time spent here when the family was still together. There were books on nature that probably helped the family better enjoy their surroundings. Of course, there was an entire section devoted to financial subjects from economic theory to exposés of fraudulent enterprises. And then there was a section devoted to what appeared to be the popular literature of the last 20 years—fiction and non-fiction. Most of the "big" books were there, perhaps a reflection of Catherine's need to remain current while tied to her role as a mother.

I assumed that the crisp order of the arrangement of all these volumes reflected Willie's need for order and efficiency in his life. Whatever the motivation, order was certainly present in this collection. Each logical subdivision of subject matter occupied a separate section of the shelves. Each section was separated from the others with some sort of knickknack, a pine cone, a rock, a model toy, almost anything to delineate one section from another as the shelves ran on. After looking at the shelves for a few minutes and imagining the family here in the lodge on a snowy evening, each choosing their own literary entertainment to absorb by the fire, it occurred to me that there should be somewhere here a section devoted to cars. After all, Willie'd poured a good deal of money into that pastime and he must have done some reading to prepare himself for his investments.

Once I'd focused on that subject, it took no time at all to find what I was looking for. Once I'd found the section I was looking for, it was even less time until I found myself engrossed in some of the volumes in the collection. There were volumes on all manner of makes, on famous race events, on the history of the automobile, on famous drivers, on and on. Before I knew it, my eyes were bleary and my stomach was growling. I hadn't eaten on the plane and now it was time to repair the damage.

I picked up the volume I'd been skimming and took it to the kitchen to help me get through the can of soup I had chosen for dinner. It wasn't until I'd finished the soup and the can of beer and had the pot full of soapy water to wash my dishes that it came to me. I was staring out the window at the lights down the mountainside when the awareness burst full bloom into my mind.

There are no Ferrari books.

I spun on my heels, grabbed a dish towel, dried my hands and went back into the sitting room. I walked up to the bookshelves and began a methodical search for any book on Ferraris, starting in the automobile section first and then moving on to the rest of the shelves. *Zip. Nada. Nothing.*

I was so astonished by this discovery that I simply sat down at the desk and stared at the far wall, while I tried to make some sense of it. *What the hell does it mean? In the first place, it can't be true*, I thought. *The man couldn't have bought $20 million dollars worth of cars and* *never one book on the make of car he was buying. Wait a minute...maybe he kept them all at Woodside? Yeah? Then why?* I thought, *did he have all these others here. And Catherine had said that he'd had them spread all over the floor once with the kids.*

No sir, I thought. *there's only one answer. Somebody removed them. Hey, that's it. Jennifer took them all back to Woodside to study. But didn't she tell me that she had someone close up the lodge after Willie died? When would she have been here? Well, this is just another mystery I'll have to ask her about when I see her tomorrow.*

I went back to the kitchen and finished the dishes, still puzzled about what I was sure were missing books. Then I built a fire and sat down to read about the careers of some of the famous drivers I had revered since childhood. Eventually, I dozed off, more than partly due to the jet lag that was beginning to stalk me wherever I was these days.

I awoke with a jerk at the popping of one of the logs in the fire and decided it was time to hit the sack.

In the morning, I was up early planning to call Jennifer and let her know that I'd arrived alright and would see her that afternoon at the beach house which, from the lodge, was an easy five or six hour drive. I looked forward to a day without pushing; a day ending with those green eyes in the light of a candle.

I waited until what I thought was a reasonable hour and then dialed her number. She answered in that cheerful morning voice that I'd begun to cherish.

"It's me," I said, "How's my sunshine?"

"If you're anywhere near California, it's shining to beat the band," she said and laughed, "but if you're not, it's a very rainy day. Which is it?"

"Fear not, sweet damsel, I am but leagues away and

well supplied with strong horses. I shall be by your side in the wink of an eye."

"Well, just don't be winking that eye at any other damsels along the way. You are expected at table."

"Really," I said, "what's for dinner?"

"Ah, kind sir, tidbits and delicacies to enthrall and amuse. Satisfaction beyond measure. Let's see, did I leave anything out?"

"I'm a no gonna' say, lady. I'm a nice a boy and it's early in the morning."

"Then here's to sundown. Hurry, sweet."

We talked for a minute about directions and her schedule for the week that would require her to be in the office during the days. But the beach house was close enough, so that she could commute until Friday. She didn't ask and I didn't volunteer anything about the lodge and what I might have found. I was happy with that. There would be time.

I was sitting at the desk with its swivel chair turned back around to the bookshelves as we talked, my feet up on one of the lower shelves resting on a stack of newspapers. As I hung up the phone and took my feet off the papers, my eye caught one of the headlines and I became interested to see what the date of the paper was. I reached down and picked up the two or three sections on top and there it was. Under the paper was a large, hardcover, coffee table book entitled simply, *Ferrari*.

What the hell, I thought, *one book? First no books, now one book.* This doesn't make any sense. Then I thought I knew what I was looking at. Whoever removed those other books, and I was convinced that somebody had, simply missed this one because Willie had carelessly put the Sunday paper on top of it. *What were they look-*

ing for? What was in those books that somebody would want? Or be afraid of?

I opened the book to see what it might be and began to casually page through it. It seemed to be a kind of encyclopedia of the marque, filled with pictures and descriptions of the cars and giving details of their introduction and history. I remembered what Romano had said about the car that concerned Willie, so I looked in the index for a listing entitled, *250GT California*. I was rewarded with a page number and immediately went there.

As I read the description of the car with only mild interest I eventually came to a passage that startled me so much that I went back to read it again. It read, *Experts estimate that approximately 50 of this type may have been built during the 2 years or so this model was in production.*

Approximately? Estimate? May have been built? What the hell does this mean? I thought. *You mean, they don't know? How can you not know how many million dollar cars you built?*

This is unbelievable, I went on mentally raving. I decided to read on. *Maybe this was a mistake? Nope.* There it was again on the page about another car — same guessing about how many of them were built.

Then I discovered something else that made the hair on the back of my neck stand straight up. After each car, the author had listed the serial numbers of the production run. To my astonishment, they were seldom completely consecutive.

A note here: Your typical bank statement will highlight any break in the sequence of checks cashed during the period. Why? To make you ponder where the missing check number might have gone. Tax Accountants pay particular attention to such gaps in the sequence.

Here, there were small gaps and large gaps in every sequence. *Holy Mary*, I thought, remembering what Alan Simpson at Sothebys had told me. "Look for the registration numbers first," he had said. *How the hell are you going to do that, if there are missing numbers?* I wondered out loud. I was now so agitated that I was talking to myself out loud.

With my head spinning, I went back to the page that had Willie's car on it and read on. As I turned the page, I got the worst chill of all. There, near the bottom of the page, was the list of numbers for that car. Someone had made two circles with a ballpoint pen. The pen had been run around and around, over and over the circles so that there was a deep impression on the paper, much like someone doodling while they think about something important.

I got an awful feeling that Willie was hovering nearby as that page gave off some kind of terrible energy. The circles were around sets of numbers where there were gaps. In other words, Willie was circling the space where there were missing numbers. *My god*, I thought, *what did Willie know about those missing numbers?*

I sat there for a while just stunned. *What in the world*, I thought, *would prevent somebody from just choosing one of those missing numbers and using it to produce a car with an apparently legitimate registration number?* I couldn't answer the question. But I knew one thing. Willie knew something and it may have gotten him killed. And that son-of-a-bitch in Modena was going to get some more questions tossed in his lap before I finished with this thing.

I took one more flip through the book just to see if Willie had made any other marks and that's when I found the piece of note paper. It was a simple piece of foolscap that one might keep by the phone. On it were two more numbers: *3951276723* and *3951325612*.

Same shit, I thought. I looked quickly through the book to see if I could find numbers like these, but eventually got impatient to get going. I closed the book, threw it in the carryall and went to get my other bag. I locked up and went out to the car. On the way down the mountain, as I passed by the shiny Armco, I thought, *Willie, wherever you are buddy, I'm on the case. If there's something to be done here, I'll do it.*

I ignored the little voice that said, *If it doesn't do you first.*

THE BEACH HOUSE

The world has become a very crowded place; too many people, too much money. But someone in California's past saw them coming and decided to put up some fences, and control some space. That's why the coastline of California enjoys long stretches of state owned beach and no housing development in view. But there were some early birds who got there in time to claim and keep the best seats in the house. Jennifer's friend's house was the legacy of one of those.

Perched on a rock outcropping, shaped like the broad bow of a giant ship, the house commanded a 270 degree view of the sea and the shore for ten miles in all directions — spectacular.

Along the way, someone had installed 176 steps leading down to the beach. Someone else thought this too primitive and installed a deck and swimming pool on the southern side of the house to avoid the strain.

And with views like that, the best thing a sensible architect can do is leave them alone. Whoever designed the house was a minimalist and let the outside in through yards of glass. *God bless.*

She had left the office early and managed to beat me to the house. When I arrived, the Mercedes was parked in the drive in front of the entry door that was actually on the back of the house, away from the sea. She had apparently not been there long because there were still some packages on the back seat. I was moving between the cars and up to the door when it burst open and she stepped out of the shadow with her arms outstretched and said, "Howdy sailor, looking for a mooring?"

I grinned, took her hands in mine and asked, "Would you think this a safe port?"

"Depends. Hearts have been stolen here." She smiled into my eyes.

"Then I have nothing to fear," I said and she looked at me closely. "Mine has been missing for three weeks. I left it somewhere on the Western shore of the Americas. Perhaps you'd help me search for it."

She punched me in the stomach, laughed and said, "Right after you help me unload the provisions from this dinghy here," she said, moving toward the Mercedes.

Whatever she'd brought, it sure smelled good and there was lots of it. It occurred to me that we could last a long time holed up here in a storm, which seemed like a really good idea. Then I got back to work unloading the groceries.

As we worked to stow the groceries and finish the organizing of the kitchen and our luggage, there was a certain tension in the air, sort of a tentativeness between us. It was if we both had thoughts about the other, but were holding them for the proper moment. I think we both knew where we were going, but somehow couldn't find the right moment to take the first step. Finally, we finished and she said, "Excuse me for a minute. I want to get out of this monkey suit." She was referring to the suit she'd worn to the office that morning. I watched as those long golden legs moved briskly down the hall toward the bedroom suite.

I walked out through the sliding glass doors onto the wraparound deck and stared out to sea. I thought, *Each time I see her, she's more wonderful than the memory. I hope she's not too good to be true.*

Soon, she was back wearing a floor length, sleeveless silk beach robe in wedgewood blue with vertical gold stripes and a pair of soft leather sandals. Belted at the waist, the robe looked almost like a roman toga and emphasized the presence of her very small waist and lovely bosom. She had swept her hair up in back and piled it carelessly on her head, all peaches and cream. She was gorgeous and I just gaped. She came on to the deck and took my hand and turned to look out to sea.

"It's glorious, isn't it? I don't know how one could stand to leave this place."

"I have no such plans," I said and she giggled.

The sun was getting low over the water and the surface was beginning to give off red and pink sparkles and reflect the ever-reddening sky. We stood there for a long time, each quietly thinking our own thoughts. Then, I felt her look at me and I turned to look into that warm quiet smile of hers. She said, "Welcome back."

I reached for her and she stepped into my arms. I pressed her to my chest and felt the full length of her through the soft fabric of the robe. Her head came up and we began a long, slow, sweet kiss that just went on and on. Finally, I raised my head enough to see her eyes and she asked, "Where the hell have you been all my life?" She laughed.

That laugh was the salvation of what turned out to be an excellent dinner because without it, we wouldn't have seen the kitchen again for the rest of the evening. As I fought to get the blood flowing back to my brain, she asked, "Getting hungry?" And she grinned that evil grin that says I know what you're thinking.

"I haven't stopped being hungry since I met you."

"Touché," she said. "Well then, what sort of an evil wench would deny a hungry man sustenance?" And she moved off toward the kitchen with my eyes watching the movement of firm hips beneath the flowing fabric of the robe.

"How can I help?"

"Well, you could start by opening the split of Moet that you'll find in the fridge." She laughed.

I followed her into the kitchen and found the champagne, opened it, and poured two glasses. I took hers over to her, where she was opening a package of herbs. We each raised our glass and I said "Bon Appétit."

"To all of them," She replied. We smiled and drank the crisp, cold champagne and I thought about the prospect of spending days and nights with this beautiful, happy, healthy, woman by the sea. She interrupted to ask if I'd mind setting the table on the deck, so that we could listen to the ocean while we ate. I obliged.

Dinner was a simple sautéed filet of grey sole, *haricots verts* and a fresh, crisp salad. We shared a bottle of dry, oaken, California chardonnay and talked about all the things that had occurred in our lives during the past three weeks. From time-to-time, a brightly lighted ship would pass slowly across the horizon and we would speculate about its destination and the lives of those on board.

After a while, the breeze began to cool so we picked up the dishes, took them into the kitchen and moved into the living room to finish our wine. I'd brought the candles inside and put them on a table behind the soft corduroy couch, so that we could still see out to sea. Jennifer made coffee and served it on the low table in front of the couch, along with two snifters of cognac and some luscious chocolate truffles she'd brought.

Our talk drifted to the past and she asked about my childhood and where I went to school, and how I became a journalist and a race driver. Time just drifted by in a warm, soft cocoon of quiet talk and touching hands and smiling eyes.

We were sitting on the couch facing each other as we talked, when she moved closer, smiled at me and turned to put her head in my lap and look up at me. I cradled her head in my left arm, so that I could look at the candlelight flickering in those lustrous green eyes. She smiled and relaxed against my chest. I felt as if I had been given an enormous trust; the responsibility to protect this soft, gentle, sweet package of warmth and hope.

I raised her head just slightly and bent to kiss her and her lips parted softly. We were together and I was tasting the sweetness of her breath and feeling the pressure of her firm breasts, as she rolled into my arms and clung to me. We stayed that way for the longest time and then I felt the heat and urgency of her delicate tongue searching for mine. They joined and the heat flooded into my loins. I thought I might swoon.

She drew back and smiled up at me; a smile filled with joy and anticipation and trust. "Darling, take me to bed, please," she whispered.

We rose from the couch. She picked up the candle

and moved gracefully down the hall toward the bed-room. As we entered the darkened room, I could see the stars twinkling over the black water and a slight moon glow diffusing the shadows. The candle reflected in the windows and mirrors, so that there was not just one but hundreds of tiny, flickering flames.

She put the candle on a side table near the door and, as I followed, moved toward the bed in the center of the room. Then she turned and stopped and held out her arms. I took her once again into my own and held her tightly against me, feeling the urgency in her body. She stepped back slightly and said, "We don't need this." She began to unbutton my shirt. In my impatience, I reached down and pulled it over my head. She gently kissed me on each nipple, caressing each softly with her warm tongue, as I removed my belt and pushed my slacks and shorts to the floor.

She then stood up on her toes, kissed me full on the lips, spun in my arms until her back was toward me and said, "Your turn." She pointed to a small clasp at the neck of the robe.

I released it and the robe fell away with a swish of silken sound, as she turned again to face me in the candlelight. As she stood there before me, naked skin glowing, as if a gift from the gods, I could think of only one word. I said it out loud. "Goddess. You are a Goddess."

She smiled and very, very slowly raised her arms behind her head and took the pins out of her hair. As she raised her arms, her luscious, taut breasts thrust upward and outward, with each slow breath. Her hair came softly cascading down through her hands and over her shoulders. I thought I might die. She left her hands in her hair for a long time and I had trouble breathing. Finally, she took my hands and backed up to the bed, sat down, leaned back on her elbows and raised her stunning left leg slowly into the air. I turned my head and looked closely at a slender, tanned feminine foot and discovered something I hadn't seen before. There, just under the anklebone, in the little hollow above the heel was a tiny, pale pink rosebud. I looked back at her smiling eyes, lowered my lips and slowly kissed the rose. Then I began the delicious trip up the inside of the calf to her knee. That's when she giggled softly and said, " My Lord, you have kissed the secret rose. Now you must make sweet love to me." And so I did

With that, I entered into the most incredible night of love in my life. She was more than a Goddess. She was also the Devil and everything in between. Everywhere I went that night, I found sweet fire and intoxicating spice. My hands and my mouth and my mind were filled with tender warm wonderful sensations and my body was consumed with the passion of this unbelievable creature.

We smiled and laughed and slept and woke and did it all over again. Finally, we drifted off to sleep in each other's arms, with my face filled with her fragrant hair and the bed floating in the warm glow of love and candlelight.

I awakened very slowly from the most peaceful sleep I'd experienced in months. Then her fragrance reached my consciousness and without even opening my eyes, I smiled. I hadn't known it but Jennifer was standing by the window, looking out to sea at a fishing fleet. When she heard me stir she came to the bed and asked, "Do you always awake with a smile on your face?"

"Only here in heaven," I said, "When I'm on earth, I frown a lot."

She laughed and kissed me. I reached for her but she was too quick. I only got a piece of her bathrobe as she spun away, so that all I got for my trouble was another look at that spectacular golden body. She slipped out of the robe and escaped into the bathroom, saying, "Naughty, naughty, mustn't dally with the upstairs maid. She's only a working girl, you know."

While she was in the shower, I brushed my teeth and got myself some orange juice from the kitchen. I had slipped back into the bed and under the sheet when she came out of the bathroom with her hair pinned up again and smelling all steamy and bath powdery. She came over to the bed and sat on the edge and asked, "What are you going to do today?"

"Stay right here and wait for you to come home from the office, dear."

"Good," she said, "I hate to see a man waste good energy on trivial pursuits when he'll need it for important things later." She giggled.

I leaned over and nuzzled behind her ear. She leaned into my kiss. Then I whispered softly, "How about a roady?"

She said, "Silly, I just got out of the shower."

I took her hand and placed it gently in my lap. Her eyes widened, she smiled and said, "You little devil, you."

So we had a roady.

HEAVEN

It was a place for peace; a place to reflect, to read, to walk — and a place to fall in love.

So that's what we did.

During the days while Jennifer was away, I walked or ran on the beach or read or wrote. Each evening when she would return to the house, we would sit on the deck. Over a glass of wine I would read the poem I had composed for her that day.

And we spent the nights as one — unable to exist without touching, holding, caressing with the warmth and love flowing between us. And when the energy was gone, we would lie quietly feeling the soft beat of each other's heart and whisper our affections to each other.

Friday came quickly and she promised to be home early, so we could have a picnic on the beach. The day was unusually warm for the end of May and I was like a child waiting to see her car appear on the highway above the house. Finally, she was there. We packed a basket with cheese and bread and meat and wine and carried a blanket, towels and umbrella down to the beach.

We found a flat spot near the huge, black lava rocks and spread the blanket and staked the umbrella for shade. Then we threw off our clothes and ran into the cold surf in bathing suits. She ran like an athlete and I enjoyed the view of those strong legs and tight buns straining against her bikini, as I chased her into the water. We romped and frolicked like puppies and both got goose bumps from the chill. She tried to duck me and I relaxed and enjoyed the feel of those strong arms and legs wrapped around me, and that warm body clinging to mine as we rolled in the surf.

Eventually tiring, we made our way back to the blanket and towels warm from the sunshine. And I had the extreme privilege and pleasure of toweling off almost every inch of that marvelous, voluptuous body. I rubbed her briskly with the towel and she stood submissively and smiled at me, as I took great care in my work. I knelt in the sand to dry her legs and found the golden fuzz of hair on the tops of her thighs irresistible and requiring of a gentle kiss or two. She rested her hand lightly on the back of my head and arched ever so slightly and my body began to send new signals.

Apparently, she got a similar message because she asked, "What about some lunch?"

"That's exactly what I had in mind," I said.

So we wrapped each other up in the blanket under the umbrella, while she lay on top of me and we made sweet, gentle love on the beach. We had dried her hair and as we made love, it fell softly around my face. It smelled clean and salty from the sea. When I reached the pinnacle—that strong, surging, lovely ache—she felt it and clung to me. Then she smiled into my eyes and I wanted to die this way.

We just held each other for a while and finally she said, reading my mind again, "If I die right now, you must promise that you will set my face in a smile before they come to carry me away. I want them to know how you killed me, you animal." She giggled.

We finally got around to the bread and wine and cheese. Afterward, we packed everything back up and left it, while we went for a long walk along the beach.

We got back to the house, as the sun was setting, and the day had made us both happily weary. We had an early dinner and climbed into bed to watch a movie and just hold each other. After the movie, we turned out the lights and made spoons, as we drifted off to sleep with murmurs of affection.

I was up early Saturday and slipped quietly out of the bedroom to let Jennifer catch up on some lost sleep. As I stood on the deck drinking my coffee, I realized that the week had flown by and soon I was going back to Europe. I also had not wanted to even mention what I had learned about Willie during these glorious last few days for fear of breaking the magic spell. But I knew that somehow I had to tell Jennifer what I knew and ask for her help again.

While I was trying to think of a good time to broach the subject, two golden arms slipped around my waist and I felt the warmth of her pressed against my back.

"Penny for your thoughts, sailor. Thinking of sailing off again to other Ports and other Maidens?"

I turned and took her in my arms and buried my face in the golden hair and whispered, "All the other maidens have been turned into toads by the magic of your beauty, my Queen. They hold no attraction for me."

"That's good, Magic Prince. Otherwise, I might

have to have your magic wand cut off."

"Perhaps I should find someplace to hide it, my dear. Any ideas?"

"Satyr," she said, "More coffee?" She moved toward the kitchen.

As she was getting her coffee, I made a decision not to put off the conversation about Willie any longer. *Besides*, I thought, *if it upsets her, I'd rather do it now than wait until there might be no time to repair the damage before I left. Let's get it over with.*

When she came back out on the deck I said, "Darling, please sit down with me. There's something we have to talk about."

She looked at me and, as she sat, she said with a laugh, perhaps steeling herself for bad news, "I know. You really are married, aren't you? Nobody as good as you could be floating around unattached."

I laughed and said, "No, I just wanted to tell you what I've learned about Willie and where he was before he died. I know you don't want to go on with this, but I have to tell you because it may be more than anybody suspected."

As I talked, her face clouded and I felt terrible but I knew it must be done. Hopefully, I could make it quick and merciful. So I told her as simply as I could of Willie's trip to Italy and his conversation with Romano about a counterfeit car. I also told her that this was consistent with Willie's plan to see the Sotheby's people in New York and the question he had asked MacIntosh about forged paintings.

I purposely left out what I'd learned from Andrews about the crash. There was no reason to hurt her any more than necessary. Then I asked her the 64 dollar question. "Did Willie have a collection of books about

Ferraris?"

"Oh sure," she said, "many."

"How many?"

"Oh, I don't know, 15 or 20, I guess. Why?"

"Think a minute, darling. Do you know where they are?"

"Let's see. He kept some at the lodge and some in Woodside. Sometimes he'd take one or two from one place to another to read on weekends. What's this all about, Ned?"

"But you don't think they're all at Woodside?"

"No, I don't, but if it's important we can go look. It's only 40 minutes from here. Hey, are you going to tell me what this is about?"

"Jennifer, when I was at the lodge, I looked at the section of the bookshelves where Willie kept his car books. There wasn't a single book there about Ferrari. Not one."

"That's crazy," she said.

"I agree, but if you didn't take them and Willie didn't, then who did'?"

She turned and looked far away out to sea. She seemed lost in thought for a moment. I said, "Jennifer?"

She looked back and said, "Oh, I was just trying to think of who else could have been there. I just don't know."

"There's one more thing and then I'm finished. By accident, I did find one Ferrari book." I then told her the story of looking up the model Willie was concerned about and finding the numbers circled and the ones on the sheet of paper. "Jennifer, didn't Willie ever tell you that he thought that one of the Ferrari's was a counterfeit?"

She looked at me for the longest time and I saw something burning deep inside those green eyes. Finally, she said, very slowly, "No. He never did." Then she asked, "What are you going to do?"

"Well, if it won't upset you too much, I'd like to take a look at the collection again to see if I can make any sense of it."

"It does upset me, darling, but I understand what you want to do so I'll cooperate as much as I can. But promise me one thing. Please get this over with as quickly as possible. I'm tired of Willie hanging in the shadows of our lives.

"I loved Willie for what he was, a lonely man who'd devoted his life to making money and nothing else; a man who ignored the needs of his wife and children on the excuse that he was being a good provider. Willie was good to me in the only ways he knew how and I was good to him. After Catherine kicked him out, he needed his ego repaired and I did that. He was proud of me and I needed someone to provide some security in my life. Not the worst basis for marriage, but not the most fulfilling either. I did what was asked of me, but now it's over. I want to stop talking about Willie and start talking about you and me. Willie's dead and I can't change that. I'm alive and so are you. You're looking like the best thing that's ever happened in my life and that's what I care about now. Can you understand that?"

It was the most passionate thing she'd said to me and I couldn't think of anything to do but put my arms around her and wait till she stopped trembling.

Eventually, we dressed and drove up to Woodside where Jennifer used the device on the key ring to open the garage door. We parked the Mercedes and went down to the barn where the collection was kept. Once again, she punched in the numbers and the lock made its metallic *snick*. We went inside. She flipped the switch and overhead light flooded the barn, as I decided where to start.

To my surprise, there were two empty slots, two cars missing. I said "Jennifer, what happened to these two cars?"

"Oh, one of Evans' people called to ask if I would mind if they put them in an exhibition somewhere in Los Angeles for some charity. Willie used to do that all the time. They're fully insured and using them for charity events makes the upkeep tax deductible. They'll be back next week."

Damn, I thought, *I'll be gone next week, so I won't be able to check those numbers. Why didn't Jennifer tell me this before? Well, I'd better make the best of it while I'm here.* So I set about looking at the small metal plates on the firewalls and door jams of each of the cars to see if I could find discrepancies against the numbers in the book that I'd brought along from the lodge. It was not easy because first I'd have to figure out which model I was looking at from the pictures in the book and then start checking the numbers shown in the book against those on the car.

After an hour of this, I gave up. Willie had two cars in the barn here where there were no numbers in the book to match, but this occurred where the book only gave a range of numbers from x to y. Willie's numbers could be in that range so nothing was clear. What I did not find was the missing numbers that Willie or somebody had circled in the book, nor did I find the two numbers on the paper.

Jennifer had gone back up to the house, so I tried to

close up myself. The problem was that I didn't have the combination, so I guessed that she would have to come back down and lock up. As I turned out the lights, I noticed that one of the lines on the wall phone was lit up and then it went out. Once again, I had that jealous feeling wondering who she was talking to. *I'm going to have to get over that*, I told myself.

I walked back up to the house and she met me on the veranda, smiling eagerly and asking, "Well, did you find anything?"

I shook my head and said, "No, not even a way to lock up so you wouldn't have to go back down."

She reached in her pocket and said, "Not to worry, my sweet." She produced the small remote for the car. She pressed one of the buttons and watched until a small light blinked twice. Then she said, "Magic. All done." She put the thing back in her pocket.

We drove quietly back to the beach house, with me pondering the missing numbers and the missing cars. Finally, she said, "Hey, sailor, you look like you lost your best friend. What's up?"

I decided that I was being dopey. I had precious little time left with Jennifer and I was wasting it worrying about something that couldn't be fixed, at least not now, so I said, "I was trying to decide between you and Mexican for lunch."

"Why decide?" she asked, "They're both available." We drove into Santa Cruz and ate tacos and enchiladas for lunch and washed it down with sangria. Afterwards, we strolled on the boardwalk and watched the tourists feed the seagulls and tried to figure out which one was Jonathon.

We got back to the house late in the afternoon, carrying the steaks we'd bought for dinner and feeling like a nap. We actually got a nap, but not until after we'd demonstrated Jennifer's sincerity about the choices for lunch and my appetite for dessert. *God, she is fantastic*, I thought.

Over the steaks and the big, fruity Cabernet, we talked about our childhoods. She grew up in Minneapolis. Her mother had died when she was 13 and she had lived with an aunt until she could leave and come to California when she was 17. She told me that she had borrowed and worked her way through UCLA, and gone to work as a secretary in a brokerage house at the beginning of a market boom. That's how she had become a successful broker and met Willie.

I told her about my family and how I felt about my dad's death and why I'd become a journalist. I also told her about my first marriage and why it ended and a little bit about Laura. She seemed really interested in that and at the end, all she said was, "Poor, silly girl," and shook her head with a sad smile.

Then she smiled softly and said, "I'd be harder to get rid of." I reached for her and she came into my arms again. I loved her so much it hurt.

Sunday was our last day. Jennifer had to be in the office on Monday and I was catching an early plane out of LAX on Monday morning to be in Nice on Tuesday and over at Paul Ricard, a racetrack near the Cote d'Azur, Tuesday afternoon. That meant that I would leave the beach house right after dinner and drive to LA and stay at the airport.

The day had that gloomy feeling of all last days, when time stretches and dread of the inevitable dampens the emotions like fog on a mountain top. We stayed in bed late, just holding each other and charting the contours of each other's bodies, building the memory file for dreams to come. Finally, we arose and fixed a big brunch and then went for a long quiet walk on the beach.

We got back to the house in the middle of the afternoon and opened a bottle of wine, fixed a snack and went out on the deck to watch the sea. For the first time since I'd arrived at the house, the phone rang. It startled me so badly that I nearly dropped my glass.

Jennifer went in and answered it. Soon, came back outside with a strange look on her face and said, "It's Rod Evans. He wants to speak to you."

I was dumbfounded. *How did he know I was here? And what could he want on a Sunday afternoon?* With my mind racing, I rose and went in to the phone and said, "Hello?"

"Mr. Pearson," came the professional announcer's voice, "please forgive me for disturbing your quiet afternoon, but I have a situation that may be of interest to you and it needs resolution fairly quickly."

"No problem," I said automatically, while my brain continued to try to answer the first question, *How did he know?*

"Here's the situation. A very good customer of mine has acquired one of the formerly factory supported Porsche 962s. He would like to improve the car's "history," as it were, that would of course, improve its value. His hope is to run the car at Le Mans and he's asked me to see if I could arrange for a crew and drivers. Well, it's very short notice with the race only two weeks away and I told him this but he is insistent on trying.

"So I did some checking and discovered that your new sponsors had decided not to go to Le Mans, which I hope means that you and your crew might be free to take on such a project?" He paused.

My, my, I thought, *when you're hot, you're hot.* I wondered, *Is this really possible?*

"Well," I said, "I've nothing in my contract, except sponsorship conflicts that would prohibit my driving at Le Mans," thinking, *And I'd sure love the exposure.*

"My client has a toiletries manufacturer as a sponsor. In fact, he owns the company. I see no conflict with IEM."

"You realize I can't speak for my crew. That would be up to Colin McDonald."

"You certainly know him better than I do. Would you be willing to explore this with him?"

"Has a fee been discussed?" *Might as well get this out on the table,* I thought.

"The budget is somewhere in the range of $70-80,000. That would include my fee of $10,000, of course."

Pretty slick, I thought. *Three phone calls and ten grand. Nice way to make a living.* Then I thought, *Colin would jump at the chance to do Le Mans with a decent car and $50,000 for him and the crew would make him very happy. That leaves $20 for me. I'm getting just like Evans,* I thought, *but then, it's my ass going 220 out there, too.*

"I'm on my way to Paul Ricard," I said, "I'll call you from there after I've had a chance to discuss it with Colin. That won't be until Tuesday morning your time because both of us are traveling."

"Excellent, Mr. Pearson. My client would drive some himself and supply two other drivers, although you would be the leader, of course." *Stroke, stroke,* I thought, but the prospect was pleasing.

I got his number again and hung up. When I went back out on the deck, Jennifer looked worried. I explained the conversation, but she didn't look happy. All she said was, "Ned, be careful with that man. I don't trust him."

After a while, she asked, "When will you be back, darling?" and I told her that right after Le Mans, we had a 30 day break in the schedule and I'd spend most of it in California. That seemed to cheer her up and we spent time talking about what we would do then.

Saying goodbye was a lot worse this time than in the coffee shop. We clung to each other for a long time and I promised to call from France.

Greed is a terrible thing. I was halfway to LA before I realized that I hadn't asked Evans how he found me.

MODENA

I knew it wouldn't go on forever, but I didn't expect it to end so soon. Our good luck stayed at home that week or went on vacation or something. It certainly never showed up at the race track. The IEM engineers had installed the new electronic engine management systems on our four race engines after Silverstone and we just hadn't allowed enough time to de-bug the system.

When it worked, which was about half the time, it was brilliant and the cars were much quicker than they had been at Silverstone and Monza. But half won't cut it and by Friday afternoon, with Colin walking around with his teeth tightly clenched and looking as if he might bite somebody in the face, the IEM engineers threw in the towel and re-installed the old system.

We'd lost so much time messing with the engines during the week that we'd never got the chassis right and the best we were able to do in Saturday qualifying was eighth on the grid. Since there are a limited number of places to pass at Paul Ricard, with an underpowered, less than perfect car, I knew that Sunday was going to be a long day.

And so it was. All afternoon, I scrapped with cars that had been well behind me earlier in the year and the leaders just disappeared into the distance. After dropping to tenth on a lousy start—my fault, I fear, I was actually thinking about Jennifer on the beach when they dropped the green flag—I was able, through hard work and attrition to finally finish seventh which dropped us to fifth in the series.

Racers are incurable optimists, so we told ourselves that the good news was that with some testing we'd have that extra 30 horsepower we needed to run up front by the time we got to Germany in a little over a month.

Sunday morning before the race I had decided that I would spend the three days between the race and my arrival at Le Mans chasing down Piero Romano to get some answers about what was really going on with Willie. I considered calling him to make an appointment and then decided that the element of surprise might be effective in cracking through the party line. I would just show up at the offices in Modena or the factory in Maranello and surprise him with what I'd found at the lodge.

Earlier in the week, Colin had agreed in an instant to do Le Mans for the privateer, particularly in light of the $50,000 for him and the crew. They'd leave the cars and transporter at Ricard and we'd come back later to continue the testing and use the privateer's equipment at Le Mans.

I'd called Evans on Tuesday morning and told him of the arrangements and given him a branch bank in Paris where half the money needed to be deposited before Friday, so that we would know that the deal was firm before leaving Ricard on Sunday. We would collect the other half upon arrival at Le Mans.

On Sunday morning at the track, I asked Vicky if she could recommend a place to stay near Maranello and she raised her eyebrows quizzically. I explained that my late cousin had a Ferrari collection and I wanted some advice from the factory.

With a wry smile, she said, "Well, Ned, we all went down there last year and they put us up in a lovely pensione, very comfortable, just west of Maranello, called Il Osteria di Principessa which means, The Inn of the Princess. The story is that Il Duce or somebody famous kept their mistress there for several years. Very romantic, but one wouldn't want to be there alone."

And she laughed, I knew I was having my leg pulled but it was nice. *Or is she coming on?* I didn't know for sure, but I was otherwise occupied, as they say, so it didn't make any difference. It was a nice thought and I was flattered. I thanked her for the recommendation and went off to find a pay phone. I made a reservation for late arrival that night.

After the race, I escaped as quickly as possible and set off in the rented Mercedes like the hammers of hell to make the 300 mile drive to Maranello, East through Monaco along the Grand Corniche, then North and around the Gulf of Genoa and finally over the mountains into the bottom of the Po River Valley through the Italian night.

The last 60 miles over the mountains North of La Spezia was the worst, partly because of the winding road and partly because the rigors of the day had caught up with me. I missed the hotel the first time by because my directions were from the east and I was traveling from the west. But I quickly caught my mistake, turned around and was climbing the stairs to my second floor room just before eleven o'clock. The kitchen was closed but the clerk agreed to bring up some sausage and cheese and a half bottle of the house wine which, when it arrived, and given my condition, tasted like food from the Cordon Bleu.

Stomach satisfied, I was quickly in bed and dreaming dreams of California sunshine, green eyes and warm, powdered, fragrant skin. *Yum.*

I was up early the next day and on the phone to the office to promise that my report on the race at Paul Ricard would be along shortly. I also wanted to let them know where I'd be for the next day or so.

Housekeeping finished, I set off to find Piero Romano. I went to the address in Modena on the card he'd given me at Monza. It was the right address, alright, but after asking if Signor Romano and I had an appointment and being told sheepishly by the impetuous American driver that we had none, the imperious assistant to Signor Romano made it clear that my visit was most unusual and perhaps I'd like to phone ahead and make an appointment — next time.

After some bowing and scraping and other obsequious behavior on my part, which I decided was the price of my bad planning, I was able to learn that Romano was en route back to the office from a weekend in Rome and would arrive late in the day; that he had an extremely full schedule prior to a Directors meeting in the evening. In other words, *not a chance, buster.*

It wasn't for nothing that I've been a journalist all these years. I asked the gatekeeper for some stationery and an envelope so that I could leave Signor Romano a "personal note of some urgency." When it was brought, I sat down and wrote;

Piero,

Please forgive my sudden arrival, but I must see you this afternoon on a matter of some urgency. I have discovered among my late cousin William's confidential papers a series of registration numbers which appear to be a problem. I'd like to discuss these with you before my meeting with the Authentication Department at Sothebys in London later this week.

I'm staying at the Principessa near Maranello until my departure early tomorrow. I can see you any time this afternoon.

I then sealed the envelope and wrote, *Personal and Confidential* across the front of it. I handed it to the gatekeeper along with one of my *International Motor Racing Monthly* business cards. *If that doesn't flush the rabbits out of the hedgerow, nothing will,* I thought. Then I went back to the hotel to settle down, write my report and wait hopefully for Romano's call.

At lunch time, I went down to the small dining room that was almost deserted since most of the weekend guests had departed the day before. Nonetheless, the kitchen was operating and I ordered Cannelloni, the veal-filled tube of pasta with two sauces that the Bolognese do so well.

As I was eating my meal, a middle aged man approached the table, smiled and asked, "Mr. Pearson?" I nodded, clearing my mouth, and he said, "Please forgive me for interrupting your lunch, but I am the owner of the inn and I've just discovered a coincidence that I should share with you."

Puzzled, I asked, "What's that?"

"Well, we don't get many Americans here and to get two Pearson's in two months is most unusual." A chill went down my spine and I put down my fork and waited.

"Would you know a William B. Pearson by any chance?"

I could hardly speak. Finally, I said, "Yes he was my cousin."

"Did you say 'was', Mr. Pearson?"

"Yes, he died three months ago."

"*Santo cielo!*" Good heavens.

"Oh, Mr. Pearson, please forgive me. I'm so sorry. I couldn't know."

"No, no," I said quickly. "It's not your fault. Tell me, how long was he here?"

"Oh, just a day or two, I think. He was meeting with the Ferrari people, I believe. He was a wealthy collector, wasn't he?"

"Yes, he was."

"I'm so sorry to hear that he passed away. He was a nice man, not like some of the wealthy Americans who come here, if you'll forgive me for saying so."

"Yes, he was a nice man," I replied, wishing this would end.

"I told him, you know, that one of the old men who tends our gardens was a cousin of old Enzo Ferrari when he was alive. Used to work in the factory years ago."

I picked up my fork, hoping to signal that I wanted to finish my meal before it got cold. It worked.

"Well, I'm keeping you from your lunch. I have things to do. Nice to meet you and I'm so sorry to hear about your cousin. What a coincidence. Enjoy your stay, Mr. Pearson. Arrivederci," he concluded and he was gone.

Well, I'll be damned, I thought, *everywhere I turn, another coincidence. So Willie stayed here in February. Well, I suppose the factory recommends it so it's no surprise. After all, that's how I found out about it from Vicky.*

I finished my lunch and went back to my room to edit the Paul Ricard story, which took two hours. I was tickled to see the clock at 4:00 because it meant that I could call Jennifer in California. I asked the hotel operator to get me long distance and after much "momento" and "prego," I heard the phone ringing in Woodside.

"Hello?" she said.

"Is this Merry Sunshine speaking? I have a message from old what's-his-name name."

She giggled. "What was your name anyway, sailor?"

"Mr. Magic Wand. How could you forget?"

"Oh, not to worry. I haven't forgotten the Wand. It's your name I've forgotten. When's the Wand coming back?"

"When it gets out of the rest home. It's recovering from exhaustion."

"Well, you tell Mr. Wand to rest up real good because Merry Sunshine has a couple more tricks she'd like to show him."

"I'll do that. How are you?"

"Missing you like crazy. When are you coming back?"

"Soon, darling. I wish you could come over for Le Mans."

"So do I but it just won't work. Are you coming back after that, or do you have more testing to do?"

"Not for a while. I should have another two weeks."

"I can't wait."

We talked about the bad luck in France and what I

was going to tell Romano when I saw him, but I decided not to mention what the hotel owner had said about meeting Willie. I couldn't see any purpose in it. Finally, I began to worry that Romano would call and I'd miss him, so we said goodbye and I promised to call when I got to Le Mans.

After we'd hung up, the clerk rang to say that Romano's assistant had called while I was on the phone and left a message. Romano could see me between 5:30 and 6:00 pm. I changed into a suit and set off for Modena, with little time to spare.

I was on time and immediately shown into Romano's corner office. There was no room for doubt in his very formal, cool demeanor that he was not pleased to see me again.

We exchanged cordial if stiff greetings, he offered coffee; I declined and sat when invited. He chose to stay behind a rather ornate desk and asked, "Now, Mr. Pearson, as you've no doubt been told, I have a very difficult schedule this afternoon. I've asked two department heads to stay late in order to accommodate your rather sudden and informal demand for a meeting. I do hope that it is as urgent as your note indicates."

Honey beats vinegar, so I stroked the guy for a couple of minutes, assuring him of my awareness of his importance and apologizing for my bad manners and pleading the pressure of Le Mans as my excuse. He didn't say that I was forgiven, but he did come out from behind the desk and sit across from me in another of the club chairs that I took to mean he wasn't going to throw me out immediately.

"Signor Romano," I began, "Since we met, I've come into possession of some of my cousin's confidential, private papers." *Well, sort of*, I thought. I continued, "These indicate to me that Mr. Pearson was interested in learning more about one of the cars in his collection; a car that he apparently was concerned might not be authentic."

Romano interrupted, "Yes, of course, Mr. Pearson. As I told you, he came here to inquire about that car. What is your new discovery, may I ask?"

"Mr. Romano, what is your procedure for verifying the authenticity of a car when asked to do so by a customer? Can you tell me that?"

His face darkened and he said, "Mr. Pearson, as I explained to you, we have several means of authentication many of which I cannot discuss with you. They are private, confidential methods maintained by us for the benefit of our customers. Of course, we begin with a check of the identification numbers placed on every car at the time of manufacture."

Aha, you bastard, *I've got you now*, I thought. I pulled out the book I had brought from the lodge and flipped it open to the page on which someone had circled the gap in the numbers. "How do you explain this, Mr. Romano?" I asked, triumphantly.

He looked at me and smiled that sad smile reserved for the idiot child. "Mr. Pearson, did you come all the way to Modena to ask me this? My dear man, have you looked at the copyright on this book? If you had, you would have seen that it was published by an Englishman. Also, if you had looked, you would have noticed the absence of any approval or endorsement by our company. Surely, Mr. Pearson, you can see that just because someone prints a list of numbers that they have compiled one way or another, that list is not necessarily complete nor official. You can see that, can't you?"

I had a sinking feeling that the SOB had me, but I wasn't ready to give up. "So is what you are telling me that you keep the official list and no one else has it?"

"Precisely, Mr. Pearson." And he smiled the cat and canary smile.

Well, well, I thought, *so the fox is watching the hens. I wonder who is watching the fox?* But I wasn't prepared to take this any further so I said, "And am I correct to think that when someone asks for confirmation that your records contain a specific number, you simply check them and provide the confirmation?"

"Exactly."

"And is that what you did for my cousin?"

"Yes."

"I see," I said, but I didn't.

"Now, Mr. Pearson if that covers the matter, I really do have to run. Please do let me know if you have any further questions. I may be able to save you the trouble of such a long journey in the future."

I stood to leave and thought about the two numbers on the note paper. I said, "Mr. Romano, just one more thing. Could you check these numbers for me?" I reached in my bag for the note.

"I could, Mr. Pearson, but not tonight I'm afraid. I really must go. Is there someplace you can be reached in France?" As I handed him the note, I started to think where I'd be staying. Then Romano started laughing.

"My dear, Mr. Pearson, I do believe that I can help you tonight." He laughed again. "I can definitely identify at least one of these numbers but I'm afraid you're going to be disappointed." He held the paper up facing me and it read:

3951276723

3951325612

"You see, Mr. Pearson, in the top number, the first two digits are the international code for Italy and the second two are the city code for Modena and the last six are for me. You have here, Mr. Pearson, the not so confidential phone number of Piero Romano. I'm afraid I cannot help you with the second number. My apologies." He laughed again.

Shit, shit, shit. God, let me out of here before I lose my grip. How could I have been so stupid? I hate this and I want to kill this smug bastard and I want to kill myself for being such an idiot.

My memory of the leave taking is not distinct. I know I could have been arrested and put away for the way I drove leaving Modena. A few innocent Italians are cursing the Germans for making cars for maniacs to drive. It was some time before I calmed down. I'd come way out of my way, only to have the door slammed in my face with a horse laugh to boot. And I had nowhere else to go.

Maybe Jennifer is right? I should just bury this damn thing along with Willie and get on with my life. I went back to the hotel and up to my room to pack. I just wanted out of Italy and out of this whole puzzle. As I took off my jacket, I went through each pocket to be sure they were empty before packing it. As I reached in the left one, there was the damn note with the two numbers on it. Apparently, in my rush to get out of Romano's office, I'd snatched it out of his hand and stuffed it into my pocket. I crumpled it up and threw it across the room in disgust, and turned back to my packing.

The note caused me to start going back over the awful scene in Romano's office. That's when I remembered what he said about the numbers. He said, "I'm afraid I can't help you with the second one."

I walked across the room, picked up the crumpled note and looked at the number. *Screw it*, I thought, *you've come this far and you can't make a bigger ass out of yourself than you already have*. And I started dialing the second number on the paper.

SASSUOLO

The ringing of the phone made an unusual sound —
very harsh with a clanking, rasping note. *This is out in
the country somewhere*, I thought. It rang for a long time
and I was close to giving up when a guttural voice
said, "Pronto"

In my best tourist Italian I said, "Parla Inglese?"

"Capisco." I understand.

"Uh, good. My name is Ned Pearson and I got this
number from my cousin William who was here two
months ago. Uh...did you speak to him by any
chance?" *Jesus, this sounds stupid.*

"No."

"Oh, I see. Well, would you know if anyone else at
this number spoke to him?" *This is not going to work.*

"No." I could hear someone speaking in rapid Italian in the background — emotionally. There was that
brief ocean sound, as the receiver was covered with the
palm. Then there was silence. The palm came away, the
other voice returned for an instant — the first voice —
now away from the mouthpiece said, "Peersown."

The voice in the background went lower and said

one word three times, each time more strongly than before. Then somebody hung up the phone.

Damn! I sat there trying to think about what to do. *Was this a family argument I walked into, or was it specifically me that they were rejecting?* Obviously, the other voice told the first person to hang up. *Why?* After a while, my journalistic instincts took over and I decided I had absolutely nothing to lose by pressing the issue one more time. I was relatively safe on the end of a phone line and the worst that could happen was that they'd hang up again. *On the other hand, maybe they'll try a different tack that will lead somewhere?* I dialed again.

"Pronto"

"Yes, excuse me, we were disconnected."

There was a long pause, followed by a question in the background. The voice on the phone said, "Si."

There were footsteps and then someone handling the receiver. A much younger voice now in broken English, said, "If you are Mr. Pearson, then you know you were told never to call this number again. We have nothing more to tell you."

"Yes, well, who is this?"

Click. They hung up again. So I redialed. Busy signal. Again. Busy signal. *Well, that's that,* I thought. *Even if I could find out whose number this is, they don't want to talk to me. To hell with this. I quit.* I decided to get a good night's sleep and drive over to Le Mans in the morning and chuck this whole wild goose chase before it ruined any other budding relationships. It was time for dinner, so I went down to the dining room and ordered some kind of veal scaloppini in a delicious sauce with asparagus and cream. *Some Mommy food to soothe my wounds. Jesus, what a lousy day.*

The food was delicious and I was starting to feel a little better, so I ordered an espresso to finish the meal. The tray with the coffee and Sambucca was brought by a little old lady dressed in black that I hadn't seen before. She scuttled up to the table with the tray and began transferring the coffee cup and saucer, the silver spoon, sugar and the Sambucca to the table. Just as she brought the bottle across with her right hand, she looked in my eyes. "Sambucca?" With her left hand, she placed a small piece of paper under the bottle, as she set it on the table.

I thought, *Now what the hell is this?* There were two other guests in the room, so I couldn't just ask. I felt like I was watching a spy movie and I wouldn't touch the bottle for a while because I was sure someone was watching. Besides, I don't even like Sambucca.

I drank half the coffee, signed the bill, filched the paper from under the bottle and left the room. When I got out in the lobby, I unfolded the paper and found this:

Cathedral di Sassuolo 10 p.m.

Oh please, I thought, *gimme a break. What the hell does this mean?* I was so tired of this business that I turned around and went back through the dining room and into the kitchen to find the woman who brought the note. She wasn't there — only a young boy washing pots and pans and dishes who hadn't a clue what the crazy American wanted in the kitchen.

Frustrated, I went back up to my room to finish packing. The more I thought about it, the more I realized that there might be some connection between the note and the phone call and maybe I should follow through. Then I realized that someone was watching me — I don't mean at that minute, but someone knew how to reach me at the dinner table.

That scared the hell out of me just like the laptop did.

I decided that I would do a little reconnaissance and not just drive right up to this Cathedral in Sassuolo, wherever that was. I got out my map of Italy and discovered that I'd already been to Sassuolo. It was the last little town I'd passed through on the way to Maranello last night. In other words, it was close.

I put on jeans, a sweater and a windbreaker and put a small flashlight, notepad and pencil in my pocket. *What in the world*, I wondered, *is this all about, skulking around in the gloomy Italian night?*

Sassuolo turned out to be bigger than a village but not much and the Mercedes looked like an elephant at a lawn party. I drove around until I found the Cathedral, not difficult in a two-story town. I drove past it just to get the feel of the neighborhood and found a place beside a small factory about a quarter mile away to park the car, kind of out of sight.

Like all small towns in Italy, the shutters had closed and the town went dark around nine o'clock. By 10:00, the place looked deserted and the only noises were the fog-muffled sound of a car door slamming and the occasional bark of a dog. On the way back to the Cathedral, I passed a small tavern with beer signs in the window and three or four workmen gathered at the bar. It looked cozy and I wished that it were my destination instead of this mysterious rendezvous.

There were ten steps leading up to the front door of the Cathedral and I was on number six feeling that there were a thousand eyes on my back when the damn bells started ringing ten. It was so loud in the night that I almost tripped and fell from the fright.

With the adrenaline surging, I burst through the heavy oak door into the vestibule where I was plunged into blackness and mortal fear. I couldn't see a thing for a moment and I just stood there listening to my heart pound.

Get a grip on yourself, I thought. *Yeah, right.* Then I saw the dim outline of the door leading into the sanctuary itself and moved cautiously across the vestibule and through the door. Inside, there was enough light from candles on the altar, as well as the votive candles in the galleries along the sides, for me to see that the church was empty.

I went a third of the way down the center aisle and moved into the row on the right. I decided that I was starting to like the protection of the dark, so I chose a row where the end nearest the outside wall was in shadow from the supporting pillars.

I'm not a practicing anything, but I've been to church enough to know what you're supposed to look like if you're here for real and not for some weirdness. I knelt and clasped my hands on the back of the bench in front of me and bowed my head. I was starting to think, *What the heck...as long as you're here, maybe you should say something to whoever might be listening up there? After all, how could it hurt?* Then I heard the rustle of cloth to my right.

Like a ghost, a tiny figure in black with a black shawl covering its head appeared next to me. I nearly wet myself. It was close enough to touch me and all I wanted to do was run. Then this deep, raspy voice said, "Do not look at me. Look straight ahead."

I did as I was told and tried to calm down.

"Why have you come to Maranello?" said the voice in a hoarse whisper.

I thought for a second how to make this simple."To learn what my cousin learned when he was here."

"Why don't you ask your cousin?"

"He's dead." I have terrific peripheral vision and while I couldn't focus on the person beside me I could see an outline without facing them. The person visibly jerked at the word.

"Dead"

Then a bony hand came out from under the shroud and made the sign of the cross. "How?"

"His car went off the side of a mountain."

"Which car?"

"A Ferrari."

Again, the sign of the cross was made. Then, the voice said, "Leave this alone."

"I can't."

"It is not safe."

"What is not safe?"

"The search."

"I don't even know what I'm searching for."

"Il Duplicatore. The one who made the car."

"The counterfeit?"

"Si."

"Tell me how to know if the car is real."

"Only the family knows everything, but I can tell you one thing. This was 40 years ago and they took secret measures to protect the cars. Now, only Rinaldo is alive from those days. When he is drunk, he mumbles, 'Scatola Ottone,' and then he smiles. He will not say more."

"What? What does he mumble? What does it mean?" I was no longer whispering and I had half-turned around in my desperation to get this clear.

The front door of the church banged and my heart

stopped. I looked over my left shoulder to see who had entered the Sanctuary. Suddenly, there was a strong set of fingers on my right shoulder and I was being pulled to my right into the musty folds of the shroud. The voice said into my ear, "Look in Santa Maria but do not be careless like your cousin." The hand released its grip. Coming down the center aisle was a young man with slick black hair in a leather jacket and shoes with a hard heel that sounded like shots, as he slowly came toward our row. He stopped, knelt and crossed himself before moving slowly into the left side of the aisle, one row in back of ours.

I had been watching this out of the corner of my eye, as I continued my imitation of a supplicant. Slowly, I turned my head back to the right and to my horror the shroud was gone.

Oh my god, I'm now alone in here with this guy. What the hell is going on?

I decided to make the first move because I just couldn't stand to sit there any longer. I stood up and moved to my right, away from my young friend and down to the end of the row. Then I turned and slowly moved back up to the rear of the sanctuary, watching him in his prayerful posture all the way. When I got to the rear, I walked softly over to the door and slid through it. Then I leaped across the darkened vestibule, threw open the outside door, slammed it shut and backed into the shadows back inside the vestibule.

My suspicions were correct. At the sound of the outside door slamming, I heard the rapping of those heels coming rapidly up the aisle. I squeezed myself as far back into the corner as I could, as the inner door burst open and a figure came sailing through on the way to the outside door. He went through it in a hurry, paused and looked both ways and chose the left, the direction from which I'd come to the church. I moved slowly over to the door and cracked it ever so gently, peeked out and saw him disappearing up the street in a hurry, looking like a man who'd lost his dog. I waited until he turned the corner and then went down the street in the other direction planning to circle back to the car. I figured I could always hear those heels coming if he circled, as well. Apparently, he didn't because I arrived back at the car without seeing him again, circled it warily to be sure I had no unwelcome guests and beat it out of town.

By the time I got back to the hotel ten minutes later, I knew that I hadn't a clue of the meaning of "Rinaldo's" mumbling, but I did know that Santa Maria must be a place and maybe I should go there. I went up to my room, got out the map again and began to search for Santa Maria. It took a long time because I was exhausted from the evening's adrenalin binge, but I finally found it just north of Naples.

This is getting like Gulliver's Travels, I thought, and decided that it was too far to drive tonight in my weary condition. I got out the directory and, even though it was in Italian, I could recognize Alitalia Airlines when I saw it and called to ask about early morning flights. There was one at 8:15 am out of Bologna and I booked it. I set my travel alarm for 6:00 am and collapsed into bed. Just before I fell asleep, I jumped out of bed and propped a chair under the doorknob.

This place gives me the creeps.

LE MANS

The only good thing about Santa Maria, for a man on a wild goose chase, was that Santa Maria wasn't big enough to hide a goose in. In two days, I could have done a strip search on the whole town, if I didn't get killed first by one of the very mean looking locals with an obvious resentment of the Yankee busybody asking a lot of nosey questions about motorista and meccanico, of which there were none.

I spent the afternoon driving around the countryside looking for promising buildings and shops, and then trying to explain to farmers in pigeon Italian that I was looking for the meccanico. Of course, the minute I'd say, "Ferrari," everyone would say "Ah, Ferrari, si, si," and point northward and tell me to go to Maranello where I'd just come from. It was very frustrating — another dead end.

So I drove sadly back to the airport and caught the last plane to Rome where I made a connection to Paris, rented another car and drove down to Le Mans, arriving in a state of complete depression and exhaustion. *A great way to prepare for a 24 hour race,* I thought.

I slept late on Wednesday since all I had to do was register, pick up my credentials and catch up with Colin and the crew, who should be busily prepping the racecar. I finally got to the course about noon and quickly found our garage and pit. Practice wouldn't begin until Thursday since the course was partly on public roads that couldn't be closed for the entire week.

I took the opportunity to stroll down pit road and say hello to a lot of old friends, catch up on the latest gossip and accept congratulations on the new sponsor and the promising start to the new season. For the privateers, Le Mans is less intense than the sprint races on the rest of the circuit because it is understood that the pace, because of the distance, must be slower and the chances of a top five finish are even less because the factories bring two, three sometimes four cars. This is really a competition for the factories and a happening for the privateers for whom simply finishing is sufficient glory.

In one of the pits, I was surprised to find one of the young IEM engineers talking with a well-known engine builder from Germany. He saw me approaching and interrupted the conversation to say hello. "What are you doing here?" he asked with a smile.

I explained the last minute arrangement with the privateer and he asked a couple of interested questions about the car. I started to move on when I had a second thought. "Aldo," I asked, "could you translate two words into English for me?"

"I can try."

"One is 'scatola,' I think and the other is, let me see, odone or otone, something like that."

"These two words, Ned," he asked, "were they spoken together?"

"Yes."

"Well, scatola means box or can, a container. The other word you said was odone?"

"Or otone, the *d* like a *t*."

"Then that would probably be *ottone*, it means 'brass'."

"Box brass or brass box?"

"Scatola was first, right?"

"Yes."

"Then it's probably brass box, even if they didn't say the di for of."

"Brass box," I mused. "Well, I'll have to work on that."

"Who said these words?" Aldo asked.

"A little old lady or a little old man. I'm not sure which and I don't know what they mean to me, either. I'll have to work on it but thanks for the translation." I left them then to go back to their conversation and went back to the pits to see Colin and get fitted for the seat in the race car.

When I arrived, Colin said, "The eagle flew over the nest while you were away. We kept your share for the party."

"What's that supposed to mean?" I asked.

"It means, Laddie, that your check for the balance due is in that briefcase over there if you're interested."

"Who delivered it?"

"His highness, Rodney Walker Evans, his-own-self, that's who."

"So," I said, "I didn't know he'd be here. Well, let's make him and the owner happy. Maybe they'll want to do this again sometime."

The next two days were spent in day practice and night practice, and trying to get my co-drivers, all experienced but amateurs nonetheless, who, along with the car owner and sponsors, were paying the fee for the team and me to calm down and think endurance racing and not fast lap of the day. None of them really needed to go too quickly because I was going to qualify the car on Friday. What we needed to teach them was how to maintain a steady pace and stay out of trouble, which is 90 percent of what endurance racing is all about unless you have three cars; a 'rabbit' to wear out the competition and two cars to guarantee at least one lasting the whole race.

They seemed competent enough and I began to think by Friday afternoon that we might have a chance of finishing. If you can finish Le Mans, you've accomplished a lot.

I didn't actually see much of Evans. Obviously, he had much business to do and I was busy sorting out the car all day. And without a sponsor, I had no need to hang around the parties every night. He did ask me once if Jennifer had made a decision about his proposal to liquidate the collection and I told him I didn't know, which was true.

I called Jennifer just before the race preparations started on Saturday afternoon. I woke her up and I apologized, but I was missing her so and I didn't want to go off without talking to her. She was sweet and sleepy and I just longed to hold her again. I left her murmuring love words into her pillow and went off to go 220 miles an hour.

The race went along uneventfully, pretty much. One of the drivers suffered a little brain fade in the middle of the night and tangled with a slower car, tearing up some body work. But we had a spare nose and the crew replaced the damage on a regular stop, so not much time was lost.

The sun came up on Sunday and we were lying ninth, which made everyone feel good about our chances for a top ten finish. All we had to do was keep the car together. I had just gotten in the car for a two-hour stint and was getting it and me back up to speed. At the south end of the 3-mile, 240mph Mulsanne straight, there is a 50 mile per hour, 130 degree hairpin back to the north where the spectators can get within 80 feet of the cars. It is a favorite place for photographers because they can get great close-ups without the distortion of a telephoto lens.

Once you've rounded this corner, its foot flat on the floor for another mile or so up to Indianapolis corner in Arnage where there is another slow corner requiring heavy braking. As I approached Indianapolis I lifted at my braking point, the car made a sudden dart to the right, then as I corrected, to the left, then back to the right, left again and then leaped into the air.

I woke up 48 hours later in the hospital in awesome pain, with my good friend Colin trying to convince me that someone had tried to kill me.

Apparently, someone had.

HOSPITAL

"Colin, how could somebody shoot a race car in broad daylight in front of hundreds of fans? I mean, somebody would surely see or at least hear the gun, wouldn't they? I mean, did anybody report anything to the Gendarmes? I don't think this is possible. Do you?"

"Well, laddie, I've had the benefit of 24 hours to think about this with a fully functioning brain. On the other hand, you've had three minutes and no one would swear you could recognize your own mother at this point, so I see why you might think it couldn't be done. Having thought about how I'd do it if I wanted to, I think I know how it was done."

"You do?"

"I do."

"You want me to beg? Tell me, for Christ's sake."

"I'd do it with a camera. You know, all those fancy Jap cameras with the humongous telephoto lenses, some of them so big they come with a leg to stand them on?"

"Sure. They're at every race track and football game in the world."

"Well, I can't think of a single reason why you couldn't take the guts outa one of them beauties and replace them with a gun."

"Holy cow. You're right, Colin. But what about the noise?"

"Good question, lad. Maybe there's no brain damage, after all. I had the same question so I asked my friend, the flic about it and he went in the house and came out with a pistol with a silencer on the end of it. He fired it twice right next to me. Sounds like compressed air; like one of our air hoses if you just flick it. Pfft. Like that."

"And the whole damn thing—pistol, silencer and all—is no longer than one a them lenses. That's how I'd do it."

"Colin, did your friend think that such a gun would be accurate? Could you actually use it?"

"That's the crazy thing, lad. It'd actually be more accurate than the pistol if it was resting on its leg and you aimed it through an eyepiece, don't ya see? It'd be like a short barreled rifle."

My god, I thought, *he's right and you'd look exactly like an ordinary photographer doing your work.* "Okay, last question. Where would you do it?"

"Why, I'd get myself right up to the fence on the inside of the old *Mulsanne* Corner. The cars slow down there and get broadside to the fence, which is not 100 feet away. Then I'd stick my lens over the fence, so nobody could see the flash. And I'd wait until you had your foot well and truly into the throttle and them turbos were starting to howl and I'd let fly. Nobody'd hear a thing."

He was right. It was so simple. Even if somebody thought they heard or saw something, you could be gone before they could figure it out.

Then Colin said, "There's just one thing I haven't figured out, lad. If this could be done," pointing at the tire, "I can't figure out why they didn't just shoot you in the head and let it be done with." He looked at me shrewdly.

I debated a moment and then decided that Colin was my friend and this concerned him, too. He deserved to be trusted with the whole story. So I began, "Because whoever wants me dead doesn't want anyone to know that I was murdered. Just like my cousin, Willie, was."

I told him the whole story. It took an hour and the nurses finally came in and chased Colin out. He promised to come back the next day and to call Jennifer that night, and tell her that I was alright and would call on Wednesday.

Then I went back to sleep for another 15 hours. I began mending pretty quickly and I had been extremely lucky. The foot problems were mostly separations and dislocations of small bones. They opened it up, put everything back where it belonged and put a cast on it to immobilize it. The hip had gone back in place by itself and it was now just sore as hell. The collar bone turned out to be more of a crack than a complete break, but they immobilized it anyway because I wasn't going anywhere right away.

I began physical therapy on the third day and the pain was unbelievable, but they assured me that sooner was better and they convinced me that the sooner I got with it the sooner I'd be back in a race car. That got my attention.

So did Jennifer's arrival on the weekend. It was a complete surprise and I almost destroyed all of the doctor's good work trying to get out of bed when she suddenly showed up in the room at noon on Saturday.

She cried when she saw me trussed up as I was and the two black eyes from the pounding didn't help, either.

"Oh my god, what have they done to my beautiful sailor," she cried and laughed at the same time and, to my surprise, I found myself crying, too. She kissed me and kissed me and as soon as I could get my breath, I whispered in her ear, "Good news, darling, they didn't wreck the Magic Wand."

"I'll be the judge of that," she said, "later."

I told her what had happened and she told me that she'd seen clips on TV and was horrified at the sight of the car destroying, itself. I didn't tell her about my conversation with Colin. *She'll only worry needlessly*, I told myself.

She lied to the nurses and told them she was my wife by showing them a drivers license reading, "Pearson," so they brought her a cot and let her stay in the room with me. The nurses were only too happy to leave their regular chores for this patient to someone else. That produced blessed privacy, so that Jennifer and I were able to very quietly, very gently test my theory about the Magic Wand. I was right — not a scratch, perfect health. She went to sleep on my good arm and didn't go to the cot until almost dawn.

She had to go back on Monday afternoon and I hated that, but I promised her I'd be back in California in two weeks.

Laying in a hospital bed provides a lot of time to think slowly and I was beginning to think that I might have this puzzle mostly solved. The doctors accelerated the physical therapy, took the cast off the foot and replaced it with a brace. I was starting to get around on crutches in the second week, although the shoulder still hurt a lot.

At the end of the third week, I felt really good. I could now walk without the crutches and put a lot of weight on the foot. This took the strain off the shoulder and the pain receded there as well. I was now doing four hours of therapy every day and getting stronger. They gave me a cane and I took long walks each day.

Finally, the big day came and I was pronounced fit to go home. As I packed, the phone rang. It was Colin from Hereford Green. He just wanted to find out how I was and to tell me that we'd resume testing in two weeks, so I'd better get a move on. Just before we hung up, I remembered a question that I'd kept forgetting to ask, "Colin, when you heard about the crash on the emergency network, was Evans in the pits with you?"

There was a long silence and then, "I'd been wondering if you never asked that question would I ever tell you the answer. Just before I radioed to bring the car in to put you in it and change tires, Evans left the pits."

"Did he say where he was going?"

"He did, lad. He picked up his big black camera case and said he was gonna go get some pictures."

"Thanks, Colin. See you in two weeks."

SANTA MARIA

"Older but wiser" is the phrase. On the way back to New York, I felt a great deal older but I wondered how much wiser I really was. I was still walking around with a lot of theories that couldn't be proven, even if I had the resources of some police department, which I didn't.

Oh, I'd thought of trying to convince Alan Andrews of the California State Police that there was foul play in Willie's death, but what did I really have as evidence? *Bupkus, that's what. Nothing but the recollections of a logger about the behavior of the car. Nothing at the scene, nothing upon examination of the car.*

Then, there was Willie's behavior prior to his death. What could I prove other than that several people thought it was odd? *So what. Lots of people have odd spells. Here's a guy married to a gorgeous woman 13 years younger than he. She says she thought maybe he was having an affair. Was it possibly the other way around? Who can say?*

His mother noticed his odd behavior, too. *What does that prove? Same for his partner, who didn't like him all that much anyway.*

So his cousin, the journalist comes along and finds some doodles in a book, finds out the guy went to Italy to ask about a counterfeit car and is told by the manufacturer that it's legit. *So what else is new?*

Then, some unknown people in the Italian countryside do weird things like invite the journalist to a church late at night and tell him that the manufacturer took steps 50 years ago to protect against forged cars. *Great. Where's the crime?*

The only crime we can prove is the wanton destruction by gunfire of a racing tire worth approximately $400. *Barely a misdemeanor — if you can find the perpetrator, a witness, the weapon and a motive.*

Maybe I was a little wiser, after all. At least I knew that I was still alone in this. I also knew that whoever was involved in this with me was not kidding around. The other thing that I knew was that I no longer had any idea where to go from here and I found that less frustrating than relieving. At least I now had a good excuse to stop because there was nothing left to do. I could tell Aunt Blake that I'd done everything I could to run this down, nearly died in the process and there was nothing more to learn. *Se terminer*, as the French say, the end.

So I switched my thoughts to the only good thing to come of all this, the most spectacular woman I'd ever known; a warm, loving, delicious confection, full of wonderful surprises and all the love to give that one man could stand. And I was the chosen one, the one with the duty to care for this creature and accept her gifts. *Tough duty. I'll do my best,* I thought.

While I'm in New York, I thought, *I'll take Aunt Blake to lunch and tell her my story. I won't tell her the whole truth, of course, no point in that, but I could tell her that there seemed to be some possible funny business with one of the cars and that they were now Jennifer's problem and I was helping her deal with that as best I could. Duty done and well away,* I thought.

I got to the apartment late in the afternoon and struggled a bit with the luggage since the left shoulder was still a bit sore, and I still had the brace on the left foot. It took two trips, but I got everything upstairs okay and then went through a month's worth of mail that the super had collected for me.

Next on to the answering machine and the usual droning of solicitations, a few people you'd really like to talk to, a couple of impromptu invitations — now too late to do anything about — and buried in the middle, a surprise. My good friend with the iron sphincter, Robert MacIntosh, Willie's loving partner. "Yes, Mr. Pearson," said the nasal voice on the tape, "I believe I've come across something that may be of interest to you. Perhaps you could give me a call at your convenience. It's about William's unexplained absences. I'll be in my office. I believe you have the number."

Oh Christ, I thought, *enough already. Why won't this thing just die? I don't want to talk to this guy for the whole rest of my lifetime and a couple more.* I thought that maybe I'd just not call him back but no, just before the end of his day in California I couldn't stand it anymore, so I called.

After some fussing that he'd called a week ago and didn't I get my messages, he got to the point, "Our travel agent called last week to tell me that they were going to have to add an extra charge to our bill this month to cover some tickets that hadn't been charged properly on an earlier billing. When I inquired as to what these tickets were for, the woman told me that they were for William's trip to Mexico. I, of course, told her that there must be a mistake in view of William's...uh, death. but she was very sure."

"I asked for the dates and, sure enough, they matched two of those that I had written in my diary when William couldn't be located. Apparently, they had first been mistakenly billed to another of the travel agency's clients and recently sent back. What do you think of that, Mr. Pearson?"

"Well. Bob, I don't know. Did you say you have no clients in Mexico?"

"None. What on earth do you suppose he was doing down there?"

I shouldn't have said it but I was really weary of this priggish sonofabitch. "Perhaps he was having an abortion before the Supreme Court overturns Roe vs. Wade?"

"I don't see the humor in that Mr. Pearson. I'm only trying to be helpful."

"Of course, Bob, please forgive me. I've been under some strain. And thank you for giving me this information. By the way, where did Willie go in Mexico?"

"I have it right here. It was Guadalajara."

"Guadalajara, you say?"

"That's correct."

"Well, thanks again, Bob, I'll certainly think about this. If I learn anything, I'll let you know, okay?"

"Fine. I hope you're feeling better. Goodbye."

"Goodbye, Bob."

What the hell is in Guadalajara? I wondered. *Why would Willie go there without telling anybody? What's the secret? Where the hell is Guadalajara anyway?*

I got up from my desk and went to the bookshelf

and took down the Atlas. I quickly found the map of Mexico and located Guadalajara, west of Mexico City. *So what?* I thought. *I still don't have a clue why Willie would go there. Maybe I'll ask Jennifer if she can figure it out? And then again, maybe I won't.*

I had started to close the book and decided to take one last glance at Guadalajara when I saw it and the hair went up on the back of my neck. *Jesus, Mary and Joseph.* There on the map, 25 miles west of Guadalajara was the small town of Santa Maria.

There are times in your life when you simply know things that you don't know why you know but you just do. This was one of those times. I knew exactly what I would find in Santa Maria, Mexico. Mexico, not Italy. And I now knew what Willie had discovered that got him killed. I even thought I knew how it was done.

I looked at my watch and said the hell with it. I dialed Colin in Hereford Green, even though it was 11:00 at night there. His sleepy voice answered, "This had better be important."

"It is," I said. "Tell me something about the electronic engine management system."

"What the bloody hell are ye calling me in the middle of the night for, to play 20 questions? Are ya daft, man?"

"Nope. I think I've never been less. Come on, tell me about the system. Is it based on telemetry?"

"Yes, that and microprocessors. Why?"

"So it's really radio controlled, right?"

"That or infra red or laser."

"So you could control the engine from outside the car, right?"

"If you had the frequency right and you could override the built-in programs to cancel outside transmissions, what's called alien signals, yes."

"You could fix the system, so that you had a radio-controlled car. Couldn't you?"

"Yes, you could. Eventually, we'll go racing without the bother of you prima donnas behind the wheel. Jesus Christ, lad, is this about your cousin?"

"Yes, it is. I think I know what happened to Willie."

"Will you please be careful? Yur not foolin' with amateurs here, you know."

"I know," I said, but did I? I hung up and called the airlines. I booked a ticket for Guadalajara on the following day. Then I called Jennifer and lied to her. I told her that I had to take care of some things in New York for an extra day and that I would be in California in two days. The last part was true.

I opened the laptop and checked my notes from the conversation with Alan Andrews. There at the bottom was the note about the insurance company picking up the wreckage of Willie's car. I checked the phone number in California and, after answering a few questions, I got to the person with the file. I asked, "Do you still have the car?"

"No, sir. That car was sold for salvage. You see, when we pay the insured for a totaled car, totaled means not repairable, then we take possession of the car and sell it for salvage value."

"I see," I replied. I already knew this, but we were making progress. "And can you tell me to whom the car was sold?"

"Yes, sir. Just a moment." I heard the click of computer keys. "Yes, sir, here it is. The Rodney Walker Evans Company in Monterey."

"Thank you. And do your records show whether the car was picked up or delivered?"

"Oh, we don't deliver, sir. The cars are always picked up by the buyer."

"Oh. Well, would your record show when this car was picked up?"

"Let me see..." She gave me the date and I wrote it down.

"You've been really helpful. I just have one more question and then I'll let you go. Can you tell me when the insured was paid?"

"One moment, sir." She went off the line and I held my breath and crossed my fingers. She came back on and said, "Sir, this is an unusual case. The insured hasn't been fully paid yet. It's pending an appraisal of the current value of the car.

"But it was released to the salvage company. Do you get the insured's permission to do that?"

"Yes, sir, it's right here. We have a release form signed by Mrs. Pearson the day the car was picked up."

"Thank you very much," I said, and slowly put the phone back on the cradle. I don't know how long I sat there in the gloom of the gathering dusk just staring at the note pad, the one on which I had written the date the car was picked up by Evans Company with Jennifer's written approval. It was the same day that I'd arrived in San Francisco and met Jennifer in Half Moon Bay for lunch.

MEXICO

All the way to Mexico City, I worried about how I was going to finish this thing, and if I found what I expected to find in Santa Maria, what would I do. I changed planes for the short flight to Guadalajara and by mid-afternoon, I was there. It was a short drive to Santa Maria, which was bigger than I had expected, but I still had no trouble finding what I was looking for.

They didn't even try to hide it. I started by going to the center of town and driving out the major roads until I was in the countryside, searching as I went for the facility I knew would be there. I had completed the trip out to the east and to the north and was now on the edge of the western side of the town. And there it was.

They were damn near advertising it. At least they made no attempt to hide the huge tractor trailer with the Rodney Walker Evans livery painted on the side. It was parked in a large dirt lot surrounded by a barbed wire fence. The fence looked like it was more to scare the local peasants than for any serious security.

The truck was parked beside a one-story metal building that had a large overhead door in the side, which looked to me as if it would accommodate the truck.

Well, I thought, *here goes nothing*, as I turned off the road and into the parking area of the building, itself. The overhead door was on the side of the building with a human sized door next to it. On the front of the building, there was another door that looked like the main entrance. I chose that one and limped confidently up to it, turned the knob and walked in as if I belonged there. I used a trick I learned in the Army. If you act like you know what you're doing, nobody will question you about it. I walked right through the offices past open doors on the right and left to a door in the back wall at the end of the hall and out into the open area of the building before anyone could tell me not to.

And there they were. Seven bright red Ferraris in various states of repair, each undergoing some sort of restoration or modification in the hands of mechanics. There were also two or three cars of other makes in the same state.

Old Rodney had himself a neat—and cheap, I'd have bet—little restoration operation going down here out of sight of prying eyes. *And maybe more.*

"May I help you, Senor?" said a deep Mexican voice in my ear. I turned and looked at the source of the voice. He was about five nine, thin and very mean looking.

I put on my best Rocky Mountain smile and said a little too loudly,

"Hey, Buddy, good to see you. So this is where that old rascal gets all that good work done? Clinton's, my name. Down from Denver. Just on my way over to the coast to catch some a them Baja marlin, if ya know what I mean, and I saw ole Rodney's truck out there so

I stopped to see what's goin' on. You don't mind if I look at a couple of these beauties, do ya?"

He thought about it for a second and decided that I'd probably be out of his hair quicker, if he indulged me than if he tried to turn me away. He'd obviously had some experience with pushy gringos. "What did you want to see, Senor?"

"Oh nuthin' special. I just love these here cars and I just like to see the different models and all. I won't be long. I gotta meet up with a boat over in Puerta Vallarta like I said."

"Fine," he said, "Perhaps ten minutes? I have to lock up after that."

I smiled, both of us knowing that that was bullshit but we had a compromise and that's all I wanted. I was looking for two things and I found one of them right away. One of the charity cars from Willie's collection was sitting there and the brazen bastards hadn't even changed the license plate which is how I spotted it. The hood was up and it looked like some electrical work was going on.

I couldn't find the second thing, so I walked back up to the office and stuck my head in where my new friend was sitting behind a desk looking at some official papers.

"Say, anybody ever wreck one of these things...you know, let it get away from them and then you guys put it back together?"

He took this in like a fish examining the bait and decided there was no hook in there. "Once in a while."

"Friend a' mine wrecked his. I thought it might be here. You got anything like that here now?"

He saw the hook in this one and telegraphed the lie by putting his hands flat on the desk before saying,

"No, not now." He stood. "Well, have you seen enough?"

I decided not to push it. I had plenty of time for what I needed to do.

"Yep. Thanks for your time. Next time I see ole Rodney, I'll tell him you're a nice feller. See ya later," and went out the door.

I went out to the car, pulled out of the lot and continued traveling west to verify my story. The building was actually on a corner, with a side road running north and slightly uphill just beyond the lot. I passed it and noted that from that road, you should get a nice view into the back lot of the complex. I went to the next right turn and circled to see if I could find the road beside the shop. Sure enough, I found it where I thought it would be and slowly traveled south to come up behind the building. When I got to the crest of the hill, I parked, got out and walked forward to see what I could see. Exactly as I expected, there behind the building, under a tarpaulin, was a rectangular shape just the right size to be a badly wrecked car. I was pretty sure I knew what was under that tarp.

I reversed and took a great circle route back to town to wait for nightfall. It was July now, so it took a long time. Finally, at nine o'clock, it seemed to be as dark as it was going to get, so I retraced my steps of the afternoon and went back to the shop. I drove by the front once to see who might be there and saw only one old battered car. *Damn,* I thought, *a night watchman. Well I'll just have to deal with that.*

I went around the circle again and parked up on the hill overlooking the back of the building. I limped down the hill to a point on the fence nearest the building, got down on the ground, stretched the barbed wire up and rolled under.

Then I made my way over to the tarp, lifted it up and smelled the distinctive, acrid aroma of burnt rubber and plastic. I shined the small flashlight under the tarp and my stomach rolled over, thinking about what Willie went through and about my own crash.

Conveniently, they had stored the car on saw horses so that it was three feet off the ground, presumably to make it easier to work on. I crawled under the tarp and began to search for what I'd come looking for. I went to where the transmission was located and shined the light on it. I studied it for a long time. It was just back of the engine and tapered down toward the rear where the drive shaft was attached. About halfway from front to back, there was a lateral brace running from one frame rail to the other that formed a support for the transmission. This support was bolted to the frame at both ends. I took out a pen knife and scraped the case of the transmission and produced some bright silver colored, aluminum shavings through the soot and grease covered surface. I looked once more at the brace and then snapped off the light.

Now for the hard part. As I crawled out from under the tarp, I heard a dog bark in the distance and prayed that there were no junkyard dogs here. If there were, I was in deep shit.

I walked along the side of the building and came to a window at shoulder height. I carefully raised up and looked in. To my relief, I was looking at a watchman sleeping on the job. He was sitting behind a desk with the remains of his supper and a girly magazine opened in front of him, but he was slouched back in the chair, his head lolling to one side and a slight drool flowing down his chin.

Fabulous, I thought, *sweet dreams, amigo. Hang in there for just ten more minutes.* I went back around the building, across the back and approached the small side door. It was locked but it was poorly made and a credit card moved the tongue out of its slot in an instant. I quietly slipped into the darkened garage and, keeping one eye on the light shining under the door to the offices, I made my way to the car with Willie's plate on it.

It was sitting nose in to the left of the office door so that at least I could keep the car between me and that door in case I got any nasty surprises. I got down on the floor and tried to perform the same test on this car's transmission that I had on the one outside, but I couldn't reach it and the damn thing was too low to get under.

Now, I thought, *I've really got a problem. How am I going to get this thing up in the air enough to do what I have to?* I stood up and looked around the darkened shop. There was just enough glow from under the office door to see the floor jack two cars away. Somebody had let the car down at quitting time, but left the jack under the car.

I thought, *Boy, are you asking for trouble now. That thing is gonna' make a lot of noise and your ass is gonna' be grass. Ah yes, said the devil, but never up never out. Here goes nothin'.*

Inch-by-inch, I rolled that damn heavy jack out from under the first car and then under Willie's. I thought, *How much longer can this guy sleep and what if the phone rings or something?* I thought of everything that could go wrong, but I finally got that damned jack under Willie's car. I worked the handle and quickly the car was just high enough for me to roll under, which I did. I snapped on the flashlight and looked over this transmission, which of course, was much cleaner than the one outside since this car hadn't been driven down a mountainside.

I had finished doing my scraping with the penknife, getting the same aluminum scraps when the office door opened and the shop was flooded with light. *Oh shit, oh dear.* My lungs locked and I couldn't breathe for the longest time. I very slowly pulled my feet up under the car and thought, *Please god, make him go away.*

Then he turned on the overhead lights. *Oh Christ, he's going to do a round.* And he started walking. I could actually see his feet, as he came into the shop and turned right, away from me, to go down the line of cars toward the other wall. Those were the biggest, ugliest, black, dirty boots I'd ever seen. Now they turned back toward me and began to move again. *What if he has a gun?* I thought. *He would, wouldn't he? All Mexicans have guns, don't they? I'm going to die on the floor of a Mexican garage, if I don't do something quick.*

The boots turned left toward the office door and I thought, *Oh, thank god.* Then they stopped and he said something in Spanish. He backed up and half turned toward my end and I thought, *What is it? What does he see? Oh shit, it's the jack. He sees the car up on the jack and it's not supposed to be.* Then he said, "Shit," a word I recognize in four languages. And the boots started my way. I curled myself up ready to spring out from under the car and attack him with a gimpy foot and a cracked collar bone. And then I realized the real truth. *If he gets to that jack handle, now just 20 feet away, he'll twist it to let the car drop and I'm pudding.*

That's when the loud jangle of the shop phone set

off and scared me so badly I jerked and banged my head on the frame of the car. It was all I could do not to cry out. The boots stopped, turned and went back to the office door, slamming it.

I took one deep breath and started out from under the car, when I remembered what I had been looking at when the door opened. When I was scraping the transmission, I noticed in the cross brace that someone had drilled two, no, three holes part way into the metal. The flashlight showed shiny aluminum up inside the holes that were in a random pattern and did not go all the way through.

I turned on the flashlight for one last look at this phenomenon and then made haste for the back door. I let myself out into the fresh air and realized that I was soaking wet from the tension. But I had to go take one more look at the wrecked car, or I'd have wasted the whole trip. So I went back to it, climbed under once more and shined the light on the cross brace. And there they were, the same kind of holes I'd seen inside. I hadn't seen them earlier because the car was so dirty. I stuck the point of the knife up into one of them and sure enough it showed silver.

That's it, I thought. *Now I know what Willie knew and I'll bet it's what got him killed.* I climbed back under the fence, walked back up to the car and drove all the way to the airport in Mexico City in the warm July night thinking about my next step.

THE BEACH HOUSE

"Is this my Merry Sunshine?"

"Ned," she squealed, "where are you? You're not in New York are you? Did you miss the plane?"

"No, my darling, I'm closer than you think. I'm in Mexico City, but I'll be at the airport in San Francisco at two o'clock. Can you pick me up?"

"Oh, yippee. When the phone rang, I was afraid it was you to tell me you'd been delayed again and I don't think I could stand it. You bet I'll pick you up, you hunk, you. Can we go directly to the beach house?"

"As fast as our little wheels can carry us, my dear."

"Oh goodie, I'm so excited to see you. Hey, what are you doing in Mexico?"

"Tell you when I see you, sweetheart. 2 o'clock, okay?"

"Right," she said and we hung up. Then I placed the second call. I was put through right away and that professional voice came on, saying, "Evans."

"Rod, it's Ned Pearson. How are you?

"Fine, fine but more to the point, how are you? I

came to the hospital but they wouldn't let me see you. I'm so glad you're alright. I was terribly worried."

I'll bet, I thought.

"Where are you? Are you coming to California soon?"

"As a matter of fact, Rod, that's why I'm calling. I'll be in San Francisco this afternoon. In fact, I'll be not too far from you. I'm driving down to a house on the beach just north of Santa Cruz. I'd really like to get together with you and discuss your proposal concerning Willie's collection. Could you make it this afternoon?"

He took his time thinking about that and finally said, "Why yes, I could do that. What time will you be there?"

"About 3:00, Rod. Will that be alright?"

"That's fine."

"Oh, by the way, Jennifer tells me that you took two of the cars for some sort of charity exhibition. Are they back yet?"

"Well one of them is. Why?"

"If it's not too much trouble, could you bring it to the meeting? There's something I'd like to look at, okay?"

"Of course, no problem." I could hear in his tone that he thought he'd won a Bluff; that I believed he didn't really have the car.

"Fine then, I'll see you at 3:00."

I did a lot of thinking on the way up to San Francisco and felt really bad about doing this to Jennifer, but I simply had to have some answers to questions that had been crawling around in the back of my mind for too long.

The plane was on time and there she was at the gate, looking spectacular and throwing her arms around me and kissing me and generally pissing off every male under the age of 70 within sight. I hugged her as tightly as I could with my one good arm and felt the warm length of her, and thought dreadfully about the next two hours.

My luggage came quickly for a change. We went out and got in the Mercedes and went off to the house with me, enjoying the smooth power of this lovely car once again.

We talked about plans she had made for the week and about my condition and the doctor I'd agreed to check in with while I was here. She didn't ask again about Mexico and I didn't volunteer anything.

We were right on time getting to the house and, as we came down the narrow driveway, she saw the red car parked in front of the door and asked, "Ned, what is this? That's one of the cars from the collection. What's it doing here?"

I looked at her and my heart was like a cold stone in my chest. I said, "Darling, there are some things that I haven't been able to make sense out of and I asked Rod Evans to stop by and have a little discussion with you and me to maybe clarify things."

Her eyes were wider and more frightened than I had ever seen them. I almost got back in the car and drove away because I didn't know if I could handle this, but I knew it had to happen.

She put her head down and walked into the house. I followed. Rod was standing on the deck when we came in. He turned around and smiled that smooth client smile that said, "I'm clearly superior and I'm happy to take your money."

"Ned...Mrs. Pearson," he said.

I thought, *Well, he's going to stick with this act to the*

bitter end, I guess?

Jennifer only nodded and looked at me again with those frightened eyes. I felt so sorry for her that I just wanted to take her in my arms and hold her but I couldn't do it. *Not yet. Later, please god, but not yet.*

"Why don't we all sit down," I said, "I want to tell you both what I've been doing for the last two months between races and flying accidents." I smiled thinly at Evans. He and Jennifer sat in the two club chairs across from the couch and I sat on the couch facing the sea. As I looked over Evans shoulder, I thought, *How can it be so beautiful out there when it's so ugly in here?*

"It goes like this," I said. "I promised my Aunt Blake that I would try to find out why my cousin Willie acted so distressed just before he died a violent death in an exotic car from his very valuable collection. I came to California to ask some questions of those who knew him and they all pretty much confirmed what Aunt Blake had said. His widow, Jennifer here, and his business partner both thought his behavior odd including some unexplained absences.

"I learned that his car went off a cliff at very high speed, which wasn't like Willie who was a very conservative man. Then I met the man who sold him the car and took care of his valuable collection, and who is now offering to take it off the widow's hands. This man stands to make a nice commission for the second time he sells the same cars. I hear he is very successful but when I go to his place of business, half the desks are empty. Same for the repair bays. Could this business be in trouble in the recession? I wonder.

"And something else bothers me. The widow acts like she is a stranger to a guy who has sold several million bucks' worth of cars to her husband and who she

is now going to trust with selling them off for her benefit. Yet, these people act like they don't like each other.
Puzzling, I think to myself.

"Then accidents start to happen. A complete
stranger walks up to me in Italy and tells me that my
cousin visited him in Italy not two weeks before his
death to tell him that he thinks he's bought a counterfeit car. This man from the factory assures me that this
couldn't happen. I'm a journalist. I don't believe anything the establishment tells me."

By now, Evans could no longer hold my eye. He
was starting to show signs of the pressure building—
fidgeting, looking at his fingernails.

"Then I go to the last place my cousin was alive and
I see how fast the car was going when it went over and
I know Willie couldn't have done this by himself.
Someone who heard the accident tells me that the motor continued at full throttle all the way down the
mountainside." I looked at Jennifer and there were
tears in her eyes. She just looked at me, silently begging
me to stop. But I couldn't.

"I also find that someone has taken every reference
book on the death car out of Willie's library. Why? I
wonder. But they missed the crucial one; the one in
which Willie left scribbles that tell you what was on his
mind those last days of his life.

"So I go back to Italy and I confront the guy at the
factory and make a complete ass of myself. But I do
learn one thing. They're hiding the records from the
world and I wonder why. Could Willie have been
right? Did he buy a counterfeit car? Then something
weird happens. Some locals, who are scared to death of
what they know, still care enough about their beloved
tradition that even after the death of the Patron, they

try to protect his name. And they tell me a couple of things that I can't understand at the time. What I do understand is that they told Willie the same things two weeks before he died." Jennifer put her hand to her mouth and looked away.

"Then I go off to go racing again having been hired by the guy who sold Willie the car he was so worried about. And somebody tries to murder me, too."

At this, both of them exclaimed. Jennifer just made a noise and looked at Evans. Evans said, "Preposterous."

"Not so, the Surete have the bullet fired into my right rear tire that almost killed me. They're looking for the gun and I've given them a suggestion as to where to look.

"But the last piece of the puzzle didn't fall into place until yesterday. You see, another accident occurred and I discovered where Willie went on his last mysterious trip. He went to Mexico where he found what the little people in Italy said he would; the source of the phony Ferraris. Your little money machine in Santa Maria, Mr. Evans."

Rodney Walker Evans rose to his full height of six feet two, spun on his heel and walked toward the deck. "It's a fascinating tale, Mr. Pearson," he said, adopting his professional voice again, "but if you think that it proves anything, you are mistaken. And it certainly doesn't implicate me in any way in Willie's death. And as to counterfeit cars, I'm afraid you'd have to prove that and I don't think you can."

He was a hell of a bluffer. You could see why he'd been so successful. But then, I wasn't born yesterday, either.

"I don't intend to Rod, old Buddy. I'm just going to

suggest in my article that everybody who has bought a car at one of your auctions or with you as broker just put it up on a jack or a lift and drill two or three little holes in the bracket that holds the transmission up. If they penetrate the aluminum casting and find brass on the inside, they got nothing to worry about. They got old Enzo's secret authentication device. But if they get solid aluminum like those that somebody who didn't know Enzo's secret manufactured in the last five years, then they got a problem car, just like that one sitting out there in the driveway. Right, Rod? Why don't we go out there right now and see what we got, brass or aluminum? But I suspect Willie already told you the answer to that, didn't he?

"Now comes the real ugly part, Rod. I'm pretty sure I know what happened to Willie. I think you took those cars away on the pretense that you were servicing them and you secretly installed electronic controls on them. You made radio controlled cars out of them, is what I think. And I think that when Willie told you what he had discovered, you simply pushed a button and ran Willie right through a guardrail to his death."

Jennifer sobbed out loud and then said, "You son-of-a-bitch. You were there, weren't you? You told me you wouldn't hurt him. You told me it was an accident but you killed him, didn't you?"

I turned to look at Evans and found myself looking up at a little Ruger 9mm. caliber automatic. It looked small in his hand, but the muzzle looked like a sewer pipe in my face.

He turned to look at Jennifer and said, "Darling, get a hold of yourself and don't start making accusations. As I've told you often enough, you're in this too deeply now to start throwing rocks."

I wanted to puke. In fact, I thought I would. This was what I had been dreading for weeks. The unexplained light on the phone, the laptop in my hotel, the flush on the back of her neck in Evans' Rolls and then her release of Willie's car to him on the day we met. *Oh Jesus, Jesus, I wanted it not to be true but here it is.*

She looked at me and the tears were running down her cheeks. She said, "Ned, please, please believe me. It's not what you think it is. I love you. I couldn't help myself. I didn't know what he'd done. Please believe me."

I couldn't look at her anymore and he cut her off, saying, "Jennifer, it's time you went home now. Mr. Pearson and I have some arrangements to discuss. I'll call you later and tell you what kind of an agreement we've reached. Now run along. Just do as I say and everything will be fine."

With the gun on me, he led her meekly toward the door. She went out and he turned and slapped me across the face with the pistol and said, "Now, Mr. Pearson, we have something to discuss. You're going to tell me the names of the people you spoke to in Italy, or I'm going to finish what I started in France."

He stepped on the top of my bad foot. I screamed and almost fainted. He was very strong and he dragged me over to a supporting pillar in the middle of the room, put the gun under my throat and told me to take off my belt. When I had it off, he pulled my hands behind me and around the pillar and wrapped the belt around my wrists.

He stepped around in front of me and, without warning, sucker punched me in the stomach. This time, I did puke—all down the front of myself. When I finished gagging, he said, "Now, Mr. Pearson, do we have a better understanding? You cannot be allowed to run around spreading those ugly rumors, can you? It would be very bad for my reputation and my business, and god knows this recession has nearly ruined me, as it is.

"Meanwhile all these superior Harvard graduate junk bond phonies continue to steal millions from the system and pretend that it is their brilliance that produces such wealth instead of their ability to purchase the services of judges and commissioners and senators like so many whores in the market.

"So what if I created an excellent replica or two? The stupid bastards don't know the difference anyway and they just bid the prices up and steal play money from each other. Who is hurt, if I sell them something for a million dollars that's only worth a hundred thousand? Certainly not the little old ladies who invested money in their crooked mortgage scams. Think of me this way Mr. Pearson. I only steal from the rich. Who stole it from the poor in the first place."

"Now tell me, shall it be painful or not? Who told you about the brass in the transmission support?"

"I don't know."

He swung his clenched fist down on the cracked collarbone. I screamed and passed out. When I came to, I smelled the propane gas from the burners that he'd turned on without lighting them. He saw me looking at them and said, "What a pity to lose this place, but you have to go and you shouldn't have been so careless with the gas stove. Now which shall it be this time...the foot or the shoulder?" He punched me in the stomach again, the sadist.

I couldn't retch anymore; I was empty.

"Come now, Mr. Pearson, I assure you that you're

going to tell me eventually. Why not tell me now?" He stepped on my foot and I screamed again.

Then, behind me, Jennifer said, "Untie him, you son-of-a-bitch."

The voice was a big surprise, but the .38 caliber, nickel-plated police special in her hand was an even bigger surprise.

Evans was reaching for my shoulder at the time and he froze and then turned his head to look at her. "I told you that this doesn't concern you. Go home." He had a crazy look in his eye.

"I said untie him, or I'll shoot you."

I knew he wasn't going to believe her. He thought she would just obey him like she always had. He turned toward her and reached out with his right hand to distract her, while he brought the gun up in his left hand. I saw the look in his eye and I knew he was going to shoot her. I tried to kick him, but she moved quicker. The look of hatred in his eyes turned to shock when the gun in her hand went off and a hole appeared in those brilliant white teeth and blood flew out of his ears.

The Ruger went off twice and I thought I was dead for sure. He stood there for an eternity with his mouth open. Then he dropped the gun and slowly put his hand in his jacket pocket. But she wasn't finished. As he groped and staggered toward her, she pulled the trigger three more times, the last one as he toppled over backward from the knees.

The noise was deafening and I will never forget the look in her eyes; a look of the coldest hatred I'd ever seen, almost the glassy look of a dead person. When it was over, she dropped the gun and started sobbing.

I said, "Jennifer untie me."

She said, "I can't. If I do you'll just make me stay and I have to go away. I have to get away from here."

"*Why* Jennifer? It was self-defense. He was trying to shoot you."

"No, Ned, that's not it. It's everything else. You don't understand anything about me," she sobbed. "I couldn't tell you the truth because you would have fled in a minute. You are the first man in my entire life who has treated me like a human being and not some possession to be used and discarded when he was through. For the first time in my life, someone wanted me as a person and not as a trophy or a piece of meat, or bait for his business. My mother didn't die. She killed herself because she couldn't stand the beatings she got from my father when she tried to keep him away from me—at 13. She left me a suicide note and told me to run away. Where could I go? My father told me if I told anyone, it would disgrace my mother. Then my 17 year old brother started and drove my father away, and told me he'd tell everyone at school about my father and me if I refused him." Her body was racked with sobbing.

"My father finally drank himself to death and I got old enough to run away. Ned, my darling, I've spent my whole life depending on one man after another, and being used and threatened and blackmailed into cooperating in my own destruction. Then Willie came along. I lied to you about how we met. Rod introduced us after he saw that I was more useful as bait than a girl friend. So Willie needed someone to repair his broken ego after Catherine threw him out. I was it. Oh, he wasn't a bad person and I figured at least now I'd have some security. Then he found out what Rod was doing and threatened to expose him. Rod made me tell him everything that Willie had learned by threatening to tell Willie about my past. Oh god, Ned, it's just a vicious circle and I have to break out of it.

"I wanted to tell you all of this, but you kept getting closer and closer to the truth that Willie discovered and Rod threatened to tell you what I did to Willie. So I made a decision and, for the first time in my life, goddamnit, I'm going to find the strength to stick to it. The reason I couldn't come to Europe is because I had to be here to transfer my money off shore, to make small enough transfers so that no one would notice. Darling, I've finally done it. Don't you see? I have enough money in foreign banks, so that you and I can live for the rest of our lives. I'll never have to depend on anyone ever again, but I can't stay here and run the risk that someone will try to prove that Willie's death was my fault. Or that horrid bastard," she said, looking at Evans.

Still sobbing, she said, "Please, my darling, don't you see? It's the only chance I'm ever going to have to break this goddamn chain. You're the only one who's ever loved me for love and not for some purpose that eventually goes away. I'm begging you, Ned, come get me and save me. I love you from the bottom of my heart like I've never loved anyone."

We were both sobbing now and my heart was breaking with her pain. I said, knowing that she'd refuse, "Jennifer, untie me. Let me hold you."

And she said, "No, I can't Ned. Don't you see? I've got to do this my way. I'm going to the airport now. On the way, I'll leave a phone number on your voice mail and I'll call someone to come turn you loose. I beg you to call me and come be with me forever. I'll love you forever, whatever you decide." Then she came to me and took my face in her hands and kissed me that long slow kiss that filled me with warmth and made all the pain go away. I tasted the salt of her tears.

She stepped back, smiled and said "Please come darling, please? Do you have my keys?"

"No, he took them."

She looked at Evans and then at the sideboard where she saw the Ferrari keys. She took them and left the room.

I struggled with the belt around my wrists, as I heard the rumble and whine of the twelve-cylinder engine as it made its way up the drive. Then it was gone.

It took me another 20 minutes until I finally worked the belt loose enough to slip one hand out. I stood there for a minute not sure what to do. The pain in my foot and shoulder was pounding. I went to the kitchen, turned off the gas burners and opened the windows. Then I decided to go after her. She didn't need to flee the country and it would look worse if she did.

I didn't want to touch the bastard on the floor, but he had my keys. I reached in the right jacket pocket and it was empty. When I rolled him over to get at the left one, I saw that his hand was in it. I pulled on his wrist to get the hand out and then reached into the pocket and got my keys. As I dropped the wrist, the hand turned over and there — clenched tightly in his fist — was a small remote control with a tiny red light blinking quietly.

Oh no. Please, please, god. No, No, NO!

THE DEAD END

I could see the ugly black smoke rising over the beach from four miles away. I stopped hurrying because I already knew the source of the smoke. When I got closer, I could see that people had stopped their cars on the curve and gotten out to see what had happened.

I was sort of moving in slow motion now, like a sleepwalker in a dream. I stopped the Mercedes and walked over to the guardrail. There was the same kind of a gap that I'd seen once before only this one was new and in a different country.

I looked down the steep slope of the rocks above the beach and there was what I expected to see. The red paint was all that you could recognize from this distance and, of course, the emergency vehicles with their flashing lights. There was also a long, narrow, green plastic envelope on the ground beside the wreckage.

I climbed painfully down the slope, slowly picking my way among the rocks until I finally reached the beach. I walked over to the crowd gathered around the car and looked for a police officer. I finally found one and asked, "Have you identified the driver?"

He said, "Yes. We found her purse. Her name was Pearson. Why, did you know her?"

"No," I said and turned away.

I decided to walk back to the house along the beach. I didn't feel much like the Mercedes right then. It was almost sunset and the sea was beautiful.

After a while, I noticed that tears were streaming down my face. Then I realized that I was quietly humming. At first, I didn't recognize the tune. Then it came to me.

"You are my Sunshine, my only Sunshine, You make me Happy when skies are gray, You'll never know Dear, how much I love you Please don't take my Sunshine away."

DECISIONS

I had made maybe a half-mile when I realized that I had been quietly crying all the way. In my mind, I had been running over and over all the irretrievable, miraculous things that had happened between Jennifer and me in the past three months and the horrid rubble left in my life by this dreadful afternoon. I knew that I was suffering from shock, the shock of the combat zone when things are happening totally beyond your control and major, incredibly valuable parts of your life are being destroyed violently. And you are helpless.

And of course, by now the adrenalin had all been dissolved and the pain came relentlessly marching back into my body parts. *Jesus, could this possibly hurt any worse. God, what am I going to do without that woman?*

I knew what the days ahead were going to be like — torture, as each distraction in everyday life temporarily served to take my focus away from reality. And then suddenly, it would desert me to this ugly pit of hopelessness, the certain knowledge that *it can never be the same.*

I am lost. And tomorrow will never be the same.

At some time in all our lives, we go through some comparable experience—a loved one dies, we lose a job, we crash a car, a romance fails. And we suffer the pain of loss and regret and the nagging torture that we might have somehow contributed to the tragedy. Yes, there is plenty of guilt to go around. Pop psychology tells us that we have a built-in mechanism to deal with that condition. They call it compartmentalizing.

All combat soldiers have it. Combat pilots have it. Racecar drivers who lose competitors experience it. Everyone must go on. After we have uncurled from the initial, little self-protecting ball of denial, we begin to pack the grief, the anger, the search for blame, for the bad deals of life into parcels and we put them away for a little while each day. They all come out again, for sure, but over time their batteries weaken and their light is not so bright. And so the pain diminishes through the act of getting on with reality—and so it goes.

Without my realizing it, the process had started with the realization that I still had three miles to go. I hurt like hell and there was a car parked up there along that highway. I couldn't very well just leave it there, so I climbed back up the rocky face and made my way back to the Mercedes that bore that faint, elegant scent; the one that brought more tears to my eyes. *Please...how am I going to endure this?*

I drove back to the beach house, absolutely dreading what I knew was awaiting me. I pulled slowly into the driveway with a shocking realization. *You are here alone with a dead son-of-a-bitch and you are the only person who knows what happened here. And you alone know what all of this is about. Can I just run? Just leave and pretend it never happened? Christ!*

I must admit that the first thought was very tempting. In my present physical and emotional condition, I just couldn't bear the thought of all the people who would want to know what I know. And then there was a dawning. Why wouldn't I be the person of "most interest," as the police types like to say? *Ace, you're the last man to see those people alive. We work on the OMM trilogy, you know? You sure had opportunity. Now all we gotta do is produce motive and means. And the holes in that corpse over there give us a hint about means.*

What the hell am I going to do? I have to get back to Europe, or the whole deal goes up in smoke. But if I just take off, even if they don't catch me at the airport they'll sure as hell catch me in New York, or have me brought back from Europe... at least I think they can. And then I'll have a cloud over my head on two continents.

Goddamnit! I didn't do anything. Yeah, but you're still here and they'll want to know why you were here in the first place. Great.

In a racecar, in a long distance race, getting near the end, you and your Crew Chief have to make some decisions. If you are in third or fourth place, you could conceivably pick up some points by pushing a little harder and overtaking a car or two ahead of you. That would make you, and the crew and the sponsor and the fans very happy — unless by trying too hard you over-stressed and broke or crashed the car and finished 10th. Then none of you would be happy. No one would say, "Nice try, stupid." They would just leave off the "Nice Try." So you have to think it through, suck it up, consolidate your gains and fight another day. In that case, truth is everything and you better realistically face it. I was going to be stuck here for a while. All this came to me, while applying the best medicine I know for the wreckage of a terrible day, a hot shower.

I went to the bedroom and stripped the soiled, damp clothes of the afternoon and dumped them in a pile. Then I looked into the mirror for the bad news. There was plenty; two purpling, fist-sized blotches with knuckle highlights on my stomach where the asshole sucker punched me for appetizers. Finger marks were on the broken collarbone and my face had a major scrape; a cut and crash damage from the pistol whipping. My knees were red and sore where I'd dropped to the floor at some point. As I showered, I ran down a list of things I should do quickly. *I need to pack and get ready to leave quickly, if I can. I have to call the Santa Cruz County Sheriff and tell him about the body. And I have to make a call that I never, ever wanted to make — ever.* And I would do those things in reverse order. A plan was forming.

As I dried and dressed, I ran the entire day back through my mind. There was no way that I could see any justice falling naturally out of this day. Let's start with the basics. *Willie is still dead. So is Rodney Evans, the evil piece of shit. And he deserves it. The injustice is that the whole thing is going to get pinned on Jennifer. Why? Because her car is here and so are her things. And worse, now she's dead so who's going to defend her? Plenty of people know she was Evan's girlfriend for a while and then married Willie who Evans killed. How will they find that out? Because your friendly journalist, stupid detective, racer guy is going to tell them, that's why. Well, why will he do that? Because if she didn't kill Evans, who did? The three of them were here together. And he must have seen her do it, or he did it. And he has no alibi because she's dead. And everybody knows the Dummy was tracking down the people who killed Willie. Motive and Opportunity. And he's going to have to tell them what he learned...and what brought him right back here. Oh shit, shit, shit, this is awful. They won't let me go for months. And if they don't hang me, they'll hang Jennifer posthumously. And that will really make me puke.*

At this point, I was wandering aimlessly through the house as my confusion bubbled over into fear. *What the hell am I going to do?* As I looked again at the corpse, my eye fell on the silver .38 Special Jennifer had dropped as she fled.

There are moments in life that are watersheds; times that change everything and you can never change them back. *Means*, I thought. Bullet holes just show how the victim died. But bullets don't function without a gun. *Means.* I slowly bent down. I straightened up, went to the kitchen and got a dishtowel off the rack. I came back and carefully wrapped the gun in the towel. I very carefully wiped it off, while I stared thoughtfully out to the sea. I then walked out on the deck and over to the platform at the top of the many stairs that went so far down to the water at the face of the cliff. I was a pretty good pitcher in high school and could throw a football an easy 60 yards. The gun felt about the same weight as the football. So with the still healthy right arm, I threw the gun, towel and all, as far as I could. I knew that the water here was quite deep, as the rock face disappeared beneath the surface. *The means are gone. Now neither one of us did it.* But one of us destroyed evidence in a murder case. *Bad Boy. Tough shit.* No one was going to hang an act of self-defense as a murder on that lady. *Not on my watch. Nor on me.*

I went to the phone and started the most difficult phone call I was ever going to make. The phone rang for a long time and I thought that I was going to fail again today. Then that deep, smooth baritone voice said, "This is Robert."

"Uncle Robert," I said, "This is Ned. Am I disturbing you?" thinking about the time difference.

"No, not at all, Ned. I was just reading a bit before bed. How are you? We haven't talked in a while."

"Yes, well, I've been back and forth from California to New York, and then to Europe and back. Been hectic."

'This about your racing?"

Here we go. "Well, some of it but also our concerns about Willie."

"Oh," he said, "Well, do you..." *have anything to report...I finished the sentence for the Chairman.* "...uh, have you learned anything?"

Fuck this, I thought, *get over it and speak to him like an equal and not the enemy.* "Yes, I have, Uncle Robert, and the news is quite bad. I hope you have a place to sit because this will take a bit. It's very complicated and somewhat unpleasant." *Well, alright, jump right on it. Easy, dude, easy.* "Uncle Robert? You there"

"Unh, yes. I just wasn't prepared. Yes, I'm okay. Please tell me."

"Fine, sir. First, I'm going to go quickly through some events that have occurred today, events that are quite tragic, then I'll explain the detail later. Okay?"

'Yes, Ned, you can...what? Oh, Blake? It's Ned. Yes, Ned, He's learned something about Willie that he wants to tell us..."

Great God A'mighty, is this shitty day never going to end. Hey, maybe it's just starting, dude. This will kill Blake.

"Ned, your Aunt Blake is going to get on the phone so she can hear, as well."

Wonderful...just swell. "Right, well I had hoped...oh, that's fine, Uncle Robert."

"Hello, Ned. That you? It's Blake. How are you?"

I adore this woman! I can't wait to get my arms around her. "Well, I'm about to tell you all about that. I have much news and not very good, I'm afraid. I need you and Uncle Robert to brace yourselves, as I give you a quick summary."

"That's fine, Ned. We'll be fine. Just go ahead and tell us what you need to and we'll not interrupt."

My god, there she goes again. "First, I'm in California. I've learned quite a bit about what happened to Willie. I joined Jennifer here today to confront a central figure, well, the auctioneer who sold Willie several of the cars in his collection. I say confront because I discovered that some of the cars were counterfeit, that is, they were not what they were represented to be...but extremely clever fakes. I also discovered how this was done. And further, I discovered that Willie had discovered the same things that I'd learned and that he'd confronted the man behind the fraud. That man and his organization tampered with the cars in such a way as to cause them under certain circumstances to go out of the driver's control and kill him. I'm afraid that Willie was intentionally killed." I paused to let those awful words sink in.

"My God," said Robert, quietly. Blake gasped.

"May I continue?"

"Yes, go on."

"I said that we had a confrontation. Well, it was more than that. After I laid out what I had discovered, Evans attacked me and tried to beat the information out of me, as to who else knew what I know. It was ugly." *And now my inventions begin. There will be no turning back.*

Robert asked, "What do you mean...ugly?"

"Evans was shot."

"Shot? Jesus, is he okay?"

"No, he's dead."

"Dead! Are you kidding? Ned, are you alright? What happened?"

"Well, I don't know everything." *The first lie.* "He had a gun and he hit me with it and knocked me out. When I woke up, he was lying on the floor, dead and Jennifer was gone."

"Oh, my god! Where is she?"

"I know this is very difficult. Jennifer left in another Ferrari, which ran off the road and a cliff...just as Willie's did. She died in the crash. I'm so sorry." I began to cry. Blake sobbed, quietly.

Robert was now in problem solving gear. "This is a nightmare! Ned, are you alright. Really? Who could have done this?"

The second lie. "I don't know. He was alive when I was knocked out and she was gone when I awoke. I just don't know." *There...the wonderful, creative, self-protective, human brain wipes the slate clean and moves on. I had figured out my story and I'll be sticking to it. Catch me, if you can.*

"What are you going to do, Ned? Is there anybody there? Why don't you just leave?"

"I thought of that, but Jennifer rented the house from a friend. If someone discovers the body, the owners will tell the police. Jennifer and I have been here before." And then I sobbed and gasped. "You and Aunt Blake probably couldn't know this, but Jennifer and I were falling in love."

Blake said quietly but firmly, "Robert, Ned is in trouble. He needs a criminal lawyer...right now."

Oh, this incredible woman. In the midst of a nightmare,

she cuts right to the chase in a nanosecond.

"He's there alone with a dead man whom he has pursued and fought with. He will be suspect number one and his life may be ruined. And if he runs, it may seal his fate."

Robert was now in command voice, "Right. Ned, please give me your phone number and the address. And please don't leave under any circumstances. If you need to call, here is the number of second line that we'll keep open. And please call me when the sheriff gets there and you know more. We'll take care of this."

"Thanks for your help, folks."

"Don't be silly, Ned," said Blake, "We got you into this and we'll get you out. I'm really sorry about Jennifer. This is a tragedy. Try to have hope, Ned."

"Ned?" Robert asked.

"Yes?"

"Ned, we have not been close for reasons we both understand, but I wish you to know this. You have pursued your own goals in an honest and honorable effort and when the family called, you came without hesitation. You are a helluva man and you have my respect. I want you to know that."

Jesus, what next? "Thank you, Uncle Robert, I appreciate that. Good night for now."

SHERIFF

Well, they did. "Take care of this," I mean. You read about power and influence, but you mostly only see it from a distance, like on TV. With me, it actually flowed into and around me, and saved my ass. I hung up from Uncle Robert and Aunt Blake, with some of the hopelessness abated. At least the "worst" telephone call was over. And the ending was much to savor. Now it was time to call the sheriff. I smiled at the "call the sheriff," feeling a little silly but that was just shock wearing off. So I did. After telling them about the dead body in the next room and giving them the address and directions, a sheriff's detective — monitoring the call — came on the line and started asking pointed questions in a thinly polite way.

"Mr. Pearson…"

Yes, monitoring, he knows my name.

"Do you know how the person died?"

"He appears to have been shot." *Oh boy, let the lying continue.*

"Did you see that?"

"No." *Oooh, be cool, man.*

"How do you know he was shot? Did you witness the shooting?"

"No, but he appears to be bleeding from several places."

"I see, so you discovered him in the house?"

"Yes, sir. Well...not exactly. I left the house and then came back."

"Okay...so you were in the house, you left and then came back?"

"That's right."

"Do you know this man and was he there when you left?"

"Yes...and he was."

"And was he alive?"

The 64 Thousand Dollar Question and the third lie. "I'm not sure."

"Uh, Mr. Pearson," he lowered his voice, puzzled, "Let me go over this. There was a man in your house..."

I interrupted, "It's not actually my house. It belongs to a friend of a friend "

"Would that be the Warren's?

Wow, the computers are whirring. He's already checked the address. "I think so, but I don't actually know because I'm a visitor."

"Okay, so let's just continue with what you know. You left and as far as you know the man was alive, and now you've returned and he appears to be dead from gunshot wounds. Is that correct?"

"Yes, sir."

"And do you know who shot him"

Zap! *Right to the heart. This may be worth 20 years.* "Detective uh..."

"Jackson"

"Right. Detective Jackson, I'm under a great deal of stress and in considerable pain. This is a very complicated situation. Should we be doing this over the phone?"

As I was finishing the sentence, the unmistakable shriek of sirens began to grow from the highway. The sheriff said, "Is that our people I hear?"

"I think so. Wait a second." The flashing blue lights came down the driveway. "Yes, sir, I believe it is."

"Mr. Pearson, please stay on the line until the officers come in and ask one of them to speak to me. Can you do that?"

"Yes, sir. Hold on," and I put the phone down. *Saved by the siren. I don't know if I've said too much, but the hole is sure getting deeper. They're going to secure this scene and cart me "downtown" — wherever that is.*

Two very large, tan-uniformed sheriff's deputies burst through the door, with the wide-eyed look of hot pursuit. They looked at me, put on the brakes and said, "Please stand right there, sir." They moved quickly to my side and asked, "Sir, are you armed?"

I shook my head. "No."

They confirmed that with a pat down and calmed a bit.

I said, "Detective Jackson is on the phone and wants to speak to you." Now I could slow down, catch my breath, lower my heartbeat, and wait for the next act.

Actual racing is slam, bam, thank you, ma'm. Start your engines, pace lap, green flag, go like Hell, checkered flag, kiss the trophy girl—if you're lucky. Testing, on the other hand, is an entire day of three laps at a time, interspersed with seemingly endless pondering and tinkering by the crew; incremental adjustments that must be tested to be confirmed or rejected. It's one thing at a time. Smart crew chiefs never change two things at one time because then you never know which of the two changes made the lap times go up or down. Or did they just cancel each other out. For the driver, those days are long days, but often very rewarding.

Soon, I had reason to wonder which it would be — jail time or just a long night.

LONG NIGHT

The Deputy turned and said, "Lt. Jackson wants to speak to you again." I took the phone and said hello.

"Mr. Pearson, did you find a gun in the house?"

"No, sir." *Here we go again...another nail in the coffin.*

"Well, was there somebody else there?"

"Sir, did you hear about the crash of a Ferrari on the beach on PCH this afternoon?"

"Yes, that's right near where you are, isn't it?"

"Yes, it is. Did you know the driver died?"

Now my eyes are moist and my throat is constricting. God! "Yes, of course. What has that to do with what we're talking about?"

"I think she came from here."

"Really? She was there when you were there the first time?"

"Yes, sir."

"Mr. Pearson, I'm going to have to ask you to come into our office and make a full statement. Will you do that?"

"Well, I need to ask--are you arresting me?"

"No, I'm asking for a voluntary statement as a witness to the events as far as you know them, although I will ask the officers on the scene to conduct a couple of simple tests before you leave. Then, they will bring you here. Are you willing to do that?"

"Well, I think so, as long as you say I'm not being arrested. I'm a public figure and an arrest might have negative consequences."

"Really? What kind of public figure?"

"I drive race cars professionally and I'm a senior correspondent for a motor sports magazine in Europe. You can see the possible headlines, which would not be good. You can check this all out with Detective Allen Andrews at CHP in Sacramento." *Thank you Patrol Officer Harmon, you angel, you.*

"Well, I might do that. In the meantime, I've sent a crime scene squad out there and I need to spend some time with you here. Is that okay?"

"Yes, sir." *So we're going to spend a long night putting together a puzzle and they are glad to have a likely suspect, beat up, exhausted, emotionally distressed — they don't know the half of it yet — and willing to talk.*

And what a long day and night it was. Before the crime scene guys got there, the Deputies had bagged my vomit-stained, sweaty clothes and sprayed something on my hands. I later learned that it was to detect gunpowder. They looked around a little for a gun, but that was really the crime scene guys' job. When they arrived, we got into the cars and set off for the Sheriff's office. On the way, I called Uncle Robert, told him what had happened so far, told him of the assurances that I was not under arrest and where we were going. With the blue-light, gumball machines whirling around above, the ride took about 30 minutes. I felt like an Arab Oil Prince. Soon, we were making the turn into the garage under the Sheriff's building; the one they use to sneak the drunken stars into the jail. I felt honored. *Maybe this will get better...or maybe not.*

The most important thing that happened in the next six hours was the arrival of the A-Team; the guys that Uncle Robert rounded up. Without going into too much detail, if you remember the OJ Trial of the Century, you will remember the A-Team. The worst thing that can befall a public figure — that happens to be in the wrong place at the wrong time, and without regard to the question of guilt or innocence — is to fall into the hands of police officials, inviting the worst and often ineradicable news reporting. It just never goes away. Getting beyond the horrible events of the day was one thing; suffering a blighted future was another. Uncle Robert knew what he was doing and so did these guys.

After letting me eat something not very good and drink a cup of coffee, the good Detective Jackson — a soft-voiced, all-pro, right defensive tackle type with a shirt one size too small gave me that bright, shining smile only the black man can produce — said, "Tell me everything, from the beginning." For me, the happy news is that the A-Team had arrived in the office two hours earlier and had insisted that they have one hour to de-brief their client, so that we all could "avoid any misunderstandings," including the fact that I was not an official suspect and certainly not under arrest. Jackson agreed because he was awaiting the return of the crime scene guys..

Of course, the A-Team goal was to get me the Hell out of there as quickly as possible, one way or the other. So, on advice of counsel, I began to tell the Assistant District Attorney, the investigating officers and the court recorder everything that had happened in the last three months. I included my conclusions about the counterfeit Ferrari and the perpetrators of that scheme and their methods. I also admitted that it might be hard to prove with two totally destroyed cars unless somebody impounded the latest and examined the throttle controls. Of course, that story was so beyond their specific interest — they were simply trying to solve a murder on their patch — that I didn't see anybody scurrying around to call for a wrecker.

So on we went right up to the confrontation at the beach house. They had examined my cuts and bruises and looked in my eyes to confirm the concussion. The crime scene guys and a medical examiner had surveyed Evans' body, so they understood that I had been abused by somebody — and that he had not until the gunplay. They also discovered his gun, recently fired, powder on his hands and errant bullet holes in the wall above and beyond my head. So far, it looked like they were getting it. My story was gliding around the room like a serpent, curling around every question smoothly — at least that's what I hoped. Evans was waiting for Jennifer and me. We started our conversation, I laid out my theories and facts, Jennifer learned for the first time my theory of how Willie was killed by the car, Jennifer became emotional and Evans made her leave, then tied me up and began to beat details out of me as to who I had spoken to. Then he hit me hard enough to knock me out. I fell onto my knees, still tied to the torture pole. Jennifer was gone and Evans was dead. Through it all, and for the third time in my head and now out loud, that amazing thing that happens to people — who are harboring an unacceptable truth and fabricating a story — happened to me. *My story's starting to be real to me. Now I believe my own story!*

Jackson, who had been quietly nodding as I moved through the drama, waited until I sighed, sat back and turned to look him in the eye with "sincerity." Without warning or any change of expression he asked, "So, what'd you do with her gun?"

Fuck! He's figured it out!

Three things happened, two of which saved me. First, the A-Team leader smacked the table with both open hands, which sounded like gunshots. Before reaching his full height, he leaned over the table and screamed into Jackson's face, "This interview has ended!! You are on record that this cooperating witness is not under suspicion or arrest. He came here voluntarily and you have just accused him of a crime. We're gone."

The second thing that happened was that the attack forced Jackson to look away from me and up at his attacker. And the third thing that happened is that my racing reflexes took over and froze me, while the scene developed. I never reacted to the explosion in my heart rate. And I thought, *Jackson, you poor bastard, you just got chop-blocked by an offensive end and now your knee is killing you.*

The room grew stunningly silent; nothing but heavy breathing. The A-Team guy cleared his throat. In a carefully modulated, courtroom voice, he looked directly at Jackson and said, "It is 3:00 am, Saturday morning. We've been in the offices of the Santa Cruz County Sheriff for approximately six hours. Mr. Pearson, the witness, has been in police custody for another two hours before arriving here. He has answered every question asked unequivocally and provided a long narrative of his involvement with the victim and another involved person. Barring an official charge of a criminal action, we now officially demand his release on his own recognizance."

I was now watching Jackson and the Assistant DA, who was waiting for her weekend to go up in smoke, as they quietly looked at each other. He stood, nodded to her and they left the room. The court recorder turned off her machines and left, as well. The A-Team said to me in a voice that could have been commenting on a used car, "No smoking gun, no murder weapon and a deceased witness, or maybe a second suspect. That's a big problem. All circumstantial. But he made a great try."

Not much later, the door opened and the ADA says, "You are free to go. Please don't leave the state for 48 hours. We may need an identification of the driver's body."

Oh Shit! Jesus give me strength.

The A-Team leader nodded and said, "No problem. You have my contact numbers. With reasonable notice, Mr. Pearson will be available for 48 hours, as agreed."

SUNRISE

Lt. Jackson's sneak attack produced so much adrenaline, along with my release, that as we left the Sheriff's office, I was nearly bouncing, despite the 3:00 am hour and the really long day. I'd had no time to think about, *What next?* The A-Team was hungry, so we found an all-night diner and rolled up to the trough. Over pecan waffles, sausage and eggs, we did a post mortem, concluding that the Department had concluded exactly what our leader had summarized. The thinking we imagined went like this: *No gun, no gunpowder residue on their present suspect's hands and a deceased alternative, who is maybe the more likely suspect if we can't break his story. Charging him — me — would be very tricky. If we do any publicity damage to this guy and if we lose, we'll certainly get Santa Cruz County's ass sued off by the gunslingers. It looks as if this guy has juice. This guy didn't kill the woman and we have the clicker device with the other deceased's prints. Let's walk him and keep looking. Or maybe close the case. The dead guy's family will accept the likelihood that the woman killed him, but can't expect us to indict a dead woman with no gun. Sorry Jackson. This one might be getting away with something, but it doesn't look like murder. Let's get some breakfast.*

At this point, we began to think about next steps. I decided that like it or not, I had to go back to the beach house. My clothes, camera, laptop and other junk were there. I had no other place to go, except maybe the Woodside house but didn't see why. And I had to stay in California for 48 hours — clean up whatever mess I can is what I'll do — and grieve, and grieve. The Deputies had let me drive the Mercedes to the Sheriff's office sandwiched, nose to tail, between their cruisers. It was the only fun I'd had in 48 hours. I guessed they figured it would save them another trip, if someone sprung me. And the A-Team had seen to that.

"Try to have some hope," Blake said. I decided that the best use of 48 hours was to write the story for Arthur Bathgate and let him decide what to do with it — and say goodbye to Jennifer.

The drive back up to the house at sunrise was as beautiful as it could be under the circumstances of the last 24 hours, with the beautiful hills on the right and the blue pacific on the left. I was now too weary and wrung out to think much of anything coherent, so I stopped trying and just drove. It was the most soothing thing I know how to do.

When I got back to the house, I unplugged the house phones, turned off my cell phone, undressed, climbed into bed and pulled a pillow over my head. My lights all went out and I slept — thank god — a dreamless sleep for four hours. After I awoke, I called Robert and Blake, thanked them for their help and told them the rest of the story, except for the part about Jennifer's involvement with Evans. Then I sent several emails to other people who needed to know my whereabouts, condition and plans before some news-hound got hold of the police blotter and began to write wire service reports. After all, Evans "The Evil" was a local hero; his death by an excess of new orifices would be big news. I didn't know whether or not the police would report my involvement and with what implications, so it was important that I get there first with the whole truth.

After some fruit and a glass of wine, I began to write, "The Tale of The Duplicata." At around four o'clock, my cell rang. A woman assigned to the A-Team introduced herself and asked me if I could meet Lt. Jackson at the County Morgue early Sunday morning. After that, I would probably be free to go. I agreed, thanked her, hung up and began to plot my return to the life I had left behind — flights from San Fran to New York and from there to London; and from there back to "home," a racetrack, where life would be rational again.

The next morning, when I arrived at the morgue, Lt. Jackson was waiting and surprisingly cordial for a man who had been chop-blocked by a gunslinger from the city. He grinned and said, "Tough weekend, eh?"

"Sure is," I replied, and thought, *I wonder if he's figured out that my worst injury is the broken heart below the surface?*

Apparently, he had because he then added, "Look, we'll try to make this as painless as we can. We just have to have an eyewitness who at least believes that the body is as it was identified by the documents found. I can tell you right now that the upper half of the body was stuffed under the dashboard, which was almost the center of the fire. There's nothing much identifiable there."

Oh puleeze, god, I know this guy is trying to be sympathetic, but I don't know if I can handle this. Heavens. Okay, just suck it up, get through this and get the Hell out of here.
"Thanks for the warning, Lieutenant."
"No prob, man."
So in we went, Jackson leading the way. Soon, we reached a large, very cold room with a powerful disinfectant odor—thank heavens—and tall, moving racks containing dead people. He walked several steps and stopped at his choice, checked a tag on the toe, slid the shelf out until the entire, heavily wrapped corpse was available for inspection. I tried not to dwell on the end of the package farthest from us, but my mind just wouldn't leave me alone. I realized that there wasn't much in that end. *Oh, let's get this over before I lose it.*

Jackson began to unwrap the plastic wrapping at the feet and loosened it, so that it could be rolled up to further reveal the body. *How can I get him to stop?* He stopped at the knees. If I had been looking at a lighter-skinned man, I'm sure I'd have seen him blushing. *Good for him,* I thought, *He's ashamed of this.* For my part, I wasn't looking at anything outside the inside of my head. I knew what those feet and legs looked like when they had a blood supply. *Just stop it, dude. The end is near. Control yourself.*

"Mr. Pearson, would you please take a look here and tell me what you think?"

So I turned my head and stared at those small, petite feet and the lower legs and began to tear. Jackson saw this and asked, quietly, "Mr. Pearson, do you believe this was Mrs. Pearson?"

Weird. I simply could not speak. I was close to bawling, so I nodded my head and then turned away. As if into a recorder, Jackson said, "The witness answered affirmatively." He then called to one of the orderlies and said to me, "Let's get the hell out of here."

Indeed. He walked me to my car and I asked, "Am I free to go?"

"Yeah. Every once in a while, we get one of these mystery events where we just can't sort it out enough to take the risk of a bad case and the blowback of a civil suit. If there's no one from the outside pressing for an indictment, the insurance risk of false accusation is so high, and our county self-insures, that the DA becomes very reluctant to charge. Between you and me, I think it was the Lady. Some people believe that you're the best suspect because you're the only one alive who knows how to frame the story. But you're believable. As soon as we got the "no gun powder" report on you and no gun from the Deputies on the scene, I knew we were in trouble. The good news for us is that the other two are gone, so you're it and you're all circumstantial. So we don't have to explain to anybody why we're not charging." Then he tried one more time. "Was it a .38?"

I said, "My friend, I have no idea what you just asked. May I go now?"

He smiled that "Howdy," smile and said. "Good luck Buddy, I'm sorry for your loss." And he walked away.

What a cool guy.

DREAM

When I arrived in New York late Sunday, I called Aunt Blake to see if we could have lunch on Monday before I flew to London later that day. I would have been happy to see Robert, as well, but I knew Monday was business for him and so I left it in her hands. She didn't mention it, so I guessed she preferred to solo. We went to a more modest trattoria on the upper east side and ate at a sidewalk table, uncrowded on a late Monday. She looked a little strained around the eyes, but was her usual calm, rational self. Over the weekend, she and Robert had learned that as soon as Willie's estate was probated, Jennifer had contacted her own lawyer and drawn a will for herself, leaving the Woodside house, the car collection and a portfolio of investments and his interest in the investment banking partnership to his children by Catherine, his first wife, Jennifer's stepchildren. This had made Blake very grateful and she had high praise for Jennifer's wisdom and generosity. The will would be keeping all that stuff out of probate and away from the tax man.

I thought it was great, too, but frankly, I didn't even

want to think about it. *Let's just get on with it,* was my mood.

And so on I went, back to London, to Arthur Bathgate, who was very excited about my story and the magazine series he envisioned and maybe the book. *Book? Oh, I don't know about any book stuff. That'd make me crawl back down in that hole that I'd just crawled out of. We'll see.*

And then I was on to Hereford Green, Colin and the crew and the gorgeous new car. We spent a day at Silverstone setting up both cars, trying some things and getting down to very respectable lap times—below those of our last visit—maybe winning times.

With the return to a rational daily life, the pains, both physical and emotional, were beginning to lose their poignancy. I began to believe that I would heal. But I never believed that I would lose my sadness over a glorious future lost.

A week later, we were sitting on the grid at Hockenheimring. It was the historic track south of Frankfurt, Germany. While waiting for another green flag, the crew was busy with dozens of last minute system checks and measurements. The crowd of race crazies were milling around the cars, laughing, gossiping and enjoying the carnival atmosphere of all major, world-class racing events. Soon, the Course Marshalls were chasing them back into the grandstands, so the racing could begin. For my part, this was the most relaxing part of race day. I was sitting in the racecar, firmly strapped in watching the circus. I had a particularly pleasant view of the Grid Girls and their colorful pennants—oh, and their long legs and lovely backsides.

Surprisingly, after the pressures building up to the

day, these last quiet moments were quite calm inside the car with my head, inside the helmet, resting on the seat back; so much so that it was not unusual for me to briefly nod off — really. This made the crew crazy when they discovered me asleep at the wheel, but what the heck. I'd done all I could do to prepare. The next few moments were in the hands of the crew and the officials. My heart rate was as low as it would be for the next three hours. I was calm and comfortable, so I snoozed. And I had a dream. My dream randomly skipped over the last two weeks and ended when I was jolted awake by a frightening scene. I was back in the morgue, looking at the feet. *What? What? My God, I can't find the rosebud.* The tiny pink rosebud. I was straining so hard that I was jolted awake, sweating and stunned.

What is this? What IS this? The wrong body? My imagination? Jesus!

Colin's firm voice jerked me back, "Have a nice nap, Laddie? Perhaps it's time to get up and come to work, fer Christ's sake."

I touched the radio button on the wheel and replied, "I'm here."

"Good," he said, "One minute to start engines."

"Got it."

Of course, I couldn't get the dream completely wiped away but before I knew it, I heard the track announcer saying, "Ladies and Gentlemen..." And Colin said, "Start it." I flipped some switches and put one finger in the air, the signal for the crew to engage the external starter. The engine burst into rumbling life, the needles on my instruments flipped to the proper readings and all was well. I put two fingers in the air to tell the crew, but the telemetry had already told the story.

We were good to go. Soon, we were on the "Reconnaissance" lap, that quaint French term for warm-up, loosen up, calm down and return to the grid for the green flag; also called the pace lap. During that lap, my final thought about the past was the voice of Super Lady, Aunt Blake. "Try to have hope, Ned."

Hmmm. Ok.

At that moment, my earpiece clicked and Colin calmly said, "Kick butt, Laddie."

Right. I will. I hope.

And so I did.

ABOUT THE AUTHOR

Here's the "30,000 foot" view of "Where has he been, why is he here, where is he going?" From my mid-teens, by which time I was peeking over the horizons at what might be out there, I formed the beginning of a lifetime expectation that if I survived, I would probably have 3 or 4 major lives, mostly in sequence. As it turns out I have needed or wanted to reinvent myself several times. It has been a lifetime of serendipity, full of surprises, many wonderful and some painful. I attended college on a football scholarship, an opportunity that, believe it or not, came as a complete surprise in the second half of my high school senior year. No one in my extended family had ever been to college.

After graduation from business school I was awarded one of the coveted, best first jobs in modern marketing at the Procter & Gamble Company. Later I moved to New York City and opened my own international consulting company, which took me to world destinations far beyond my teenage dreams. And my last formal, creative, business experience was the creation and publishing of a training curriculum for teenage drivers, "New Driver Car Control-From Kamikaze To Competent," designed to cope with crisis behind the wheel, crash avoidance. That business has now trained over 50,000 young drivers and parents. It is now in the fine hands of a new generation. http://www.carcontrol.com.

So what has this all to do with "The Duplicata?" Several things. I have always written for a living; but not fiction. For example, in addition to advertising and marketing communications, I have been an automotive columnist for a newspaper and for magazines. Second, I have been, since childhood, obsessed with motor vehicles. Over the years, when I search for the earliest memories I can recall, one is of small, cast metal toy cars in the sand alongside the foundation of a neighbor's house. I know how old I was because of where my family lived at the time. I was in my 3rd year of life. On my blog you can read about my car history and automotive highlights. And that is the motivation behind my favorite, lifetime avocation, motor sports. In addition to being a fan, as a high-level amateur racer I won several championships and set track records at 7 major US racetracks.

And for a lifetime an avid reader of fiction. Fiction is my sleeping pill. I go to sleep or back to sleep under all conditions with a book in my hand. For me, novels calm the seas. So it was logical that I would eventually set to writing fiction. In the Dedication here, the Pablo Picasso comment "...doing that which I cannot do..." has been a theme in my life. It also explains the name of my boat, incidentally the first and only one I've ever owned, and it would be my message to you, young or old, up or down, rich or poor, happy or unhappy. The name of the boat is "PERSIST."

And if you like this beginner's work, and you say so by going to Amazon.com, clicking on this title and leaving a 4 or 5 star review, the magical software of the Amazon geniuses who led us here will decide to put "The Duplicata" on a best seller list and more like you will come and we can all learn more about Ned Pearson and his future. Of course, I already know a few things about that. That is the fun of writing fiction. But without the reader's important feelings first, those adventures may remain a secret. Poor Ned. And thanks a lot for your time.

And finally, I must say that this project has been one of the most satisfying of my life. The opportunity to imagine, to design, to craft, to problem solve, to build something that is uniquely your own is delicious. Even the most modest control freak among us will take guilty pleasure in the obedience of the characters. But a warning; like precocious children, they will also shock and surprise you by lurching off in directions you never anticipated, and for that, may make a better story. What fun! Maybe you should try it.

E publishing is an incredible new frontier in creativity and story telling. Emancipation is the best word I can think of. Now the public, not publishers, shall decide between the talented and the not so. A little scary because the writer no longer has a big brother or a daddy (a publisher) to nurture them into (or keep them out of) print. It's just the writer and the readers. At the same time, whatever happens to the popularity of "The Duplicata," no one can ever take away this journey of 100,004 words. And it has been fabulous. I'd like to do it again. Perhaps I will. Maybe starting tomorrow.

Melbourne Beach
July 4th 2012

ACKNOWLEDGEMENTS

In my life and career I have traveled light. In "The Du-plicata" there is the muse that "you inherit your family and choose your friends." I have been fortunate on both counts, but unlike some acknowledgements pages in recent works, head count has never been my goal. As wise women of modest means know, a few good pieces, well chosen, will endure when the fads have faded.

Here I have singled out a few good persons who have been of spiritual or technical help. There are others, of course, who have influenced my life and to them I will be eternally grateful. But as it relates to "The Du-plicata" the influence of these is preeminent.

Jane Lee Sears Thompson — My late wife, business partner and best friend for life who, unfortunately for all of us who benefited from her time on earth, went away too soon. But she was there through the birth of "The Duplicata," its construction and final shape — ever urging that it should someday be published. And so it is.

Daniel Nolan Neil, WSJ — The only, that is *only*, newspaper or magazine critic ever to win the Pulitzer Prize for automobile criticism. My first professional editor at a small-town newspaper, and an April-September friendship forged in shared experiences at race tracks around the world, yelling at one another from political poles, roaring around in the Nevada desert at 3am attempting to navigate the diabolical challenges of Rally-Masters and a lifetime learning experience hearing opposing ideas expressed with vigor. Friends and relatives seek solace from our exercises with fingers in their ears. But we always learn something we didn't know — and the friendship ripens. Dan has known about "The Duplicata" from early on and will be proud to see it presented to the world.

Steven Manchester — Editor, author and all-quality professional, Steve took this work from a novice fiction writer with a high school grammar education and killed a plague of commas and parenthetical phrases, re-arranged the furniture properly and gave me back something readable. I am forever indebted to his diligence, good works and encouragement. If you are a "newbie" too, you couldn't do better. http://www.stevenmanchester.com.

Robert Bidinotto — Best-selling Author of "Hunter: A Thriller" is an amazing man who has a world-class reputation as a non-fiction writer of award-winning articles on Crime and Criminal Justice, but like this author, had never written fiction. Robert has preceded me and a thousand other would-be novelists down the bunny trail, publishing his book just one year ago and subsequently rocketing up the bestseller lists. But the difference here is that Robert, with the heart of the saints, has chosen not to stand on a lofty perch smiling at his personal success while watching the swimmers still struggling in the chilly waters. Instead he has become a cheerleader, a coach, an inspiration and a professor of "indie" publishing. This author sent him a simple note of congratulations on a recent award and instead of a polite thank-you; got in return a crash course on the do's and don'ts of this unfamiliar territory called Independent Publishing. Again, if you are planning such a journey, enrich your life and increase your odds of success. Hie yourself to Bidinotto.com and steal everything that isn't tied down. In the land of the blind, the one-eyed man is king. As mentors go, Robert is Royalty.

Some others who have made a specific difference in the outcome of "The Duplicata:"

Todd Engel — Designer of Beautiful Covers. Todd is the dream of all producers needing graphic arts support; Todd views the process as a collaboration and takes as well as gives. With great taste and vision he is a real professional and a pleasure to work with. He also understands timetables and budgets. Engel Creative, FaceBook

Mark Levine — E-Book Publisher/Author — Mark publishes an e-book entitled "The Fine Print of Self-Publishing," principally a rating system of Author Services companies and with a great deal of specifics from 20 years in the publishing business. Excellent and actionable advice.

Ron Susser — Auctioneer. Ron secured the photo of the replica Ferrari on the cover of "The Duplicata." He has what Tom Peterson, author of the landmark study of successful companies, "In Search of Excellence," calls "a bias toward action," that rare instinct to move forward and manage the risk instead of "leading from behind.

Cindy Buccieri — My Managing Editor for Social Media like Facebook and Twitter. If you heard from me during our marketing campaign it was because Cindy spied you from her tree house, hot air balloon or satellite camera or however she does this stuff. This newbie novelist is also a social media newbie and Cindy is my navigator. Thank heavens. www.cbvirtualservices.com

And finally a couple of my favorite authors, one modern and one not so, both of whom most certainly influenced my "style" in the writing of "The Duplicata." Please note that I make no pretense of achieving their successes, but I am a wannabe.

Robert B. Parker—Called the "Dean of American Crime Fiction," Parker's, easy-going, quipping characters with one-liners galore plus his good-guy heroes like Spenser and Hawk helping those in distress and battling with the hoodlums and crooks produced 70 best sellers. I always wanted to meet the "Joan" in every dedication, (real fans know she's Mrs. Parker) and ask that boring, predictable question, "What's he really like?" Didn't happen and now he's gone. And is missed.

John D. MacDonald—Author of 78 novels in the 60's, 70's and 80's and a well-known character named Travis McGee who appeared in 28 of those. By modern standards, a little cerebral, moralistic, (living and writing in Florida during the real estate development years, MacDonald's characters and plots often commented on the environmental impact of development) and maybe predictable (McGee was not going to fail) and seen by some female reviewers in the era of liberation as chauvinistic. (McGee liked the ladies; eat your heart out.) But very entertaining.

To those I missed, hopefully, there is hope. There may be further opportunities in the next adventure of Ned Pearson. We shall see what we shall see. All the best.